THE WHITE ROAD

"Darkly brilliant, spellbinding, and disturbing."
—Harlan Coben

"The malevolence here is almost palpable."
—*Publishers Weekly* (starred review)

THE KILLING KIND

"Unfolds with the force and logic of a nightmare."
—*The Washington Post*

"Connolly has that rare ability to hit you head-on with a great crime story while giving you goose bumps in the process."

—*Clarion Ledger* (Jackson, MS)

DARK HOLLOW

"Grim, hard-edged and compulsively readable."
—*Publishers Weekly*

"A frightening, disturbing, and brutal tale interspersed with moments of dark humor."
—*Yorkshire Evening Press* (UK)

EVERY DEAD THING

"Speeds us through a harrowing plot to a riveting climax."
—*New York Times* bestselling author Jeffery Deaver

"A spellbinding book. . . . holds the reader fast in a comfortless stranglehold."
—*The Los Angeles Times*

Books by
JOHN CONNOLLY

The Reapers
The Unquiet
The Book of Lost Things
The Black Angel
Nocturnes
Bad Men
The White Road
The Killing Kind
Dark Hollow
Every Dead Thing

JOHN CONNOLLY

EVERY DEAD THING

POCKET BOOKS

New York London Toronto Sydney

Pocket Books
A Division of Simon & Schuster, Inc.
1230 Avenue of the Americas
New York, NY 10020

This book is a work of fiction. Names, characters, places, and incidents either are products of the author's imagination or are used fictitiously. Any resemblance to actual events or locales or persons, living or dead, is entirely coincidental.

For information about special discounts for bulk purchases, please contact Simon & Schuster Special Sales at 1-800-456-6798 or business@simonandschuster.com

Cover design by Jae Song.
Cover photo © Christopher Shafer/stock.xchng.

Manufactured in the United States of America

10 9 8 7 6 5 4 3 2 1

ISBN-13: 978–1–4165–9598–4

ISBN-10:   1–4165–9598–8

1

For I am every dead thing . . . I am re-begot
Of absence, darknesse, death; things which are not.

John Donne
"A Nocturnall Upon S. Lucies Day"

PROLOGUE

IT IS COLD in the car, cold as the grave. I prefer to leave the a/c on full, to let the falling temperature keep me alert. The volume on the radio is low but I can still hear a tune, vaguely insistent over the sound of the engine. It's early R.E.M., something about shoulders and rain. I've left Cornwall Bridge about eight miles behind and soon I'll be entering South Canaan, then Canaan itself, before crossing the state line into Massachusetts. Ahead of me, the bright sun is fading as day bleeds slowly into night.

The patrol car arrived first on the night they died, shedding red light into the darkness. Two patrolmen entered the house, quickly yet cautiously, aware that they were responding to a call from one of their own, a policeman who had become a victim instead of the resort of victims.

I sat in the hallway with my head in my hands as they entered the kitchen of our Brooklyn home and glimpsed the remains of my wife and child. I watched as one conducted a brief search of the upstairs rooms while the other checked the living room, the dining room, all the time the kitchen calling them back, demanding that they bear witness.

I listened as they radioed for the Major Crime Scene Unit, informing them of a probable double homicide. I could hear the shock in their voices, yet they tried to communicate what they had seen as dispassionately as they could, like good cops should. Maybe, even then, they suspected me. They were policemen and they, more than anyone else, knew what people were capable of doing, even one of their own.

And so they remained silent, one by the car and the other in the hallway beside me, until the detectives pulled up outside, the ambulance following, and they entered our home, the neighbors already gathering on their stoops, at their gates, some moving closer to find out what had happened, what could have been visited on the young couple beyond, the couple with the little blond girl.

"Bird?" I ran my hands over my eyes as I recognized the voice. A sob shuddered through my system. Walter Cole stood over me, McGee farther back, his face bathed by the flashes of the patrol car lights but still pale, shaken by what he had seen. Outside there was the sound of more cars pulling up. An EMT arrived at the door, distracting Cole's attention from me. "The medical technician's here," said one of the patrolmen as the thin, whey-faced young man stood by. Cole nodded and gestured toward the kitchen.

"Birdman," Cole repeated, this time with greater urgency and a harder tone to his voice. "Do you want to tell me what happened here?"

I pull into the parking lot in front of the flower shop. There is a light breeze blowing and my coattails play at my legs like the hands of children. Inside, the store is cool, cooler than it should be, and redolent with the scent of roses. Roses never go out of style, or season.

A man is bending down, carefully checking the thick waxy leaves of a small green plant. He rises up slowly and painfully as I enter.

"Evening," he says. "Help you?"

"I'd like some of those roses. Give me a dozen. No, better make it two dozen."

"Two dozen roses, yessir." He is heavy-set and bald, maybe in his early sixties. He walks stiffly, hardly bending his knees. The joints of his fingers are swollen with arthritis.

"Air-conditioning is playing up," he says. As he passes by the ancient control unit on the wall, he adjusts a switch. Nothing happens.

The store is old, with a long glass-fronted hothouse along the far wall. He opens the door and begins lifting roses carefully from a bucket inside. When he has counted twenty-four, he closes the door again and lays them on a sheet of plastic on the counter.

"Gift wrap 'em for ya?"

"No. Plastic is fine."

He looks at me for a moment and I can almost hear the tumblers fall as the process of recognition begins.

"Do I know you from someplace?"

In the city, they have short memories. Farther out, the memories last longer.

Supplemental Crime Report

NYPD	**Case Number:** 96-12-1806
Offense:	Homicide
Victim:	Susan Parker, W/F
	Jennifer Parker, W/F
Location:	1219 Hobart Street, kitchen
Date:	Dec. 12, 1996
Time:	Around 2130 hrs
Means:	Stabbing
Weapon:	Edged weapon, possibly knife (not found)
Reporting Officer:	Walter Cole, Detective Sergeant

Details: On December 13, 1996, I went to 1219 Hobart Street in response to a request by Officer Gerald Kersh for detectives to work a reported homicide.

Complainant Detective Second Grade Charles Parker stated he left house at 1900 hrs following argument with wife, Susan Parker. Went to Tom's Oak Tavern and remained there until around 0130 hrs on December 13. Entered house through front door and found furniture in hallway disturbed. Entered kitchen and found wife and daughter. Stated that wife was tied to kitchen chair but daughter's body appeared to have been moved from adjacent chair and arranged over mother's body. Called police at 0155 hrs and waited at scene.

Victims, identified to me by Charles Parker as Susan Parker (wife, 33 years old) and Jennifer Parker (daughter, 3 years old), were in kitchen. Susan Parker was tied to a kitchen chair in center of floor, facing door. A second chair was placed beside it, with some ropes still · attached to rear struts. Jennifer Parker was lying across her mother, faceup.

Susan Parker was barefoot and wearing blue jeans and white blouse. Blouse was ripped and had been pulled down to her waist, exposing breasts. Jeans and underwear had been pulled down to her calves. Jennifer Parker was barefoot, wearing a white nightdress with blue flower pattern.

I directed Crime Scene Technician Annie Minghella to make a full investigation. After victims were confirmed dead by Medical Examiner Clarence Hall and released, I accompanied bodies to hospital. I observed Dr. Anthony Loeb as he used rape kit and turned it over to me. I collected following items of evidence:

96-12-1806-M1: white blouse from body of
  Susan Parker (Victim No. 1)
96-12-1806-M2: blue denim jeans from body
  of Victim 1
96-12-1806-M3: blue cotton underwear from
  body of Victim 1
96-12-1806-M4: combings from pubic hair of
  Victim 1
96-12-1806-M5: washings from vagina of
  Victim 1
96-12-1806-M6: scrapings from under Victim
  1's fingernails, right hand

96-12-1806-M7: scrapings from under Victim
    1's fingernails, left hand
96-12-1806-M8: combings from Victim 1's
    hair, right front
96-12-1806-M9: combings from Victim 1's
    hair, left front
96-12-1806-M10: combings from Victim 1's
    hair, right rear
96-12-1806-M11: combings from Victim 1's
    hair, left rear
96-12-1806-M12: white/blue cotton
    nightdress from body of Jennifer Parker
    (Victim No. 2)
96-12-1806-M13: washings from vagina of
    Victim 2
96-12-1806-M14: scrapings from under Victim
    2's fingernails, right hand
96-12-1806-M15: scrapings from under Victim
    2's fingernails, left hand
96-12-1806-M16: combings from Victim 2's
    hair, right front
96-12-1806-M17: combings from Victim 2's
    hair, left front
96-12-1806-M18: combings from Victim 2's
    hair, right rear
96-12-1806-M19: combings from Victim 2's
    hair, left rear

It had been another bitter argument, made worse by the fact that it followed our lovemaking. The embers of previous fights were stoked back into glowing life: my drinking, my neglect of Jenny, my bouts of bitterness and self-pity. When I stormed from the house, Susan's cries followed me into the cold night air.

It was a twenty-minute walk to the bar. When the first shot of Wild Turkey hit my stomach, the tension dissipated from my body and I relaxed into the familiar routine of the drunk: angry, then maudlin, sorrowful, remorseful, resentful. By the time I left the bar only the hard core remained, a chorus of drunks and sots battling with Van Halen on the jukebox. I stumbled at the door and fell down the steps outside, barking my knees painfully on the gravel at their base.

And then I stumbled home, sick and nauseous, cars swerving wildly to avoid me as I swayed onto the road, the faces of the drivers wide with alarm and anger.

I fumbled for my keys as I arrived at the door, and scraped the white paint beneath the lock as I struggled to insert the key. There were a lot of scrapes beneath the lock.

I knew something was wrong as soon as I opened the front door and stepped into the hall. When I had left, the house had been warm, the heating on full blast because Jennifer especially felt the winter cold. She was a beautiful but fragile child, as delicate as a china vase. Now the house was as cold as the night outside. A mahogany flower stand lay fallen on the carpet, the flowerpot broken in two pieces amid its own soil. The roots of the poinsettia it had contained were exposed and ugly.

I called Susan's name once, then again, louder this time. Already the drunken haze was clearing and I had my foot on the first step of the stairs to the bedrooms when I heard the back door bang against the sink unit in the kitchen. Instinctively I reached for my Colt DE but it lay upstairs on my desk, upstairs where I had discarded it before facing Susan and another chapter in the story of our dying marriage. I cursed myself then. Later, it would come to symbolize all of my failures, all of my regrets.

I moved cautiously toward the kitchen, the tips of my fingers glancing against the cold wall on my left. The kitchen door was almost closed and I edged it open slowly with my hand. "Susie?" I called as I stepped into the kitchen. My foot slid gently on something sticky and wet. I looked down and I was in Hell.

In the florist's, the old man's eyes are narrowed in puzzlement. He shakes his finger good-naturedly in front of me.

"I'm sure I know you from someplace."

"I don't think so."

"You from around here? Canaan, maybe? Monterey? Otis?"

"No. Someplace else." I give him a look that tells him this is a line of inquiry he doesn't want to pursue, and I can see him backing off. I am about to use my credit card but decide not to. Instead, I count out the cash from my wallet and lay it on the counter.

"Someplace else," he says, nodding as if it has some deep, inner meaning for him. "Must be a big place. I meet a lot of fellers from there."

But I am already leaving the store. As I pull away, I can see him at the window, staring after me. Behind me, water drips gently from the rose stems and pools on the floor of the car.

Supplemental Crime Report (Contd.)
Case Number: 96-12-1806

Susan Parker was seated in a pine kitchen chair, facing north toward the kitchen door. Top of the head was ten feet, seven inches from north wall and six feet, three inches from east wall. Her arms were pulled behind her back and . . .

tied to the bars at the back of the chair with thin cord. Each foot was in turn tied to a leg of the chair, and I thought her face, mostly concealed by her hair, seemed so awash with blood that no skin could be seen. Her head hung back so that her throat gaped open like a second mouth, caught in a silent, dark red scream. Our daughter lay splayed across Susan, one arm hanging between her mother's legs.

The room was red around them, like the stage of some terrible revenger's tragedy where blood was echoed with blood. It stained the ceiling and the walls as if the house itself had been mortally wounded. It lay thick and heavy on *the floor and seemed to swallow my reflection in a scarlet darkness.*

Susan Parker's nose had been broken. Injury
was consistent with impact against wall or
floor. Bloodstain on wall near kitchen door
contained fragments of bone, nasal hair, and
mucus . . .

Susan had tried to run, to get help for our daughter and herself, but she had made it no farther than the door. Then he had caught her, had grabbed her by the hair and smashed her against the wall before dragging her, bleeding and in pain, back to the chair and to her death.

Jennifer Parker was stretched, facing upward,
across her mother's thighs, and a second pine
kitchen chair was positioned beside that of
her mother. Cord wrapped around the back of
the chair matched marks on Jennifer Parker's
wrists and ankles.

There was not so much blood around Jenny, but her nightdress was stained by the flow from the deep cut in her throat. She faced the door, her hair hanging forward, obscuring her face, some strands sticking to the blood on her chest, the toes of her naked feet dangling above the tiled floor. I could only look at her for a moment because Susan drew my eyes toward her in death as she had in life, even amid the wreckage of our time together.

And as I looked upon her I felt myself slide down the wall and a wail, half-animal, half-child, erupted from deep inside me. I gazed at the beautiful woman who had been my wife, and her bloody, empty sockets seemed to draw me in and envelop me in darkness.

The eyes of both victims had been mutilated,
probably with a sharp, scalpel-like blade.
There was partial flensing of the chest of

Susan Parker. The skin from the clavicle to
the navel had been partially removed, pulled
back over the right breast and stretched over
the right arm.

*The moonlight shone through the window behind
them, casting a cold glow over the gleaming countertops,
the tiled walls, the steel faucets on the sink. It caught
Susan's hair, coated her bare shoulders in silver, and shone
through parts of the thin membrane of her skin pulled
back over her arm like a cloak, a cloak too frail to ward off
the cold.*

There was considerable mutilation . . .

And then he had cut off their faces.

It is darkening rapidly now and the headlights catch the
bare branches of trees, the ends of trimmed lawns, clean
white mailboxes, a child's bicycle lying in front of a garage.
The wind is stronger now, and when I leave the shelter of
the trees I can feel it buffeting the car. Now I am heading
toward Becket, Washington, the Berkshire Hills. Almost
there.

There was no sign of forcible entry. Complete
measurements and a sketch of the entire room
were noted. Bodies were then released.
    Dusting for fingerprints gave the follow-
ing results:
    Kitchen / hall / living room—usable prints
later identified as those of Susan Parker
(96-12-1806-7), Jennifer Parker (96-12-1806-
8), and Charles Parker (96-12-1806-9).
    Rear door of house from kitchen—no usable
prints; water marks on surface indicate that
door was wiped down. No indication of robbery.
    No prints were developed from tests on
victims' skin.

Charles Parker was taken to Homicide and gave statement (attached).

I knew what they were doing as I sat in the interrogation room: I had done it so many times myself. They questioned me as I had questioned others before, using the strange formal locutions of the police interrogation. "What is your recollection as to your next move?" "Do you recall in relation to the bar the disposition of the other drinkers?" "Did you notice the condition as to the lock on the rear door?" It is an obscure, convoluted jargon, an anticipation of the legalese that clouds any criminal proceedings like smoke in a bar.

When I gave my statement Cole checked with the bartender from Tom's and confirmed that I was there when I said I was, that I could not have killed my own wife and child.

Even then, there were whispers. I was questioned again and again about my marriage, about my relations with Susan, about my movements in the weeks coming up to the killings. I stood to gain a considerable sum in insurance from Susan, and I was questioned about that as well.

According to the ME, Susan and Jennifer had been dead for about four hours when I found them. Rigor mortis had already taken hold at their necks and lower jaws, indicating that they had died at around 21.30, maybe a little earlier.

Susan had died from severing of the carotid artery, but Jenny . . . Jenny had died from what was described as a massive release of epinephrine into her system, causing ventricular fibrillation of the heart and death. Jenny, always a gentle, sensitive child, a child with a traitor-weak heart, had literally died of fright before her killer had a chance to cut her throat. She was dead when her face was taken, said the ME. He could not say the same for Susan. Neither could he say why Jennifer's body had been moved after death.

Further reports to follow.
            Walter Cole, Detective Sergeant

I had a drunk's alibi: while someone stole away my wife and my child, I downed bourbon in a bar. But they still come to me in my dreams, sometimes smiling and beautiful as they were in life and sometimes faceless and bloodied as death left them, beckoning me further into a darkness where love has no place and evil hides, adorned with thousands of unseeing eyes and the flayed faces of the dead.

It is dark when I arrive and the gate is closed and locked. The wall is low and I climb it easily. I walk carefully, so as not to tread on memorial stones or flowers, until I stand before them. Even in the darkness, I know where to find them, and they in their turn can find me.

They come to me sometimes, in the margin between sleeping and waking, when the streets are silent in the dark or as dawn seeps through the gap in the curtains, bathing the room in a dim, slow-growing light. They come to me and I see their shapes in the darkness, my wife and child together, watching me silently, ensanguined in unquiet death. They come to me, their breath in the night breezes that brush my cheek and their fingers in the tree branches tapping at my window. They come to me and I am no longer alone.

1

□

THE WAITRESS was in her fifties, dressed in a tight black miniskirt, white blouse, and black high heels. Parts of her spilled out of every item of clothing she wore, making her look like she had swollen mysteriously sometime between dressing and arriving for work. She called me "darlin' " each time she filled my coffee cup. She didn't say anything else, which was fine by me.

I had been sitting at the window for over ninety minutes now, watching the brownstone across the street, and the waitress must have been wondering exactly how long I was planning to stay and if I was ever going to pay the check. Outside, the streets of Astoria buzzed with bargain hunters. I had even read the *New York Times* from start to finish without nodding off in between as I passed the time waiting for Fat Ollie Watts to emerge from hiding. My patience was wearing thin.

In moments of weakness, I sometimes considered ditching the *New York Times* on weekdays and limiting my purchase to the Sunday edition, when I could at least justify buying it on the grounds of bulk. The other option was to begin reading the *Post,* although then I'd have to start clipping coupons and walking to the store in my bedroom slippers.

Maybe in reacting so badly to the *Times* that morning I was simply killing the messenger. It had been announced that Hansel McGee, a state Supreme Court judge and, according to some, one of the worst judges in New York, was retiring in December and might be nominated to the board of the city's Health and Hospitals Corporation.

Even seeing McGee's name in print made me ill. In the

1980s, he had presided over the case of a woman who had been raped when she was nine years old by a fifty-four-year-old man named James Johnson, an attendant in Pelham Bay Park who had convictions for robbery, assault, and rape.

McGee overturned a jury award to the woman of $3.5 million with the following words: "An innocent child was heinously raped for no reason at all; yet that is one of the risks of living in a modern society." At the time, his judgment had seemed callous and an absurd justification for overturning the ruling. Now, seeing his name before me again after what had happened to my family, his views seemed so much more abhorrent, a symptom of the collapse of goodness in the face of evil.

Erasing McGee from my mind, I folded the newspaper neatly, tapped a number on my cell phone, and turned my eyes to an upper window of the slightly run-down apartment building opposite. The phone was picked up after three rings and a woman's voice whispered a cautious hello. It had the sound of cigarettes and booze to it, like a bar door scraping across a dusty floor.

"Tell your fat asshole boyfriend that I'm on my way to pick him up and he'd better not make me chase him," I told her. "I'm real tired and I don't plan on running around in this heat." Succinct, that was me. I hung up, left five dollars on the table, and stepped out onto the street to wait for Fat Ollie Watts to panic.

The city was in the middle of a hot, humid summer spell, which was due to end the following day with the arrival of thunderstorms and rain. Currently, it was hot enough to allow for T-shirts, chinos, and overpriced sunglasses, or, if you were unlucky enough to be holding down a responsible job, hot enough to make you sweat like a pig under your suit as soon as you left the a/c behind. There wasn't even a gust of wind to rearrange the heat.

Two days earlier, a solitary desk fan had struggled to make an impact on the sluggish warmth in the Brooklyn Heights office of Benny Low. Through an open window I could hear Arabic being spoken on Atlantic Avenue and I could smell the cooking scents coming from the Moroccan

Star, half a block away. Benny was a minor-league bail bondsman who had banked on Fat Ollie staying put until his trial. The fact that he had misjudged Fat Ollie's faith in the justice system was one reason why Benny continued to remain a minor-league bondsman.

The money being offered on Fat Ollie Watts was reasonable, and there were things living on the bottom of ponds that were smarter than most bail jumpers. There was a fifty-thousand-dollar bond on Fat Ollie, the result of a misunderstanding between Ollie and the forces of law and order over the precise ownership of a 1993 Chevy Beretta, a 1990 Mercedes 300 SE, and a number of well-appointed sport utility vehicles, all of which had come into Ollie's possession by illegal means.

Fat Ollie's day started to go downhill when an eagle-eyed patrolman familiar with Ollie's reputation as something less than a shining light in the darkness of a lawless world spotted the Chevy under a tarpaulin and called for a check on the plates. They were false and Ollie was raided, arrested, and questioned. He kept his mouth shut but packed a bag and headed for the hills as soon as he made bail, in an effort to avoid further questions about who had placed the cars in his care. That source was reputed to be Salvatore "Sonny" Ferrera, the son of a prominent capo. There had been rumors lately that relations between father and son had deteriorated in recent weeks, but nobody was saying why.

"Fuckin' goomba stuff," as Benny Low had put it that day in his office.

"Anything to do with Fat Ollie?"

"Fuck do I know? You want to call Ferrera and ask?"

I looked at Benny Low. He was completely bald and had been since his early twenties, as far as I knew. His glabrous skull glistened with tiny beads of perspiration. His cheeks were ruddy and flesh hung from his chin and jowls like melted wax. His tiny office, located above a halal store, smelled of sweat and mold. I wasn't even sure why I had said I would take the job. I had money—insurance money, money from the sale of the house, money from what had once been a shared account, even some cash from my retirement fund—and Benny Low's money wasn't going to make me any happier. Maybe Fat Ollie was just something to do.

Benny Low swallowed once, loudly. "What? Why are you lookin' at me like that?"

"You know me, Benny, don't you?"

"Fuck does that mean? Course I know you. You want a reference? What?" He laughed halfheartedly, spreading his pudgy hands wide as if in supplication. "What?" he said again. His voice faltered, and for the first time, he actually looked scared. I knew that people had been talking about me in the months since the deaths, talking about things I had done, things I might have done. The look in Benny Low's eyes told me that he had heard about them too and believed that they could be true.

Something about Fat Ollie's flight just didn't sit right. It wouldn't be the first time that Ollie had faced a judge on a stolen vehicles rap, although the suspected connection to the Ferreras had forced the bond up on this occasion. Ollie had a good lawyer to rely on; otherwise his only connection to the automobile industry would have come from making license plates on Rikers Island. There was no particular reason for Ollie to run, and no reason why he would risk his life by fingering Sonny over something like this.

"Nothing, Benny. It's nothing. You hear anything else, you tell me."

"Sure, sure," said Benny, relaxing again. "You'll be the first to know."

As I left his office, I heard him mutter under his breath. I couldn't be sure what he said but I knew what it sounded like. It sounded like Benny Low had just called me a killer like my father.

It had taken me most of the next day to locate Ollie's current squeeze through some judicious questioning, and another fifty minutes that morning to determine if Ollie was with her through the simple expedient of calling the local Thai food joints and asking them if they had made any deliveries to the address in the last week.

Ollie was a Thai food freak and, like most skips, stuck to his habits even while on the run. People don't change very much, which usually makes the dumb ones easy to find. They take out subscriptions to the same magazines, eat in the same places, drink the same beers, call the same women, sleep with the same men. After I threatened to call the health inspectors, an Oriental roach motel called the Bangkok Sun House confirmed deliveries to one Monica Mulrane at an address in Astoria, leading to coffee, the *New York Times,* and a phone call to wake Ollie up.

True to form and dim as a ten-watt bulb, Ollie opened the door of 2317 about four minutes after my call, stuck his head out, and then commenced an awkward, shambling run down the steps toward the sidewalk. He was an absurd figure, strands of hair slicked across his bald pate, the elasticated waistband of his tan pants stretched across a stomach of awesome size. Monica Mulrane must have loved him a whole lot to stay with him, because he didn't have money and he sure as hell didn't have looks. It was strange, but I kind of liked Fat Ollie Watts.

He had just set foot on the sidewalk when a jogger wearing a gray sweat suit with the hood pulled up appeared at the corner, ran up to Ollie, and pumped three shots into him from a silenced pistol. Ollie's white shirt was suddenly polka-dotted with red and he folded to the ground. The jogger, left-handed, stood over him and shot him once more in the head.

Someone screamed and I saw a brunette, presumably the by now recently bereaved Monica Mulrane, pause at the door of her apartment block before she ran to the sidewalk to kneel beside Ollie, passing her hands over his bald, bloodied head and crying. The jogger was already backing off, bouncing on the balls of his feet like a fighter waiting for the bell. Then he stopped, returned, and fired a single shot into the top of the woman's head. She folded over the body of Ollie Watts, her back shielding his head. Bystanders were already running for cover behind cars, into stores, and the cars on the street ground to a halt.

I was almost across the street, my Smith & Wesson in my hand, when the jogger ran. He kept his head down and moved fast, the gun still held in his left hand. Even though he wore black gloves, he hadn't dropped the gun at the scene. Either the gun was distinctive or the shooter was dumb. I was banking on the second option.

I was gaining on him when a black Chevy Caprice with tinted windows screeched out from a side street and stood waiting for him. If I didn't shoot, he was going to get away. If I did shoot, there would be hell to pay with the cops. I made my choice. He had almost reached the Chevy when I squeezed off two shots, one hitting the door of the car and the second tearing a bloody hole in the right arm of the jogger's top. He spun, firing two wild shots in my direction as he did so, and I could see his eyes were wide and ultra-bright. The killer was wired.

As he turned toward the Chevy it sped away, the driver spooked by my shots, leaving Fat Ollie's killer stranded. He fired off another shot, which shattered the window of the car to my left. I could hear people screaming and, in the distance, the wail of approaching sirens.

The jogger sprinted toward an alley, glancing over his shoulder at the sound of my shoes hammering on the road behind him. As I made the corner a bullet whined off the wall above me, peppering me with pieces of concrete. I looked up to see the jogger moving beyond the midpoint of the alley, staying close to the wall. If he got around the corner at the end, I would lose him in the crowds.

The gap at the end of the alley was, briefly, clear of people. I decided to risk the shot. The sun was behind me as I straightened, firing twice in quick succession. I was vaguely aware of people at either side of me scattering like pigeons from a stone as the jogger's right shoulder arched back with the impact of one of my shots. I shouted at him to drop the piece but he turned awkwardly, his left hand bringing the gun up. Slightly off balance, I fired two more shots from around twenty feet. His left knee exploded as one of the hollow points connected, and he collapsed against the wall of the alley, his pistol skidding harmlessly away toward some trash cans and black bags.

As I closed on him I could see he was ashen faced, his mouth twisted in pain and his left hand gripping the air around his shattered knee without actually touching the

2

□

FIVE HOURS had elapsed since the death of Fat Ollie Watts, his girlfriend, Monica Mulrane, and the shooter, as yet unidentified. I had been interviewed by a pair of detectives from Homicide, neither of whom I knew. Walter Cole did not participate. I was brought coffee twice but otherwise I was left alone after the questionings. Once, when one of the detectives left the room to consult with someone, I caught a glimpse of a tall, thin man in a dark linen suit, the ends of his shirt collar sharp as razors, his red silk tie unwrinkled. He looked like a fed, a vain fed.

The wooden table in the interrogation room was pitted and worn, caffeine-stamped by the edges of hundreds, maybe thousands, of coffee cups. At the left-hand side of the table, near the corner, someone had carved a broken heart into the wood, probably with a nail. And I remembered that heart from another time, from the last time I sat in this room.

"Shit, Walter . . ."
"Walt, it ain't a good idea for him to be here."
Walter looked at the detectives ranged around the walls, slouched on chairs around the table.
"He's not here," he said. "As far as everyone in this room is concerned, you never saw him."
The interrogation room was crowded with chairs and an additional table had been brought in. I was still on compassionate leave and, as it happened, two weeks away from quitting the force. My family had been dead for two weeks

and the investigation had so far yielded nothing. With the agreement of Lieutenant Cafferty, soon to retire, Walter had called a meeting of detectives involved in the case and one or two others who were regarded as some of the best homicide detectives in the city. It was to be a combination of brainstorm and lecture, the lecture coming from Rachel Wolfe.

Wolfe had a reputation as a fine criminal psychologist, yet the Department steadfastly refused to consult her. It had its own deep thinker, Dr. Russell Windgate, but as Walter once put it: "Windgate couldn't profile a fart." He was a sanctimonious, patronizing bastard but he was also the commissioner's brother, which made him a sanctimonious, patronizing, influential bastard.

Windgate was attending a conference of committed Freudians in Tulsa, and Walter had taken the opportunity to consult Wolfe. She sat at the head of the table, a stern but not unattractive woman in her early thirties, with long, dark red hair that rested on the shoulders of her dark blue business suit. Her legs were crossed and a blue pump hung from the end of her right foot.

"You all know why Bird wants to be here," continued Walter. "You'd all want the same thing, if you were in his place." I had bullied and cajoled him to let me sit in on the briefing. I had called in favors I didn't even have the right to call in, and Walter had relented. I didn't regret doing what I had done.

The others in the room remained unconvinced. I could see it in their faces, in the way they shifted their gaze from us, in the shrug of a shoulder and the unhappy twist of a mouth. I didn't care. I wanted to hear what Wolfe had to say. Walter and I took seats and waited for her to begin.

Wolfe took a pair of glasses from the tabletop and put them on. Beside her left hand, the carved broken heart shone wood-bright. She glanced through some notes, pulled out two sheets from the sheaf, and began.

"Right, I don't know how familiar you are with all this, so I'll take it slowly." She paused for a moment. "Detective Parker, you may find some of this difficult." There was no apology in her voice; it was a simple statement of fact. I nodded and she continued. "What we're dealing with here appears to be sexual homicide, sadistic sexual homicide."

I traced the carved heart with the tip of my finger, the texture of the grain briefly returning me to the present. The door of the interrogation room opened, and through the gap, I saw the fed pass by. A clerk entered with a white *I Love NY* cup. The coffee smelled as if it had been brewing since that morning. When I put in the creamer it created only the slightest difference in the color of the liquid. I sipped it and grimaced.

"A sexual homicide generally involves some element of sexual activity as the basis for the sequence of events leading to death," continued Wolfe, sipping at her coffee. "The stripping of the victims and the mutilation of the breasts and genitals indicate a sexual element to the crime, yet we have no evidence of penetration in either victim by either penis, fingers, or foreign objects. The child's hymen was undamaged and there was no evidence of vaginal trauma in the adult victim.

"We also have evidence of a sadistic element to the homicides. The adult victim was tortured prior to death. Flensing took place, specifically on the front of the torso and the face. Combined with the sexual elements, you're dealing with a sexual sadist who obtains gratification from excessive physical and, I would think, mental torture.

"I think he—and I'm assuming it's a white male, for reasons I'll go into later—wanted the mother to watch the torture and killing of her child before she herself was tortured and killed. A sexual sadist gets his kicks from the victim's response to torture; in this case, he had two victims, a mother and child, to play off against each other. He's translating sexual fantasies into violent acts, torture, and, eventually, death."

Outside the door of the interrogation room I heard voices suddenly raised. One of them was Walter Cole's. I didn't recognize the other. The voices subsided again, but I knew that they were talking about me. I would find out what they wanted soon enough.

"Okay. The largest focus group for sexual sadists consists of white, female adults who are strangers to the killer, although they may also target males and, as in this case, children. There is also sometimes a correspondence between the victim and someone in the offender's own life.

"Victims are chosen through systematic stalking and surveillance. The killer had probably been watching the family for some time. He knew the husband's habits, knew that if he went to the bar then he would be missing for long enough to allow him to complete what he wanted to do. In this case, I don't think the killer managed that completion.

"The crime scene is unusual in this case. Firstly, the nature of the crime means that it requires somewhere solitary to give the offender time with his victim. In some cases, the offender's residence may have been modified to accommodate his victim, or he may use a converted car or van for the killing. In this case, the killer chose not to do this. I think he may like the element of risk involved. I also think he wanted to make, for want of a better term, an 'impression.' "

An impression, like wearing a bright tie to a funeral.

"The crime was carefully staged to impact in the most traumatic way on the husband when he returned home."

Maybe Walter had been right. Maybe I shouldn't have come to the briefing. Wolfe's matter-of-factness reduced my wife and child to the level of another gruesome statistic in a violent city, but I hoped that she would say something that would resonate inside me and provide some clue to drive the investigation forward. Two weeks is a long time in a murder case. After two weeks with no progress, unless you get very, very lucky, the investigation starts to grind to a halt.

"This seems to indicate a killer of above-average intelligence, one who likes playing games and gambling," said Wolfe. "The fact that he appeared to want the element of shock to play a part could lead us to conclude that there was a personal element to what he did, directed against the husband, but that's just speculation, and the general pattern of this type of crime is impersonal.

"Generally, crime scenes can be classified as organized, disorganized, or some mix of the two. An organized killer plans the murder and targets the victim carefully, and the crime scene will reflect this element of control. The victims will meet certain criteria which the killer has set: age, hair color maybe, occupation, lifestyle. The use of restraints, as we have in this case, is typical. It reflects the elements of control and planning, since the killer will usually have to bring them to the scene.

"In cases of sexual sadism, the act of killing is generally eroticized. There's a ritual involved; it's usually slow, and every effort is made to ensure that the victim remains conscious and aware up to the point of death. In other words, the killer doesn't want to end the lives of his victims prematurely.

"Now, in this case he didn't succeed, because Jennifer Parker, the child, had a weak heart and it failed following the release of epinephrine into her system. Combined with her mother's attempted escape and the damage caused to her face by striking it against the wall, which may have resulted in temporary loss of consciousness, I believe the killer felt he was losing control of the situation. The crime scene moved from organized to disorganized, and shortly after he commenced flensing, his anger and frustration got the better of him and he mutilated the bodies."

I wanted to leave then. I had made a mistake. Nothing could come of this, nothing good.

"As I said earlier, mutilation of the genitals and breasts is a feature of this type of crime, but this case doesn't conform to the general pattern in a number of crucial ways. I think the mutilation in this case was either a result of anger and loss of control, or it was an attempt to disguise something else, some other element of the ritual which had already commenced and from which the killer was trying to divert attention. In all likelihood, the partial flensing is the key. There's a strong element of display—it's incomplete, but it's there."

"Why are you so sure it's a white male?" asked Joiner, a black Homicide detective with whom I'd worked once or twice.

"The most frequent perpetrators of sexual sadism are white males. Not women, not black males. White males."

"You're off the hook, Joiner," someone said. There was a burst of laughter, an easing of the tension that had built up in the room. One or two of the others glanced at me but for the most part they acted as if I wasn't there. They were professionals, concentrating on amassing any information that might lead to a greater understanding of the killer.

Wolfe let the laughter fade. "Research indicates that as many as forty-three percent of sexual murderers are married. Fifty percent have children. Don't make the mistake of thinking that you're looking for some crazy loner. This guy may be the hero of his local PTA meetings, the coach of the Little League team.

"He could be engaged in a profession that brings him into contact with the public, so he's probably socially adept and he may use that to target his victims. He may have engaged in antisocial behavior in the past, although not necessarily something serious enough to have gotten him a police record.

"Sexual sadists are often police buffs or weapons freaks. He may try to stay in touch with the progress of the investigation, so keep an eye on individuals who ring in with leads or who try to trade off information. He also owns a clean, well-maintained car: clean so it doesn't attract attention, well maintained because he has to be sure he doesn't get stranded at or near the crime scene. The car could have been modified to allow him to transport victims; the door and window handles in the rear will have been removed, the trunk may have been soundproofed. If you think you have a possible suspect, check the trunk for extra fuel, water, ropes, cuffs, ligatures.

"If you go for a search warrant, you'll be looking for any items relating to sexual or violent behavior: pornographic magazines, videos, low-end true-crime stuff, vibrators, clamps, women's clothing, particularly undergarments. Some of these may have belonged to victims or he may have taken other personal items from them. Look out also for diaries and manuscripts; they may contain details of victims, fantasies, even the crimes themselves. This guy may also have a collection of police equipment and almost certainly has a knowledge of police procedures." Wolfe took a deep breath and sat back in her chair.

"Is he going to do it again?" asked Walter. There was silence in the room for a moment.

"Yes, but you're making one assumption," said Wolfe. Walter looked puzzled.

"You're assuming this is the first. I take it a VICAP has been done?"

VICAP, operational since 1985, is the FBI's Violent Criminal Apprehension Program. Under VICAP, a report is completed on solved or unsolved homicides or attempted homicides, particularly those involving abductions or that are apparently random or motiveless or sexually oriented; on missing persons cases, when foul play is suspected; and on unidentified dead bodies, when the manner of death is known or suspected to be homicide. The report is then submitted to the National Center for the Analysis of Violent Crime at the FBI's academy in Quantico, in an effort to determine if similar pattern characteristics exist elsewhere in the VICAP system.

"It was submitted."

"Have you requested a profile?"

"Yes, but no profile as yet. Unofficially, the MO doesn't match. The removal of the faces marks it out."

"Yeah, what about the faces?" It was Joiner again.

"I'm still trying to find out more," said Wolfe. "Some killers take souvenirs from their victims. There may be some kind of pseudo-religious or sacrificial element to this case. I'm sorry, I'm really not sure yet."

"You think he could have done something like this before?" said Walter.

Wolfe nodded. "He may have. If he has killed before, then he may have hidden the bodies, and these killings could represent an alteration in a previous pattern of behavior. Maybe, after killing quietly and unobtrusively, he wanted to bring himself to a more public arena. He may have wanted to draw attention to his work. The unsatisfactory nature of these killings, from his point of view, may now cause him to revert to his old pattern. Alternatively, he could recede into a period of dormancy; that's another possibility.

"But if I was to gamble, I'd say that he's been planning his next move carefully. He made mistakes this time and I don't think he achieved the effect he was looking for. The next time, he won't make any mistakes. The next time, unless you catch him first, he's really going to make an impact."

The door of the interrogation room opened and Walter entered with two other men.

"This is Special Agent Ross, FBI, and Detective Barth from Robbery," said Walter. "Barth was working the Watts case. Agent Ross here deals with organized crime."

Close up, Ross's linen suit looked expensive and tailored. Barth, in his JCPenney jacket, looked like a slob by comparison. The two men stood against opposite walls and nodded. When Walter sat, Barth sat as well. Ross remained standing against the wall.

"Anything you're not telling us here?" Walter asked.

"No," I said. "You know as much as I do."

"Agent Ross believes that Sonny Ferrera was behind the killing of Watts and his girlfriend and that you know more than you're saying." Ross picked at something on the sleeve of his shirt and dropped it to the floor with a look of distaste. I think it was meant to represent me.

"There was no reason for Sonny to kill Ollie Watts," I replied. "We're talking stolen cars and fake license plates here. Ollie wasn't in a position to scam anything worthwhile from Sonny and he didn't know enough about Sonny's activities to take up ten minutes of a jury's time."

Ross stirred and moved forward to sit on the edge of the table. "Strange that you should turn up after all this time— what is it? six, seven months?—and suddenly we're knee deep in corpses," he said, as if he hadn't heard a word I'd said. He was forty, maybe forty-five, but he looked to be in good condition. His face was heavily lined with wrinkles that didn't seem like they came from a life of laughter. I'd heard a little about him from Woolrich, after Woolrich left New York to become the feds' assistant special agent in charge in the New Orleans field office.

There was silence then. Ross tried to stare me out, then looked away in boredom.

"Agent Ross here thinks that you're holding out on us," said Walter. "He'd like to sweat you for a while, just in case." His expression was neutral, his eyes bland. Ross had returned to staring at me.

"Agent Ross is a scary guy. He tries to sweat me, there's no telling what I'll confess to."

"This is not getting us anywhere," said Ross. "Mr. Parker is obviously not cooperating in any way and I—"

Walter held up a hand, interrupting him. "Maybe you'd both leave us alone for a while, get some coffee or something," he suggested. Barth shrugged and left. Ross remained seated on the table and looked like he was going to say more, then he stood up abruptly and quickly walked out, closing the door firmly behind him. Walter exhaled deeply, loosened his tie, and opened the top button of his shirt.

"Don't dump on Ross. He'll bring a ton of shit down on your head. And on mine."

"I've told you all I know on this," I said. "Benny Low may know more, but I doubt it."

"We talked to Benny Low. The way Benny tells it, he didn't know who the president was until we told him." He twisted a pen in his hand. " 'Hey, it's just bidness,' that's what he said." It was a pretty fair imitation of one of Benny Low's verbal quirks. I smiled thinly and the tension in the air dissipated slightly.

"How long you been back?"

"Couple of weeks."

"What have you been doing?"

What could I tell him? That I wandered the streets, that I

visited places where Jennifer, Susan, and I used to go together, that I stared out of the window of my apartment and
thought about the man who had killed them and where he
might be, that I had taken on the job for Benny Low because I was afraid that, if I did not find some outlet, I would
eat the barrel of my gun?

"Not a lot. I plan to look up some old stoolies, see if
there's anything new."

"There isn't, not at this end. You got anything?"

"No."

"I can't ask you to let it go, but—"

"No, you can't. Get to it, Walter."

"This isn't a good place for you to be right now. You
know why."

"Do I?"

Walter tossed the pen hard on the table. It bounced to
the edge and then hung there briefly before dropping to the
floor. For a moment I thought he was going to take a swing
at me but then the anger went from his eyes.

"We'll talk about this again."

"Okay. You going to give me anything?" Among the papers on the table, I could see reports from Ballistics and
Firearms. Five hours was a pretty short time in which to get
a report. Agent Ross was obviously a man who got what he
wanted.

I nodded at the report. "What did Ballistics say about the
bullet that took out the shooter?"

"That's not your concern."

"Walter, I watched the kid die. The shooter took a pop at
me and the bullet went clean through the wall. Someone's
got distinctive taste in weaponry."

Walter stayed silent.

"No one picks up hardware like that without someone
knowing," I said. "You give me something to go on, maybe I
might find out more than you can."

Walter thought for a minute and then flicked through
the papers for the Ballistics report. "We got submachine bullets, five-point-seven millimeters, weighing less than fifty
grains."

I whistled. "That's a scaled-down rifle round, but fired from a handgun?"

"The bullet is mainly plastic but has a full-metal jacket, so it doesn't deform on impact. When it hits something—like your shooter—it transfers most of its force. There's almost no energy when it exits."

"And the one that hit the wall?"

"Ballistics reckons a muzzle velocity of over two thousand feet per second."

That was an incredibly fast bullet. A Browning 9 millimeter fires bullets of one hundred ten grains at only eleven hundred feet per second.

"They also reckon that this thing could blow through Kevlar body armor like it was rice paper. At two hundred yards, the thing could penetrate almost fifty layers." Even a .44 Magnum will only penetrate body armor at very close range.

"But once it hits a soft target . . ."

"It stops."

"Is it domestic?"

"No, Ballistics say European. Belgian. They're talking about something called a Five-seveN—that's big *F*, big *N*, after the manufacturers. It's a prototype made by FN Herstal for antiterrorist and hostage rescue operations, but this is the first time one has turned up outside national security forces."

"You contacting the maker?"

"We'll try, but my guess is we'll lose it in the middlemen."

I stood up. "I'll ask around."

Walter retrieved his pen and waved it at me like an unhappy schoolteacher lecturing the class wise guy. "Ross still wants your ass."

I took out a pen and scribbled my cell phone number on the back of Walter's legal pad.

"It's always on. Can I go now?"

"One condition."

"Go on."

"I want you to come over to the house tonight."

"I'm sorry, Walter, I don't make social calls anymore."

He looked hurt. "Don't be an asshole. This isn't social. Be there, or Ross can lock you in a cell till doomsday for all I care."

I stood up to leave.

"You sure you've told us everything?" he asked to my back.

I didn't turn around. "I've told you all I can, Walter."

Which was true, technically at least.

Twenty-four hours earlier, I had found Emo Ellison. Emo lived in a dump of a hotel on the edge of East Harlem, the kind where the only guests allowed in the rooms are whores, cops, or criminals. A Plexiglas screen covered the front of the super's office, but there was no one inside. I walked up the stairs and knocked on Emo's door. There was no reply but I thought I heard the sound of a hammer cocking on a pistol.

"Emo, it's Bird. I need to talk."

I heard footsteps approach the door.

"I don't know nothin' about it," said Emo, through the wood. "I got nothin' to say."

"I haven't asked you anything yet. C'mon, Emo, open up. Fat Ollie's in trouble. Maybe I can do something. Let me in."

There was silence for a moment and then the rattle of a chain. The door opened and I stepped inside. Emo had retreated to the window but he still had the gun in his hand. I closed the door behind me.

"You don't need that," I said. Emo hefted the gun once in his hand and then put it on a bedside cabinet. He looked more comfortable without it. Guns weren't Emo's style. I noticed that the fingers of his left hand were bandaged. I could see yellow stains on the tips of the bandages.

Emo Ellison was a thin, pale-faced, middle-aged man who had worked on and off for Fat Ollie for five years or so. He was an average mechanic but he was loyal and knew when to keep his mouth shut.

"Do you know where he is?"

"He ain't been in touch."

He sat down heavily on the edge of the neatly made bed. The room was clean and smelled of air freshener. There were one or two prints on the walls, and books, magazines, and some personal items were neatly arrayed on a set of Home Depot shelves.

"I hear you're workin' for Benny Low. Why you doin' that?"

"It's work," I replied.

"You hand Ollie over and he's dead, that's your work," said Emo.

I leaned against the door.

"I may not hand him over. Benny Low can take the loss. But I'd need a good reason not to."

The conflict inside him played itself out on Emo's face. His hands twisted and writhed over each other and he looked once or twice at the gun. Emo Ellison was scared.

"Why did he run, Emo?" I asked softly.

"He used to say you were a good guy, a stand-up guy," said Emo. "That true?"

"I don't know. I don't want to see Ollie hurt, though."

Emo looked at me for a time and then seemed to make a decision.

"It was Pili. Pili Pilar. You know him?"

"I know him." Pili Pilar was Sonny Ferrera's right-hand man.

"He used to come once, twice a month, never more than that, and take a car. He'd keep it for a couple of hours, then bring it back. Different car each time. It was a deal Ollie made, so he wouldn't have to pay off Sonny. He'd fit the car with false plates and have it ready for Pili when he arrived.

"Last week, Pili comes, collects a car, and drives off. I came in late that night, 'cause I was sick. I got ulcers. Pili was gone before I got there.

"Anyway, after midnight I'm sittin' up with Ollie, talkin' and stuff, waitin' for Pili to bring back the car, when there's this bang outside. When we get out there, Pili's wrapped the car around the gate and he's lying on the wheel. There's a dent in the front, too, so we figure maybe Pili was in a smash and didn't want to wait around after.

"Pili's head is cut up bad where he smacked the windshield and there's a lot of blood in the car. Ollie and me push it into the yard and then Ollie calls this doc he knows, and the guy tells him to bring Pili around. Pili ain't movin' and he's real pale, so Ollie drops him off at the doc's in his own car, and the doc insists on packing him off to the hospital 'cause he thinks Pili's skull is busted."

It was all flowing out of Emo now. Once he began the tale he wanted to finish it, as if he could diminish the burden of knowing by telling it out loud. "Anyway, they argue for a while but the doc knows this private clinic where they won't ask too many questions, and Ollie agrees. The doc calls the clinic and Ollie comes back to the lot to sort out the car.

"He has a number for Sonny but there's no answer. He's got the car in back but he doesn't want to leave it there in case, y'know, it's a cop thing. So he calls the old man and lets him know what happened. So the old man tells him to sit tight, he'll send a guy around to take care of it.

"Ollie goes out to move the car out of sight but when he comes back in, he looks worse than Pili. He looks sick and his hands are shakin'. I say to him, 'What's wrong?' but he just tells me to get out and not to tell no one I was there. He won't say nothin' else, just tells me to get goin'.

"Next thing I hear, the cops have raided the place and then Ollie makes bail and disappears. I swear, that's the last I heard."

"Then why the gun?"

"One of the old man's guys came by here a day or two back." He gulped. "Bobby Sciorra. He wanted to know about Ollie, wanted to know if I'd been there the day of Pili's accident. I said to him, 'No,' but it wasn't enough for him."

Emo Ellison started to cry. He lifted up his bandaged fingers and slowly, carefully, began to unwrap one of them.

"He took me for a ride." He held up the finger and I could see a ring-shaped mark crowned with a huge blister that seemed to throb even as I looked at it. "The cigarette lighter. He burned me with the car cigarette lighter."

Twenty-four hours later, Fat Ollie Watts was dead.

3

□

WALTER COLE lived in Richmond Hill, the oldest of the Seven Sisters neighborhoods in Queens. Begun in the 1880s, it had a village center and town common and must have seemed like Middle America recreated on Manhattan's doorstep when Walter's parents first moved there from Jefferson City shortly before World War II. Walter had kept the house, north of Myrtle Avenue on 113th Street, after his parents retired to Florida. He and Lee ate almost every Friday in Triangle Hofbräu, an old German restaurant on Jamaica Avenue, and walked in the dense woods of Forest Park during the summer.

I arrived at Walter's home shortly after nine. He answered the door himself and showed me into what, for a less educated man, would have been called his den, although "den" didn't do justice to the miniature library he had assembled over half a century of avid reading: biographies of Keats and Saint-Exupéry shared shelf space with works on forensics, sex crimes, and criminal psychology. Fenimore Cooper stood back to back with Borges; Barthelme looked uneasy surrounded by various Hemingways.

A Macintosh PowerBook sat on a leather-topped desk beside three filing cabinets. Paintings by local artists adorned the walls, and a small glass-fronted case in the corner displayed shooting trophies, haphazardly thrown together as if Walter was simultaneously proud of his ability yet embarrassed by his pride. The top half of the window was open and I could smell freshly mown grass and hear the sound of kids playing street hockey in the warm evening air.

The door to the den opened and Lee entered. She and Walter had been together for twenty-four years and they shared each other's lives with an ease and grace that Susan and I had never approached, even at the best of times. Lee's black jeans and white blouse hugged a figure that had survived the rigors of two children and Walter's love of Oriental cuisine. Her ink black hair, through which strands of gray wove like moonlight on dark water, was pulled back in a ponytail. When she reached up to kiss me lightly on the cheek, her arms around my shoulders, the scent of lavender enfolded me like a veil and I realized, not for the first time, that I had always been a little in love with Lee Cole.

"It's good to see you, Bird," she said, her right hand resting lightly on my cheek, lines of anxiety on her brow giving the lie to the smile on her lips. She glanced at Walter and something passed between them. "I'll be back later with some coffee." She closed the door softly behind her on the way out.

"How are the kids doing?" I asked as Walter poured himself a glass of Redbreast Irish whiskey—the old stuff with the screw top.

"Good," he replied. "Lauren still hates high school. Ellen's going to study law in Georgetown in the fall, so at least one member of the family will understand the way it works." He inhaled deeply as he raised the glass to his mouth and sipped. I gulped involuntarily and a sudden thirst gripped me. Walter noticed my discomfiture and reddened.

"Shit, I'm sorry," he said.

"It's all right," I responded. "It's good therapy. I notice you're still swearing in the house." Lee hated swearing, routinely telling her husband that only oafs resorted to profanity in speech. Walter usually countered by pointing out that Wittgenstein once brandished a poker in the course of a philosophical argument, proof positive in his eyes that erudite discourse sometimes wasn't sufficiently expressive for even the greatest of men.

He moved to a leather armchair at one side of the empty fireplace and motioned to its opposite number. Lee entered with a silver coffeepot, a creamer, and two cups on a tray and then left, glancing anxiously at Walter as she did. I knew they had been talking before I arrived; they kept no secrets from each other and their unease seemed to indicate that they had discussed more than their concerns about my well-being.

"Do you want me to sit under a light?" I asked. A small smile moved across Walter's face with the swiftness of a breeze and then was gone.

"I heard things over the last few months," he began, looking into his glass like a mystic examining a crystal ball. I stayed silent.

"I know you talked to the feds, pulled in some favors so you could take a look at files. I know you were trying to find the man who killed Susan and Jenny." He looked at me for the first time since he had begun talking.

I had nothing to say, so I poured some coffee for both of us, then picked up my own cup and sipped. It was Javan, strong and dark. I breathed deeply. "Why are you asking me this?"

"Because I want to know why you're here, why you're back. I don't know what you've become if some of the things I've heard are true." He swallowed and I felt sorry for him, for what he had to say and the questions he had to ask. If I had answers to some of them, I wasn't sure that I wanted to give them, or that Walter really wanted to hear them. Outside, the kids had finished their game as darkness drew in, and there was a stillness in the air that made Walter's words sound like a portent.

"They say you found the guy who did it," he said, and this time there was no hesitation, as if he had steeled himself to say what he had to say. "That you found him and killed him. Is that true?"

The past was like a snare. It allowed me to move a little, to circle, to turn, but in the end, it always dragged me back. More and more, I found things in the city—favorite restaurants, bookshops, tree-shaded parks, even hearts carved bone white into the wood of an old table—that reminded me of what I had lost, as if even a moment of forgetfulness was a crime against their memories. I slipped from present to past, sliding down the snake heads of memory into what was and what would never be again.

And so, with Walter's question, I fell back to late April, back to New Orleans. They had been dead for almost four months.

Woolrich sat at a table at the rear of the Café du Monde, beside a bubble gum machine, with his back against the wall of the main building. On the table before him stood a steaming cup of café au lait and a plate of hot beignets covered in powdered sugar. Outside, people bustled down Decatur, past the green-and-white pavilion of the café, heading for the cathedral or Jackson Square.

He wore a tan suit, cheaply made, and his silk tie was stretched and faded so that he didn't even bother to button his shirt at the collar, preferring instead to let the tie hang mournfully at half mast. The floor around him was white with sugar, as was the only visible part of the green vinyl chair upon which he sat.

Woolrich was an assistant SAC of the local FBI field office over at 1250 Poydras. He was also one of the few people from my police past with whom I'd stayed in touch in some small way, and one of the only feds I had ever met who didn't make me curse the day Hoover was born. More than that, he was my friend. He had stood by me in the days following the killings, never questioning, never doubting. I remember him standing, rain-soaked, by the grave, water dripping from the rim of his outsized fedora. He had been transferred to New Orleans soon after, a promotion that reflected a successful apprenticeship in at least three other field offices and his ability to keep his head in the turbulent environment of the New York field office in downtown Manhattan.

He was messily divorced, the marriage over for maybe twelve years. His wife had reverted to her maiden name, Karen Stott, and lived in Miami with an interior decorator whom she had recently married. Woolrich's only daughter, Lisa—now, thanks to her mother's efforts, Lisa Stott—had joined some religious group in Mexico, he said. She was just eighteen. Her mother and her new husband didn't seem to care about her, unlike Woolrich, who cared but couldn't get his act together enough to do anything about it. The disintegration of his family pained him in a very particular way, I knew. He came from a broken family himself, a white-trash mother and a father who was well meaning but inconsequential, too inconsequential to hold on to his hellcat wife. Woolrich had always wanted to do better, I think. More than the rest, I believed, he shared my sense of loss when Susan and Jennifer were taken.

He had put on more weight since I last saw him, and the hair on his chest was visible through his sweat-soaked shirt. Rivulets rolled down from a dense thatch of rapidly graying hair and into the folds of flesh at his neck. For such a big man, the Louisiana summers would be a form of torture. Woolrich may have looked like a clown, may even have acted that way when it suited him, but no one in New Orleans who knew him ever underestimated him. Those who had in the past were already rotting in Angola penitentiary.

"I like the tie," I said. It was bright red and decorated with lambs and angels.

"I call it my metaphysical tie," Woolrich replied. "My George Herbert tie."

We shook hands, Woolrich wiping beignet crumbs from his shirtfront as he stood. "Damn things get everywhere," he said. "When I die, they'll find beignet crumbs up the crack of my ass."

"Thanks, I'll hold that thought."

An Asian waiter in a white paper cap bustled up and I ordered coffee. "Bring you beignets, suh?" he asked. Woolrich grinned. I told the waiter I'd skip the beignets.

"How you doin'?" asked Woolrich, taking a gulp of coffee hot enough to scarify the throat of a lesser man.

"I'm okay. How's life?"

"Same as it ever was: gift wrapped, tied with a red bow, and handed to someone else."

"You still with . . . what was her name? Judy? Judy the nurse?"

Woolrich's face creased unhappily, as if he'd just encountered a cockroach in his beignet. "Judy the nut, you mean. We split up. She's gone to work in La Jolla for a year, maybe more. I tell you, I decide to take her away for a romantic vacation a couple of months back, rent us a room in a two-hundred-dollar-a-night inn near Stowe, take in the country air if we left the window of the bedroom open, you know the deal. Anyway, we arrive at this place and it's older than Moses's dick, all dark wood and antique furniture and a bed you could lose a team of cheerleaders in. But Judy, she turns whiter than a polar bear's ass and backs away from me. You know what she says?"

I waited for him to continue.

"She says that I murdered her in the very same room in a previous life. She's backed up against the door, reaching for the handle and looking at me like she's expecting me to turn into the Son of Sam. Takes me two hours to calm her down and even then she refuses to sleep with me. I end up sleeping on a couch in the corner, and let me tell you, those goddamned antique couches may look like a million bucks and cost more, but they're about as comfortable to sleep on as a concrete slab."

He finished off the last bite of beignet and dabbed at himself with a napkin.

"Then I get up in the middle of the night to take a leak and she's sitting up in bed, wide awake, with the bedside lamp upside down in her hand, waiting to knock my head off if I come near her. Needless to say, this put an end to our five days of passion. We checked out the next morning, with me over a thousand dollars in the hole.

"But you know what the really funny thing is? Her regression therapist has told her to sue me for injuries in a past life. I'm about to become a test case for all those donut heads who watch a documentary on PBS and think they were once Cleopatra or William the Conqueror."

His eyes misted over at the thought of his lost thousand and the games Fate plays on those who go to Vermont looking for uncomplicated sex.

"You heard from Lisa lately?"

His face clouded over and he waved a hand at me. "Still

with the Jesus huggers. Last time she called me, it was to say that her leg was fine and to ask for more money. If Jesus saves, he must have had all his cash tied up with the savings and loan." Lisa had broken her leg in a roller-skating accident the previous year, shortly before she found God. Woolrich was convinced that she was still concussed.

He stared at me for a time, his eyes narrowed. "You're not okay, are you?"

"I'm alive and I'm here. Just tell me what you've got."

He puffed his cheeks and then blew out slowly, marshaling his thoughts as he did so.

"There's a woman, down in St. Martin Parish, an old Creole. She's got the gift, the locals say. She keeps away the gris-gris. You know, bad spirits, all that shit. Offers cures for sick kids, brings lovers together. Has visions." He stopped and rolled his tongue around his mouth, and squinted at me.

"She's a psychic?"

"She's a witch, you believe the locals."

"And do you?"

"She's been . . . helpful, once or twice in the past, according to the local cops. I've had nothing to do with her before."

"And now?"

My coffee arrived and Woolrich asked for a refill. We didn't speak again until the waiter had departed and Woolrich had drained half of his coffee in a steaming mouthful.

"She's got about ten children and thousands of goddamn grandchildren and great-grandchildren. Some of them live with her or near her, so she's never alone. She's got a bigger extended family than Abraham." He smiled but it was a fleeting thing, a brief release before what was to come.

"She says a young girl was killed in the bayou a while back, in the marshlands where the Barataria pirates used to roam. She told the sheriff's office but they didn't pay much attention. She didn't have a location, just said a young girl had been murdered in the bayou. Said she had seen it in a dream.

"Sheriff didn't do nothing about it. Well, that's not entirely true. He told the local boys to keep an eye out and then pretty much forgot all about it."

"What brings it up again now?"

"The old woman says she hears the girl crying at night."

I couldn't tell whether Woolrich was spooked or just embarrassed by what he was saying, but he looked toward the window and wiped his face with a giant grubby handkerchief.

"There's something else, though." He folded the handkerchief and stuffed it back in his trouser pocket.

"She says the girl's face was cut off." He breathed in deeply. "And that she was blinded before she died."

We drove north on I-10 for a time, past an outlet mall and on toward West Baton Rouge with its truck stops and gambling joints, its bars full of oil workers and, elsewhere, blacks, all drinking the same rotgut whiskey and watery Dixie beer. A hot wind, heavy with the dense, decayed smell of the bayou, pulled at the trees along the highway, whipping their branches back and forth. Then we crossed onto the raised Atchafalaya highway, its supports embedded beneath the waters, as we entered the Atchafalaya swamp and Cajun country.

I had been here only once before, when Susan and I were younger and happier. Along the Henderson Levee Road we passed the sign for McGee's Landing, where I'd eaten tasteless chicken and Susan had picked at lumps of deep-fried alligator so tough even other alligators would have had trouble digesting it. Then a Cajun fisherman had taken us on a boat trip into the swamps, through a semisubmerged cypress forest. The sun sank low and bloody over the water, turning the tree stumps into dark silhouettes like the fingers of dead men pointing accusingly at the heavens. It was another world, as far removed from the city as the moon was from the earth, and it seemed to create an erotic charge between us as the heat made our shirts cling to our bodies and the sweat drip from our brows. When we returned to our hotel in Lafayette we made love urgently and with a passion that superseded love, our drenched bodies moving together, the heat in the room as thick as water.

Woolrich and I did not go as far as Lafayette. We abandoned the highway for a two-lane road that wove through the bayou country for a time before turning into little more than a rutted track, pitted by holes filled with dank, foul-smelling swamp water around which insects buzzed in thick swarms. Cypress and willow lined the road and, through them, the stumps of trees were visible in the waters of the swamp, relics of the harvestings of the last century. Lily pads clustered at the banks, and when the car slowed and the light was right, I could see bass moving languidly in their shadows, breaking the water occasionally.

I had heard once that Jean Lafitte's brigands had made their home here. Now others had taken their place, killers and smugglers who used the canals and marshes as hiding places for heroin and marijuana, and as dark, green graves for the butchered, their bodies adding to the riotous growth of nature, their decay masked by the rich stench of vegetation.

We took one further turn, and here the cypress overhung the road. We rattled over a wooden bridge, the wood gradually returning to its original color as the paint flaked and disintegrated. In the shadows at its far end I thought I saw a giant figure watching us as we passed, his eyes white as eggs in the darkness beneath the trees.

"You see him?" said Woolrich.

"Who is he?"

"The old woman's youngest son. Tee Jean, she calls him. Petit Jean. He's kinda slow, but he looks out for her. They all do."

"All?"

"Six of 'em live in the house. The old woman, her son, three kids from her second-eldest's marriage—he's dead; died with his wife in a car crash three years back—and a daughter. She has five more sons and three daughters all living within a few miles of here. Then the local folks, they look after her too. She's kind of the matriarch around these parts, I guess. Big magic."

I looked to see if he was being ironic. He wasn't.

We left the trees and arrived in a clearing before a long, single-story house raised above the ground on stripped stumps of trees. It looked old but lovingly built, the wood on the front unwarped and carefully overlapped, the shingles on the roof undamaged but, here and there, darker where they had been replaced. The door stood open, blocked only by a wire screen, and chairs and children's toys littered the porch, which ran the length of the front of the house and disappeared around the side. From behind, I could hear the sound of children and the splashing of water.

The screen door was opened and a small, slim woman appeared at the top of the steps. She was about thirty, with delicate features and lush dark hair drawn back in a ponytail from her light coffee-colored skin. Yet as we stepped from the car and drew nearer, I could see her skin was pitted with scars, probably from childhood acne. She seemed to recognize Woolrich for, before we said anything, she held the door open so I could step inside. Woolrich didn't follow. I turned back toward him.

"You coming in?"

"I didn't bring you here, if anyone asks, and I don't even want to see her," he said. He took a seat on the porch and rested his feet on the rail, watching the water gleam in the sunlight.

Inside, the wood was dark and the air cool. Doors at either side opened into bedrooms and a formal-looking living room with old, obviously hand-carved furniture, simple but carefully and skillfully crafted. An ancient radio with an illuminated dial and a band dotted with the names of far-flung places played a Chopin nocturne. The music followed me through the house and into the last bedroom, where the old woman waited.

She was blind. Her pupils were white, set in a huge moon face from which rolls of fat hung to her breastbone. Her arms, visible through the gauze sleeves of her multicolored dress, were bigger than mine and her swollen legs were like the trunks of small trees ending in surprisingly small, almost dainty, feet. She sat, supported by a mountain of pillows, on a giant bed in a room lit only by a hurricane lamp, the drapes closed against the sunlight. She was at least three hundred and fifty pounds, I guessed, probably more.

"Sit down, chile," she said, taking one of my hands in her own and running her fingers lightly over mine. Her eyes stared straight ahead, not looking at me, as her fingers traced the lines on my palm.

"I know why you here," she said. Her voice was high, girlish, as if she were a huge speaking doll whose tapes had been mixed up with a smaller model. "You hurtin'. You burnin' inside. Little girl, you woman, they gone." In the dim light, the old woman seemed to crackle with hidden energy.

"*Tante,* tell me about the girl in the swamp, the girl with no eyes."

"Poor chile," said the old woman, her brow furrowing in sorrow. "She the fust here. She was runnin' from sumpin' and she los' her way. Took a ride wi' him and she never came back. Hurt her so, so bad. Didn't touch her, though, 'cept with the knife."

She turned her eyes toward me for the first time and I realized she was not blind, not in any way that mattered. As her hands traced the lines of my palm, my eyes closed and I felt that she had been there with the girl in her final moments, that she might even have brought her some comfort as the blade went about its business. "Hush, chile, you come with *Tante* now. Hush, chile, take my hand, you. He done hurtin' you now."

As she touched me, I heard and felt, deep within myself, the blade cutting, grating, separating muscle from joint, flesh from bone, soul from body, the artist working on his canvas; and I felt pain dancing through me, arcing through a fading life like a lightning flash, welling like the notes of a hellish song through the unknown girl in the Louisiana swamp. And in her agony I felt the agony of my own child, my own wife, and I was certain that this was the same man. Even as the pain faded to its last for the girl in the swamp, she was in darkness and I knew he had blinded her before he killed her.

"Who is he?" I said.

She spoke, and in her voice there were four voices: the voices of a wife and a daughter, the voice of an old obese woman on a bed in a wine-dark room, and the voice of a nameless girl who died a brutal, lonely death in the mud and water of a Louisiana swamp.

"He the Travelin' Man."

Walter shifted in his chair and the sound of his spoon against the china cup was like the ringing of chimes.

"No," I said. "I didn't find him."

4

□

WALTER HAD BEEN silent for a while, the whiskey now almost drained from his glass. "I need a favor. Not for me but for someone else."

I waited.

"It has to do with the Barton Trust."

The Barton Trust had been founded in his will by old Jack Barton, an industrialist who made his fortune by supplying parts for the aeronautical industry after the war. The trust provided money for research into child-related issues, supported pediatric clinics, and generally provided child-care money that the state would not. Its nominal head was Isobel Barton, old Jack's widow, although the day-to-day running of the business was the responsibility of an attorney named Andrew Bruce and the trust's chairman, Philip Kooper.

I knew all this because Walter did some fund-raising for the trust on occasion—raffles, bowling tournaments—and also because, some weeks before, the trust had entered the news for all the wrong reasons. During a charity fete held on the grounds of the Barton house on Staten Island, a young boy, Evan Baines, had disappeared. In the end, no trace of the boy had been found and the cops had pretty much given up hope. They believed he had somehow strayed from the grounds and been abducted. It merited some mention in the newspapers for a time and then was gone.

"Evan Baines?"

"No, at least I don't think so, but it may be a missing person. A friend of Isobel Barton, a young woman, seems to have gone missing. It's been a few days and Mrs. Barton's worried. Her name's Catherine Demeter. Nothing to link her with the Baines disappearance; she hadn't even met the Bartons at that point."

"Bartons plural?"

"Seems she was dating Stephen Barton. You know anything about him?"

"He's an asshole. Apart from that, he's a minor drug pusher for Sonny Ferrera. Grew up near the Ferreras on Staten Island and fell in with Sonny as a teenager. He's into steroids, also coke, I think, but it's minor stuff."

Walter's brow furrowed. "How long have you known about this?" he asked.

"Can't remember," I replied. "Gym gossip."

"Jesus, don't tell us anything we might find useful. I've only known since Tuesday."

"You're not supposed to know," I said. "You're the police. Nobody tells you things you're supposed to know."

"You used to be a cop too," Walter muttered. "You've picked up some bad habits."

"Gimme a break, Walter. How do I know who you're checking up on? What am I supposed to do, go to confession to you once a week?" I poured some hot coffee into my cup. "Anyway, you think there might be a connection between this disappearance and Sonny Ferrera?" I continued.

"It's possible," said Walter. "The feds were tracking Stephen Barton for a while, maybe a year ago, before he was supposed to have started seeing Catherine Demeter. They were chasing their tails with that kid, so they let it go. According to the Narcotics file she doesn't seem to have been involved, at least not openly, but what do they know? Some of them still think a crack pipe is something a plumber fixes. Maybe she could have seen something she wasn't supposed to see."

His face betrayed how lame he thought the link was, but he left me to voice it. "C'mon, Walter, steroids and minor coke? There's money in it but it's strictly Little League compared to the rest of Ferrera's business. If he knocked off someone over musclehead drugs, then he's even more stu-

pid than we know he is. Even his old man thinks he's the result of a defective gene."

Ferrera senior, sick and decrepit but still a respected figure, had been known to refer to his only son as "that little
prick" on occasion. "Is that all you've got?"

"As you say, we're the police. No one tells us anything
useful," he replied dryly.

"Did you know Sonny is impotent?" I offered.

Walter stood up, waving his empty glass in front of his
face and smiling for the first time that evening. "No. No, I
didn't. I'm not sure I wanted to know, either. What the hell
are you, his urologist?" He glanced over at me as he reached
for the Redbreast. I waved my fingers in a gesture of disregard that went no farther than my wrist.

"Pili Pilar still with him?" I asked, testing the waters.

"Far as I know. I hear he pushed Nicky Glasses out of a
window a few weeks back because he fell behind on the
vig."

The World Bank had loans out that attracted lower interest than Sonny Ferrera's financial operations. Then again,
the World Bank probably didn't throw people out of the
tenth floor because they couldn't keep up with the interest,
at least not yet.

"Tough on Nicky. Another hundred years and he'd have
had the loan paid off. Pili'd better ease up on his temper or
he's gonna run out of people to push through windows."

Walter didn't smile.

"Will you talk to her?" he asked as he resumed his seat.

"MPs, Walter . . ." I sighed. Fourteen thousand people
disappear in New York every year. It wasn't even clear if this
woman was missing—in which case she didn't want to be
found or someone else didn't want her found—or simply
misplaced, which meant that she had merely upped sticks
and moved off to another town without breaking the news
to her good friend Isobel Barton or to her lovely boyfriend,
Stephen Barton.

Those are the kinds of issues PIs have to consider when
faced with missing persons cases. Tracing missing persons is
bread and butter for PIs, but I wasn't a PI. I had taken on Fat

Ollie's skip because it was easy work, or seemed to be at the time. I didn't want to file for a PI license with the state licensing services in Albany. I didn't want to get involved in missing persons work. Maybe I was afraid it would distract me too much. Maybe I just didn't care enough, not then.

"She won't go to the cops," said Walter. "The woman isn't even officially missing yet, since no one has reported her."

"So how come you know about it?"

"You know Tony Loo-Loo?" I nodded. Tony Loomax was a small-time PI with a stammer who had never graduated beyond skips and white trash divorces.

"Loomax is an unusual candidate for Isobel Barton's patronage," I said.

"It seems he did some work for one of the household staff a year or two back. Traced her husband, who'd run off with their savings. Mrs. Barton told him she wanted something similar done, but wanted it done quietly."

"Still doesn't explain your involvement."

"I have some stuff on Tony, mild overstepping of legal boundaries, which he would prefer I didn't act on. Tony figured I might like to know that Isobel Barton had been making low-key approaches. I spoke to Kooper. He believes the trust doesn't need any more bad publicity. I figured maybe I could do him a favor."

"If Tony has the call, then why are you approaching me?"

"We've encouraged Tony to pass it on. He's told Isobel Barton that he's passing her on to someone she can trust because he can't take the case. Seems his mother just died and he has to go to the funeral."

"Tony Loo-Loo doesn't have a mother. He was brought up in an orphanage."

"Well, *someone's* mother must have died," said Walter testily. "He can go to *that* funeral."

He stopped and I could see the doubt in his eyes as the rumors he had heard flicked a fin in the depths of his mind. "And that's why I'm approaching you. Even if I tried to do this quietly through the usual channels, someone would know. Christ, you take a drink of water at headquarters and ten guys piss it out."

"What about the girl's family?"

He shrugged. "I don't know much more but I don't think there is one. Look, Bird, I'm asking you because you're good. You were a smart cop. If you'd stayed on the force the rest of us would have been cleaning your shoes and polishing your shield. Your instincts were good. I reckon they still are. Plus you owe me one: people who go shooting up the boroughs don't usually walk away quite so easily."

I was silent for a while. I could hear Lee banging around in the kitchen while a TV show played in the background. Perhaps it was a remnant of what had taken place earlier, the apparently senseless killing of Fat Ollie Watts and his girlfriend, the death of the shooter, but it felt as if the world had shifted out of joint and that nothing was fitting as it should. Even this felt wrong. I believed Walter was holding back on me.

I heard the doorbell ring and then there was a muffled exchange of voices, one of them Lee's and the other a deep male voice. Seconds later there was a knock on the door and Lee showed in a tall, gray-haired man in his fifties. He wore a dark blue double-breasted suit—it looked like Boss—and a red Christian Dior tie with an interlocking gold *CD* pattern. His shoes sparkled like they'd been shined with spit, although, since this was Philip Kooper, it was probably someone else's spit.

Kooper was an unlikely figure to act as chairman and spokesman of a children's charity. He was thin and pale faced, and his mouth managed the unique trick of being simultaneously slim and pursed. His fingers were long and tapering, almost like claws. Kooper looked like he had been disinterred for the express purpose of making people uneasy. If he had turned up at one of the trust's kids' parties, all of the children would have cried.

"This him?" he asked Walter, after declining a drink. He flicked his head at me like a frog swallowing a fly. I played with the sugar bowl and tried to look offended.

"This is Parker," nodded Walter. I waited to see if Kooper

would offer to shake hands. He didn't. His hands remained clasped in front of him like a professional mourner at a particularly uninvolving funeral.

"Have you explained the situation to him?"

Walter nodded again but looked embarrassed. Kooper's manners were worse than a bad child's. I stayed seated and didn't say anything. Kooper sniffed and then stood in silence while he looked down on me. He gave the impression that it was a position with which he was entirely familiar.

"This is a delicate situation, Mr. Parker, as I'm sure you'll appreciate. Any communication in this matter will be made to me in the first instance before you impart any information to Mrs. Barton. Is that clear?"

I wondered if Kooper was worth the effort of annoying and decided, after looking at Walter's look of discomfort, that he probably wasn't, at least not yet. But I was starting to feel sorry for Isobel Barton and I hadn't even met her.

"My understanding was that Mrs. Barton was hiring me," I said eventually.

"That's correct, but you will be answerable to me."

"I don't think so. There's a small matter of confidentiality. I'll look into it, but if it's unconnected with the Baines kid or the Ferreras, I reserve the right to keep what I learn between Isobel Barton and myself."

"That is not satisfactory, Mr. Parker," said Kooper. A faint blush of color rose in his cheeks and hung there for a moment, looking lost in the tundra of his complexion. "Perhaps I am not making myself clear: in this matter, you will report to me first. I have powerful friends, Mr. Parker. If you do not cooperate, I can ensure that your license is revoked."

"They must be very powerful friends because I don't have a license," I said. I stood up and Kooper's fists tightened slightly. "You should consider yoga," I said. "You're too tense."

I thanked Walter for the coffee and moved to the door.

"Wait," he said. I turned back to see him staring at Kooper. After a few moments, Kooper gave a barely perceptible shrug of his shoulders and moved to the window. He didn't look at me again. Kooper's attitude and Walter's expression conspired against my better judgment, and I decided to talk to Isobel Barton.

"I take it she's expecting me?" I asked Walter.

"I told Tony to tell her you were good, that if the girl was alive you'd find her."

There was another brief moment of silence.

"And if she's dead?"

"Mr. Kooper asked that question as well," said Walter.

"What did you say?"

He swallowed the last of his whiskey, the ice cubes rattling against the glass like old bones. Behind him, Kooper was a dark silhouette against the window, like a promise of bad news.

"I told him you'd bring back the body."

In the end, that's what it all came down to: bodies—bodies found and yet to be found. And I recalled how Woolrich and I stood outside the old woman's house on that April day and looked out over the bayou. I could hear the water lapping gently at the shore, and farther out, I watched a small fishing boat bobbing on the water, two figures casting out from either side. But both Woolrich and I were looking deeper than the surface, as if, by staring hard enough, we could penetrate to the depths and find the body of a nameless girl in the dark waters.

"Do you believe her?" he said at last.

"I don't know. I really don't know."

"There's no way we're gonna find that body, if it exists, without more than we've got. We start trawling for bodies in bayous and pretty soon we're gonna be knee deep in bones. People been dumping bodies in these swamps for centuries. Be a miracle if we didn't find something."

I walked away from him. He was right, of course. Assuming there was a body, we needed more from the old woman than she had given us. I felt like I was trying to grip smoke, but what the old woman had said was the closest thing yet to a lead on the man who had killed Jennifer and Susan.

I wondered if I was crazy, taking the word of a blind woman who heard voices in her sleep. I probably was.

"Do you know what he looks like, *Tante?*" I had asked her, watching as her head moved ponderously from side to side in response.

"Only see him when he comes for you," she replied. "Then you know him."

I reached the car and looked back to see a figure on the porch with Woolrich. It was the girl with the scarred face, standing gracefully on the tips of her toes as she leaned toward the taller man. I saw Woolrich run his finger tenderly across her cheek and then softly speak her name: "Florence." He kissed her lightly on the lips, then turned and walked toward me without looking back at her. Neither of us said anything about it on the journey back to New Orleans.

5

□

IT RAINED throughout that night, breaking the shell of heat that had surrounded the city, and the streets of Manhattan seemed to breathe easier the next morning. It was almost cool as I ran. The pavement was hard on my knees but large areas of grass were sparse in this part of the city. I bought a newspaper on the way back to my apartment, then showered, changed, and read over breakfast. Shortly after 11 A.M. I headed out to the Barton house.

Isobel Barton lived in the secluded house her late husband had built in the seventies on Todt Hill, an admirable if unsuccessful attempt to replicate the antebellum houses of his native Georgia in an East Coast setting and on a smaller scale. Old Jack Barton, an amiable soul by all accounts, had apparently made up with money and determination for what he lacked in good taste.

The gate to the drive was open as I arrived, and the exhaust fumes of another car hung in the air. The cab turned in just as the electronic gates were about to rumble closed, and we followed the lead car, a white BMW 320i with tinted windows, to the small courtyard in front of the house. The cab looked out of place in that setting, although how the Barton household might have felt about my own battered Mustang, currently undergoing repairs, I wasn't so sure.

As I pulled up, a slim woman dressed conservatively in a gray suit emerged from the BMW and watched me curiously as I paid the cabdriver. Her gray hair was tied back in a bun that did nothing to soften her severe features. A large black man wearing a chauffeur's uniform appeared at the door of the house and moved quickly to intercept me as I walked from the departing cab.

"Parker. I believe I'm expected."

The chauffeur gave me a look that told me, if I was lying, he'd make me wish I'd stayed in bed. He told me to wait, before turning back to the woman in gray. She glanced at me briefly but nastily before exchanging a few words with the chauffeur, who moved off to the back of the house as she approached me.

"Mr. Parker, I'm Ms. Christie, Mrs. Barton's personal assistant. You should have stayed at the gate until we were sure who you were." In a window above the door, a curtain twitched slightly and then was still.

"If you have a staff entrance I'll use that in future." I got the impression from Ms. Christie that she hoped that eventuality wouldn't arise. She eyed me coldly for a moment, then turned on her heel.

"If you'll come with me, please," she said over her shoulder as she moved toward the door. The gray suit was threadbare at the edges. I wondered if Mrs. Barton would haggle over my rates.

If Isobel Barton was short of cash she could simply have sold off some of the antiques that furnished the house, because the interior was an auctioneer's wet dream. Two large rooms opened out at either side of a hallway, filled with furniture that looked like it was used only when presidents died. A wide staircase curved up to the right; a closed door lay straight ahead while another nestled under the stairs. I followed Ms. Christie through the latter and into a small but surprisingly bright and modern office with a computer in a corner and a TV and video unit built into the bookshelves. Maybe Mrs. Barton wouldn't haggle about the rates after all.

Ms. Christie sat down behind a pine desk, removed some papers from her valise, and shuffled through them in obvious irritation before finding what she wanted.

"This is a standard confidentiality agreement drawn up by the trust's legal advisers," she began, pushing it toward me with one hand while clicking a pen simultaneously with the other. "It is an undertaking on your behalf to keep all communication relating to the matter in hand between Mrs. Barton, myself, and yourself." She used the pen to point to the relevant sections on the agreement, like an insurance salesman trying to slip a bum contract past a sucker. "I'd like you to sign it before we proceed any further," she concluded.

It seemed like nobody involved with the Barton Trust had a particularly trusting nature. "I don't think so," I said. "If you're concerned about possible breaches of confidentiality, then hire a priest to do your work. Otherwise you'll have to take my word that what passes between us will go no further." Perhaps I should have felt guilty about lying to her. I didn't. I was a good liar. It's one of the gifts God gives alcoholics.

"That's not acceptable. I am already unconvinced about the necessity of hiring you and I certainly feel it is inappropriate to do so without—"

She was interrupted by the sound of the office door opening. I turned to see a tall, attractive woman enter, her age indeterminable through a combination of the gentleness of nature and the magic of cosmetics. At a glance I would have guessed she was in her late forties, but if this was Isobel Barton, then I knew she was closer to fifty-five, maybe older. She wore a pale blue dress that was too subtly simple to be anything but expensive and displayed a figure that was either surgically enhanced or extremely well preserved.

As she drew closer and the tiny wrinkles in her face became clearer, I guessed it was the latter: Isobel Barton did not look like the sort of woman who resorted to plastic surgery. Around her neck gold and diamonds glittered, and a pair of matching earrings sparkled as she walked. Her hair too was gray, but she let it hang long and loose on her shoulders. She was still an attractive woman and she walked like she knew it.

Philip Kooper had borne the brunt of the media attention following the disappearance of the Baines boy, but that attention had not been significant. The Baines boy was from a family of dopers and no-hopers. His disappearance merited a mention only because of the trust, and even then the trust's lawyers and patrons had called in enough favors to ensure that speculation was kept to a minimum. The boy's mother was separated from his father and they hadn't been getting along any better since he left.

The police were still trying to trace the father in case of a possible snatch, even though every indication was that the father, a petty criminal, hated his child. In some cases, that might be enough to justify taking the child and killing him to get at his estranged wife. When I was a rookie patrolman, I once arrived at a tenement to find a man had abducted his baby daughter and drowned her in the bath because his ex-wife wouldn't let him have the TV after they separated.

Only one piece of coverage of the Baines disappearance stuck in my mind: a picture of Mrs. Barton, snapped head-bowed as she visited the mother of Evan Baines in a run-down project. It was supposed to have been a private visit. The photographer, returning from the scene of a drug killing, just happened to be passing. One or two papers took the picture, but they ran it small.

"Thank you, Caroline. I'll talk to Mr. Parker alone for a while." She smiled as she said it but her tone brooked no argument. Her assistant affected a lack of concern at the dismissal but her eyes flashed fire. When she had left the room, Mrs. Barton seated herself on a stiff-backed chair away from the desk and motioned me toward a black leather couch, then turned her smile on me.

"I'm sorry about that. I didn't authorize any such agreement but Caroline can be overprotective of me at times. Can we offer you coffee, or would you prefer a drink?"

"Neither, thank you. Before you go any further, Mrs. Barton, I should tell you that I don't really do missing persons work." In my experience, searching for missing persons was best left to specialist agencies with the manpower to chase up leads and possible sightings. Some solo investigators who took on that kind of work were at best ill equipped and at worst little better than parasites who preyed on the hopes of those who remained to keep funding minimal efforts for even smaller returns.

"Mr. Loomax said you might say that, but only out of modesty. He told me to say he would regard it as a personal favor."

I smiled, despite myself. The only favor I would give Tony Loo-Loo would be not to piss on his grave when he died.

According to Mrs. Barton, she had met Catherine Demeter through her son, who had seen the girl working at DeVries's department store and had pestered her for a date. Mrs. Barton and her son—her stepson, to be accurate, since Jack Barton had been married once before, to a Southern woman who had divorced him after eight years and moved to Hawaii with a singer—were not close. She was aware that her son was engaged in activities that were, as she put it, "unsavory," and had tried to get him to change his ways, "both for his own sake and the sake of the trust." I nodded sympathetically. Sympathy was the only possible emotion to feel for anyone involved with Stephen Barton.

When she heard he was seeing a new girlfriend she asked if they could all meet together, she said, and a date had been arranged. In the end her son had failed to appear but Catherine had turned up, and after an initial awkwardness, the two quickly struck up a friendship far more amicable than the relationship that existed between the girl and Stephen Barton. The two had continued to meet occasionally for coffee and lunch. Despite invitations, the girl had politely refused offers from Mrs. Barton to come out to the house, and Stephen Barton had never brought her.

Then Catherine Demeter had simply dropped out of sight. She had left work early on Saturday and had failed to keep an early dinner appointment on Sunday with Mrs. Barton. That was the last anyone had heard of Catherine Demeter, said Mrs. Barton. Two days had now passed and she had heard nothing from her.

"Because of, well, the publicity that the trust has received recently over the disappearance of that poor child, I was reluctant to cause a fuss or draw any further adverse attention down on us," she said. "I called Mr. Loomax and he seemed to think that Catherine may simply have drifted on somewhere else. It happens a lot, I believe."

"Do you think there's something more to it than that?"

"I really don't know, but she was so happy with her job and she appeared to be getting on well with Stephen." She stopped for a moment at this mention of her son's name, as if considering whether or not to proceed. Then: "Stephen has been running wild for some time—since before his father's death, in fact. Do you know the Ferrera family, Mr. Parker?"

"I'm aware of them."

"Stephen fell in with their youngest son, despite all of our efforts. I know he keeps bad company and I know he's involved with drugs. I'm afraid he may have dragged Catherine into something. And . . ." She paused again, briefly. "I enjoyed her company. There was something gentle about her and she seemed so sad sometimes. She said that she was anxious to settle down here, after moving around for so long."

"Did she say where she had been?"

"All over. I gather that she had worked in a number of states."

"Did she say anything about her past, give any indication that something might be troubling her?"

"I think something may have happened to her family when she was young. She told me that she had a sister who died. She didn't say any more. She said she couldn't talk about it and I didn't press her on it."

"Mr. Loomax may be right. She may simply have moved on again."

Mrs. Barton shook her head insistently. "No, she would have told me, I'm sure of it. Stephen hasn't heard from her and neither have I. I'm afraid for her and I want to know that she is safe. That's all. She doesn't even have to know that I hired you, or that I was concerned for her. Will you take the case?"

I was still reluctant to do Walter Cole's dirty work and to take advantage of Isobel Barton, but I had little else on my plate except an appearance in court the following day on behalf of an insurance firm, another case I had taken for the money and to pass the time.

If there was a connection between the disappearance of Catherine Demeter and Sonny Ferrera, then she was almost certainly in trouble. If Sonny had been involved in the killing of Fat Ollie Watts, it was clear that he was going off the rails.

"I'll give it a few days," I said. "As a favor," I added. "Do you want to know my rates?"

She was already writing a check, drawn on her private account and not that of the trust. "Here's three thousand dollars in advance and this is my card. My private number is on the back."

She moved her chair forward. "Now, what else do you need to know?"

That evening, I had dinner at River on Amsterdam Avenue, close to Seventieth Street, where the classic beef made it the best Vietnamese in town and where the staff moved by so softly that it was like being waited on by shadows or passing breezes. I watched a young couple at a nearby table intertwining their hands, running their fingers over each other's knuckles and fingertips, tracing delicate circles in their palms, then gripping their hands together and pressing the heel of each hand forcefully against the other. And as they simulated their lovemaking, a waitress drifted by and smiled knowingly at me as I watched.

6

THE DAY AFTER I visited Isobel Barton, I made a brief visit to court in connection with the insurance case. A claim had been made against a phone company by a contracted electrician, who said he had fallen down a hole in the road while examining underground cables and was no longer able to work as a result.

He may not have been able to work, but he had still been able to power lift five hundred pounds in a cash contest in a Boston gymnasium. I had used a palm-size Panasonic video camera to capture his moment of glory. The insurance company presented the evidence to a judge, who suspended any further decision on the matter for one week. I didn't even have to give evidence. Afterward I had coffee in a diner and read the paper before heading over to Pete Hayes's old gym in Tribeca.

I knew Stephen Barton worked out there sometimes. If his girlfriend had disappeared, then there was a strong possibility that Barton might know where she had gone or, equally important, why. I remembered him vaguely as a strong, Nordic-looking type, his body obscenely pumped from steroid use. He was in his late twenties but the combination of training and tanning salons had worn his face to the consistency of old leather, adding at least ten years to his age.

As artists and Wall Street lawyers had started moving into the Tribeca area, attracted by loft space in the cast iron and masonry buildings, Pete's gym had moved upmarket, filling what used to be a spit and sawdust place with mirrors and potted palms and, sacrilege upon sacrilege, a juice bar. Now heavyweight boneheads and serious power lifters worked out alongside accountants with paunches and female executives with power-dress business suits and cell phones. The bulletin board at the door advertised something called "spinning," which involved sitting on a bike for an hour and sweating yourself into a red agony. Ten years ago, even the suggestion that the gym might be used for such a purpose would have caused Pete's regular clientele to bust the place up.

A wholesome-looking blonde in a gray leotard buzzed me into Pete's office, the last bastion of what the gym had once been. Old posters advertising power lifting competitions and Mr. Universe shows shared wall space with pictures of Pete alongside Steve Reeves, Joe Weider, and, oddly, the wrestler Hulk Hogan. Bodybuilding trophies sat in a glass-fronted cabinet while behind a battered pine desk sat Pete himself, his muscles slackening in old age but still a powerful, impressive figure, his salt-and-pepper hair cut in a short military style. I had trained in the gym for almost six years, until I was promoted to detective and started to destroy myself.

Pete stood and nodded, his hands in his pockets and his loose-fitting top doing nothing to conceal the size of his shoulders and arms.

"Long time," he said. "Sorry about what happened to . . ." He trailed off and moved his chin and shoulders in a kind of combination shrug, a gesture to the past and what it contained.

I nodded back and leaned against an old gunmetal gray filing cabinet adorned with decals advertising health supplements and lifting magazines.

"*Spinning*, Pete?"

He grimaced. "Yeah, I know. Still, spinning makes me two hundred dollars an hour. I got forty exercise bikes on the floor above us and I couldn't make more money with a printing press and green ink."

"Stephen Barton around?"

Pete kicked at some imaginary obstacle on the worn wooden floor. "Not for a week or so. He in trouble?"

"I don't know," I replied. "Is he?"

Pete sat down slowly and, wincing, stretched his legs out in front of him. Years of squatting had taken their toll on his knees, leaving them weak and arthritic. "You're not the first person to come here asking about him this week. Couple of guys in cheap suits were in here yesterday trying to find him. Recognized one of them as Sal Inzerillo. Used to be a good light-middleweight until he started taking falls."

"I remember him." I paused. "Works for old man Ferrera now, I hear."

"Might do," nodded Pete. "Might do. Might have worked for the old man in the ring too, if you believe the stories. This about drugs?"

"I don't know," I replied. Pete glanced at me quickly to see if I was lying, decided I wasn't, and went back to examining the tops of his sneakers. "You hear of any trouble between Sonny and the old man, anything that might have involved Stephen Barton?"

"There's trouble between them, sure, otherwise what's Inzerillo doing damaging my floor with his black rubber soles? Don't know that it involves Barton, though."

I moved on to the subject of Catherine Demeter.

"Do you remember a girl with Barton recently? She may have been around here sometimes. Short, dark hair, slight overbite, maybe in her early thirties."

"Barton has lots of girls but I don't remember that one. Don't notice, mostly, unless they're smarter than Barton, which makes me wonder."

"Not difficult," I said. "This one probably was smarter. Is Barton a hitter?"

"He's mean, sure. Popping pills frazzled his brain, gave him bad 'roid rage. It's fight or fuck with him. Fuck, mainly. My old lady could take him in a fight." He looked at me intently. "I know what he was into, but he didn't sell here. I'd have force-fed his shit to him till he burst if he tried it." I didn't believe Pete but I let it go. Steroids were part of the game now and there was nothing Pete could do except bluster.

He pursed his lips and pulled his legs slowly in. "A lot of women were attracted to him by his size. Barton was a big

guy and he sure talked big. Some women just want the protection someone like him seems to offer. They believe if
they give the guy what he wants he'll look out for them.

"Pity she chose Stephen Barton, then," I said.

"Yeah," agreed Pete. "Maybe she wasn't so smart after all."

I had brought my training gear with me and did ninety
minutes in the gym, the mirrored walls reflecting my efforts back at me from every angle. It had been some time
since I trained properly. To avoid embarrassment I skipped
the bench and stuck to shoulders, back, and light arm
work, enjoying the sensation of strength and movement in
the bent-over rows and the pressure on my biceps during
the curls.

I still looked pretty good, I thought, although the assessment was a result of insecurity instead of vanity. At just
under six feet, I still retained some of my lifter's build—the
wide shoulders, definition in the biceps and triceps, and a
chest that was at least bigger than two eggs frying on the
sidewalk—and I hadn't regained much of the fat I had lost
during the year. I still had my hair, although there was gray
creeping back from the temples and sprinkling the fringe.
My eyes were clear enough to be recognizably gray-blue, set
in a slightly long face now deeply etched at the eyes and
mouth with the marks of remembered grief. Clean shaven,
with a decent haircut, a good suit, and some flattering light,
I could look almost respectable. In the right light, I could
even have claimed to be thirty-two without making people
snigger too loudly. It was only two years less than my age on
my driver's license, but these little things become more important as you get older.

When I was finished, I packed my gear, declined Pete's
offer of a protein shake—it smelled like rotten bananas—
and stopped off for a coffee instead. I felt relaxed for the first
time in weeks, the endorphins pumping through my system
and a pleasant tightness developing across my shoulders
and back.

The next call I made was to DeVries's department store on
Fifth Avenue. The personnel manager called himself a human

resources manager and, like personnel managers the world over, was one of the least personable people one could meet. Sitting opposite him, it was difficult not to feel that anyone who could happily reduce individuals to resources, to the same level as oil, bricks, and canaries in coal mines, probably shouldn't be allowed to have any human relations that didn't involve locks and prison bars. In other words, Timothy Cary was a first-degree prick from the tip of his close-cropped dyed hair to the toes of his patent leather shoes.

I had contacted his secretary earlier that afternoon to make the appointment, telling her that I was acting for an attorney in the matter of an inheritance coming to Ms. Demeter. Cary and his secretary deserved each other. A wild dog on a chain would have been more helpful than Cary's secretary, and easier to get past.

"My client is anxious that Ms. Demeter be contacted as soon as possible," I told him as we sat in his small, prissy office. "The will is extremely detailed and there are a lot of forms to be filled out."

"And your client would be . . . ?"

"I'm afraid I can't tell you that. I'm sure you understand."

Cary looked like he understood but didn't want to. He leaned back in his chair and gently rubbed his expensive silk tie between his fingers. It had to be expensive. It was too tasteless to be anything else. Crisp lines showed along his shirt as if it had just been removed from its packaging, assuming Timothy Cary would have anything to do with something so plebeian as a plastic wrapper. If he ever visited the shop floor it must have been like an angel descending, albeit an angel who looked like he'd just encountered a bad smell.

"Miss Demeter was due in work yesterday." Cary glanced down at a file on his desk. "She had Monday off, so we haven't seen her since Saturday."

"Is that usual, to have Monday off?" I wasn't anxious to know, but the question distracted Cary from the file. Isobel Barton didn't have Catherine Demeter's new address. Catherine would usually contact her, or Mrs. Barton would

have her assistant leave a message at DeVries's. As Cary
brightened slightly at the opportunity to discuss a subject
close to his heart and started mouthing off about work
schedules, I memorized her address and SSN. I eventually
managed to interrupt him for long enough to ask if Catherine Demeter had been ill on her last day at work or had
complained of being disturbed in any way.

"I'm not aware of any such communication. Miss
Demeter's position with DeVries is currently under review as
a result of her absence," he concluded smugly. "I hope, for
her sake, that her inheritance is considerable." I don't think
he meant it.

After some routine delaying tactics, Cary gave me permission to speak with the woman who had worked with
Catherine on her last shift in the store. I met her in a supervisor's office off the shop floor. Martha Friedman was
in her early sixties. She was plump, with dyed red hair and
a face so caked with cosmetics that the floor of the Ama-
zon jungle probably saw more natural light, but she tried
to be helpful. She had been working with Catherine
Demeter in the china department on Saturday. It was her
first time to work with her, since Mrs. Friedman's usual assistant had been taken ill and someone was needed to
cover for her.

"Did you notice anything unusual about her behavior?" I
asked, as Mrs. Friedman took the opportunity afforded by
some time in the supervisor's office to discreetly examine
the papers on his desk. "Did she seem distressed or anxious
in any way?"

Mrs. Friedman furrowed her brow slightly. "She broke a
piece of china, an Aynsley vase. She had just arrived and was
showing it to a customer when she dropped it. Then, when I
looked around, she was running across the shop floor, heading for the escalators. Most unprofessional, I thought, even
if she was sick."

"And was she sick?"

"She *said* she felt sick, but why run for the escalators? We
have a staff washroom on each floor."

I got the feeling that Mrs. Friedman knew more than she

was saying. She was enjoying the attention and wanted to draw it out. I leaned toward her confidentially.

"But what do *you* think, Mrs. Friedman?"

She preened a little and leaned forward in turn, touching my hand lightly to emphasize her point.

"She saw someone, someone she was trying to reach before they left the store. Tom, the security guard on the east door, told me she ran out by him and stood looking around the street. We're supposed to get permission to leave the store when on duty. He should have reported her, but he just told me instead. Tom's a *schvartze,* but he's okay."

"Do you have any idea who she might have seen?"

"No. She just refused to discuss it. She doesn't have any friends among the staff, far as I can tell, and now I can see why."

I spoke to the security guard and the supervisor, but they couldn't add anything to what Mrs. Friedman had told me. I stopped at a diner for coffee and a sandwich, returned to my apartment to pick up a small black bag my friend Angel had given me, and then took another cab, to Catherine Demeter's apartment.

7

THE APARTMENT was in a converted four-story redbrick in Greenpoint, a part of Brooklyn that was populated mainly by Italians, Irish, and Poles, the latter counting a large number of former Solidarity activists among them. It was from Greenpoint's Continental Iron Works that the ironclad *Monitor* had emerged to fight the Confederate ship *Merrimac,* when Greenpoint was Brooklyn's industrial center.

The cast iron manufacturers, the potters, and printers were all gone now, but many of the descendants of the original workers still remained. Small clothing boutiques and Polish bakeries shared frontage with established kosher delis and stores selling used electrical goods.

Catherine Demeter's block was still a little down at heel, and kids wearing sneakers and low-slung jeans sat on the steps of most of the buildings, smoking and whistling and calling at passing women. She lived in apartment 14, probably near the top of the building. I tried the bell but wasn't surprised when there was no answer from the intercom. Instead I tried 20, and when an elderly woman's voice responded, I told her I was from the gas company and had a report of a leak but the super's apartment was empty. She was silent for a moment, then buzzed me in.

I guessed she'd probably check with the super, so time was limited, although if the apartment didn't reveal anything about where Catherine Demeter might have gone, I'd have to talk to the super anyway, or approach the neighbors, or maybe even talk to the mailman. As I passed into the lobby I used a pick to open the mailbox for apartment

14, finding only a copy of the most recent *New York* magazine and what looked like two junk mail drops. I closed the box and took the stairs up to the third floor.

The third floor was silent, with six newly varnished apartment doors along the hall, three on each side. I walked quietly to number 14 and took the black bag from under my coat. I knocked once more on the door, just to be sure, and removed the power rake from the bag. Angel was the best B&E man I knew, and even as a cop I'd had reasons to use him. In return, I'd never hassled Angel and he'd stayed out of my way professionally. When he did go down, I'd done my best to make things a little easier for him inside. The rake had been a thank-you of sorts. An illegal thank-you.

It looked like an electric drill but was smaller and slimmer, with a prong at its tip that acted as a pick and tension tool. I stuck the prong in the lock and squeezed the trigger. The rake clattered noisily for a couple of seconds and then the lock turned. I slipped in quietly and closed the door behind me, seconds before another door in the corridor opened. I stayed still and waited until it closed again, then put the rake back in the bag, reopened the door, and took a toothpick from my pocket. I snapped it into four pieces and jammed them into the lock. It would give me time to get to the fire escape if someone tried to enter the apartment while I was there. Then I closed the door and turned on the lights.

A short hallway with a threadbare rug led to a clean living room, cheaply furnished with a battered TV and a mismatched sofa and chairs. To one side was a small kitchen and to the other a bedroom.

I checked the bedroom first. Some paperback novels stood on a small shelf beside the bed. The only other furniture consisted of a wardrobe and dressing table, both of which appeared to have been made up from IKEA kits. I checked under the bed and found an empty suitcase. There were no cosmetics on the dressing table, which meant that she had probably packed a small overnight bag when she left and taken them with her. She probably hadn't intended to stay away for long and she certainly didn't appear to have left for good.

I checked the closet but there were only clothes and a few pairs of shoes inside. The first two drawers in the dresser also contained only clothes, but the last one was filled with papers, the accumulated documents, tax forms, and employment records of a life spent moving from city to city, from job to job.

Catherine Demeter had spent a long time in the waitressing game, moving from New Hampshire to Florida and back again with the social season. She had also spent some time in Chicago, Las Vegas, and Phoenix, as well as numerous small towns, judging by the collection of wage slips and tax documents in her drawer. There were also various bank statements. She had about nineteen thousand dollars in a savings account in a Citibank, as well as some stocks and bonds, bound carefully with a thick blue ribbon. Finally, there was a passport, updated recently, and within it three extra passport-size photos of herself.

Catherine Demeter, true to Isobel Barton's description, was a small attractive woman in her mid-thirties, five-two, with dark hair cut short in a bob, pale blue eyes, and a fair complexion. I took the extra photos and put them in my wallet, then turned to examine the only item of a very personal nature in the drawer.

It was a photo album, thick and worn at the corners. Within it was what I assumed to be a history of the Demeter family, from sepia-tinted photos of grandparents through the wedding of what I guessed were her parents and on through the photos of two girls growing up, sometimes with parents and friends, sometimes together, sometimes alone. Pictures from the beach, from family holidays, from birthdays and Christmas and Thanksgiving, the memories of two sisters starting off in life. The resemblance between the two was clear. Catherine was the younger, the overbite visible even then. The girl I took to be her sister was perhaps two or three years older, with sandy-colored hair, a beautiful girl even at eleven or twelve.

There were no more pictures of the older girl after that age. The rest consisted of Catherine alone or with her parents, and the record of her growth was more periodic, the sense of celebration and joyfulness gone. Eventually, the photos dwindled away to nothing, with a final picture of Catherine on the day of her high school graduation, a solemn-looking young woman with dark rings beneath eyes that seemed close to tears. The testimonial attached came from the principal of Haven High School, in Virginia.

Something had been removed from the final pages of the album. Small pieces of what appeared to be newspaper rested at the base of the album pages, most merely tiny fragments as thin as threads, but one about an inch square. The paper was yellowing with age, with a fragment of a weather report on one side and part of a picture on the other, the tip of some sand-blond hair visible in one corner. Tucked into the last page were two birth certificates, one for Catherine Louise Demeter, dated March 5, 1962, and the other for Amy Ellen Demeter, dated December 3, 1959.

I returned the album to the drawer and went into the bathroom next door. It was clean and neat like the rest of the apartment, with soap, shower gels, and foam bath arranged neatly on the white tiles by the bath and towels stored in a small cabinet under the sink. I opened one side of the mirrored cabinet on the wall. It contained toothpaste, floss, and mouthwash, as well as some nonprescription medicines for cold relief and water retention, evening primrose capsules, and assorted vitamin pills. There were no birth control pills or other contraceptives. Maybe Stephen Barton took care of that, although I doubted it. Stephen didn't seem like the sensitive type.

The other side of the cabinet contained a miniature pharmacy with enough uppers and downers to keep Catherine moving like a roller coaster. There were Librium, for mood swings; Ativan, to combat agitation; and Valium, Thorazine and Lorazepam for anxiety. Some were empty, others half empty. The most recent came from a prescription from Dr. Frank Forbes, a psychiatrist. I knew the name. "Fucking Frank" Forbes had screwed or attempted to screw so many of his patients that it was sometimes suggested that they should charge him. He had been on the verge of losing his license on a number of occasions, but the complaints were either withdrawn, never got to court, or were suppressed through the judicious application of some of Fucking Frank's funds. I heard he had been unusually quiet lately after one of his patients had contracted a dose of the clap after an encounter with Frank and then had promptly slapped a lawsuit on him. This one, I gathered, was proving difficult for Fucking Frank to bury.

Catherine Demeter was clearly a very unhappy woman and was unlikely to get any happier if she was seeing Frank Forbes. I wasn't too keen on visiting him. He had once tried to come on to Elizabeth Gordon, the daughter of one of Susan's divorced friends, and I'd paid him a visit to remind him of his duties as a doctor and to threaten to throw him from his office window if it ever happened again. After that, I tried to take a semiprofessional interest in Frank Forbes's activities.

There was nothing else of note in Catherine's bathroom, or in the rest of her apartment. As I was leaving I stopped at her telephone, picked it up, and pressed the redial button. After the beeps subsided a voice answered.

"Haven County Sheriff's Office, hello?"

I hung up and called a guy I knew in the telephone company. Five minutes later he came back with a list of local numbers called from Friday to Sunday. There were only three and they were all mundane—a Chinese take-out, a local laundry, and a movie information line.

The local company couldn't give me any details of any long distance calls made, so I tried a second number. This one connected me with one of the many agencies that offer PIs and those with a deep and abiding interest in other people's business the opportunity to purchase confidential information illegally. The agency was able to tell me within twenty minutes that fifteen calls had been made to Haven, Virginia, numbers on Saturday evening through Sprint, seven to the sheriff's office and eight to a private residence in the town. I was given both numbers and I went with the second. The message on the answering machine was terse: "This is Earl Lee Granger. I'm not here right now. Leave a message after the beep or, if it relates to police business, contact the sheriff's office at . . ."

I punched in the number, got the Haven County Sheriff's Office again, and asked to speak to the sheriff.

I was told that Sheriff Granger wasn't available, so I asked to speak to whoever was in charge in his absence. The ranking deputy was Alvin Martin, I learned, but he was out on a case. The deputy on the phone didn't know when the sheriff would be back. From his tone, I guessed the sheriff hadn't simply gone out to buy cigarettes. He asked me my name and I thanked him and hung up.

It seemed that something had caused Catherine Demeter to get in touch with the sheriff in her hometown, but not with the NYPD. If there was nothing else, I'd have to pay a visit to Haven. First, though, I decided to pay a visit to Fucking Frank Forbes.

I STOPPED OFF at Azure on Third Avenue and bought myself some expensive fresh strawberries and pineapple from the deli, then took them around to the Citicorp Center to eat in the public space. I liked the building's simple lines and its strange, angled top. It was also one of the few new developments where a similar imagination had been applied to its interior: its seven-story atrium was still green with trees and shrubs, its shops and restaurants were packed with people, and a handful of worshipers sat silently in its simple, sunken church.

Two blocks away, Fucking Frank Forbes had a swank office in a seventies smoked-glass development, at least for the present. I took the elevator up and entered the reception area, where a young and pretty brunette was typing something on the computer. She looked up as I entered and smiled brightly. I tried not to let my jaw hang as I smiled back.

"Is Dr. Forbes available?" I asked.

"Do you have an appointment?"

"I'm not a patient, thankfully, but Frank and I go way back. Tell him Charlie Parker wants to see him."

Her smile faltered a little but she buzzed Frank's office and gave him the message. Her face paled slightly as she listened to his response but she held herself together remarkably well, all things considered.

"I'm afraid Dr. Forbes can't see you," she said, the smile now fading rapidly.

"Is that really what he said?"

She blushed slightly. "No, not quite."

"Are you new here?"

"This is my first week."

"Frank select you personally?"

She looked puzzled. "Ye-es."

"Get another job. He's a deviant and he's on his way out of business."

I walked past her and entered Frank's office while she took all this in. There was no patient in Frank's consulting room, just the good doctor himself leafing through some notes on his desk. He didn't look pleased to see me. His thin mustache curled in distaste like a black worm, and a red bloom spread from his neck to his high-domed forehead before disappearing into his brush of wiry black hair. He was tall, over six feet, and he worked out. He looked real good, but looks were as far as it went. There was nothing good about Fucking Frank Forbes. If he handed you a dollar, the ink would be running before it got to your wallet.

"Get the fuck out, Parker. In case you've forgotten, you can't come barging in here anymore. You're not a cop now and the force is probably all the richer for your absence." He leaned toward the intercom button but his receptionist had already entered behind me.

"Call the police, Marcie. Better still, call my lawyer. Tell him I'm about to file for harassment."

"Hear you're giving him a lot of business at the moment, Frank," I said, taking a seat in a leather upright opposite his desk. "I also hear Maibaum and Locke are handling the lawsuit for that unfortunate woman with the social disease. I've done some business with them in the past and they're real hot. Maybe I could put them onto Elizabeth Gordon. You remember Elizabeth, don't you, Frank?"

Frank cast an instinctive glance over his shoulder at the window and twisted his chair away from it.

"It's okay, Marcie," he said, nodding uneasily to the receptionist. I heard the door close softly behind me. "What do you want?"

"You have a patient called Catherine Demeter."

"Come on, Parker, you know I can't discuss my patients. Even if I could, I wouldn't share shit with you."

"Frank, you're the worst shrink I know. I wouldn't let a dog be treated by you because you'd probably try to fuck it, so save the ethics for the judge. I think she may be in trouble and I want to find her. If you don't help me I'll be in touch with Maibaum and Locke so fast you'll think I'm telepathic."

Frank tried to look like he was wrestling with his conscience, although he couldn't have found his conscience without a shovel and an exhumation order.

"She missed an appointment yesterday. She didn't give any notice."

"Why was she seeing you?"

"Involutional melancholia, mainly. That's depression to you, characteristic of middle to later stages of life. At least that's what it seemed like, initially."

"But . . . ?"

"Parker, this is confidential. Even I have standards."

"You're joking. Go on."

Frank sighed and fiddled with a pencil on his blotter, then moved to a cabinet, removed a file, and sat back down. He opened it, leafed through it, and began to talk.

"Her sister died when Catherine was eight, or rather her sister was killed. She was one of a number of children murdered in a town called Haven, in Virginia, in the late sixties, early seventies. The children, males and females, were abducted, tortured, and their remains dumped in the cellar of an empty house outside the town." Frank was detached now, a doctor running through a case history that might have been as distant as a fairy tale to him for all the emotion he put into the telling.

"Her sister was the fourth child to die, but the first white child. After she disappeared the police began to take a real interest. A local woman, a wealthy local woman, was suspected. Her car had been seen near the house after one of the children disappeared, and then she tried an unsuccessful snatch on a kid from another town about twenty miles away. The kid, a boy, scratched up her face, then gave a description to the cops.

"They went after her but the locals heard and got to the house first. Her brother was there. He was a homosexual, according to locals, and the cops believed she had an accomplice, a male who might have driven the car while she made the snatches. The locals figured the brother was a likely suspect. He was found hanged in the basement."

"And the woman?"

"Burned to death in another of the old houses. The case simply . . . faded away."

"But not for Catherine?"

"No, not for her. She left the town after graduating from high school, but her parents stayed. The mother died about ten years ago, father shortly after. And Catherine Demeter just kept moving."

"Did she ever go back to Haven?"

"No, not after the funerals. She said everything was dead to her there. And that's it, pretty much. It all comes back to Haven."

"Any boyfriends, or casuals?"

"None that she mentioned to me, and question time is over. Now get out. If you ever bring this up again, in public or in private, I'll sue your ass for assault, harassment, and anything else my lawyer can come up with."

I got up to leave.

"One more thing," I said. "For Elizabeth Gordon and her continued nonacquaintance with Maibaum and Locke."

"What?"

"The name of the woman who burned to death."

"Modine. Adelaide Modine and her brother William. Now please, get the fuck out of my life."

9

WILLIE BREW'S auto shop looked run down and unreliable, if not blatantly dishonest, from the outside. Inside it wasn't a whole lot better, but Willie, a Pole whose name was unpronounceable and had been shortened to Brew by generations of customers, was just about the best mechanic I knew.

I had never liked this area of Queens, only a short distance north from the roars of the cars on the Long Island Expressway. Ever since I was a boy, I seemed to associate it with used car lots, old warehouses, and cemeteries. Willie's garage, close by Kissena Park, had been a good source of information over the years, since every deadbeat friend of Willie's with nothing better to do than listen in on other people's business tended to congregate there at some time or another, but the whole area still made me uneasy. Even as an adult, I hated the drive from JFK to Manhattan as it skirted these neighborhoods, hated the sight of the rundown houses and liquor stores.

Manhattan, by comparison, was exotic, its skyline capable of seemingly endless change, depending upon one's approach. My father had moved out to Westchester County as soon as he could afford to, buying a small house near Grant Park. Manhattan was somewhere we went on weekends, my friends and I. Sometimes we would traverse the entire length of the island to stand on the walkway over the Brooklyn Bridge and stare back at the evolving skyline. Beneath us, the boards would vibrate with the passage of the traffic, but to me, it seemed like more than that: it was the vibration and hum of life itself. The cables linking the towers of the bridge would cut and dissect the cityscape before us, as if it had been clipped by a child's scissors and reassembled against the blue sky.

After my father's death, my mother had moved us back to Maine, to her hometown of Scarborough, where tree lines replaced cityscapes and only the racing enthusiasts, traveling from Boston and New York to the races at Scarborough Downs, brought with them the sights and smells of the big cities. Maybe that was why I always felt like a visitor when I looked at Manhattan: I always seemed to be seeing the city through new eyes.

Willie's place was situated in a neighborhood that was fighting gentrification tooth and nail. Willie's block had been bought by the owner of the Japanese noodle house next door—he had other interests in downtown Flushing's Little Asia and seemed to want to extend his reach farther south—and Willie was involved in a partially legal battle to ensure that he wasn't shut down. The Japanese responded by sending fish smells through the vents into Willie's garage. Willie sometimes got his own back by getting Arno, his chief mechanic, to drink some beers and eat a Chinese meal, then stumble outside, stick his fingers down his throat, and vomit outside the noodle house. "Chinese, Vietnamese, Japanese—all that shit looks the same when it comes out," Willie used to say.

Inside, Arno—small, wiry, and dark—was working on the engine of a beat-up Dodge. The air was thick with the smell of fish and noodles. My '69 Mustang was raised up on a platform, unrecognizable bits and pieces of its internal workings strewn around on the floor. It looked no more likely to be on the road again in the near future than James Dean. I'd called earlier to tell Willie I'd be dropping by. The least he could have done was pretend to be doing something with it when I arrived.

The sound of loud swearing came from inside Willie's office, which was up a set of wooden stairs to the right of the garage floor. The door flew open and Willie rumbled down the steps, grease on his bald head and his blue mechanic's overalls open to the waist to show a dirty white T-shirt

straining over his huge belly. He climbed arduously up a set
of boxes placed beneath the vent in a step pattern and put
his mouth to the grille.

"You slant-eyed sons of bitches," he shrieked. "Quit
stinkin' my garage out with fish or I'm gonna get nuclear on
your ass." There was the sound of something shouted in
Japanese from the other end of the vent, and then a burst of
Oriental laughter. Willie thumped the grille with the heel of
his hand and climbed down. He squinted at me in the semidarkness before recognizing me.

"Bird, how you doin'? You want a coffee?"

"I want a car. My car. The car you've had for over a week
now."

Willie looked crestfallen. "You're angry with me," he said
in mock-soothing tones. "I understand your anger. Anger is
good. Your car, on the other hand, is not good. Your car is
bad. The engine's shot to shit. What have you been running
it on, nuts and old nails?"

"Willie, I need my car. The taxi drivers are treating me
like an old friend. Some of them have even stopped trying
to rip me off. I've considered hiring a rental car to save myself embarrassment. In fact, the only reason I haven't hit
you for a car is that you said the repairs would take a day or
two at most."

Willie slouched over to the car and nudged a cylindrical
piece of metal with the toe of his boot.

"Arno, what's the deal on Bird's Mustang?"

"It's shit," said Arno. "Tell him we'll give him five hundred dollars to scrap it."

"Arno says to give you five hundred to scrap it."

"I heard him. Tell Arno I'll burn his house down if he
doesn't fix my car."

"Day after tomorrow," came a voice from under the
hood. "Sorry for the delay."

Willie clapped me on the shoulder with a greasy hand.

"Come up for a coffee, listen to the local gossip." Then,
quietly: "Angel wants to see you. I told him you'd be
around."

I nodded and followed him up the stairs. Inside the office,

which was surprisingly neat, four men sat around a desk drinking coffee and whiskey from tin mugs. I nodded to Tommy Q, who I'd busted once for handling pirated video-cassettes, and a thickly mustached hot-wire guy known, unsurprisingly, as Groucho. Beside him sat Willie's other assistant, Jay, who, at sixty-five, was ten years older than Willie but looked at least ten years older than that again. Beside him sat Coffin Ed Harris.

"You know Coffin Ed?" said Willie.

I nodded. "Still boosting dead guys, Ed?"

"Naw, man," said Coffin Ed. "I gave all that up a long time ago. I got a bad back."

Coffin Ed Harris had been the kidnapper to beat all kidnappers. Coffin Ed figured that live hostages were too much like real work, since there was no telling what they might do or who might come looking for them. The dead were easier to handle, so Coffin Ed took to robbing mortuaries.

He would watch the death notices, pick a decedent who came from a reasonably wealthy family, and then steal the corpse from the mortuary or the funeral home. Until Coffin Ed came along and bucked the system, funeral homes weren't usually well guarded. Coffin Ed would store the corpses in an industrial freezer he kept in his basement and then ask for a ransom, usually nothing too heavy. Most of the relatives were quite happy to pay in order to get their loved ones back before they started to rot.

He did well until some old Polish aristocrat took offense at his wife's remains being held for ransom and hired a private army to go looking for Coffin Ed. They found him, although Coffin Ed just about got away through a bolt-hole in his cellar that led to his neighbor's yard. He got the last laugh, too. The power company had cut off Ed's electricity three days before because he hadn't been paying his bills. The old Pole's wife stank like a dead possum by the time they found her. Since then, things had gone downhill for Coffin Ed, and he now presented a down-at-the-heel figure in the back of Willie Brew's garage.

There was an uneasy silence for a moment, which was broken by Willie.

"You remember Vinnie No Nose?" said Willie, handing me a steaming cup of black coffee, which was already turning the tin mug red hot but still couldn't hide the smell of gasoline from its interior. "Wait'll you hear Tommy Q's story. You ain't missed nothing yet."

Vinnie No Nose was a B&E guy out of Newark who had taken one fall too many and had decided to reform, or at least to reform as far as any guy can who has made a living for forty years by ripping off other people's apartments. He got his nickname from a long, unsuccessful involvement with amateur boxing. Vinnie, small and a potential victim for any New Jersey lowlife with a penchant for inflicting violence, saw an ability to use his fists as his potential salvation, like lots of other short guys from rough neighborhoods. Sadly, Vinnie's defense was about as good as the Son of Sam's, and his nose was eventually reduced to a mush of cartilage with two semiclosed nostrils like raisins in a pudding.

Tommy Q proceeded to tell a story involving Vinnie, a decorating company, and a dead gay client that could have put him in court if he'd told it in a respectable place of employment. "So the fruit ends up dead, in a bathroom, with this chair up his ass, and Vinnie ends up back in jail for peddling the pics and stealing the dead guy's video," he concluded, shaking his head at the strange ways of non-heterosexual males. He was still laughing his ass off at the story when the smile died on his face and the laugh turned into a kind of choking sound in his throat. I looked behind me to see Angel in the shadows, curly black hair spilling out from under his blue watch cap and with a sparse growth of beard that would have made a thirteen-year-old laugh. A dark blue longshoreman's jacket hung open over a black T-shirt, and his blue jeans ended in dirty, well-worn Timberlands.

Angel was no more than five-six, and to the casual onlooker, it was difficult to see why he should have struck fear into Tommy Q. There were two reasons. The first was that Angel was a far better boxer than Vinnie No Nose and could have pummeled Tommy Q to horse meat if he wanted to, which might well have been the case since Angel was gay and might have found the source of Tommy's humor less than amusing.

The second and probably more compelling reason for Tommy Q's fear was that Angel's boyfriend was a man known only as Louis. Like Angel, Louis had no visible means of support, although it was widely known that Angel, now semiretired at the age of forty, was one of the best thieves in the business, capable of stealing the fluff from the president's navel if the money was good enough.

Less widely known was the fact that Louis, tall, black, and sophisticated in his dress sense, was a hit man almost without equal, a killer who had been reformed somewhat by his relationship with Angel and who now chose his rare targets with what might be termed a social conscience.

Rumor had it that the killing of a German computer expert named Gunther Bloch in Chicago the previous year had been the work of Louis. Bloch was a serial rapist and torturer who preyed on young, sometimes very young, women in the sex resorts of Southeast Asia, where much of his business was transacted. Money usually covered all ills, money paid to pimps, to parents, to police, to politicians.

Unfortunately for Bloch, someone in the upper reaches of the government in one of his nations of choice couldn't be bought, especially after Bloch strangled an eleven-year-old girl and dumped her body in a trash bin. Bloch fled the country, money was redirected to a "special project," and Louis drowned Gunther Bloch in the bathroom of a thousand-dollar-a-night hotel suite in Chicago.

Or, like I said, so rumor had it. Whatever the truth of the matter, Louis was regarded as very bad news and Tommy Q wanted in future to be able to take a bath, however rarely, without fear of drowning.

"Nice story, Tommy," said Angel.

"It's just a story, Angel. I didn't mean nothing by it. No offense meant."

"None taken," said Angel. "At least, not by me."

Behind him there was a movement in the darkness, and Louis appeared. His bald head gleamed in the dim light, his muscular neck emerging from a black silk shirt within an immaculately cut gray suit. He towered over Angel by more than a foot, and as he did so, he eyed Tommy Q intently for a moment.

"Fruit," he said. "That's a . . . *quaint* term, Mr. Q. To what does it refer, exactly?"

The blood had drained from Tommy Q's face and it seemed to take him a very long time to find enough saliva to enable him to gulp. When he did eventually manage, it sounded like he was swallowing a golf ball. He opened his mouth but nothing came out, so he closed it again and looked at the floor in the vain hope that it would open up and swallow him.

"It's okay, Mr. Q, it was a good story," said Louis in a voice as silky as his shirt. "Just be careful how you tell it." Then he smiled a bright smile at Tommy Q, the sort of smile a cat might give a mouse to take to the grave with it. A drop of sweat ran down Tommy Q's nose, hung from the tip for a moment, and then exploded on the floor. By then, Louis had gone.

"Don't forget my car, Willie," I said, then followed Angel from the garage.

10

□

WE WALKED a block or two to a late-night bar and diner Angel knew. Louis strolled a few yards ahead of us, the late evening crowds parting before him like the Red Sea before Moses. Once or twice women glanced at him with interest. The men mostly kept their eyes on the ground, or found something suddenly interesting in the boarded-up storefronts or the night sky.

From inside the bar came the sound of a vaguely folky singer performing open-guitar surgery on Neil Young's "Only Love Can Break Your Heart." It didn't sound like the song was going to pull through.

"He plays like he hates Neil Young," said Angel as we entered.

Ahead of us, Louis shrugged. "Neil Young heard that shit, he'd probably hate himself."

We took a booth. The owner, a fat, dyspeptic man named Ernest, shambled over to take our order. Usually the waitresses in Ernest's took the orders, but Angel and Louis commanded a degree of respect, even here.

"Hey, Ernest," said Angel, "how's business?"

"If I was an undertaker, people'd stop dying," replied Ernest. "And before you ask, my old lady's still ugly." It was a long-established exchange.

"Shit, you been married forty years," said Angel. "She ain't gonna get no better lookin' now."

Angel and Louis ordered club sandwiches and Ernest wandered away. "I was a kid and looked like him, I'd cut my dick off and make money singin' castrato, 'cause it ain't gonna be no use no other way," remarked Angel.

"Bein' ugly ain't done you no harm," said Louis.

"I don't know." Angel grinned. "I was better looking, I coulda screwed a white guy."

They stopped bickering and we waited for the singer to put Neil Young out of his misery. It was strange meeting these two, now that I was no longer a cop. When we had encountered one another before—in Willie's garage, or over coffee, or in Central Park if Angel had some useful information to impart, or if he simply wanted to meet to talk, to ask after Susan and Jennifer—there had been an awkwardness, a tension between us, especially if Louis was nearby. I knew what they had done, what Louis, I believed, still did, silent partnerships in assorted restaurants, dealerships, and Willie Brew's garage notwithstanding.

On this occasion, that tension was no longer present. Instead, I felt for the first time the strength of the bond of friendship that had somehow grown between Angel and me. More than that, from both of them I felt a sense of concern, of regret, of humanity, of trust. They would not be here, I knew, if they felt otherwise.

But maybe there was something more, something I had only begun to perceive. I was a cop's nightmare. Cops, their families, their wives and children, are untouchables. You have to be crazy to go after a cop, crazier still to take out his loved ones. These are the assumptions we live by, the belief that after a day spent looking at the dead, questioning thieves and rapists, pushers and pimps, we can return to our own lives, knowing that our families are somehow apart from all this, and that through them we can remain apart from it too.

But that belief system had been shaken by the deaths of Jennifer and Susan. Someone wasn't respecting the rules, and when no easy answer was forthcoming, when no perp with a grudge could conveniently be apprehended, enabling all that had taken place to be explained away, another reason had to be found: I had somehow drawn it on myself, and on those closest to me. I was a good cop who was well on the way to becoming a drunk. I was falling apart and that made me weak, and someone had exploited that weakness. Other cops looked at me and they saw not a fellow officer in need, but a source of infection, of corruption. No one was sorry to see me go, maybe not even Walter.

And yet what had taken place had somehow brought me closer to both Angel and Louis. They had no illusions about the world in which they lived, no philosophical constructions that allowed them to be at once a part of, and apart from, that world. Louis was a killer: he couldn't afford delusions of that kind. Because of the closeness of the bond that existed between them, Angel couldn't afford those delusions either. Now they had also been taken away from me, like scales falling from my eyes, leaving me to reestablish myself, to find a new place in the world.

Angel picked up an abandoned paper from the booth next door and glanced at the headline. "You see this?" I looked and nodded. A guy had tried to pull some heroic stunt during a bank raid in Flushing earlier in the day and ended up with both barrels of a sawed-off emptied into him. The papers and news bulletins were full of it.

"Here's some guys out doin' a job," began Angel. "They don't want to hurt nobody, they just want to go in, take the money—which is insured anyway, so what does the bank care?—and get out again. They only got the guns 'cause no one's gonna take them seriously otherwise. What else they gonna use? Harsh words?

"But there's always gotta be some asshole who thinks he's immortal 'cause he's not dead yet. This guy, he's young, keeps himself in good condition, thinks he's gonna get more pussy than Long Dong Silver if he busts up the bank raid and saves the day. Look at him: realtor, twenty-nine, single, pulling down one-fifty a year, and he gets a hole blown in him bigger'n the Holland Tunnel. Lance Petersen." He shook his head in wonderment. "I never met anyone called Lance in my whole life."

"That's 'cause they all dead," said Louis, glancing seemingly idly around the room. "Fuckers keep standing up in banks and getting shot. Guy was probably the last Lance left alive."

The clubs arrived and Angel started eating. He was the only one who did. "So how you doin'?"

"Okay," I said. "Why the ambush?"

"You don't write, you don't call." He smiled wryly. Louis glanced at me with mild interest and then returned his attention to the door, the other tables, the doors to the restrooms.

"You been doin' some work for Benny Low, I hear. What you doin' working for that fat piece of shit?"

"Passing time."

"You want to pass time, stick pins in your eyes. Benny's just using up good air."

"Come on, Angel, get to it. You're rattling away and Louis here is acting like he expects the Dillinger gang to walk in and spray the counter."

Angel put down his half-eaten section of club and dabbed almost daintily at his mouth with a napkin. "I hear you've been asking after some girlfriend of Stephen Barton's. Some people are very curious to know why that might be."

"Such as?"

"Such as Bobby Sciorra, I hear."

I didn't know if Bobby Sciorra was psychotic or not, but he was a man who liked killing and had found a willing employer in old man Ferrera. Emo Ellison could testify to the likely result of Bobby Sciorra taking an interest in one's activities. I had a suspicion that Ollie Watts, in his final moments, had found that out as well.

"Benny Low was talking about some kind of trouble between the old man and Sonny," I said. " 'Fuckin' goombas fighting among themselves' was how he put it."

"Benny always was a diplomat," said Angel. "Only surprise is the UN didn't pick up on him before now. There's something weird going on there. Sonny's gone to ground and taken Pili with him. No one's seen them, no one knows where they are, but Bobby Sciorra's looking real hard for all of them." He took another huge bite of his sandwich. "What about Barton?"

"I figure he's gone underground too, but I don't know.

He's minor league and wouldn't have much to do professionally with Sonny or the old man beyond some muling, though he may once have been close to Sonny. May be nothing to it. Barton may not be connected."

"Maybe not, but you've got bigger problems than finding Barton or his girl."

I waited.

"There's a hit out on you."

"Who?"

"It's not local. It's out of town. Louis don't know who."

"Is it over the Fat Ollie thing?"

"I don't know. Even Sonny isn't such a moron that he'd put a contract out over some hired gun who got himself wasted 'cause you stepped in. The kid didn't mean anything to anyone and Fat Ollie's dead. All I know is you're irritating two generations of the Ferrera family and that can't be good."

Walter Cole's favor was turning into something more complicated than a missing persons case, if it was ever that simple.

"I've got one for you," I said. "Know anyone with a gun that can punch holes through masonry with a five-point-seven-millimeter bullet weighing less than fifty grains? Submachine rounds."

"You gotta be fuckin' kidding. Last time I saw something like that it was hangin' on top of a tank turret."

"Well, that's what killed the shooter. I saw him blown away and there was a hole knocked through the wall behind me. The gun's Belgian made, designed for antiterrorist police. Someone local picked up a piece of hardware like that and took it to the range, it's gotta get around."

"I'll ask," said Angel. "Any guesses?"

"My guess would be Bobby Sciorra."

"Mine too. So why would he be cleaning up after Sonny's mess?"

"The old man told him to."

Angel nodded. "Watch your back, Bird."

He finished his sandwich and then stood to go. "C'mon. We can give you a ride."

"No, I want to walk for a while."

Angel shrugged. "You packing?"

I nodded. He said he'd be in touch. I left them at the door. As I walked, I was conscious of the weight of the gun beneath my arm, of every face I passed in the crowd, and of the dark pulse of the city throbbing beneath my feet.

11

☐

BOBBY SCIORRA: a malevolent demon, a vision of ferocity and sadism that had appeared before the old man, Stefano Ferrera, when he was on the verge of insanity and death. Sciorra seemed to have been conjured up from some bleak corner of Hell by the old man's anger and grief, a physical manifestation of the torture and destruction he wished to inflict on the world around him. In Bobby Sciorra he found the perfect instrument of pain and ugly death.

Stefano had watched his own father build a small empire from the family's modest house in Bensonhurst. In those days Bensonhurst, bordered by Gravesend Bay and the Atlantic Ocean, still had a small-town feel. The scent of deli food mingled with that of wood-burning ovens from the local pizza parlors. People lived in two-family houses with wrought iron gates, and when the sun shone, they would sit out on their porches and watch their kids play in their tiny gardens.

Stefano's ambition would take him beyond his roots. When his time came to take over the operation, he built a big house on Staten Island; when he stood at his rear-facing windows, he could see the edge of Paul Castellano's mansion on Todt Hill, the $3.5 million White House, and probably, from his topmost window, the grounds of the Barton estate. If Staten Island was good enough for the head of the Gambino family and a benevolent million-aire, then it was good enough for Stefano. When Castellano died after being shot six times at Sparks Steak House in Manhattan, Stefano was, briefly, the biggest boss on Staten Island.

Stefano married a woman from Bensonhurst named Louisa. She hadn't married him out of any kind of love familiar from romantic novels: she loved him for his power, his violence, and mainly, his money. Those who marry for money usually end up earning it. Louisa did. She was emotionally brutalized and died shortly after giving birth to her third son. Stefano didn't remarry. There was no grief there; he just didn't need the bother of another wife, especially after the first had produced his heirs.

The first child, Vincent, was intelligent and represented the best hope for the family's future. When he died in a swimming pool from a massive brain hemorrhage at twenty-three, his father didn't speak for a week. Instead, he shot Vincent's pair of Labradors and retired to his bedroom. Louisa had been dead for seventeen years.

Niccolo, or Nicky, two years younger than his brother, took his place at his father's right hand. As a rookie, I watched him roam the city in his huge bullet-proofed Cadillac, surrounded by soldiers, carving himself a reputation as a thug to match his father. By the early 1980s, the family had overcome an initial distaste for the drug trade and was flooding the city with every kind of poison it could lay its hands on. Most people stayed out of the way, and any potential rivals were warned off or ended up as fish chum.

The Yardies were another matter. The Jamaican gangs had no respect for established institutions, for the old ways of doing business. They looked at the Italians and saw dead meat; a shipment of cocaine worth two million dollars was boosted from the Ferreras and two soldiers were left dead. Nicky responded by ordering a cull of the Yardies: their clubs were hit, their apartments, even their women. In a three-day period, twelve of them died, including most of those responsible for the cocaine theft.

Maybe Nicky imagined that would be the end of it and things would return to normal again. He still cruised the streets in his car, still ate in the same restaurants, still acted as if the threat of violence from the Jamaicans had dissipated in the face of this show of force.

His favorite haunt was Da Vincenzo, an upscale mom-and-pop operation in his father's old Bensonhurst neighborhood that was smart enough not to forget its roots. Maybe Nicky also liked the echoes of his brother in the name, but his paranoia led him to have the glass in the windows and doors replaced with some military-strength panes, the sort used by the president. Nicky could enjoy his fusilli in peace, undisturbed by the imminent threat of assassination.

He had only just ordered one Thursday evening in November when the black van pulled into the side street opposite, its back facing toward the window. Nicky may have glanced at it as it stopped, may have noticed that its windshield had been removed and replaced with a black wire grille, may even have frowned as the rear doors sprang open and something white flared briefly in the darkness of its interior, the back blast rattling the grille.

He may even have had time to register the RPG-7 warhead as it powered toward the window at six hundred feet per second, smoke trailing it from behind, its roar penetrating the thick panes before they exploded inward, glass and hot metal fragments and the slug from the missile's copper liner tearing Nicky Ferrera into so many pieces that his coffin weighed less than sixty pounds when it was carried up the aisle of the church three days later.

The three Jamaicans responsible disappeared into the underworld and the old man vented his fury on his enemies and his friends in an orgy of abuse, of violence, and of death. His business fell apart around him and his rivals closed in, recognizing in his madness the opportunity to rid themselves of him once and for all.

Just as his world seemed about to implode on itself, a figure appeared at the gates of his mansion and asked to speak with the old man. He told the guard he had some news about the Yardies, the guard passed on the message, and after a search, Bobby Sciorra was admitted. The search was not a complete one: Sciorra held a black plastic bag, which he refused to open. Guns were trained on him as he approached the house, and he was told to halt on the lawn, about fifty feet from the steps of the house, where the old man stood in wait.

"If you're wasting my time, I'll have you killed," said the old man. Bobby Sciorra just smiled and tipped the contents of the bag on the illuminated lawn. The three heads rolled and bumped against one another, the dreadlocks coiled like dead snakes, with Bobby Sciorra smiling above them like some obscene Perseus. Thick, fresh blood hung languorously from the edges of the bag before dripping slowly onto the grass.

Bobby Sciorra "made his bones" that night. Within one year he was a made guy, an ascent up the family ladder made doubly unique by its speed and the relative obscurity of Sciorra's background. The feds had no file on him, and Ferrera appeared able to add little more. I heard rumors that he had crossed the Colombos once, that he had operated out of Florida for a while on a freelance basis, but nothing more than that. Yet the killing of the linchpins of the Jamaican posse was enough to earn him the trust of Stefano Ferrera and a ceremony in the basement of the Staten Island house that resulted in the pricking of Sciorra's trigger finger over a holy picture and his tie-in to Ferrera and his associates.

From that day on, Bobby Sciorra was the power behind the Ferrera throne. He guided the old man and his family through the trials and tribulations of post-RICO New York, when the FBI's Racketeer Influenced Corruption Organization statutes allowed the feds to prosecute organizations and conspirators that benefited from crime, instead of just the individuals who committed those crimes. The major New York families—Gambino, Lucchese, Colombo, Genovese, and Bonanno—numbering maybe four thousand made guys and associates, all took big hits, losing the heads of their families to jail or the Reaper. But not the Ferreras. Bobby Sciorra took care of that, sacrificing some minor players along the way to ensure the survival of the family.

The old man might have preferred to take even more of a backseat in the family operation if it hadn't been for Sonny.

Poor dumb, vicious Sonny, a man without the intelligence of either of his brothers but with at least their combined capacity for violence. Any operations he controlled degenerated into bloodshed, but none of it bothered Sonny. Corpulent and bloated even in his twenties, he enjoyed the mayhem and the killing. The death of the innocent in particular seemed to give him an almost sexual thrill.

Gradually, his father sidelined him and left him to his own devices—steroids, small-time drug deals, prostitution, and occasional violence. Bobby Sciorra tried to keep him under some sort of control, but Sonny was beyond control or reason. Sonny was vicious and evil, and when his father died, a line of men would form to ensure Sonny joined him as soon as possible.

12

□

I NEVER EXPECTED to end up living in the East Village. Susan, Jennifer, and I had lived out in Park Slope, in Brooklyn. On Sundays we could stroll up to Prospect Park and watch the kids playing ball, Jennifer kicking at the grass with her sneakers, before heading to Raintree's for a soda, the sound of the band in the band shell drifting in through the stained-glass windows.

On such days, life seemed as long and welcoming as the green vista of Long Meadow. We would walk Jenny between us, Susan and I, and exchange glances over her head as she burst forth with an endless stream of questions, observations, strange jokes that only a child could understand. I would hold her hand in mine, and through her, I could reach out to Susan and believe that things would work out for us, that we could somehow bridge the gap that was growing between us. If Jenny ran ahead, I would move close to Susan and take her hand and she would smile at me as I told her that I loved her. Then she would look away, or look at her feet, or call Jenny, because we both knew that telling her I loved her was not enough.

When I decided to return to New York at the start of the summer, after months of searching for some sign of their killer, I informed my lawyer and asked him to recommend a realtor. In New York, there are about three hundred million square feet of office space and not enough places to put the people who work in them. I couldn't say why I wanted to live in Manhattan. Maybe it was just because it wasn't Brooklyn.

Instead of a realtor, my lawyer produced a network of friends and business acquaintances that eventually led to me renting an apartment in a redbrick house in the East Village with white shutters on the windows and a stoop that led up to a fanlighted front door. It was a little closer to St. Mark's Place than I would have preferred, but it was still a good deal. Since the days when W. H. Auden and Leon Trotsky had roomed there, St. Mark's had become the East Village with a vengeance, full of bars, cafés, and overpriced boutiques.

The apartment was unfurnished and I pretty much left it that way, adding only a bed, a desk, some easy chairs, and a stereo and small TV. I removed books, tapes, CDs, and vinyl from storage, along with one or two personal belongings, and set up a living space to which I had only the minimum attachment.

It was dark outside as I lined the guns before me on the desk, stripped them down, and cleaned each one carefully. If the Ferreras were coming after me, I wanted to be prepared.

In all my time on the force, I had been forced to draw my weapon to protect myself on only a handful of occasions. I had never killed a man while on duty and had only once fired at another human being, when I shot a pimp in the stomach as he came at me with a long-bladed knife.

As a detective, I had spent most of my time in Robbery and Homicide. Unlike Vice, which was a world in which the threat of violence and death to a cop was a real possibility, Homicide involved a different type of police work. As Tommy Morrison, my first partner, used to say, anybody who's going to die in a Homicide investigation is already dead by the time the cops arrive.

I had abandoned my Colt Delta Elite after the deaths of Susan and Jennifer. Now I had three guns in my possession. The .38 Colt Detective Special had belonged to my father, the only thing of his that I had retained. The prancing-pony badge on the left side of the rounded butt was worn and the frame was scratched and pitted, but it remained a useful weapon, light at about a pound in weight and easily concealed in an ankle holster or a belt. It was a simple, powerful revolver, and I kept it in a holster taped beneath the frame of my bed.

I had never used the Heckler & Koch VP70M outside a range. The 9 millimeter semiautomatic had belonged to a pusher who had died after becoming hooked on his own product. I had found him dead in his apartment after a neighbor had complained about the smell. The VP70M, a semiplastic military pistol holding eighteen rounds, lay, still unused, in its case, but I had taken the precaution of filing away the serial number.

Like the .38, it had no safety. The attraction of the gun lay in the accessory shoulder stock that the pusher had also acquired. When fitted, it made an internal adjustment to the firing mechanism that turned the weapon into a full-automatic submachine gun that could fire twenty-two hundred rounds per minute. If the Chinese ever decided to invade, I could hold them off for at least ten seconds with all the ammunition I had for it. After that, I'd have to start throwing furniture at them. I had removed the H&K from the compartment in the Mustang's trunk where I usually stored it. I didn't want anyone stumbling across it while the car was being serviced.

The third-generation Smith & Wesson was the only gun I carried, a 10 millimeter model specially developed for the FBI and acquired through the efforts of Woolrich. After cleaning it, I loaded it carefully and placed it in my shoulder holster. Outside, I could see the crowds making for the bars and restaurants of the East Village. I was just about to join them when the cell phone buzzed beside me, and thirty minutes later I was preparing to view the body of Stephen Barton.

Red lights flashed, bathing everything in the parking lot with the warm glow of law and order. A patch of darkness marked the nearby McCarren Park, and to the southwest, traffic passed over the Williamsburg Bridge heading for the Brooklyn-Queens Expressway. Patrolmen lounged by cars, keeping the curious and the ghoulish behind barriers. One reached out to block my way—"Hey, gotta keep back"—when we recognized each other. Tyler, who remembered my father and would never make it beyond sergeant, withdrew his hand.

"It's official, Jimmy. I'm with Cole." He looked over his shoulder and Walter, who was talking with a patrolman, glanced over and nodded. The arm went up like a traffic barrier and I passed through.

Even yards from the sewer I could smell the stench. A frame had been erected around the area and a lab technician in boots was climbing out of the manhole.

"Can I go down?" I asked. Two men in neatly cut suits and London Fog raincoats had joined Cole, who barely nodded. The FBI letters weren't visible on the backs of their coats so I assumed they were keeping a low profile. "Uncanny," I said as I passed. "They could almost be regular people." Walter scowled. They joined in.

I slipped on a pair of gloves and climbed down the ladder into the sewer. I gagged with my first breath, the river of filth that ran beneath the tree-lined avenues of the city forcing a taste of bile into the back of my throat. "It's easier if you take shallow breaths," said a sewer worker who stood at the base of the ladder. He was lying.

I didn't step from the ladder. Instead, I pulled my Maglite from my pocket and pointed it to where a small group of maintenance workers and cops stood around an arc-lit area, their feet sloshing through stuff about which I didn't even want to think. The cops gave me a brief glance, then returned with bored looks to watching the med guys go about their business. Stephen Barton lay about five yards from the base of the ladder in a tide of shit and waste, his blond hair moving wildly with the current. It was obvious that he had simply been dumped through the manhole at street level, his body rolling slightly when it hit the bottom.

The ME stood up and pulled the rubber gloves from his hands. A plainclothes Homicide detective, one I didn't recognize, directed a quizzical look at him. He returned one of frustration and annoyance. "We'll need to look at him in the lab. I can't tell shit from shit down here."

"Come on, give us a fucking break," the detective whined lamely.

The ME hissed through his teeth in irritation. "Strangled," he said as he elbowed his way through the small group. "Knocked unconscious first with a blow to the back of the head, then strangled. Don't even ask for a time of death. He could have been down here for a day or so, probably no longer. The body's pretty flaccid." Then the sound of his feet echoed through the sewer as he began to clack up the ladder.

The detective shrugged. "Ashes to ashes, shit to shit," he said, then turned back toward the body.

I climbed up to street level, the ME behind me. I didn't need to look at Barton's body. The blow to the head was unusual, but not extraordinary. It can take as long as ten minutes to kill a man by strangulation, assuming he doesn't manage to break free in the process. I had heard of would-be assassins losing handfuls of hair, patches of skin, and in one case, an ear to a struggling victim. Far better, where possible, to tap him on the head first. Tap him hard enough and strangling him might not be necessary at all.

Walter was still talking to the feds, so I moved as far away from the sewer as I could get while still remaining within the police cordon and drew deep breaths of night air. The smell of human waste underpinned everything, clinging to my clothes with the grim resolution of death itself. Eventually the feds returned to their car and Walter walked slowly toward me, hands stuck in his trouser pockets.

"They're going to bring Sonny Ferrera in," he said.

I snorted. "For what? His lawyer will have him out before he even has time to take a leak. That's assuming he was even involved, or that they can find him. This bunch couldn't find the ground if they fell over."

Walter wasn't in the mood. "What do you know? The kid was running shit for Ferrera; he fucks him over and ends up dead, strangled what's more." Strangulation had become the mob's preferred method of dispatch in recent years: quiet and no mess. "That's the feds' line, and anyway, they'd bring Sonny Ferrera in on suspicion of ignoring a no-smoking sign if they thought it would stick."

"C'mon, Walter, this isn't a Ferrera job. Dumping a guy in a sewer isn't . . ." But he was already walking away, a raised right hand indicating that he didn't want to hear any more. I followed him. "What about the girl, Walter? Maybe she fits in somewhere?"

He turned back to me and put a hand on my shoulder. "When I called you, I didn't think you were going to come running in like Dick Tracy." He glanced back at the feds. "Any sign of her?"

"I think she blew town. That's all I'm saying for the present."

"The ME thinks Barton could have been killed early Tuesday. If the girl left town after that, it could tie her in."

"Are you going to mention her to the feds?"

Walter shook his head. "Let them go chasing after Sonny Ferrera. You stay on the girl."

"Yassuh," I said. "I'ma keep lookin'." I hailed a cab, conscious that the feds were looking at me even as I got in and we drove away into the night.

13

□

IT WAS common knowledge that the old man was having trouble keeping his only surviving son under control. Ferrera had watched the Cosa Nostra tear itself apart back in Italy as it tried, with increasing brutality, to intimidate and destroy the state's investigators. Instead, its methods had served to reinforce the determination of the braver ones to continue the fight; the families were now like one of their own victims bound in the *incaprettamento,* the method of execution known as the goat strangling. Like a victim bound with ropes to his arms, legs, and neck, the more the families struggled, the more the rope around them grew tighter. The old man was determined that this should not happen to his own organization.

By contrast, Sonny saw in the violence of the Sicilians a method of tyranny that suited his own aspirations for power. Maybe that was the difference between father and son. Wherever possible old Ferrera had used the "white *lupara*" when an assassination was necessary, the complete disappearance of the victim without even a trace of blood to give away the truth of what had taken place. The strangling of Barton was certainly a Mafia hallmark, but the dumping was not. If the old man had been responsible for his death, then his final resting place would probably have been the sewers, but not before he had been dissolved in acid and poured down a drain.

So I didn't believe the old man had ordered the killing of Isobel Barton's stepson. His death and the sudden disappearance of Catherine Demeter had come too close together to be mere coincidence. It was possible, of course, that Sonny had ordered them both to be killed for some reason, for if he was as crazy as he seemed to be, then another corpse would be unlikely to trouble him. On the other hand, it was also possible that Demeter had killed her own boyfriend and then fled. Perhaps he hit her once too often, in which case Mrs. Barton was now paying me to find someone who was not only a friend but, potentially, her son's killer.

The Ferrera house was set in tree-shrouded grounds. Entry was by a single iron gate, electronically operated. An intercom was set into the pillar on the left-hand side. I buzzed, gave my name, and told the voice I wanted to see the old man. From the top of the pillar a remote camera was focused on the cab, and although no one was visible in the grounds, I guessed three to five guns were in my immediate vicinity.

Some one hundred yards from the house sat a dark Dodge sedan with two males sitting in the front seat. I could expect a visit from the feds as soon as I got back to my apartment, possibly sooner.

"Walk through. Wait inside the gate," said the voice from the intercom. "You'll be escorted to the house." I did as I was told and the cab pulled away. A gray-haired man in a dark suit and standard-issue shades appeared from behind the trees, a Heckler & Koch MP5 held at port arms. Behind him was another younger man, similarly dressed. To my right I could see two more guards, also armed.

"Lean against the wall," said the gray-haired man. He frisked me professionally while the others watched, removing the clip from my own Smith & Wesson along with the spare clip on my belt. He pulled back the slide to eject the round in the chamber and handed the gun back to me. Then he motioned me toward the house, walking to my right and slightly behind me so that he could keep an eye on my hands. One man shadowed us at either side of the road. It was hardly surprising that old man Ferrera had lived so long.

The house was surprisingly modest from the outside, a

long two-story dwelling with narrow windows at the front
and a gallery running along the upper level. More men pa-
trolled the meticulously kept garden and the graveled driveway. A black Mercedes stood at the right of the house, its
driver waiting nearby if needed. The door was already open
as we approached, and Bobby Sciorra stood in the hallway,
his right hand clasping his left wrist like a priest waiting for
the offerings.

Sciorra was six feet five inches tall and probably weighed
less than one-sixty, his long thin limbs like blades beneath
his gray single-breasted suit, his striated neck almost feminine in its length, its pallor enhanced by the pristine white-
ness of the collarless shirt buttoned beneath it. Short dark
hair surrounded a bald pate, which ended in a cone so sharp
as to appear pointed. Sciorra was a knife made flesh, a
human instrument of pain, both surgeon and scalpel. The
FBI believed that he had personally committed more than
thirty killings. Most of those who knew Bobby Sciorra believed the FBI was conservative in its estimate.

He smiled as I approached, revealing perfectly white
teeth glistening behind narrow, slash lips, but the smile
never reached his blue eyes. Instead it disappeared in the
jagged scar that ran from his left ear across the bridge of his
nose and ended just below the right earlobe. The scar devoured his smile like a second mouth.

"You got some balls coming here," he said, still smiling,
his head shaking gently from side to side as he said it.

"That an admission of guilt, Bobby?" I asked.

The smile never faltered. "Why do you want to see the
boss? He's got no time for shit like you." The smile broad-
ened perceptibly. "By the way, how are your wife and kid?
Kid must be—what?—four by now."

A dull red throbbing began to pulse in my head but I
held it back, my hands tightening at my sides. I knew I'd be
dead before my hands closed on Sciorra's white skin.

"Stephen Barton turned up dead in a sewer this evening.
The feds are looking for Sonny and probably for you as well.
I'm concerned for your welfare. I wouldn't want anything
bad to happen to either of you that I wasn't a part of."

Sciorra's smile remained the same. He seemed about to answer when a voice, low but authoritative, sounded over the house intercom system. Age gave it a gravelly resonance from which the rattle of death was not absent, lurking in the background like the traces of Don Ferrera's Sicilian roots.

"Let him in, Bobby," it said. Sciorra stepped back and opened a set of draft-excluding double doors halfway down the hall. The gray-haired guard walked behind me as I followed Sciorra, who waited until he had closed the draft doors before opening a second door at the end of the hall.

Don Ferrera sat in an old leather armchair behind a big office desk, not entirely dissimilar from Walter Cole's desk, although its gilt inlay raised it into a different league from Walter's comparatively Spartan possession. The curtains were drawn and wall lights and table lamps gave a dim yellow glow to the pictures and bookshelves that lined the walls. I guessed from their age that the books were probably worth a lot and had never been read. Red leather chairs stood against the walls, complementing Don Ferrera's own chair and some sofas that surrounded a long low table at the far end of the room.

Even sitting down and stooped by age, the old man was an impressive figure. His hair was silver and greased back from his temples, but an unhealthy pallor seemed to underlie his tanned complexion and his eyes appeared rheumy. Sciorra closed the door and once more assumed his priest-like stance, my escort remaining outside.

"Please, sit," said the old man, motioning toward an armchair. He opened an inlaid box of Turkish cigarettes, each ringed with small gold bands. I thanked him but refused. He sighed: "Pity. I like the scent but they are forbidden me. No cigarettes, no women, no alcohol." He closed the box and looked longingly at it for a moment, then clasped his hands and rested them on the desk before him.

"You have no title now," he said. Among "men of honor," to be called Mister when you had a title was a calculated insult. Federal investigators sometimes used it to belittle mob suspects, dispensing with the more formal Don or Tio.

"I understand no insult is intended, Don Ferrera," I said. He nodded and was silent.

As a detective I had some dealings with the men of honor and always approached them cautiously and without arrogance or presumption. Respect had to be met with respect and silences had to be read like signs. Among them, everything had meaning and they were as economical and efficient in their modes of communication as they were with their methods of violence.

Men of honor spoke only of what concerned them directly, answered only specific questions and would stay silent rather than tell a lie. A man of honor had an absolute obligation to tell the truth and only when the behavior of others altered so far as to make it necessary to break these rules of behavior would he do so. All of which assumed that you believed pimps and killers and drug dealers were honorable in the first place, or that the code was anything more than the incongruous trapping of another age, pressed into service to provide a sheen of aristocracy for thugs and murderers.

I waited for him to break the silence.

He stood and moved slowly, almost painfully, around the room and stopped at a small side table on which a gold plate gleamed dully.

"You know, Al Capone used to eat off gold plates. Did you know that?" he asked. I told him that I hadn't known.

"His men used to carry them in a violin case to the restaurant and lay them on the table for Capone and his guests, and then they'd all eat off them. Why do you think a man would feel the need to eat from a gold plate?" He waited for an answer, trying to catch my reflection in the plate.

"When you have a lot of money, your tastes can become peculiar, eccentric," I said. "After a while, even your food doesn't taste right unless it's served on bone china, or gold. It's not fitting for someone with so much money and power to eat from the same plates as the little people."

"It goes too far, I think," he replied, but he no longer seemed to be talking to me and it was his own reflection he was examining in the plate. "There's something wrong with it. There are some tastes that should not be indulged, because they are vulgar. They are obscene. They offend nature."

"I take it that isn't one of Capone's plates."

"No, my son gave it to me as a gift on my last birthday. I told him the story and he had the plate made."

"Maybe he missed the point of the story," I said. The old man's face looked weary. It was the face of a man who had not enjoyed his sleep for some time.

"The boy who was killed, you think my son was involved? You think this was a piece of work?" he asked eventually, moving back into my direct line of vision and staring away from me at something in the distance. I didn't look to see what it was.

"I don't know. The FBI appears to think so."

He smiled an empty, cruel smile that reminded me briefly of Bobby Sciorra. "And your interest in this is the girl, no?"

I was surprised, although I should not have been. Barton's past would have been common knowledge to Sciorra at least and would have been passed on quickly when his body was discovered. I thought my visit to Pete Hayes might have played a part too. I wondered how much he knew, and his next question gave me the answer: not much.

"Who are you working for?"

"I can't say."

"We can find out. We found out enough from the old man at the gym."

So that was it. I shrugged gently. He was silent again for a while.

"Do you think my son had the girl killed?"

"Did he?" I responded. Don Ferrera turned back toward me, the rheumy eyes narrowing.

"There is a story told about a man who believes he is being cuckolded by his wife. He approaches a friend, an old, trusted friend, and says: 'I believe my wife is cheating on me but I don't know with whom. I have watched her closely but I cannot find out the identity of this man. What do I do?'

"Now his friend is the man who is cheating with his wife, but to divert the other's attention he says that he saw the wife with another man, a man with a reputation for dishonorable conduct with other men's wives. And so the cuckold turns his gaze on this man and his wife continues to cheat on him with his best friend." He finished and gazed intently at me.

Everything has to be interpreted, everything is codified. To live with signs is to understand the necessity of finding meanings in seemingly irrelevant pieces of information. The old man had spent most of his life looking for the meanings in things and expected others to do likewise. In his cynical little anecdote lay his belief that his son was not responsible for Barton's death but that whoever was responsible stood to benefit from the concentration of the police and FBI on Sonny's assumed guilt. I glanced at Bobby Sciorra and wondered how much Don Ferrera really knew about what went on behind those eyes. Sciorra was capable of anything, even of undermining his boss for his own gains.

"I hear maybe Sonny has taken a sudden interest in my good health," I said.

The old man smiled. "What kind of interest in your health, Mr. Parker?"

"The kind of interest that could result in my health suddenly ceasing to be good."

"I don't know anything about that. Sonny is his own man."

"That may be, but if anyone pulls anything on me, I'll see Sonny in Hell."

"I'll have Bobby look into it," he said.

That didn't make me feel a whole lot better. I stood up to leave.

"A clever man would be looking for the girl," said the old man, also standing up and moving toward a door in a corner of the room behind the desk. "Alive or dead, the girl is the key."

Maybe he was right, but the old man must have had his own reasons for pointing me toward her. And as Bobby

Sciorra escorted me to the front door, I wondered if I was the only person looking for Catherine Demeter.

There was a cab waiting at the gates of the Ferrera house to take me back to the East Village. As it turned out, I had enough time to shower and make a pot of coffee at my apartment before the FBI came knocking on my door. I had changed into tracksuit bottoms and a sweatshirt so I felt a little casual next to Special Agents Ross and Hernandez. The Blue Nile was playing in the background, "A Walk Across the Rooftops," causing Hernandez to wrinkle his nose in distaste. I didn't feel the need to apologize.

Ross did most of the talking, while Hernandez ostentatiously examined the contents of my bookshelf, looking at covers and reading the dust jackets. He hadn't asked if he could and I didn't like it.

"There are some picture ones on the lower shelf," I said. "No Crayolas, though. I hope you brought your own."

Hernandez scowled at me. He was in his late twenties and probably still believed everything he had been taught about the agency in Quantico. He reminded me of the tour guides in the Hoover Building, the ones who herd the Minnesota housewives around while dreaming of gunning down drug dealers and international terrorists. Hernandez probably still refused to believe that Hoover had worn a dress.

Ross was a different matter. He had been involved with the feds' Truck Hijack Squad in New York in the seventies and his name had been linked to a number of high-profile RICO cases since then. I believed he was probably a good agent, but a lousy human being. I had already decided what I was going to tell him: nothing.

"Why were you at the Ferrera house this evening?" he began, after declining an offer of coffee like a monkey refusing a nut.

"I've got a paper route." Ross didn't even grin. Hernandez's scowl deepened. If I'd had a nervous disposition, the strain might have proved too much for me.

"Don't be an asshole," said Ross. "I could arrest you on

suspicion of involvement with organized crime, hold you for a while, let you go, but what good would that do either of us? I'll ask you again: why were you at the Ferrera house this evening?"

"I'm conducting an investigation. Ferrera might have been connected to it."

"What are you investigating?"

"That's confidential."

"Who hired you?"

"Confidential." I was tempted to put on a singsong voice, but I didn't think Ross was in the right frame of mind. Maybe he was right, maybe I was an asshole; but I was no nearer to finding Catherine Demeter than I had been twenty-four hours ago, and her boyfriend's death had opened up a range of possibilities, none of which was particularly appealing. If Ross was out to nail Sonny Ferrera or his father, then that was his problem. I had enough of my own.

"What did you tell Ferrera about Barton's death?"

"Nothing he didn't know already, seeing as how Hansen was at the scene before you were," I replied. Hansen was a reporter with the *Post,* a good one. There were flies that envied Hansen's ability to sniff out a corpse, but if someone had time to tip Hansen off it was pretty certain that someone had informed Ferrera even earlier. Walter was right: parts of the Police Department leaked like a poor man's shoes.

"Look," I said, "I don't know any more than you do. I don't think Sonny was involved, or the old man. As for anyone else . . ."

Ross's eyes flicked upward in frustration. After a pause, he asked if I'd met Bobby Sciorra. I told him I'd had that pleasure. Ross stood and picked at some microscopic speck on his tie. It looked like the sort you picked up in Filene's Basement after the good stuff has gone.

"Sciorra's been mouthing off about teaching you a lesson, I hear. He thinks you're an interfering prick. He's probably right."

"I hope you'll do everything in your power to protect me."

Ross smiled, a minute hitching of the lips that revealed small, pointed canines. He looked like a rat reacting to a stick poked in its face.

"Rest assured, we'll do everything in our power to find the culprit when something happens to you." Hernandez smiled too as they headed for the door. Like father, like son.

I smiled back. "You can let yourselves out. And Hernandez . . ." He stopped and turned.

"I'm gonna count those books."

Ross was right to be concentrating his energies on Sonny. He may have been strictly minor league in many ways—a few porn parlors near Port Authority, a social club on Mott with a handwritten notice taped above the phone reminding members that it was bugged, assorted petty drug deals, shylocking, and running whores hardly made him Public Enemy Number One—but Sonny was also the weak link in the Ferrera chain. If he could be broken, then it might lead to Sciorra and to the old man himself.

I watched the two FBI men from my window as they climbed into their car. Ross paused at the passenger side and stared up at the window for a time. It didn't crack under the pressure. Neither did I, but I had a feeling that Agent Ross wasn't really trying, not yet.

14

□

It was after ten the next morning when I arrived at the Barton house. An unidentified flunky answered the door and showed me into the same office in which I had met Isobel Barton the day before, with the same desk and the same Ms. Christie wearing what looked like the same gray suit and the same unwelcoming look on her face.

She didn't offer me a seat so I stood with my hands in my pockets to stop my fingers getting numb in the chilly atmosphere. She busied herself with some papers on the desk, not sparing me a second look. I stood by the fireplace and admired a blue china dog that stood at the far end of the mantelpiece. It was part of what had probably once been a pair, since there was an empty space on the opposite side. He looked lonely without a friend.

"I thought these things usually came in pairs?"

Ms. Christie glanced up, her face crumpled in annoyance like an image on old newspaper.

"The dog," I repeated. "I thought china dogs like that came in matching pairs." I wasn't particularly concerned about the dog but I was tired of Ms. Christie ignoring me and I derived some petty pleasure from irritating her.

"It was once part of a pair," she replied after a moment. "The other was . . . damaged some time ago."

"That must have been upsetting," I said, trying to look like I meant it while simultaneously failing to do so.

"It was. It had sentimental value."

"For you, or Mrs. Barton?"

"For both of us." Ms. Christie realized she had been

forced to acknowledge my presence despite her best efforts, so she carefully put the cap on her pen, clasped her hands together, and assumed a businesslike expression.

"How is Mrs. Barton?" I asked. What might have been concern moved swiftly across Ms. Christie's features and then disappeared, like a gull gliding over a cliff face.

"She has been under sedation since last night. As you can imagine, she took the news badly."

"I didn't think she and her stepson were that close."

Ms. Christie tossed me a look of contempt. I probably deserved it.

"Mrs. Barton loved Stephen as if he were her own son. Don't forget that you are merely an employee, Mr. Parker. You do not have the right to impugn the reputation of the living or the dead." She shook her head at my insensitivity. "Why are you here? There's a great deal to be done before . . ."

She stopped and, for a moment, looked lost. I waited for her to resume. "Before Stephen's funeral," she finished, and I realized that there might be more to her apparent distress at the events of last night than simple concern for her employer. For a guy who had all the higher moral qualities of a hammerhead shark, Stephen Barton had certainly attracted his share of admirers.

"I have to go to Virginia," I said. "It may take more than the advance I was given. I wanted to let Mrs. Barton know before I left."

"Is this to do with the killing?"

"I don't know." It was becoming a familiar refrain. "There may be a connection between Catherine Demeter's disappearance and Mr. Barton's death but we won't know unless the police find something or the girl turns up."

"Well, I can't authorize that kind of spending at the present time," began Ms. Christie. "You'll have to wait until after—"

I interrupted her. Frankly, I was getting tired of Ms. Christie. I was used to people not liking me, but most at least had the decency to get to know me first, however briefly.

"I'm not asking you to authorize it, and after my meeting with Mrs. Barton, I don't think you have anything to do with it. But as a common courtesy I thought I'd offer my sympathies and tell her how far I've got."

"And how far have you got, *Mr.* Parker?" she hissed. She was standing now, her knuckles white against the desk. In her eyes something vicious and poisonous raised its head and flashed its fangs.

"I think the girl may have left the city. I think she went home, or back to what used to be home, but I don't know why. If she's there I'll find her, make sure she's okay, and contact Mrs. Barton."

"And if she isn't?" I let the question hang without a reply. There was no answer, for if Catherine Demeter wasn't in Haven, then she might as well have dropped off the face of the earth until she did something that made her traceable, like using a credit card or making a telephone call to her worried friend.

I felt tired and frayed at the edges. The case seemed to be fragmenting, the pieces spinning away from me and glittering in the distance. There were too many elements involved to be merely coincidental, and yet I was too experienced to try to force them all together into a picture that might be untrue to reality, an imposition of order upon the chaos of murder and killing. Still, it seemed to me that Catherine Demeter was one of those pieces and that she had to be found so that her place in the order of things could be determined.

"I'm leaving this afternoon. I'll call if I find anything." Ms. Christie's eyes had lost their shine and the bitter thing that lived within her had curled back on itself to sleep for a while. I was not even sure that she heard me. I left her like that, her knuckles still resting on the desk, her eyes vacant, seemingly staring somewhere within herself, her face slick and pale as if troubled by what she saw.

As it turned out, I was delayed by further problems with my car and it was 4 P.M. before I drove the Mustang back to my apartment to pack my bag.

A welcome breeze blew as I walked up the steps, fumbling for my keys. It sent candy wrappers cartwheeling across the street and set soft drink cans tolling like bells. A discarded newspaper skimmed the sidewalk with a sound like the whisperings of a dead lover.

I walked the four flights of stairs to my door, entered the apartment, and turned on a lamp. I prepared a pot of coffee and packed as it percolated. About thirty minutes later I was finishing my coffee, my overnight bag at my feet, when the cell phone rang.

"Hello, Mr. Parker," said a man's voice. The voice was neutral, almost artificial, and I could hear small clicks between the words as if they had been reassembled from a completely different conversation.

"Who is this?"

"Oh, we've never met, but we had some mutual acquaintances. Your wife and daughter. You might say I was with them in their final moments." The voice alternated between sets of words: now high, then low, first male, then female. At one point, there seemed to be three voices speaking simultaneously, then they became a single male voice once again.

The apartment seemed to drop in temperature and then fall away from me. There was only the phone, the tiny perforations of the mouthpiece, and the silence at the other end of the line.

"I've had freak calls before," I said, with more confidence than I felt. "You're just another lonely man looking for a house to haunt."

"I cut their faces off. I broke your wife's nose by slamming her against the wall by the kitchen door. Don't doubt me. I am the one you've been looking for." The last words were all spoken by a child's voice, high-pitched and joyous.

I felt a stabbing pain behind my eyes and my blood sounded loudly in my ears like waves crashing against a headland bleak and gray. There was no saliva in my mouth, just a dry dusty sensation. When I swallowed the feeling was that of dirt traveling down my throat. It was painful and I struggled to find my voice.

"Mr. Parker, are you okay?" The words were calm, solicitous, almost tender, but spoken by what sounded like four different voices.

"I'll find you."

He laughed. The synthesized nature of the sound was more obvious now. It seemed to break up into tiny units, just as a TV screen does when you get too close and the picture becomes merely a series of small dots.

"But I've found *you*," he said. "You wanted me to find you, just as you wanted me to find them and to do what I did. You brought me into your life. For you, I flamed into being.

"I had been waiting so long for your call. You wanted them to die. Didn't you hate your wife in the hours before I took her? And don't you sometimes, in the deep dark of the night, have to fight back your sense of guilt at the feeling of freedom it gave you knowing she was dead? I freed you. The least you could do is show some gratitude."

"You're a sick man, but that isn't going to save you." I checked caller ID on the phone and froze. It was a number I recognized. It was the number of the public phone at the corner of the street. I moved toward the door and began making my way down the stairs.

"No, not 'man.' In her final moments your wife knew that, your Susan, mouth to mouth's kiss as I drew the life from her. Oh, I lusted for her in those last, bright red minutes, but then, that has always been a weakness of our kind. Our sin was not pride, but lust for humanity. And I chose her, Mr. Parker, and I loved her in my way." The voice was now deep and male. It boomed in my ear like the voice of a god, or a devil.

"Fuck you," I said, the bile rising in my throat as I felt sweat bead my brow and run in rivulets down my face, a sick, fearful sweat that defied the fury in my voice. I had come down three flights of stairs. There was one flight left to go.

"Don't go yet." The voice became that of a female child, like my child, my Jennifer, and in that moment I had some inkling of the nature of this Traveling Man. "We'll talk again soon. By then, maybe my purpose will be clearer to you. Take what I give you as a gift. I hope it will ease your suffering. It should be coming to you right . . . about . . . *now.*"

I heard the buzzer sound in my apartment upstairs. I dropped the phone to the floor and drew the Smith & Wesson from my holster. I took the remaining steps two at a time, racing down the stairs with adrenaline pumping through my system. My neighbor Mrs. D'Amato, startled by the noise, stood at her apartment door, the one nearest the front entrance, a housecoat held tight at her neck. I rushed past her, wrenched open the door, and came out low, my thumb already clicking down the safety.

On the step stood a black child of no more than ten years, a cylindrical, gift-wrapped parcel in his hand and his eyes wide in fear and shock. I grabbed him by the collar and flung him inside, shouting for Mrs. D'Amato to hold him, to get both of them away from the package, and ran down the steps of the redbrick and on to the street.

It was deserted except for the papers and the rolling cans. It was a strange desertion, as if the East Village and its inhabitants had conspired with the Traveling Man against me. At the far end of the street, beneath the streetlight, a telephone booth stood. There was no one there and the handset was hanging in its place. I ran toward it, moving away from the corner wall as I approached in case anyone was waiting at the other side. Here, the street was alive with passersby, gay couples hand in hand, tourists, lovers. In the distance I saw the lights of traffic and I heard around me the sounds of a safer, more mundane world I seemed to have left behind.

I spun at the sound of footsteps behind me. A young woman was approaching the telephone, fumbling in her purse for change. She looked up as she saw me approach and backed off at the sight of the gun.

"Find another," I said. I took one last look around, clicked the safety, and stuck the gun in the waistband of my pants. I braced my foot against the pillar of the phone booth and with both hands I wrenched the connecting cable from the phone with a strength that was not natural to me. Then I returned to my apartment house, ca___ receiver before me like a fish on the end of a line.

Inside her apartment Mrs. D'Amato was holding the k___ by his arms while he struggled and fought, with tears rolling down his cheeks. I held his shoulders and squatted down to his level.

"Hey, it's okay. Take it easy. You're not in any trouble, I just want to ask you some questions. What's your name?"

The boy quieted down a little, although he still shook with sobs. He glanced around nervously at Mrs. D'Amato and then made an attempt to break for the door. He nearly made it, too, his jacket slipping from his body as he pulled out his arms, but the force of his efforts made him slip and fall and I was on him. I hauled him to a chair, sat him down, and gave Mrs. D'Amato Walter Cole's number. I told her to tell him it was urgent and to get over here fast.

"What's your name, kid?"

"Jake."

"Okay, Jake. Who gave you this?" I nodded toward the parcel that stood on the table beside us, wrapped in blue paper decorated with teddy bears and candy canes, and topped with a bright blue ribbon.

Jake shook his head, the force sending tears flying off in both directions.

"It's all right, Jake. There's no need to be scared. Was it a man, Jake?" Jake, Jake. Keep using his name, calm him, get him to concentrate.

His face swiveled toward me, the eyes huge. He nodded.

"Did you see what he looked like, Jake?"

His chin crumpled and he started to cry in loud sobs that brought Mrs. D'Amato back to the kitchen door.

"He said he'd hurt me," said Jake. "He said he'd *cu-cut my face off*."

Mrs. D'Amato moved beside him and he buried his face in the folds of her housecoat, wrapping his small arms around her thick waist.

"Did you see him, Jake? Did you see what he looked like?"

He turned from the housecoat.

"He had a knife, like doctors use on TV." The boy's mouth hung wide with terror. "He showed it to me, touched me with it here." He lifted a finger to his left cheek.

"Jake, did you see his face?"

"He was all dark," said Jake, his voice rising in hysteria. "There was nuh-nuhthin' there." His voice rose to a scream: "*He didn't have no face.*"

I told Mrs. D'Amato to take Jake into the kitchen until Walter Cole arrived, then sat down to examine the gift from the Traveling Man. It was about ten inches high and eight inches in diameter and it felt like glass. I took out my pocket knife and gently pulled back an edge of the wrapping, examining it for wires or pressure pads. There was nothing. I cut the two strips of tape holding the paper in place and gently removed the grinning bears, the dancing candy canes.

The surface of the jar was clean and I smelled the disinfectant he had used to erase any traces of himself. In the yellowing liquid it contained I saw my own face doubly reflected, first on the surface of the glass and then, inside, on the face of my once-beautiful daughter. It rested gently against the side of the jar, now bleached and puffy like the face of a drowning victim, scraps of flesh like tendrils rising from the edges and the eyelids closed as if in repose. And I moaned in a rising tide of agony and fear, hatred and remorse. In the kitchen, I could hear the boy named Jake sobbing, and mingled with his cries, I suddenly heard my own.

I don't know how much time elapsed before Cole arrived. He stared ashen faced at the thing in the jar and then called Forensics.

"Did you touch it?"

"No. There's a phone as well. The number matches the caller ID but there won't be any traces. I'm not even sure he was at that phone: that number shouldn't have come up on the cell phone ID. His voice was synthesized in some way. I think he was running his words through some form of sophisticated software, something with voice recognition and tone manipulation, and maybe bouncing it off that number. I don't know. I'm guessing, that's all." I was babbling, words tripping over one another. I was afraid of what might happen if I stopped talking.

"What did he say?"

"I think he's getting ready to start again."

He sat down heavily and ran his hand over his face and through his hair. Then he picked up the paper by one edge with a gloved hand and almost gently used it to cover the front of the jar, like a veil.

"You know what we have to do," he said. "We'll need to know everything he said, anything at all that might help us to get a lead on him. We'll do the same with the kid."

I kept my eyes on Cole, on the floor, anywhere but on the table and the remains of all that I had lost.

"He thinks he's a demon, Walter."

Cole looked once again at the shape of the jar.

"Maybe he is."

As we left for the station, cops milled around the front of the building, preparing to take statements from neighbors, passersby, anyone who might possibly have witnessed the actions of the Traveling Man. The boy, Jake, came with us, his parents arriving shortly after with that frightened, sick look that poor, decent people get in the city when they hear that one of their children is with the police.

The Traveling Man must have been following me throughout the day, watching my movements so he could put into action what he had planned. I traced back my movements, trying to remember faces, strangers, anyone whose gaze might have lingered for just a moment too long. There was nothing.

At the station, Walter and I went through the conversation again and again, pulling out anything that might be useful, that might stamp some distinguishing feature on this killer.

"You say the voices changed?" he asked.

"Repeatedly. At one point, I even thought I heard Jennifer."

"There may be something in that. Voice synthesis of that

kind would have to be done using some sort of computer. Shit, he could simply have routed the call through that number, like you said. The kid says he was given the jar at four P.M. and told to deliver it at four-thirty-five P.M. exactly. He waited in an alley, counting the seconds on his Power Rangers digital watch. That could have given this guy enough time to get to his home base and bounce the call. I don't know enough about these things. Maybe he needed access to an exchange to do what he did. I'll have to get someone who knows to check it out."

The mechanics of the voice synthesis were one thing, but the reasons for the synthesis were another. It might have been that the Traveling Man wanted to leave as few traces of himself as possible: a voice pattern could be recognized, stored, compared, and even used against him at some point in the future.

"What about the kid's comment, that this guy with the scalpel had no face?" asked Walter.

"A mask of some kind, maybe, to avoid any possibility of identification. He could be marked in some way, that's another option. The third choice is that he is what he seems to be."

"A demon?"

I didn't reply. I didn't know what a demon was, if an individual's inhumanity could cause him to cross over in some way, to become something less than human; or if there were some things that seemed to defy any conventional notion of what it meant to be human, of what it meant to exist in the world.

When I returned to the apartment that night, Mrs. D'Amato brought me up a plate of cold cuts and some Italian bread and sat with me for a time, fearful for me after what had taken place that afternoon.

When she left, I stood beneath the shower for a long time, the water as hot as I could take it, and I washed my hands again and again. I lay awake then for a long time, sick with anger and fear, watching the cell phone on my desk. My senses were so heightened that I could hear them hum.

15

□

"Read me a story, Daddy."

"What story do you want to hear?"

"A funny story. The three bears. The baby bear is funny."

"Okay, but then you have to go to sleep."

"Okay."

"One story."

"One story. Then I go to sleep."

In an autopsy, the body is first photographed, clothed and naked. Certain parts of the body may be X-rayed to determine the presence of bone fragments or foreign objects embedded in the flesh. Every external feature is noted: the hair color, the height, the weight, the condition of the body, the color of the eyes.

"Baby Bear opened his eyes wide. 'Somebody's been eating my porridge, and it's all gone!' "

"All gone!"

All gone.

The internal examination is conducted from top to bottom, but the head is examined last. The chest is examined for any sign of rib fractures. A Y-shaped incision is made by cutting from shoulder to shoulder, crossing over the breasts, then moving down from the lower tip of the sternum to the pubic region. The heart and lungs are exposed. The pericardial sac is opened and a sample of blood is taken to determine the blood type of the victim. The heart, lungs, esophagus, and trachea are removed. Each organ is weighed, examined, and sliced into sections. Fluid in the thoracic pleural cavity is removed for analysis. Slides of organ tissue are prepared for analysis under a microscope.

"And then Goldilocks ran away and the three bears never saw her again."

"Read it again."

"No, we agreed. One story. That's all we have time for."

"We have more time."

"Not tonight. Another night."

"No, tonight."

"No, another night. There'll be other nights, and other stories."

The abdomen is examined and any injuries are noted before the removal of the organs. Fluids in the abdomen are analyzed and each separate organ is weighed, examined, and sectioned. The contents of the stomach are measured. Samples are taken for toxicological analysis. The order of removal is usually as follows: the liver, the spleen, the adrenals and kidneys, the stomach, pancreas, and intestines.

"What did you read?"

" 'Goldilocks and the Three Bears.' "

"Again."

"Again."

"Are you going to tell me a story?"

"What story would you like to hear?"

"Something dirty."

"Oh, I know lots of stories like that."

"I know you do."

The genitalia are examined for injuries or foreign material. Vaginal and anal swabs are obtained and any foreign matter collected is sent to a DNA lab for analysis. The bladder is removed and a urine sample is sent to toxicology.

"Kiss me."

"Kiss you where?"

"Everywhere. On my lips, my eyes, my neck, my nose, my ears, my cheeks. Kiss me everywhere. I love your kisses on me."

"Suppose I start with your eyes and move down from there."

"Okay. I can live with that."

The skull is examined in an effort to find evidence of injury. The intermastoid incision is made from one ear to the other, across the top of the head. The scalp is peeled away and the skull exposed. A saw is used to cut through the skull. The brain is examined and removed.

"Why can't we be like this more often?"

"I don't know. I want us to be, but I can't."

"I love you like this."

"Please, Susan . . ."

"No . . ."

"I could taste the booze on your breath."

"Susan, I can't talk about this now. Not now."

"When? When are we going to talk about it?"

"Some other time. I'm going out."

"Stay, please."

"No. I'll be back later."

"Please . . ."

Rehoboth Beach in Delaware has a long boardwalk bordered on one side by the beach and on the other by the sort of amusement arcades you remember from your childhood: twenty-five-cent games played with wooden balls that you roll into holes to score points; horse races with metal horses loping down a sloped track, with a glass-eyed teddy bear for the winner; a frog pond game played with magnets on the end of a child's fishing line.

They've been joined now by noisy computer games and space flight simulators, but Rehoboth still retains more charm than, say, Dewey Beach, farther up the coast, or even Bethany. A ferry runs from Cape May in New Jersey to Lewes on the Delaware coast, and from there, it's maybe five or six miles south to Rehoboth. It's not really the best way to approach Rehoboth, since you run the gamut of burger joints, outlet stores, and shopping malls on U.S.1. The approach north through Dewey is better, running along the shore with its miles of dunes.

From that direction, Rehoboth benefits from the contrast with Dewey. You cross into the town proper over a kind of ornamental lake, go past the church, and then you're on Rehoboth's main street, with its bookstores, its T-shirt shops, its bars and restaurants set in big old wooden houses, where you can drink on the porch and watch people walk their dogs in the quiet evening air.

Four of us had decided on Rehoboth as the place to go for a weekend break to celebrate Tommy Morrison's promotion to lieutenant, despite its reputation as something of a gay hot spot. We ended up staying in the Lord Baltimore, with its comfortable, antiquated rooms harking back to another era, less than a block away from the Blue Moon bar, where crowds of well-tanned, expensively dressed men partied loudly into the night.

I had just become Walter Cole's partner. I suspected Walter had pulled strings to have me assigned as his partner, although nothing was ever said. With Lee's agreement, he traveled with me to Delaware, along with Tommy Morrison and a friend of mine from the academy named Joseph Bonfiglioli, who was shot dead a year later while chasing a guy who had stolen eighty dollars from a liquor store. Each evening at 9 P.M., without fail, Walter would call Lee to check on her and the kids. He was a man acutely aware of the vulnerability of a parent.

Walter and I had known each other for some time—four years by then, I think. I met him first in one of the bars in which cops used to hold court. I was young, just out of uniform, and still admiring my reflection in my new tin. Great things were expected of me. It was widely believed that I would get my name in the papers. I did that, although not in the way that anyone would have imagined.

Walter was a stocky figure wearing slightly worn suits, a

dark shadow of a beard on his cheeks and chin even when he had shaved only an hour before. He had a reputation as a dogged, concerned investigator, one who had occasional flashes of brilliance that could turn an investigation around when legwork had failed to produce a result and the necessary quota of luck upon which almost every investigation depends was not forthcoming.

Walter Cole was also an avid reader, a man who devoured knowledge in the same way that certain tribes devour their enemies' hearts in the hope that they will become braver as a result. We shared a love of Runyon and Wodehouse, of Tobias Wolff, Raymond Carver, Donald Barthelme, the poetry of e. e. cummings, and, strangely, of the earl of Rochester, the Restoration dandy tortured by his failings: his love of alcohol and women and his inability to be the husband that he believed his wife deserved.

I recall Walter wandering along the boardwalk at Rehoboth with a Popsicle in his hand, a garish shirt hanging over a pair of khaki shorts, his sandals slapping lightly on the sand-scattered wood, and a straw hat protecting his already balding head. Even as he joked with us, examining menus and losing money on the slots, stealing fries from Tommy Morrison's big Thrasher's paper tub, paddling in the cool Atlantic surf, I knew that he was missing Lee.

And I knew, too, that to live a life like Walter Cole's—a life almost mundane in the pleasure it derived from small happinesses and the beauty of the familiar, but uncommon in the value it attached to them—was something to be envied.

I met Susan Lewis, as she then was, for the first time in Lingo's Market, an old-style general store that sold produce and cereals alongside expensive cheeses and boasted its own in-store bakery. It was still a family-run operation—a sister, a brother, and their mother, a tiny, white-haired woman with the energy of a terrier.

On our first morning in the resort, I stumbled out to buy coffee and a newspaper in Lingo's, my mouth dry, my legs still unsteady from the night before. She stood at the deli counter, ordering coffee beans and pecans, her hair tied loosely in a ponytail. She wore a yellow summer dress, her eyes were a deep, dark blue, and she was very, very beautiful.

I, on the other hand, was very much the worse for wear, but she smiled at me as I stood beside her at the counter, oozing alcohol from my pores. And then she was gone, trailing a hint of expensive scent behind her.

I saw her a second time that day, at the YMCA as she stepped from the pool and entered the dressing rooms, while I tried to sweat out the alcohol on a rowing machine. It seemed to me that, for the next day or two, I caught glimpses of her everywhere: in a bookshop, examining the covers of glossy legal thrillers; passing the launderette, clutching a bag of donuts; peering in the window of the Irish Eyes bar with a girlfriend; and finally I came upon her one night as she stood on the boardwalk, the sound of the arcades behind her and the waves breaking before her.

She was alone, caught up in the sight of the surf gleaming white in the darkness. Few people strolled on the beach to obscure her view, and at the periphery, away from the arcades and the fast food stalls, it was startlingly empty.

She looked over at me as I stood beside her. She smiled.

"Feeling better now?"

"A little. You caught me at a bad time."

"I could *smell* your bad time," she said, her nose wrinkling.

"I'm sorry. If I'd known you were going to be there, I'd have dressed up." And I wasn't kidding.

"It's okay. I've had those times."

And from there it began. She lived in New Jersey, commuted to Manhattan each day to work in a publisher's office, and every second weekend she visited her parents in Massachusetts. We were married a year later and we had Jennifer one year after that. We had maybe three very good years together before things started to deteriorate. It was my fault, I think. When my parents married they both knew the toll a policeman's life could take on a marriage, he because he lived that life and saw its results reflected in the lives around him, she because her father had been a deputy in

Maine and had resigned before the cost became too high. Susan had no such experience.

She was the youngest of four children, both of her parents were still alive, and they all doted on her. When she died, they ceased to speak to me. Even at the graveside, no words passed between us. With Susan and Jennifer gone, it was as if I had been cut adrift from the tide of life and left to float in still, dark waters.

16

□

THE DEATHS OF SUSAN and Jennifer attracted a great deal of attention, although it soon faded. The more intimate details of the killing—the skinning, the removal of the faces, the blindings—were kept from the public, but it didn't stop the freaks from coming out of the woodwork. For a time, murder tourists would drive up to the house and videotape one another standing in the yard. A local patrolman even caught one couple trying to break in through the back door in order to pose in the chairs where Susan and Jennifer had died. In the days after they had been found, the phone rang regularly with calls from people who claimed to be married to the killer, or who felt certain that they had met him in a past life or, on one or two occasions, called only to say they were glad my wife and child were dead. Eventually I left the house, remaining in touch by phone and fax with the lawyer who had been entrusted with the business of selling it.

I had found the community in southern Maine, when I was returning to Manhattan from Chicago after chasing up one more obscure non-lead, a suspected child killer named Myron Able, who was dead by the time I arrived, killed in the parking lot of a bar after he tangled with some local thugs. Maybe I was also looking for some peace in a place I knew, but I never got as far as the house in Scarborough, the house that my grandfather had left me in his will.

I was sick by that time. When the girl found me retching and crying in the doorway of a boarded-up electronics store and offered me a bed for the night, I could only nod. When her comrades, huge men with muddied boots and shirts that smelled of sweat and pine needles, dragged me to their pickup and dumped me in the back, I half hoped that they were going to kill me. They nearly did. By the time I left their community, out by Sebago Lake, six weeks later, I had lost more than twelve pounds and my stomach muscles stood out like the plates on an alligator's back. During the day, I worked on their small farm and attended group sessions where others like me tried to purge themselves of their demons. I still craved alcohol but fought back the desire as I had been taught. There were prayers in the evenings and every Sunday a pastor would give a sermon on abstinence, tolerance, the need for each man and woman to find a peace within himself or herself. The community funded itself through the produce it sold, some furniture it made, and donations from those who had availed themselves of its services, some of them now wealthy men and women.

But I was still sick, consumed by a desire to revenge myself upon those around me. I felt trapped in a limbo: the investigation had ground to a halt and would not resume again until a similar crime was committed and a pattern could be established.

Someone had taken my wife and child from me and escaped unpunished. Inside me, the hurt and anger and guilt ebbed and flowed like a red tide waiting to spill its banks. I felt it as a physical pain that tore at my head and gnawed at my stomach. It led me back to the city, where I tortured and killed the pimp Johnny Friday in the toilet of the bus station where he had been waiting to feast on the waifs and strays drifting into New York.

I think now that I had always set out to kill him but that I had hidden the knowledge of what I intended to do in some corner of my mind. I draped it with self-serving justifications and excuses, the sort I had used for so long each time I watched a shot of whiskey poured in front of me, or heard the gassy snap of a bottle cap. Frozen by my own inability and the inability of others to find the killer of Susan and Jennifer, I saw a chance to strike out and I took it. From the moment I packed my gun and gloves and set out for the bus station, Johnny Friday was a dead man.

Friday was a tall, thin black man who looked like a preacher in his trademark dark three-buttoned suits and his collarless shirts fastened at the neck. He would hand out small Bibles and religious pamphlets to the new arrivals and offer them soup from a flask, and as the barbiturates it contained began to take effect, he would lead them from the station and into the back of a waiting van. Then they would disappear, as surely as if they had never arrived, until they turned up on the streets as beaten junkies, whoring for the fix that Johnny supplied at inflated prices while they pulled in the tricks that kept him rich.

His was a hands-on operation, and even in a business not noted for its humanity, Johnny Friday was beyond any kind of redemption. He supplied children to pedophiles, delivering them to the doors of selected safe houses, where they were raped and sodomized before being returned to their owner. If they were rich and depraved enough, Johnny would give them access to "the basement," in an abandoned warehouse in the garment district. There, for a cash payment of ten thousand dollars, they could take one of Johnny's stable, boy or girl, child or teen, they could torture, rape, and if they wished, kill, and Johnny would take care of the body. He was noted, in certain circles, for his discretion.

In my search for the killer of my wife and child, I had learned of Johnny Friday. From a former snitch I learned that Johnny sometimes dealt in pictures and videos of sexual torture, that he was a leading source of this material, and that anyone whose tastes ran in that direction would, at some point, come into contact with Johnny Friday or one of his agents.

And so I watched him for five hours from an Au Bon Pain in the station, and when he went to the washroom, I followed him. It was divided into sections, the first mirrored, with sinks, the second lined with urinals along the end wall and two sets of stalls opposite, divided by a central aisle. An old man in a stained uniform sat in a small, glass-lined cubicle beside the sinks but he was engrossed in a magazine when I entered behind Johnny Friday. Two men were washing their hands at the sinks, two were standing at the urinals, and three of the stalls were occupied, two in the section to the left, one in the section to the right. Piped music was playing, some unrecognizable tune.

Johnny Friday walked, hips swinging, to the urinal at the far right of the wall. I stood two urinals away from him as I waited for the other men to finish. As soon as they had finished I moved behind Johnny Friday, clasping my hand on his mouth and pressing the Smith & Wesson into the soft skin beneath his chin as I pushed him into the end stall, the farthest away from the other occupied stall on that side.

"Hey, don't, man, don't," he whispered, his eyes wide. I brought my knee up hard into his groin and he fell down heavily on his knees as I locked the door behind us. He tried weakly to rise and I hit him hard in the face. I brought the gun close to his head again.

"Don't say a word. Turn your back to me."

"Please, man, don't."

"Shut up. Turn."

He inched slowly round on his knees. I pulled his jacket down over his arms and then cuffed him. From my other pocket I took a rag and a roll of duct tape. I stuffed the rag in his mouth and wrapped the tape around his head two or three times. Then I pulled him to his feet and pushed him down on to the toilet. His right foot came up and caught me hard on the shin and he tried to push himself up, but he was off balance and I hit him again. This time he stayed down. I held the gun on him and listened for a moment in case anyone came to see what the noise was. There was only the sound of a toilet flushing. No one came.

I told Johnny Friday what I wanted. His eyes narrowed as he realized who I was. Sweat poured from his forehead and he tried to blink it from his eyes. His nose was bleeding slightly and a thin trickle of red ran from beneath the duct tape and rolled down his chin. His nostrils flared as he breathed heavily through them.

"I want names, Johnny. Names of customers. You're going to give them to me."

He snorted in disdain and blood bubbled from a nostril. His eyes were cold now. He looked like a long, black snake with his slicked-back hair and slitted, reptilian eyes. When I broke his nose they widened in shock and pain.

I hit him again, once, twice, hard blows to the stomach and head. Then I pulled the tape down hard and dragged the bloodied rag from his mouth.

"Give me names."

He spat a tooth from his mouth.

"Fuck you," he said. "Fuck you and your dead bitches."

What happened after is still not clear to me. I remember hitting him again and again, feeling bone crunch and ribs break and watching my gloves darken with his blood. There was a black cloud in my mind and streaks of red ran through it like strange lightning.

When I stopped, Johnny Friday's features seemed to have melted into a bloody blur. I held his jaw in my hands as blood bubbled from his lips.

"Tell me," I hissed. His eyes rolled toward me, and like a vision of some craggy entrance to Hell, his broken teeth showed behind his lips as he managed one last smile. His body arched and spasmed once, twice. Thick black blood rolled from his nose and mouth and ears, and then he died.

I stood back, breathing heavily. I wiped my blood-spattered face as best I could and cleaned some of the blood from the front of my jacket, although it hardly showed against the black leather and my black jeans. I took the gloves from my hands, stuffed them in my pocket, and then flushed the toilet before peering carefully out and pulling the door closed behind me as I left. Blood was already seeping out of the stall and pooling in the cracks between the tiles.

I realized that the noise of Johnny Friday's dying must have echoed around the washroom but I didn't care. As I left I passed only an elderly black man at the urinals and he, like a good citizen who knows when to mind his own business, didn't even glance at me. There were other men at the sinks, who gave me a cursory look in the mirror. But I noticed that the old man was gone from his glass cubicle and I ducked into an empty departure gate as two cops came running toward the washroom from the upper level. I made my way to the street through the ranks of buses beneath the station.

Perhaps Johnny Friday deserved to die. Certainly no one mourned his passing and the police made little more than a cursory effort to find his killer. But there were rumors, for Walter, I think, had heard them.

But I live with the death of Johnny Friday as I live with the deaths of Susan and Jennifer. If he did deserve to die, if what he got was no more than he merited, yet it was not for me to act as his judge and executioner. "In the next life we get justice," someone once wrote. "In this one we have the law." In Johnny Friday's last minutes there was no law and only a kind of vicious justice that was not for me to give.

I did not believe that my wife and child were the first to die at the hands of the Traveling Man, if that was who he was. I still believed that somewhere in a Louisiana swamp lay another and in her identity was the clue that would open up the world of this man who believed he was not a man. She was part of a grim tradition in human history, a parade of victims stretching back to ancient times, back to the time of Christ and before that, back to a time when men sacrificed those around them to placate gods who knew no mercy and whose natures they both created and imitated in their actions.

The girl in Louisiana was part of a bloody succession, a modern-day Windeby Girl, a descendant of that anonymous woman found in the fifties in a shallow grave in a peat bog in Denmark, where she had been led nearly two thousand years before, naked and blindfolded, to be drowned in twenty inches of water. A path could be traced through history leading from her death to the death of another girl at the hands of a man who believed he could appease the demons within himself by taking her life but who, once blood had been spilled and flesh torn, wanted more and took my wife and child.

We do not believe in evil anymore, only evil acts that can be explained away by the science of the mind. There is no evil and to believe in it is to fall prey to superstition, like checking beneath the bed at night or being afraid of the dark. But there are those for whom we have no easy answers, who do evil because that is their nature, because they are evil.

Johnny Friday and others like him prey on those who live on the periphery of society, on those who have lost their way. It is easy to get lost in the darkness on the edge of modern life, and once we are lost and alone, there are things waiting for us there. Our ancestors were not wrong in their superstitions: there is reason to fear the dark.

And just as a trail could be followed from a bog in Denmark to a swamp in the South, so I came to believe that evil, too, could be traced throughout the life of our race. There was a tradition of evil that ran beneath all human existence like the sewers beneath a city, that continued on even after one of its constituent parts was destroyed, because it was simply one small part of a greater, darker whole.

Perhaps that was part of what made me want to find out the truth about Catherine Demeter, for as I look back, I realize that evil had found its way to touch her life too and taint it beyond retrieval. If I could not fight evil as it came in the form of the Traveling Man, then I would find it in other forms. I believe what I say. I believe in evil because I have touched it, and it has touched me.

17

□

WHEN I TELEPHONED Rachel Wolfe's private practice the following morning, the secretary told me that she was giving a seminar at a conference at Columbia University. I took the subway from the Village and arrived early at the main entrance to the campus. I wandered for a while around the Barnard Book Forum, students jostling me as I stood browsing in the literature section, before making my way to the main college entrance.

I passed through the university's large quadrangle, with the Butler Library at one end, the administration building at the other, and like a mediator between learning and bureaucracy, the statue of Alma Mater in the grass center. Like most city residents, I rarely came to Columbia, and the sense of tranquillity and study only feet away from the busy streets outside was always surprising to me.

Rachel Wolfe was just finishing her lecture as I arrived, so I waited for her outside the theater until the session ended. She emerged talking to a young, earnest-looking man with curly hair and round spectacles, who hung on her every word. When she saw me she stopped and smiled a good-bye at him. He looked unhappy and seemed set to linger, but then turned and walked away, his head low.

"How can I help you, Mr. Parker?" she asked, with a puzzled but not uninterested look.

"He's back."

We walked over to the Hungarian Pastry Shop on Amsterdam Avenue, where intense-looking young men and women sat reading textbooks and sipping coffee. Rachel Wolfe was wearing jeans and a chunky jumper with a heart-shaped design on the front.

Despite all that had happened the previous night, I was curious about her. I had not been attracted to a woman since Susan's death, and my wife was the last woman with whom I had slept. Rachel Wolfe, her long red hair brushed back over her ears, aroused a sense of longing in me that was more than sexual. I felt a deep loneliness within myself and an ache in my stomach. She looked at me curiously.

"I'm sorry," I said. "I was thinking of something."

She nodded and picked at a poppy-seed roll before pulling off a huge chunk and stuffing it in her mouth, sighing with satisfaction. I must have looked slightly shocked, because she covered her mouth with her hand and giggled softly.

"Sorry, but I'm a sucker for these things. Daintiness and good table manners tend to go out the window when someone puts one in front of me."

"I know the feeling. I used to be like that with Ben & Jerry's until I realized that I was starting to look like one of the cartons."

She smiled again and pushed at a piece of roll that was trying to make a break for freedom from the side of her mouth. The conversation sagged for a time.

"I take it your parents were jazz fans," she said eventually.

I must have looked puzzled for a moment, because she smiled in amusement as I tried to take in the question. I had been asked it many times before but I was grateful for the diversion, and I think she knew that.

"No, my father and mother didn't know the first thing about jazz," I replied. "My father just liked the name. The first time he heard about Bird Parker was at the baptismal font, when the priest mentioned it to him. The priest was a big jazz fan, I was told. He couldn't have been happier if my father had announced that he was naming all of his children after the members of the Count Basie Orchestra. My father, by contrast, wasn't too happy at the idea of naming his firstborn after a black jazz musician, but by then it was too late to think of another name."

"What did he call the rest of his children?"

I shrugged. "He didn't get the chance. My mother couldn't have any more children after me."

"Maybe she thought she couldn't do any better?" She smiled.

"I don't think so. I was nothing but trouble for her as a child. It used to drive my father crazy."

I could see in her eyes that she was about to ask me about my father but something in my face stopped her. She pursed her lips, pushed away her empty plate, and settled herself back in her chair.

"Can you tell me what happened?"

I went through the events of last night, leaving nothing out. The words of the Traveling Man were burned into my mind.

"Why do you call him that?"

"A friend of mine led me to a woman who said that she was receiving, uh, messages from a dead girl. The girl had died in the same way as Susan and Jennifer."

"Was the girl found?"

"No one looked. An old woman's psychic messages aren't enough to launch an investigation."

"Even if she exists, are you sure it's the same guy?"

"I believe it is, yes."

Wolfe looked like she wanted to ask more, but she let it go. "Go back over what this caller, this Traveling Man, said, again, slowly this time."

I did until she lifted her hand to stop me. "That's a quote from Joyce: 'mouth to mouth's kiss.' It's the description of the 'pale vampire' in *Ulysses*. This is an educated man we're dealing with. The stuff about 'our kind' sounds biblical; I'm not sure of it. I'll have to check it. Give it to me again." I spoke the words slowly as she took them down in a wire-bound note-book. "I have a friend who teaches theology and biblical studies. He might be able to identify a source for these."

She closed the notebook. "You know that I'm not supposed to get involved in this case?"

I told her that I hadn't known.

"Following our earlier discussions, someone got in touch with the commissioner. He wasn't pleased at the snub to his relative."

"I need help with this. I need to know all I can." Suddenly I felt nauseous, and when I swallowed, my throat hurt.

"I'm not sure that's wise. You should probably leave this to the police. I know that's not what you want to hear, but after all that's happened, you risk damaging yourself. Do you understand what I mean?"

I nodded slowly. She was right. Part of me wanted to draw back, to immerse myself once again in the ebb and flow of ordinary life. I wanted to unburden myself of what I felt, to restore myself to some semblance of a normal existence. I wanted to rebuild but I felt frozen, suspended, by what had happened. And now the Traveling Man had returned, snatching any possibility of that normality from me and, simultaneously, leaving me as powerless to act as I had been before.

I think Rachel Wolfe understood that. Perhaps that was why I had come to her, in the hope that she might understand.

"Are you okay?" She reached over and touched my hand and I almost cried. I nodded again.

"You're in a terribly difficult situation. If he has decided to contact you, then he wants you to be involved and there may be a link that can be exploited. From an investigative point of view, you probably shouldn't deviate from your routine in case he contacts you again, but from the point of view of your own well-being . . ." She let the unstated hang in the air. "You might even want to consider some professional help. I'm sorry for being so blunt about it, but it has to be said."

"I know, and I appreciate the advice." It was strange to find myself attracted to someone after all this time and then have her advise me to see a psychiatrist. It didn't hold out the promise of any relationship that wasn't conducted on an hourly basis. "I think the investigators want me to stay."

"I get the feeling you're not going to do it."

"I'm trying to find someone. It's a different case, but I think this person may be in trouble. If I stay here, there's no one to help her."

"It may be a good idea to get away from this for a time, but from what you're saying, well . . ."

"Go on."

"It sounds like you're trying to save this person but you're not even sure if she needs saving."

"Maybe I need to save her."

"Maybe you do."

I told Walter Cole later that morning that I would continue looking for Catherine Demeter and that I would be leaving the city to do so. We were sitting in the quietness of Chumley's, the Village's old speakeasy on Bedford. When Walter called, I had surprised myself by nominating it for our meeting, but as I sat sipping a coffee I realized why I had chosen it.

I enjoyed its sense of history, its place in the city's past, which could be traced back like an old scar or the wrinkle at the corner of an eye. Chumley's had survived the Prohibition era, when customers had escaped raids by leaving hastily through the back door, which led onto Barrow Street. It had survived world wars, stock market crashes, civil disobedience, and the gradual erosion of time, which was so much more insidious than all the rest. Right now, I needed its stability.

"You have to stay," said Walter. He still had the leather coat, now hanging loosely over the back of his chair. Someone had whistled at him when he entered wearing it.

"No."

"What do you mean, no?" he said angrily. "He's opened an avenue of communication. You stay, we wire up the phone, and we try to trace him when he calls again."

"I don't think he will call again, at least not for a while, and I don't believe we could trace him anyway. He doesn't want to be stopped, Walter."

"All the more reason to stop him, then. My God, look at

what he's done, what he's going to do again. Look at what you've done for his—"

I leaned forward and broke in on him, my voice low. "What have I done? Say it, Walter. Say it!"

He stayed silent and I saw him swallow the words back. We had come close to the edge, but he had pulled back.

The Traveling Man wanted me to remain. He wanted me to wait in my apartment for a call that might never come. I could not let him do that to me. Yet both Walter and I knew that the contact he had established could well be the first link in a chain that would eventually lead us to him.

A friend of mine, Ross Oakes, had worked in the police department of Columbia, South Carolina, during the Bell killings. Larry Gene Bell abducted and smothered two girls, one aged seventeen and abducted close to a mailbox, the other aged nine and taken from her play area. When investigators eventually found the bodies of the children they were too decomposed to determine if they had been sexually assaulted, although Bell later admitted to assaulting both.

Bell had been tracked through a series of phone calls he made to the family of the seventeen-year-old, conversing primarily with the victim's older sister. He also mailed them her last will and testament. In the phone calls he led the family to believe that the victim was still alive, until her body was eventually found one week later. After the abduction of the younger girl he contacted the first victim's sister and described the abduction and killing of the girl. He told the first victim's sister that she would be next.

Bell was found through indented writing on the victim's letter, a semiobliterated telephone number that was eventually tracked through a process of elimination. Larry Gene Bell was a thirty-six-year-old white male, formerly married and now living with his mother and father. He told Investigative Support Unit agents from the FBI that "the bad Larry Gene Bell did it."

I knew of dozens of similar cases where contact with the killer by the victim's family sometimes led to his capture, but I had also seen what this form of psychological torture had done to those who were left behind. The family of Bell's first victim were lucky because they had to suffer Bell's sick wanderings for only two weeks.

Amid the anger and pain and grief that I had felt the night before, there was another feeling that caused me to fear any further contact with the Traveling Man, at least for the present.

I felt relief.

For over seven months there had been nothing. The police investigation had ground to a halt, my own efforts had brought me no nearer to identifying the killer of my wife and child, and I feared that he might have disappeared.

Now he had come back. He had reached out to me and, by doing so, opened the possibility that he might be found. He would kill again, and in the killing, a pattern would emerge that would bring us closer to him. All these thoughts had raced through my head in the darkness of the night, but in the first light of dawn, I had realized the implications of what I felt.

The Traveling Man was drawing me into a cycle of dependency. He had tossed me a crumb in the form of a telephone call and the remains of my daughter, and in doing so had caused me to wish, however briefly, for the deaths of others in the hope that their deaths might bring me closer to him. With that realization came the decision that I would not form such a relationship with this man. It was a difficult decision to make but I knew that if he decided to contact me again, then he would find me. Meanwhile, I would leave New York and continue to hunt for Catherine Demeter.

Yet deep down, perhaps only half recognized by me and suspected by Rachel Wolfe, there was another reason for continuing the search for Catherine Demeter.

I did not believe in remorse without reparation. I had failed to protect my wife and child, and they had died as a result. Perhaps I was deluded, but I believed that if Catherine Demeter died because I stopped looking for her, then I would have failed twice, and I was not sure that I could live with that knowledge. In her, maybe wrongly, I saw a chance to atone.

Some of this I tried to explain to Walter—my need to

avoid a dependent relationship with this man, the necessity of continuing the search for Catherine Demeter, for her sake and my own—but most of it I kept to myself. We parted uneasily and on bad terms.

Tiredness had gradually taken hold of me throughout the morning and I slept fitfully for an hour before setting off for Virginia. I was bathed in sweat and almost delirious when I awoke, disturbed by dreams of endless conversations with a faceless killer and images of my daughter before her death.

Just as I awoke, I dreamed of Catherine Demeter surrounded by darkness and flames and the bones of dead children. And I knew then that some terrible blackness had descended on her and that I had to try to save her, to save us both, from the darkness.

11

Eadem mutata resurgo.
(Though changed, I shall arise the same.)

Epitaph of Jakob Bernoulli,
Swiss pioneer of fluid dynamics
and spiral mathematics

18

□

I DROVE DOWN to Virginia that afternoon. It was a long ride but I told myself that I wanted time to open up the car's engine, to let it cut loose after its time off the road. As I drove, I tried to sort through what had happened in the last two days, but my thoughts kept coming back to the remains of my daughter's face resting in a jar of formaldehyde.

I spotted the tail after about an hour, a red Nissan four wheel drive with two occupants. They kept four or five vehicles behind but when I accelerated, so did they. When I fell back they kept me in view for as long as they could, then they began to fall back too. The plates were deliberately obscured with mud. A woman drove, her blond hair pulled back behind her and sunglasses masking her eyes. A dark-haired male sat beside her. I put them both in their thirties but I didn't recognize them.

If they were feds, which was unlikely, then they were lame. If they were Sonny's hired killers, then it was just like Sonny to hire cheap. Only a clown would use a 4WD for a tail, or to try to take out another vehicle. A 4WD has a high center of gravity and rolls easier than a drunk on a slope. Maybe I was just being paranoid, but I didn't think so.

They didn't make a move and I lost them in the backroads between Warrenton and Culpeper as I headed toward the Blue Ridge. If they came after me again, I'd know: they stood out like blood in snow.

As I drove, sunlight speared the trees, causing the weblike cocoons of caterpillars to glisten. I knew that, beneath the strands, the white bodies of the larvae were twisting and writhing like victims of Tourette's syndrome as they reduced the leaves to brown lifelessness. The weather was beautiful and there was a kind of poetry to the names of the towns that skirted Shenandoah: Wolftown, Quinque, Lydia, Roseland, Sweet Briar, Lovingston, Brightwood. To that list could be added the town of Haven, but only if you decided not to spoil the effect by actually visiting it.

It was raining heavily by the time I reached Haven. The town lay in a valley southeast of the Blue Ridge, almost at the apex of a triangle formed with Washington and Richmond. A sign at the limits read, *A Welcome in the Valley,* but there was little that was welcoming about Haven. It was a small town over which a pall of dust appeared to have settled that even the driving rain seemed unable to dislodge. Rusting pickups sat outside some of the houses, and apart from a single fast food joint and a convenience store attached to a gas station, only the weak neon of the Welcome Inn bar and the lights of the late-night diner opposite beckoned the casual visitor. It was the sort of place where, once a year, the local Veterans of Foreign Wars got together, hired a bus, and went somewhere else to commemorate their dead.

I checked into the Haven View Motel at the outskirts of the town. I was the only guest and a smell of paint hung around the halls of what might once have been a considerable house but had now been converted into a functional, anonymous three-story inn.

"Second floor's being redecorated," said the clerk, who told me his name was Rudy Fry. "Have to put you upstairs, top floor. Technically, we shouldn't be accepting guests at all but . . ." He smiled to indicate the big favor he was doing me by letting me stay. Rudy Fry was a small overweight man in his forties. There were long-dried yellow sweat stains under his arms and he smelled vaguely of rubbing alcohol.

I looked around. The Haven View Motel didn't look like the sort of place that would attract visitors in the best of times.

"I know what you're thinkin'," said the clerk, his smile revealing sparkling dentures. "You're thinkin', 'Why throw good money away by decoratin' a motel in a shit hole like this?' " He winked at me before leaning over the desk conspiratorially. "Well, I'm tellin' you, sir, it ain't gonna be a shit hole much longer. Them Japanese is comin' and when they do, this place is gonna be a gold mine. Where else they gonna stay round here?" He shook his head and laughed. "Shit, we gonna be wipin' our asses with dollar bills." He handed me a key with a heavy wooden block chained to it. "Room twenty-three, up the stairs. Elevator's busted."

The room was dusty but clean. A connecting door led into the room next door. It took me less than five seconds to break the lock with my pocketknife, then I showered, changed, and drove back into town.

The recession of the seventies had hit Haven hard, putting an end to what little industry there was. The town might have recovered, might have found some other way to prosper, had its history been other than it was, but the killings had tainted it and the town had fallen into decay. And so, even after the rain had sluiced its way over the stores and streets, over the people and the houses, over trees and pickups and cars and Tarmac, there was no freshness about Haven. It was as if the rain itself had been sullied by the contact.

I stopped in at the Sheriff's Office but neither the sheriff nor Alvin Martin was available. Instead, a deputy named Wallace sat scowling behind the desk and shoveling Doritos into his mouth. I decided to wait until the morning in the hope of finding someone more accommodating.

The diner was closing as I walked through the town, which left only the bar or the burger joint. The interior of the bar was ill lit, as if it was expending too much power on the pink neon sign outside. *The Welcome Inn:* the sign glowed brightly, but the interior seemed to give the lie to the sign.

Some kind of bluegrass music was playing over a speaker, and a TV above the bar was showing a basketball game with the volume turned down, but no one seemed to be listening or watching anyway. Maybe twenty people were scattered around the tables and the long, dark wood bar, including a mountainous couple who looked like they'd left the third bear with a baby-sitter. There was a low tide of conversation, which ebbed slightly when I entered, although it refused to cease entirely, and then resumed at its previous level.

Near the bar, a small knot of men lounged around a battered pool table, watching a huge, heavy-set man with a thick dark beard playing an older man who shot pool like a hustler. They eyed me as I walked by but continued playing. No conversation passed between them. Pool was obviously a serious business in the Welcome Inn. Drinking wasn't. The hard men around the pool table were all clutching bottles of Bud Light, the real drinker's equivalent of a club soda and lime.

I took an empty stool at the bar and asked for a coffee from a bartender whose white shirt seemed dazzlingly clean for such a place. He studiously ignored me, his eyes seemingly intent on the basketball game, so I asked again. His glance moved lazily to me, as if I were a bug crawling on the bar and he had just had his fill of squashing bugs but was wondering whether he couldn't squash one more for the road.

"We don't do coffee," he said.

I glanced along the bar. Two stools down an elderly man in a lumber jacket and a battered Cat cap sipped at a mug of what smelled like strong black coffee.

"He bring his own?" I inquired, gesturing with a nod down the bar.

"Yep," said the bartender, still looking at the TV.

"A Coke'll do. Right behind your knees, second shelf down. Don't hurt yourself leaning over."

For a long time it seemed he wasn't going to move, then he shifted slowly, leaned down without taking his eyes from the screen, and found the opener on the edge of the counter by instinct. Then he placed the bottle in front of me and set an iceless glass beside it. In the mirror behind the bar, I saw the amused smiles of some of the other patrons and heard a woman's laugh, low and boozy with a promise of sex in it. In the mirror over the bar, I traced the laugh to a coarse-featured woman in the corner, her hair huge and dark. Beside her, a stout man whispered sour somethings in her ear like the cooings of a sick dove.

I poured the drink and took a long swig. It was warm and sticky and I felt it cleave to my palate, my tongue, and my teeth. The bartender spent a while idly polishing glasses with a bar towel that looked like it had last been cleaned for Reagan's inauguration. When he got bored with redistributing the dirt on the glasses he wandered back toward me and put the bar towel down in front of me.

"Passin' through?" he asked, although there was no curiosity in his voice. It sounded more like advice than a question.

"Nope," I said.

He took it in and then waited for me to say more. I didn't. He gave in first.

"Whatcha doin' here, then?" He looked over my shoulder at the pool players behind and I noticed that the sound of balls colliding had suddenly ceased. He smiled a big shit-eating grin. "Maybe I can"—he stopped and the grin got wider, his tone changing to one of mock formality—"be of some *a*-ssistance."

"You know anyone named Demeter?"

The shit-eating grin froze and there was a pause.

"No."

"Then I don't believe you can be of any *a*-ssistance."

I stood up to leave, placing two dollar bills on the counter.

"For the welcome," I said. "Put it toward a new sign."

I turned to find a small, rat-featured guy in a worn blue denim jacket standing in front of me. His nose was dotted with blackheads and his teeth were prominent and yellow-stained like walrus tusks. His black baseball cap was marked with the words *Boyz N the Hood*, but this wasn't any logo John Singleton would have liked. Instead of homies, the words were surrounded by the hooded heads of Klan figures.

Beneath his denim jacket, I could see the word *Pulaski* under a seal of some sort. Pulaski was the birthplace of the Ku Klux Klan and the site of an annual rally for Aryan crackers everywhere, although I bet the face of old Thom Robb, grand high ass-wipe of the Klan, must have just lit up at the sight of Rat Features and his pinched, subintelligent face arriving to take in the Pulaski air. After all, Robb was trying to make the Klan appeal to the educated elite, the lawyers and the schoolteachers. Most lawyers would have been reluctant to have Rat Features as a client, still less a brother in arms.

But there was probably still a place for Rat Features in the new Klan. Every organization needs its foot soldiers, and this one had cannon fodder written all over him. When the time came for the Boyz to storm the steps of the Capitol and reclaim the Jewnited States for their own, Rat Features would be in the front line, where he could be certain to lay down his life for the cause.

Behind him, the bearded pool player loomed, his eyes small, piggy, and dumb looking. His arms were enormous but without definition, and his gut bulged beneath a camouflage T-shirt. The T-shirt bore the legend *Kill 'em all—Let God sort 'em out,* but the big guy was no marine. He looked as close to retarded as you can get without someone coming by twice a day to feed you and clean up your mess.

"How you doin'?" said the Rat. The bar was quiet now and the group of men at the pool table were no longer lounging but stood rigid in anticipation of what was to come. One of them smiled and poked his neighbor with an elbow. Obviously, the Rat and his buddy were the local double act.

"Great till now."

He nodded as if I'd just said something deeply profound with which he had a natural empathy.

"You know," I said, "I once took a leak in Thom Robb's garden."

Which was true.

"It'd be better if you just got back on the road and kept driving, I reckon," said the Rat, after a pause to figure out who Thom Robb was. "So why don't you just do that?"

"Thanks for the advice." I moved to go past him but his pal put a hand like a shovel against my chest and pushed me back against the bar by flexing his wrist slightly.

"It wasn't advice," said the Rat. He gestured back at the big guy with his thumb.

"This here's Six. You don't get back in your fuckin' car

now and start raisin' dust on the highway, Six is gonna fuck you up bad."

Six smiled dimly. The evolutionary curve obviously sloped pretty gently where Six came from.

"You know why he's called Six?"

"Let me guess," I replied. "There are another five assholes like him at home?"

It didn't look like I was going to find out how Six got his name, because he stopped smiling and lunged past the Rat, his hand clutching for my neck. He moved fast for a man his size, but not that fast. I brought my right foot up and released it heel first onto Six's left knee. There was a satisfying crunching sound, and Six faltered, his mouth wide with pain, and stumbled sideways and down.

His friends were already coming to his aid when there was a commotion from behind them and a small, tubby deputy in his late thirties pushed his way through, one hand on the butt of his pistol. It was Wallace, Deputy Dorito. He looked scared and edgy, the kind of guy who became a cop to give him some sort of advantage over the people who used to laugh at him in school, steal his lunch money, and beat him up, except he found that now those people still laughed at him and didn't look like they'd let the uniform stand in the way of another beating. Still, on this occasion he had a gun and maybe they figured he was scared enough to pull it on them.

"What's goin' on here, Clete?"

There was silence for a moment and then the Rat spoke up. "Just some high spirits got out of hand, Wallace. Ain't nothin' to concern the law."

"I wasn't talking to you, Gabe."

Someone helped Six to his feet and brought him to a chair.

"Looks like more than high spirits to me. I reckon you boys better come on down to the cells, cool off for a time."

"Let it go, Wallace," said a low voice. It came from a thin, wiry man with cold, dark eyes and a beard flecked with gray. He had an air of authority about him and an intelligence that went beyond the low cunning of his associates. He watched me carefully as he spoke, the way an undertaker might eye up a prospective client for his casket.

"Okay, Clete, but . . ." Deputy Dorito's words trailed off as he realized there was nothing he could say that would matter to any of the men before him. He nodded to the crowd, as if the decision not to pursue things any further had been his to make.

"You'd better leave, mister," he said, looking at me.

I stood up and walked slowly to the door. No one said anything as I left. Back at the motel, I rang Walter Cole to find out if anything had developed in the Stephen Barton killing, but he was out of the office and his machine was on at home. I left the number of the motel and tried to get some sleep.

19

□

THE SKY WAS GRAY and dark the next morning, heavy with impending rain. My suit was wrinkled from the previous day's travel, so I abandoned it for chinos, a white shirt, and a black jacket. I even dug out a black silk-knit tie, so I wouldn't look like a bum. I drove once through the town. There was no sign of a red jeep or the couple I had seen driving it.

I parked outside the Haven Diner, bought a copy of the *Washington Post* in the gas station across the road, and then went into the diner for breakfast. It was after nine but people still lounged around at the counter or at the tables, mumbling about the weather and, I guessed, about me, since some of them glanced knowingly in my direction, directing the attention of their neighbors toward me.

I sat at a table in the corner and scanned the paper. A mature woman in a white apron and blue uniform with *Dorothy* embossed at her left breast walked over to me carrying a pad and took my order of white toast, bacon, and coffee. She hovered over me after I finished ordering. "You the fella who whupped that Six boy in the bar last night?"

"That's me."

She nodded in satisfaction.

"I'll give you your breakfast for free, then." She smiled a hard smile, then added: "But don't you go confusin' my generosity with an invitation to stay. You ain't that good lookin'." She strolled back behind the counter and pinned my order to a wire.

There wasn't much traffic on Haven's main street, or

much human activity in sight. Most of the cars and trucks seemed to be passing through on their way to someplace else. The town seemed to be permanently stuck in a grim Sunday morning.

I finished my food and left a tip on the table. Dorothy slouched forward over the counter, her breasts resting on its polished surface. "Bye now," she said as I left. The other diners briefly looked over their shoulders at me before returning to their breakfast and coffee.

I drove to the Haven Public Library, a new single-story building at the far side of the town. A pretty black woman in her early thirties stood behind the counter with an older white woman whose hair was like steel wool and who eyed me with obvious distaste as I entered.

"Morning," I said. The younger woman smiled slightly anxiously while the older one tried to tidy the already immaculate area behind the counter. "What's the local paper around here?"

"Used to be the *Haven Leader*," answered the younger woman after a slight pause. "It's gone now."

"I was looking for something older, back issues."

She glanced at the other woman as if for guidance, but she continued to shift pieces of paper behind the counter.

"They're on microfiche, in the cabinets beside the viewer. How far back do you want to go?"

"Not far," I said, and strolled over to the cabinets. The *Leader* files were arranged in date order in small square boxes in ten drawers, but the boxes of files for the years of the Haven killings were not in their place. I ran through them all, in case they had been misfiled, although I had a feeling that those files weren't available to the casual visitor.

I returned to the counter. The elderly woman was no longer in sight.

"The files I'm looking for don't appear to be there," I said. The younger girl looked confused but I didn't get the impression that she was.

"What year were you looking for?"

"Years. Nineteen sixty-nine, nineteen seventy, maybe nineteen seventy-one."

"I'm sorry, those files aren't"—she seemed to search for an excuse that might be plausible—"available. They've been borrowed for research."

"Oh," I said. I smiled my best smile. "Never mind, I'll manage with what's there."

She seemed relieved and I returned to the viewer, idly flicking through the files for anything useful with no return other than boredom. It took thirty minutes before the opportunity presented itself. A party of schoolchildren entered the junior section of the library, separated from the adult section by a half-wood, half-glass screen. The younger woman followed them and stood with her back to me, talking to the children and their teacher, a young blonde who didn't look long out of school herself.

There was no sign of the older woman, although a brown door was half open in the small lobby beyond the adult section. I slipped behind the counter and began rifling through drawers and cupboards as quietly as I could. At one point I passed, crouching, by the entry door to the junior section, but the librarian was still dealing with her young clients.

I found the missing files in a bottom drawer, beside a small coin box. I slipped them into my jacket pockets and was just leaving the counter area when the office door outside slammed and I heard soft footsteps approaching. I darted beside a shelf as the senior librarian entered. She stopped short at the entrance to the counter and shot an unpleasant look in my direction and at the book in my hand. I smiled gamely and returned to the viewer. I wasn't sure how long it would be before the dragon behind the counter checked that drawer and decided to call for backup.

I tried the 1969 files first. It took some time, even though the *Haven Leader* had been only a weekly newspaper in 1969. There was nothing about any disappearances in the paper. Even in 1969, it seemed that black folks didn't count for much. The paper contained a lot about church socials, history society lectures, and local weddings. There was some minor crime stuff, mostly traffic offenses and drunk-and-disorderlies, but nothing that might lead a casual reader to suppose that children were disappearing in the town of Haven.

Then, in a November issue, I came upon a reference to a man named Walt Tyler. There was a picture of Tyler beside the piece, a good-looking man being led away in handcuffs by a white deputy. *Man Held in Sheriff Attack,* read the headline above the picture. The details contained in the piece below were sketchy but it seemed Tyler had come into the Sheriff's Office and started busting the place up before taking a swing at the sheriff himself. The only indication of a reason for the attack came in the last paragraph.

"Tyler was among a number of Negroes questioned by the Sheriff's Office in connection with the disappearance of his daughter and two other children. He was released without charge."

The 1970 files were more productive. On the night of February 8, 1970, Amy Demeter had disappeared after heading out to a friend's house to deliver a sample of her mother's jam. She never made it to the house and the jar was found broken on a sidewalk about five hundred yards from her home. A picture of her was printed beside the story, along with details of what she had been wearing and a brief history of the family: father Earl an accountant, mother Dorothy a housewife and a schoolteacher, younger sister Catherine a well-liked child with some artistic potential. The story ran for the next few weeks: *Search Goes On for Haven Girl; Five More Questioned in Demeter Mystery;* and, finally, *Little Hope Left for Amy.*

I spent another half hour going back and forth through the *Haven Leader* but there was nothing more on the killings or their resolution, if any. The only indication was a report of the death of Adelaide Modine in a fire four months later, with a reference to her brother's death buried in the piece. There was no description of the circumstances of the death of either, but there was one hint, once again in the last paragraph. "The Haven Sheriff's Office had been anxious to talk to both Adelaide and William Modine in their ongoing investigation into the disappearance of Amy Demeter and a number of other children."

It didn't take a genius to read between the lines and see that either Adelaide Modine or her brother William, or possibly both, had been the main suspects. Local newspapers don't necessarily print all the news; there are some things everyone knows already and sometimes the local press merely prints enough to throw outsiders off the scent. The old librarian was giving me the evil eye so I finished printing off copies of the relevant articles, then gathered them and left.

A Haven County Sheriff's Office cruiser, a brown-and-yellow Crown Victoria, was pulled up in front of my car and a deputy, wearing a clean, well-pressed uniform, was leaning against my driver's door, waiting. As I drew closer I could see the long muscles beneath his shirt. His eyes were dull and lifeless. He looked like an asshole. A fit asshole.

"This your car?" he asked in a Virginia drawl, his thumbs tucked inside a gun belt that glittered with the spotless tools of his trade. On his chest, the name *Burns* stood out on his perfectly straight identity badge.

"Sure is," I said, mimicking his accent. It was a bad habit I had. His jaw tightened, if it was actually possible for it to tighten more than it was already.

"Hear you were looking up some old newspapers?"

"I'm a crossword fan. They were better in the old days."

"You another writer?"

Judging from his tone I didn't think he read much, at least nothing that didn't have pictures or a message from God. "No," I said. "You get a lot of writers around here?"

I don't think he believed I wasn't a writer. Maybe I looked bookish to him or maybe anyone with whom he wasn't personally acquainted was immediately suspected of covert literary leanings. The librarian had sold me out, believing me to be simply another hack trying to make a buck out of the ghosts of Haven's past.

"I'm escorting you to the town line," he said. "I've got your bag." He moved to the patrol car and took my traveling bag from the front seat. I was starting to get very tired of Deputy Burns.

"I'm not planning on leaving just yet," I said, "so maybe

you could put it back in my room. By the way, when you're unpacking, I like my socks on the left side of the drawer."

He dropped the bag on the road and started toward me. "Look," I began, "I have ID." I reached into the inside pocket of my jacket. "I'm—"

It was a dumb thing to do but I was hot and tired and pissed at Deputy Burns, and I wasn't thinking straight. He caught one flash of the butt of my gun and his own piece was in his hands. Burns was quick. He probably practiced in front of the mirror. Within seconds I was up against his car, my gun was gone, and Deputy Burns's shiny cuffs were biting into my wrists.

20

I WAS LEFT cooling my heels in a cell for what I reckoned to be three or four hours, since the careful Deputy Burns had taken my watch along with my gun, my wallet and ID, my notes, and my belt and laces, in case I decided to hang myself in a fit of remorse for annoying the librarians. These had been entrusted to the safe care of Deputy Wallace, who made some passing reference to Burns of my involvement in the previous night's incident in the bar.

Still, the cell was just about the cleanest one I had ever visited in my life—even the can looked like it could safely be used without needing a course of penicillin later. I passed the time by mulling over what I had learned from the library microfiche, trying to fit the pieces of the puzzle into some recognizable picture and refusing to let my mind drift to the Traveling Man and what he might be doing.

Eventually there was a noise outside and the cell door opened. I looked up to see a tall black man in a uniform shirt watching me. He looked to be in his late thirties but something about the way he walked and the light of experience in his eyes told me he was older. I guessed he might have boxed at one time, probably middle to light-heavy, and he moved gracefully on his feet. He looked smarter than Wallace and Burns put together, although no one was likely to hand out gold stars for that particular feat. This, I guessed, was Alvin Martin. I didn't rush to get up, in case he thought I didn't like his nice, clean cell.

"You want to stay there another couple of hours, or you

waiting for someone to carry you out?" he asked. The voice wasn't Southern; Detroit, Chicago maybe.

I stood and he moved aside to let me pass. Wallace waited at the end of the corridor, his thumbs tucked into his belt to take the weight off his shoulders.

"Give him back his things, Deputy."

"Even his gun?" asked Wallace, not making a move to do as he was told. Wallace had that look about him, the look that told you he wasn't used to taking orders from a black guy and didn't like it when he had to. It struck me that he might have more in common with the Rat and his friends than was really wise for a conscientious lawman.

"Even his gun," replied Martin calmly but wearily, giving Wallace the eye. Wallace shoved off from the wall like a particularly ugly ship setting out to sea and steamed behind the counter, surfacing eventually with a brown envelope and my gun. I signed and Martin nodded me toward the door.

"Get in the car, please, Mr. Parker." Outside, the light was starting to fade and there was a cool wind blowing from the hills. A pickup rattled by on the road beyond, a covered shotgun rack on the back guarded by a mangy hound.

"Back or front?" I asked.

"Get in the front," he replied. "I trust you."

He started the cruiser and we drove for a time in silence, the a/c blasting cool air into our faces and onto our feet. The town limits receded behind us and we entered woods thick with trees, the road twisting and winding as it followed the contours of the land. Then, in the distance, a light shone. We pulled up in the parking lot of a white diner, topped by a green neon sign blinking *Green River Eatery* on the road beyond.

We took a booth at the rear, far away from the handful of other patrons, who cast curious glances at us before returning to their food. Martin took off his hat, ordered coffee for both of us, then sat back and looked at me. "It's usually considered good manners for an unlicensed investigator packing a pistol to drop into the local lawmen and state his business, at least before he goes around beating up pool players and stealing library files," he said.

"You weren't around when I called," I said. "Neither was the sheriff, and your friend Wallace wasn't too keen on offering me cookies and swapping race jokes."

The coffee arrived. Martin added creamer and sugar to his. I stuck with milk.

"I made some calls about you," said Martin, stirring his coffee. "A guy called Cole vouched for you. That's why I'm not kicking your ass out of town, least not yet. That and the fact that you weren't afraid to whip some cracker ass in the bar last night. Shows you got a sense of civic pride. So maybe now you'd like to tell me why you're here."

"I'm looking for a woman named Catherine Demeter. I think she might have come to Haven in the last week."

Martin's brow furrowed.

"She anything to Amy Demeter?"

"Sister."

"I figured. Why do you think she might be here?"

"The last call she made from her apartment was to the home of Sheriff Earl Lee Granger. She made a number of calls to your office as well the same night. Since then, there's been no sign of her."

"You hired to find her?"

"I'm just looking for her," I replied neutrally.

Martin sighed.

"I came here from Detroit six months ago," he said after about a minute of silence. "Brought my wife and child. My wife's an assistant librarian. I think you may have met her."

I nodded.

"The governor decided there weren't enough blacks in the police force here and that relations between the local minority population and the cops might not be the best. So, a post came up here and I applied, mainly to get my kid away from Detroit. My father came from Gretna, just a ways from here. I didn't know about the killings before I came here. I know more now.

"This town died along with those kids. No new people came to live here and anyone with an ounce of sense or ambition got the hell out. Now the gene pool here's so shallow you couldn't drown a rat in it.

"In the last month or two there's been signs that something might happen to change that. There's a Japanese firm interested in locating around half a mile out of town. They do research and development of computer software, I hear, and they like the idea of privacy and a quiet little backwater they can call Nippon. They'd bring a lot of money to this town, a lot of jobs for locals, and maybe a chance to put the past to rest. Frankly, the people here don't much care for the idea of working for the Japanese but they know they're sucking shit as it is, so they'll work for anyone as long as he's not black.

"The last thing they want is someone sniffing around ancient history, digging up the past to come up with the bones of dead children. They may be dumb in a lot of cases. They may also be racists and shit kickers and wife beaters, but they're desperate for a second chance and they'll mess up anyone who gets in their way. If they don't do it, Earl Lee will."

He raised a finger and waved it purposefully in my face. "Do you understand what I'm saying here? Nobody wants questions asked about child killings that took place thirty years ago. If Catherine Demeter came back here, and frankly I don't know why she would since she ain't got no one here to come back to, then she wouldn't be welcome either. But she ain't here, because if she had come back it would be all over this town like shit on a shoe."

He took a sip of his coffee and gritted his teeth. "Damn, it's cold." He gestured to the waitress and called for a fresh mug.

"I don't want to stay here any longer than I have to," I said. "But I think Catherine Demeter may have come back here, or tried to come back here. She certainly wanted to talk to the sheriff and I want to talk to him too. So where is he?"

"He took a couple of days' leave to get out of town for a while," said Martin, twisting the brim of his hat so that the hat spun on the vinyl seat. "He's due back—well, he was due back today but he may leave it until tomorrow. We don't have too much crime here beyond drunks and domestics and the usual shit that goes with a place like this. But he may not be too pleased to see you waiting for him when he returns. I'm not so pleased to see you myself, no offense meant."

"None taken. I think I'll wait around for the sheriff anyway." I was also going to have to find out more about the Modine killings, whether Martin liked it or not. If Catherine Demeter had reached into her past, then I was going to have to reach into that past too, or I would understand nothing about the woman for whom I was searching.

"I'll also need to talk to someone about the killings. I need to know more."

Martin closed his eyes and ran his hand over them in weariness. "You're not listening to me . . . ," he began.

"No, *you're* not listening. I'm looking for a woman who may be in trouble and who may have turned to someone here for help. Before I leave town I'm going to find out whether or not she's here, even if it means rattling every cage in this godforsaken dump and scaring your Japanese saviors back to Tokyo. But if you help me, then this can all be done quietly and I'll be out of your hair in a couple of days."

We were both tensed now, leaning toward each other across the table. Some of the other diners were staring at us, their food ignored. Martin looked around at them, then turned back to me again. "Okay," he said. "Most of the people who were around then and might know something useful have either left, or died, or won't talk about it for love or money. There are two who might, though. One is the son of the doc who was around at that time. His name's Connell Hyams and he has a law office in town. You'll have to approach him yourself.

"The other is Walt Tyler. His daughter was the first to die and he lives outside town. I'll talk to him first and maybe he'll see you." He stood up to leave. "When you've got your business done you'd better leave, and I never want to see your face again, understand?"

I said nothing and followed him toward the door. He stopped and turned toward me, placing his hat on his head as he did so. "One more thing," he said. "I've had a word with those boys from the bar, but remember, they ain't got no reason to like you. Frankly, I can see a lot of people thinking the same way once they know why you're here. And they're going to find out. So, you'd best step lightly while you're in town."

"I noticed one of them, I think his name was Gabe, had a Klan shirt on," I said. "You got much of that around here?"

Martin blew breath heavily from puffed cheeks. "There's no klavern, but in a poor town, the dumb ones always look for someone to blame for being poor."

"There was one guy—your deputy called him Clete—who didn't look so dumb."

Martin eyed me from under his hat brim. "No, Clete's not dumb. He sits on the council, says the only way anyone's gonna get him off it is with a gun barrel. Whipping you could be good for another twenty, thirty votes, if he had a mind to do it. Shit, maybe he'll send you a campaign badge.

"But as for the Klan, this ain't Georgia or North Carolina, or even Delaware. Don't go reading too much into this. You can pay for the coffee."

I left a couple of bucks at the till and walked out toward the car, but Martin was already pulling away. I noticed that he'd taken his hat off again inside the car. The man just didn't seem comfortable with that damn hat. I went back into the diner, called Haven's only cab operator, and ordered another coffee.

21

□

IT WAS AFTER SIX when I got back to the motel. Connell Hyams's office and home address were listed but when I drove by his office all the lights were out. I called Rudy Fry at the motel and got directions for Bale's Farm Road, where not only Hyams but also Sheriff Earl Lee Granger had homes.

I drove cautiously along the winding roads, looking for the concealed entrance Fry had mentioned and still glancing occasionally in my mirror for any sign of the red jeep. There was none. I passed the entrance to Bale's Farm Road once without seeing it and had to go back over my tracks again. The sign was semiobscured by undergrowth and pointed toward a winding, rutted track heavy with evergreens, which eventually opened out on a small but well-kept row of houses with long yards and what looked like plenty of space out back. Hyams's home was near the end, a large, two-story white wooden house. A lamp blazed by a screen door, which shielded a solid oak front door with a fan of frosted glass near the top. There was a light on in the hallway.

A gray-haired man, wearing a red wool cardigan over gray slacks and a striped, open-necked shirt, opened the inner door as I pulled up and watched me with mild curiosity.

"Mr. Hyams?" I said as I approached the door.

"Yes?"

"I'm an investigator. My name's Parker. I wanted to talk to you about Catherine Demeter."

He paused for a long time in silence with the screen door between us.

"Catherine, or her sister?" he inquired eventually.

"Both, I guess."

"May I ask why?"

"I'm trying to find Catherine. I think she may have come back here."

Hyams opened the screen door and stood aside to let me enter. Inside, the house was furnished in dark wood, with large, expensive-looking mats on the floors. He led me into an office at the back of the house, where papers were strewn over a desk on which a computer screen glowed.

"Can I offer you a drink?" he asked.

"No. Thank you."

He took a brandy glass from his desk and gestured me toward a chair at the other side before seating himself. I could see him more clearly now. He was grave and patrician in appearance, his hands long and slim, the nails finely manicured. The room was warm and I could smell his cologne. It smelled expensive.

"That all took place a long time ago," he began. "Most people would rather not talk about it."

"Are you 'most people'?"

He shrugged and smiled. "I have a place in this community and a role to play. I've lived here almost all my life, apart from the time I spent in college and in practice in Richmond. My father spent fifty years practicing here and kept working until the day he died."

"He was the doctor, I understand."

"Doctor, counselor, legal adviser, even dentist when the resident dentist wasn't around. He did everything. The killings hit him particularly hard. He helped perform the autopsies on the bodies. I don't think he ever forgot it, not even in his sleep."

"And you? Were you around when they took place?"

"I was working in Richmond at the time, so I was back and forth between Haven and Richmond. I knew of what took place here, yes, but I'd really rather not talk about it. Four children died and they were terrible deaths. Best to let them rest now."

"Do you remember Catherine Demeter?"

"I knew the family, yes, but Catherine would have been much younger than I. She left after graduating from high school, as I recall, and I don't think she ever came back, except to attend the funerals of her parents. The last time she returned was probably ten years ago at the very least and her family home has been sold since then. I supervised the sale. Why do you believe she might have come back now? There's nothing here for her, nothing good at any rate."

"I'm not sure. She made some calls to here recently and hasn't been seen since."

"It's not much to go on."

"No," I admitted, "it's not."

He twisted the glass in his hand, watching the amber liquid swirl. His lips were pursed in appraisal but his gaze went through the glass and rested on me.

"What can you tell me about Adelaide Modine and her brother?"

"I can tell you that, from my point of view, there was nothing about them that might have led one to suspect that they were child killers. Their father was a strange man, a philanthropist of sorts, I suppose. He left most of his money tied up in a trust when he died."

"He died before the killings?"

"Five or six years before, yes. He left instructions that the interest on the trust fund should be divided among certain charities in perpetuity. Since then, the number of charities receiving donations has increased considerably. I should know, since it is my duty to administer the trust, with the assistance of a small committee."

"And his daughter and son? Were they provided for?"

"Very adequately, I understand."

"What happened to their money, their property, when they died?"

"The state brought an action to take over the property and assets. We contested it on behalf of the townspeople and eventually an agreement was reached. The land was sold and all assets absorbed into the trust, with a portion of the trust used to fund new developments in the town. That is why we have a good library, our own modern sheriff's office, a fine school, a top-class medical center. This town doesn't have much, but what it does have comes from the trust."

"What it has, good or otherwise, comes from four dead children," I replied. "Can you tell me anything more about Adelaide and William Modine?"

Hyams's mouth twitched slightly. "As I've said, it was a long time ago and I really would prefer not to go into it. I had very little to do with either of them; the Modines were a wealthy family, their children went to a private school. We didn't mix very much, I'm afraid."

"Did your father know the family?"

"My father delivered both William and Adelaide. I do remember one curious thing, but it will hardly be of any great help to you: Adelaide was one of twins. The male twin died in the womb and their mother died from complications shortly after the birth. The mother's death was surprising. She was a strong, domineering woman. My father thought she'd outlive us all." He took a long sip from his glass and his eyes grew sharp with a remembered perception. "Do you know anything about hyenas, Mr. Parker?"

"Very little," I admitted.

"Spotted hyenas frequently have twins. The cubs are extremely well developed at birth: they have fur and sharp incisor teeth. One cub will almost invariably attack the other, sometimes while still in the amniotic sac. Death is usually the result. The victor is also typically female and, if she is the daughter of a dominant female, will in turn become the dominant female in the pack. It's a matriarchal culture. Female spotted hyena fetuses have higher levels of testosterone than adult males, and the females have masculine characteristics, even in the womb. Even in adulthood the sexes can be difficult to differentiate."

He put his glass down. "My father was an avid amateur naturalist. The animal world always fascinated him and I think he liked to find points of comparison between the animal world and the human world."

"And he found one in Adelaide Modine?"

"Perhaps, in some ways. He was not fond of her."

"Were you here when the Modines died?"

"I returned home the evening before Adelaide Modine's body was found and I attended the autopsy. Call it gruesome curiosity. Now, I'm sorry, Mr. Parker, but I have nothing more to say and a great deal of work to do."

He led me to the door and pushed open the screen to let me out.

"You don't seem particularly anxious to help me find Catherine Demeter, Mr. Hyams."

He breathed in heavily. "Who suggested that you talk to me, Mr. Parker?"

"Alvin Martin mentioned your name."

"Mr. Martin is a good, conscientious deputy and an asset to this town, but he is still a comparatively recent arrival," said Hyams. "The reason why I am reluctant to talk is a matter of client confidentiality. Mr. Parker, I am the only lawyer in this town. At some point, nearly everyone who lives here, regardless of color, income, religious or political belief, has passed through the door of my office. That includes the parents of the children who died. I know a great deal about what happened here, Mr. Parker, more than I might wish to know and certainly much more than I plan to share with you. I'm sorry, but that's the end of the matter."

"I see. One more thing, Mr. Hyams."

"Yes?" he asked, wearily.

"Sheriff Granger lives on this road too, doesn't he?"

"Sheriff Granger lives next door, the house on the right here. This house has never been burgled, Mr. Parker, a fact that is surely not unconnected. Good night."

He stood at the screen door as I drove away. I cast a glance at the sheriff's house as I passed but there were no lights within and there was no car in the yard. As I drove back to Haven, raindrops began to strike the windshield and by the time I reached the outskirts of the town it had turned into a harsh, ceaseless downpour. The lights of the motel appeared through the rain. I could see Rudy Fry standing at the door, staring out into the woods and the gathering darkness beyond.

By the time I had parked, Fry had resumed his position behind the reception desk.

"What do folks do around here for fun, apart from trying to run other folks out of town?" I asked.

Fry grimaced as he tried to separate the sarcasm from the substance of the question. "There ain't much to do around here outside of drinking at the Inn," he replied, after a while.

"I tried that. Didn't care for it."

He thought for a little while longer. I waited for the smell of smoke but it didn't come.

"There's a restaurant in Dorien, 'bout twenty miles east of here. Milano's, it's called. It's Italian." He pronounced it *Eye-talian,* in a tone that suggested Rudy Fry was not over-fond of any Italian food that didn't come in a box with grease dripping from the vents. "Never eaten there myself." He sniffed, as if to confirm his suspicion of all things European.

I thanked him, then went to my room, showered, and changed. I was getting tired of the unrelenting hostility of Haven. If Rudy Fry didn't like somewhere, then that was somewhere I probably wanted to be. I checked the parking lot carefully before I stepped out and then I was leaving Haven behind and heading for Dorien.

Dorien wasn't much bigger than Haven but it had a bookstore and a couple of restaurants, which made it a cultural oasis of sorts. I bought a typescript copy of e. e. cummings in the bookstore and wandered into Milano's to eat.

Milano's had red-and-white check tablecloths and candles set in miniatures of the Colosseum, but it was almost full and the food looked pretty good. A slim maitre d' in a red bow tie bustled over and showed me to a table in the corner where I wouldn't scare the other diners. I took out the copy of cummings to reassure them and read "somewhere i have never traveled" while I waited for a menu, enjoying the cadence and gentle eroticism of the poem.

Susan had never read cummings before we met, and I sent her copies of his poems during the early days of our relationship. In a sense, I let cummings do my courting for me. I think I even incorporated a line of cummings into the first letter I sent her. When I look back on it, it was as much a prayer as a love letter, a prayer that Time would be gentle with her, because she was very beautiful.

A waiter strolled over and I ordered bruschetta and a carbonara from the menu, with water. I cast a glance around the restaurant but no one seemed to be paying me much attention, which was fine with me. I had not forgotten the warning Angel and Louis had given to me, or the couple in the red jeep.

The food, when it arrived, was excellent. I was surprised at my appetite, and while I ate, I turned over in my mind what I had learned from Hyams and the microfiche, and I remembered the handsome face of Walt Tyler, surrounded by police.

And I wondered, too, about the Traveling Man, before forcing him from my mind along with the images that came with him. Then I got back in my car and returned to Haven.

22

□

MY GRANDFATHER used to say that the most terrifying sound in the world was the sound of a shell being loaded into a pump-action shotgun, a shell that was meant for you. It woke me from my sleep in the motel as they came up the stairs, the hands of my watch glowing the time at 3:30 A.M. They came through the door seconds later, the sound of the explosions deafeningly loud in the silence of the night as shot after shot was fired into my bed, sending feathers and shreds of cotton into the air like a cloud of white moths.

But by then I was already on my feet, my gun in my hand. The sound of the shots was blocked slightly by the closed connecting door, just as the sound of the door opening into the hall was blocked from them, even when the firing had stopped and their ears sang with the hard notes of the gun. The decision not to make myself an easy target by sleeping in my assigned room had paid off.

I came into the hall quickly, turned, and aimed. The man from the red jeep stood in the hall, the barrel of the Ithaca 12 gauge pump close to his face. Even in the dim hall light I could see that there were no shell casings on the ground at his feet. It had been the woman who fired the shots.

Now he spun toward me as the woman swore from inside the room. The barrel of the shotgun came down as he turned in my direction. I fired one shot and a dark rose bloomed at his throat and blood fell like a shower of petals on his white shirt. The shotgun dropped to the carpet as his hands clutched for his neck. He folded to his knees and fell flat on the floor, his body thrashing and jerking like a fish on dry ground.

The barrel of a shotgun appeared from behind the door-jamb and the woman fired indiscriminately into the hall, plaster leaping from the walls. I felt a tug at my right shoulder and then sharp white pain through my arm. I tried to hold on to my gun but I lost it on the ground as the woman continued firing, deadly shot zinging through the air and exploding into the walls around me.

I ran down the hall and through the door leading to the fire stairs, tripping and tumbling down the steps as the shooting stopped. I knew she would come after me as soon as she had made certain that her partner was dead. If there had been any chance of him surviving, I think she might have tried to save him, and herself.

I made it to the second floor but I could hear her steps pounding on the stairs above me. The pain in my arm was intense and I felt certain she would reach me before I got to the ground level.

I slipped through the door into the hallway. Plastic sheeting lay upon the ground and two stepladders stood like steeples at either wall. The air was heavy with the smell of paint and thinner. Twenty feet from the door was a small alcove, almost invisible until you were upon it, which contained a fire hose and a heavy, old-fashioned water-based extinguisher. There was an identical alcove near my own room. I slipped into it, leaning against the wall and trying to control my breathing. Lifting the extinguisher with my left hand, I tried to hold it underneath with my right in a vain effort to use it as a weapon, but my arm, bleeding heavily by now, was useless and the extinguisher was too awkward to be effective. I heard the woman's steps slowing and the door sighed softly as she moved into the hall. I listened to her steps on the plastic. There was a loud bang as she kicked open the door of the first room on the floor, then a second bang as she repeated the exercise at the next door. She was almost upon me now, and though she walked softly, the plastic betrayed her. I could feel blood pouring down my arm and dripping from the ends of my fingers as I unwound the hose and waited for her to come.

She was almost level with the alcove when I swung the hose forward like a whip. The heavy brass nozzle caught her in the middle of her face and I heard bone crunch. She staggered back, harmlessly loosing off a blast from the shotgun as she raised her left hand instinctively to her face. I swung the hose again, the rubber glancing against her outstretched hand while the nozzle connected with the side of her head. She moaned and I slipped from the alcove as quickly as I could, the brass nozzle of the hose now in my left hand, and wrapped the rubber around her neck like the coils of a snake.

She tried to move her hand on the shotgun, the stock against her thigh, in an effort to pump a cartridge as blood from her battered face flowed between the fingers of her right hand. I kicked hard at the gun and it fell from her hands as I pulled her tightly against my body, bracing myself against the wall, one leg entwined with hers so she could not pull away, the other holding the hose pipe taut. And there we stood like lovers, the nozzle now warm with blood in my hand and the hose tight against my wrist, as she struggled and then went limp in my grip.

When she stopped moving I released her and she slumped to the ground. I unwound the hose from her neck, and, taking her by the hand, I pulled her down the stairs to ground level. Her face was reddish purple and I realized I had come close to killing her, but I still wanted her where I could see her.

Rudy Fry lay gray on the floor of his office, blood congealing on his face and around the dent in his fractured skull. I called the sheriff's office and, minutes later, heard the sirens and saw the red-and-blue glow of the lights spinning and reflecting around the darkened lobby, the blood and the lights reminding me once again of another night and other deaths. When Alvin Martin entered with his gun in his hand I was nauseous with shock and barely able to stand, the red light like fire in my eyes.

□

"You're a lucky man," said the elderly doctor, her smile a mixture of surprise and concern. "Another couple of inches and Alvin here would have been composing a eulogy."

"I bet that would have been something to hear," I replied.

I was sitting on a table in the emergency room of Haven's small but well-equipped medical center. The wound in my arm was minor but had bled heavily. Now it had been cleaned and bandaged, and my good hand clutched a bottle of painkillers. I felt like I'd been sideswiped by a passing train.

Alvin Martin stood beside me. Wallace and another deputy I didn't recognize were down the hall, guarding the room in which the woman was being kept. She had not regained consciousness, and from what I had heard of the doctor's hurried conversation with Martin, I believed that she might have lapsed into a coma. Rudy Fry was also still unconscious, although he was expected to recover from his injuries.

"Anything on the shooters?" I asked Martin.

"Not yet. We've sent photos and prints to the feds. They're going to send someone from Richmond later today." The clock on the wall read 6:45 A.M. Outside the rain continued to fall.

Martin turned to the doctor. "Could you give us a minute or two in private, Elise?"

"Certainly. Don't strain him, though." He smiled at her as she left, but when he turned back to me the smile was gone. "You came here with a price on your head?"

"I'd heard a rumor, that's all."

"Fuck you and your rumor. Rudy Fry almost died in there and I've got an unidentified corpse in the morgue with a hole in his neck. You know who called out the hit?"

"I know who did it."

"You gonna tell me?"

"No, not yet anyway. I'm not going to tell the feds, either. I need you to keep them off my back for a while."

Martin almost laughed. "Now, why am I gonna do that?"

"I need to finish what I came down here to do. I need to find Catherine Demeter."

"This shooting have anything to do with her?"

"I don't know. It could have but I don't see where she fits in. I need your help."

Martin bit his lip. "The town council's running wild. They reckon if the Japanese get wind of this they'll open up a plant in White Sands before they come here. Everyone wants you gone. In fact, they want you arrested, beaten, then gone."

A nurse entered the room and Martin stopped talking, preferring instead to seethe quietly as she spoke. "There's a call for you, Mr. Parker," she said. "A Lieutenant Cole from New York."

I winced at the pain in my arm as I rose, and she seemed to take pity on me. I wasn't above accepting pity at that point.

"Stay where you are," she said with a smile. "I'll bring in an extension and we can patch the call through."

She returned minutes later with the phone and plugged the jack into a box on the wall. Alvin Martin hovered uncertainly for a moment beside me and then stomped out, leaving me alone.

"Walter?"

"A deputy called. What happened?"

"Two of them tried to take me out in the motel. A man and a woman."

"How badly are you hurt?"

"A nick on the arm. Nothing too serious."

"The shooters get away?"

"Nope. The guy's dead. The woman's in a coma, I think. They're patching in the pics and the prints at the moment. Anything at your end? Anything on Jennifer?" I tried to block out the image of her face but it hung at the edge of my consciousness, like a figure glimpsed at the periphery of one's vision.

"The jar was spotless. It was a standard medical storage jar. We've tried checking the batch number with the manufacturers but they went out of business in nineteen ninety-two.

We'll keep trying, see if we can access old records, but the chances are slim. The wrapping paper must be sold in every damn gift shop in the country. Again, no prints. The lab is looking at skin samples to see if we can pick up anything from them. Technical guys figure he bounced the call—no other way the cell phone could have shown a callbox number—and there's probably no way we can trace it. I'll let you know if there's anything further."

"And Stephen Barton?"

"Nothing there either. The amount I know, I'm starting to think that I may be in the wrong business. He was knocked unconscious by a blow to the head, like the ME said, and then strangled. Probably driven to the parking lot and tipped into the sewer."

"The feds still looking for Sonny?"

"I haven't heard otherwise but I assume they're out of luck too."

"There doesn't seem to be much luck around at the moment."

"It'll break."

"Does Kooper know what happened here?"

I could hear what sounded like a choked laugh at the other end of the line. "Not yet. Maybe I'll tell him later in the morning. Once the name of the trust is kept out of it he should be okay, but I don't know how he feels about the hired help whacking people outside motel rooms. I don't imagine it's happened before. What's the situation at your end?"

"The natives aren't exactly greeting me with open arms and leis. No sign of her so far, but something isn't sitting right here. I can't explain it, but everything feels wrong."

He sighed. "Keep in touch. Anything I can do here?"

"I guess there's no way you can keep Ross off my back?"

"None whatsoever. Ross couldn't dislike you more if he heard that you screwed his mother and wrote her name on the wall of the men's room. He's on his way."

Walter hung up. Seconds later, there was a click on the line. I kind of guessed Deputy Martin might be the cautious sort. He came back in after allowing enough time to elapse so that it didn't look like he'd been listening. The expression on his face had changed, though. Maybe it hadn't been such a bad thing that Martin heard what he did.

"I need to find Catherine Demeter," I said. "That's why I'm here. When that's done, I'll be gone."

He nodded.

"I had Burns call some of the motels in the area earlier," he said. "There's no Catherine Demeter checked in at any of them."

"I checked before I left the city. She could be using another name."

"I thought of that. If you give me a description, I'll send Burns around to talk to the desk clerks."

"Thanks."

"Believe me, I ain't doing this out of the kindness of my heart. I just want to see you gone from here."

"What about Walt Tyler?"

"If we get time, I'll drive out there with you later." He went to check with the deputies guarding the shooter. The elderly doctor appeared again and checked the dressing on my arm.

"Are you sure you won't rest up here for a while?" she asked.

I thanked her for the offer but turned her down.

"I partly guessed as much," she said. She nodded toward the vial of painkillers. "They may make you drowsy."

I thanked her for the warning and slipped them in my pocket as she helped me to put on my jacket over my shirt-less chest. I had no intention of taking the painkillers. Her expression told me that she knew that as well.

Martin drove me to the sheriff's office. The motel had been sealed up and my clothes had been moved to a cell. I showered, wrapping my bandaged arm with plastic first, and then slept fitfully in the cell until the rain stopped falling.

Two federal agents arrived shortly after midday and questioned me about what had taken place. The questioning was perfunctory, which surprised me until I remembered that

Special Agent Ross was due to fly in later that evening. The woman had still not regained consciousness by 5:00 P.M., when Martin came into the Haven Diner.

"Did Burns turn up anything on Catherine Demeter?"

"Burns has been tied up with the feds since this afternoon. He said he'd check some of the motels before calling it a day. He'll let me know if there's any sign of her. You still want to see Walt Tyler, we'd better get going now."

23

WALT TYLER lived in a dilapidated but clean white clapboard house, against one side of which leaned a teetering pile of car tires that were, according to a sign on the road, *For Sale*. Other items of varying degrees of sellability that rested on the gravel and the well-trimmed lawn included two semirestored mowers, various engines and parts of engines, and some rusting gym equipment, including a full set of bars and weights.

Tyler himself was a tall, slightly stooped man with a full head of gray hair. He had been handsome once, as his picture had suggested, and he still held himself with a kind of loose-limbed grace, as if unwilling to admit that those looks were now largely gone, lost to cares and worries and the never-ending sorrow of a parent who has lost an only child.

He greeted Alvin warmly enough, although he shook my hand less cordially and seemed reluctant to invite us in. Instead he suggested that we sit on the porch, despite the prospect of further rain. Tyler sat in a comfortable-looking wicker chair and Martin and I on two ornate metal lawn chairs, the lost elements of a more complete set and also, according to the sign hung from the back of mine, *For Sale*.

Without Tyler making any effort to ask for it, coffee was brought out in clean china cups by a woman younger than he by maybe ten years. She, too, had been more beautiful once, although in her the beauty of youth had matured into something perhaps more attractive yet, the calm elegance of a woman for whom old age held no fears and in whom lines and wrinkles would alter but not erase her looks. She cast a glance at Tyler, and for the first time since we arrived, he smiled slightly. She returned the smile and went back into the house. We didn't see her on the porch again.

The deputy began to speak but Tyler stopped him with a slight movement of his hand. "I know why you're here, Deputy. There's only one reason why you'd bring a stranger to my home." He looked hard at me, his eyes yellowing and rimmed with red but with an interested, almost amused, look in them.

"You the fella been shooting up folks in the motel?" he asked, and the smile flickered briefly. "Excitin' life you lead. Your shoulder hurt?"

"A little."

"I was shot once, in Korea. Shot in the thigh. Hurt more'n a little. Hurt like hell." He winced exaggeratedly at the memory and then was quiet again. I heard thunder rumble above us, and the porch seemed to grow dark for a time, but I could still see Walt Tyler looking at me and now the smile was gone.

"Mr. Parker's an investigator, Walt. He used to be a detective," said Alvin.

"I'm looking for someone, Mr. Tyler," I began. "A woman. You probably remember her. Her name is Catherine Demeter. She's Amy Demeter's younger sister."

"I knew you weren't no writer. Alvin wouldn't bring one o' them"—he searched for the word—"*leeches* here." He reached for his coffee and sipped long and quietly, as if to stop himself from saying more on the subject and, I thought, to give him time to consider what I had said. "I remember her, but she ain't been back since her pappy died and that's better'n ten years. She ain't got no reason to come back here."

That statement was taking on the sensation of an echo. "Still, I think she did, and I think it can only be connected with what happened before," I replied. "You're one of the only ones left, Mr. Tyler, you and the sheriff and one or two others, the only ones involved with what took place here."

I think it had been a long time since he had spoken of it aloud, yet I knew that no long period went by without him returning to it in his thoughts or without him being dimly or acutely aware of it, like an old ache that never fades but that is sometimes forgotten in the throes of some other activity and then returns in the forgetting. And I thought that each return had etched a line in his face, and so a once handsome man could lose his looks like a fine marble statue being slowly chipped away to a memory of its former self.

"I still hear her sometimes, y'know. Can hear her step on the porch at night, can hear her singing in the garden. At first, I used to run out when I heard her, not knowing but I was sleeping or waking. But I never saw her and after a while I stopped running, though I still waked to her. She don't come as often now."

Perhaps he saw something in my face, even in the slow-darkening evening, that led him to understand. I do not know for certain, and he gave no sign that he knew or that there was anything more between us than a need to know and a desire to tell, but he stopped for a moment in the telling and in that pause we all but touched, like two travelers who pass on a long, hard road and offer comfort to each other in the journey.

"She was my only child," he continued. "She disappeared on the way back from town on a fall day and I never saw her alive again. Next I saw her, she was bone and paper and I didn't know her. My wife—my late wife—she reported her missing to the police, but nobody came for a day or two and in that time we searched the fields and the houses and anywhere we could. We walked from door to door, knocking and asking, but nobody could tell us where she was or where she might have been. And then, three days after she went, a deputy came and arrested me and accused me of killing my child. They held me for two days, beat me, called me a rapist, an abuser of children, but I never said anything but what I knew to be true, and after a week they let me go. And my little girl never appeared."

"What was her name, Mr. Tyler?"

"Her name was Etta Mae Tyler and she was nine years old."

I could hear the trees whispering in the wind and the

boards of the house creaking and settling. In the yard, a child's swing moved back and forth as the wind caught it. It seemed that there was movement all around us as we spoke, as if our words had awoken something that had been asleep for a long time.

"Two other children disappeared three months later, black children both, one within a week of the other. Cold it was. Folks thought the first child, Dora Lee Parker, might have fallen through some ice while playing. She was the very devil for ice, that child. But all the rivers were searched, all the ponds dredged, and they didn't find her. The police, they came and questioned me again, and for a while even some of my own neighbors looked at me kinda funny. But then the police's interest all died away again. These were black children and they saw no reason to go connectin' the two vanishings.

"The third child didn't come from Haven, he came from Otterville, about forty miles away. 'Nother black child, little boy named"—he stopped and put the palm of his hand to his forehead, pressing lightly, his eyes closed tight—"Bobby Joiner," he finished quietly, nodding slightly. "By then, people was getting scared and a deputation was sent to the sheriff and the mayor. People started keeping their children inside, specially after dark, and the police, they questioned every black man for miles around, and some white folks too, poor men they knew to be homosexuals, mostly.

"I think then there was a waiting period. Those people waited for the black folks to breathe easy again, to get careless, but they did not. It went on and on, for months, till early in nineteen seventy. Then the little Demeter girl disappeared and everything changed. The police, they questioned people for miles around, took statements, organized searches. But nobody saw a thing. It was like the little girl had disappeared into thin air.

"Things got bad then for black folks. The police figured there might be a connection between the disappearances after all and they called in the FBI. After that, black men walking around town after dark were liable to get arrested or beaten, or both. But those people . . ." He used the phrase again and there was a kind of mental shake of the head in his voice, a gesture of horror at the ways of men. "Those people had a taste for what they were doing, and couldn't stop. The woman tried to snatch a little boy in Batesville but she was alone and the boy fought and kicked and scratched her face and ran away. She chased after him, too, but then she gave up. She knew what was coming.

"The boy was a sharp one. He remembered the make of the car, described the woman, even recalled some of the numbers on the license plate. But it wasn't till the next day that someone else recalled the car and they went looking for Adelaide Modine."

"The police?"

"No, not the police. A mob of men, some from Haven, others from Batesville, two or three from Yancey Mill. The sheriff, he was out of town when it happened and the FBI men had left. But Deputy Earl Lee Granger, as was, he was with them when they arrived at the Modine house, but she was gone. There was only the brother there and he shut himself in the basement, but they broke in."

He was silent then and I heard him swallow in the gathering dark, and I knew that he had been with them. "He said he didn't know where his sister was, didn't know nothing about no dead children. So they hanged him from a beam in the roof and called it suicide. Got Doc Hyams to certify it, though that basement was fourteen feet from floor to ceiling and there was no way that boy could have gotten up there to hang hisself 'less he could climb walls. Folks after used to joke that the Modine boy wanted to hang hisself real bad to get up without help."

"But you said the woman was alone when she tried to snatch the last child," I said. "How did they know the Modine boy was involved?"

"They didn't, at least they weren't sure. But she needed someone to help her do what she did. A child is a hard thing to take sometimes. They struggle and kick and cry for help. That's why she failed the last time, because she had nobody to help her. At least, that's what they figured."

"And you?"

The porch was quiet again. "I knew that boy and he wasn't no killer. He was weak and . . . soft. He was a homosexual—he'd been caught with some boy back in his private school and they asked him to leave. My sister heard that when she was cleaning for white folks in the town. It was hushed up, though there were stories about him. I think maybe some people had suspected him for a while, just for that. When his sister tried to take the child, well, folks just decided he must have known. And he must have, I guess, or maybe suspected at least. I don't know but . . ."

He glanced at Deputy Martin and the deputy stared right back at him. "Go on, Walt. There's some things I know myself. You won't say anything I haven't thought or guessed."

Tyler still looked uneasy but nodded once, more to himself than to us, and went on. "Deputy Earl Lee, he knew the boy wasn't involved. He was with him the night Bobby Joiner was taken. Other nights too."

I looked at Alvin Martin, who stared at the floor nodding slowly. "How did you know?" I asked.

"I saw 'em," he said simply. "Their cars were parked out of town, under some trees, on the night Bobby Joiner was taken. I used to walk the fields sometimes, to get away from here, though it was dangerous given all that was happenin'. I saw the cars parked and crept up and saw them. The Modine boy was . . . down . . . on the sheriff and then they got in the back and the sheriff took him."

"And you saw them together after that?"

"Same place, couple of times."

"And the sheriff let them hang the boy?"

"He wasn't going to say nothin'," Tyler spat, "case someone found out about him. And he watched them hang that boy."

"And his sister? What about Adelaide Modine?"

"They searched for her too, searched the house and then the fields, but she was gone. Then someone saw a fire in the shell of an old house on the East Road about ten miles from town and pretty soon the whole place was ablaze. Thomas Becker, he used to store old paint and inflammables there, away from the children. And when the fire was out, they found a body, badly burned, and they said it was Adelaide Modine."

"How did they identify her?"

Martin answered. "There was a bag near the body, with the remains of a lot of money, some personal papers, bank account details mostly. Jewelry she was known to have was found on the body, a gold and diamond bracelet she always wore. It was her mother's, they said. Dental records matched too. Old Doc Hyams produced her chart; he shared a surgery with the dentist, but the dentist was out of town that week.

"Seems she had holed up, maybe waiting for her brother or someone else to come to her, and fell asleep with a cigarette in her hand. She'd been drinking, they said, maybe to try to keep warm. The whole place went up. Her car was found nearby, with a bag of clothes in the trunk."

"Do you remember anything about Adelaide Modine, Mr. Tyler? Anything that might explain . . ."

"Explain what?" he interrupted. "Explain why she did it? Explain why someone helped her to do what she did? I can't explain those things, not even to myself. She had somethin', sure enough, somethin' strong inside her, but it was a dark thing, a vicious thing. I'll tell you somethin', Mr. Parker: Adelaide Modine was as close to pure evil as I've met on this earth, and I've seen brothers hanged from trees and burned while they were hangin'. Adelaide Modine was worse than the people who did the hangin' because, try as I might, I can't see any reason for the things she did. They're beyond explainin', 'less you believe in the Devil and Hell. That's the only way I can explain her. She was a thing out of Hell."

I stayed silent for a while, trying to sort and balance what I had been told. Walt Tyler watched while these thoughts went through my head and I think he knew what I was thinking. I couldn't blame him for not telling what he knew of the sheriff and the Modine boy. An allegation like that could get a man killed and it didn't provide conclusive proof that the Modine boy wasn't directly involved in the killings, although if Tyler's character assessment was right, then William Modine was an unlikely child killer. But the knowledge that someone involved in the death of his child might have eluded capture must have tortured Tyler all these years.

One part of the story still remained.

"They found the children the next day, just as the search had begun," concluded Tyler. "A boy out hunting took shelter in an abandoned house on the Modine estate and his dog started scraping at the cellar door. It was built into the floor, like a trapdoor. The boy shot the lock off and the dog went down and he followed. Then he ran home and called the police.

"There were four bodies down there, my little girl and the three others. They . . ." He stopped and his face creased but he did not cry.

"You don't have to go on," I said softly.

"No, you gotta know," he said. Then louder, like the cry of a wounded animal: "You've gotta *know* what they did, what they did to those children, to my child. My little girl, all her fingers were broken, crushed, and the bones pulled away from the sockets." He was crying openly now, his large hands open before him like a supplicant before God. "How could they do those things, to children? How?" And then he seemed to retreat into himself and I thought I saw the woman's face at the window, and her fingertips brushing the pane.

We sat with him for a while and then stood up to leave. "Mr. Tyler," I said gently, "just one more thing: where is the house where the children were found?"

"About three, four miles up the road from here. The old Modine estate starts there. There's a stone cross at the start of the track leading up to it. The house is pretty much gone now. There's just a few walls, part of a roof. State wanted to knock it down but some of us protested. We wanted to remind them of what had happened here, so the Dane house still stands."

We left him then, but as I was going down the porch steps I heard his voice behind me.

"Mr. Parker." The voice was strong again and there was

no quaver in it, although there was the lingering sound of grief in its tones. I turned to look at him. "Mr. Parker, this is a dead town. The ghosts of dead children haunt it. You find the Demeter girl, you tell her to go back where she came from. There's only grief and misery for her here. You tell her that, now. You tell her that when you find her, y'hear?"

At the margins of his cluttered garden the whispering grew in the trees and it seemed that just beyond the line of vision, where the darkness became almost too dark to penetrate, there was movement. Figures drifted back and forth, skipping just outside the light from the house, and there was childish laughter in the air.

And then there were only the limbs of evergreens fanning the darkness and the empty jangling of a chain in the wreckage of the yard.

24

□

ON THE Casuarina Coast of Indonesian New Guinea lives a tribe called the Asmat. They are twenty thousand strong and the terror of every other tribe near them. In their language Asmat means "the people, the human beings," and if they define themselves as the only humans, then all others are relegated to the status of nonhuman, with all that that entails. The Asmat have a word for these others: they call them *manowe*. It means "the edible ones."

Hyams had no answers that would have indicated why Adelaide Modine behaved as she did, and neither did Walt Tyler. Maybe she, and others like her, had something in common with the Asmat. Maybe they, too, saw others as less than human so that their suffering ceased to matter, was below notice apart from the pleasure it gave.

I recalled a conversation with Woolrich, after the meeting with *Tante* Marie Aguillard. Back in New Orleans, we walked in silence down Royal Street, past Madame Lelaurie's old mansion, where slaves were once chained and tortured in the attic until some firefighters found them and a mob ran Madame Lelaurie out of town. We ended up at Tee Eva's on Magazine, where Woolrich ordered sweet potato pie and a Jax beer. He ran his thumb down the side of the bottle, clearing a path through the moisture, and then rubbed his damp thumb along his upper lip.

"I read a Bureau report last week," he began. "I guess it was a 'state of the nation' address on serial killers, on where we stand, where we're goin'."

"And where are we going?"

"We're goin' to hell is where we're goin'. These people are like bacteria spreading and this country is just one big petri dish to them. The Bureau reckons we could be losing a couple of thousand victims a year to them. The folks watching Oprah and Jerry Springer, or subscribin' to Jerry Falwell, they don't wanna know that. They read about them in the crime mags or see them on the TV, but that's only when we catch one of them. The rest of the time, they don't have the least idea what's goin' on around them."

He took a deep swig of Jax. "There are at least two hundred of these killers operating at the present time. *At least* two hundred." He was reeling off the numbers now, emphasizing each statistic with a stab of the beer bottle. "Nine out of ten are male, eight out of ten are white, and one in five is never goin' to be found. Never.

"And you know what the strangest thing is? We've got more of them than anywhere else. The good old U.S. of A. is breedin' these fuckers like fuckin' Elmo dolls. Three-quarters of them live and work in this country. We're the world's leading producer of serial killers. It's a sign of sickness, is what it is. We're sick and weak and these killers are like a cancer inside us: the faster we grow, the quicker they multiply.

"And you know, the more of us there are, the more distant from each other we become. We're practically livin' on top of each other but we're further away from each other in every other way than we've ever been before. And then these guys come in, with their knives and their ropes, and they're even further removed than the rest of us. Some of them even have cop's instincts. They can sniff each other out. We found a guy in Angola in February who was communicating with a suspected killer in Seattle using biblical codes. I don't know how these two freaks found each other, but they did.

"Strange thing is, most of them are even worse off than the rest of humanity. They're inadequate—sexually, emotionally, physically, whatever—and they're taking it out on those they see around them. They have no"—he shook his hands in the air, searching for the word—"no vision. They have no larger vision of what they're doing. There's no purpose to it. It's just an expression of some kind of fatal flaw.

"And the people they're killing, they're so dumb that they can't understand what's happening around them. These killers should be a wake-up call, but nobody's listening, and that widens the gap even more. All they see is the distance, and they reach across it and pick us off, one by one. All we can do is hope that, if they do it often enough, we'll spot the pattern and put together a link between us and them, a bridge across the distance." He finished his beer and raised the bottle up, calling for another.

"It's the distance," he said, his eyes on the street but his gaze beyond it, "the distance between life and death, Heaven and Hell, us and them. They have to cross it to get close enough to us to take us but it's all a matter of distance. They love the distance."

And it seemed to me, as rain poured down on the window, that Adelaide Modine, the Traveling Man, and the others like them who roamed the country were all united by this distance from the common crowd of humanity. They were like small boys who torture animals or take fish from tanks to watch them squirm and gasp in their death throes.

Yet Adelaide Modine seemed even worse than so many of the others, for she was a woman and to do what she had done not only went against law and morality and whatever other titles we give to the common bonds that hold us together and prevent us from tearing each other apart; it went against nature, too. A woman who kills a child seems to bring out something in us that exceeds revulsion or horror. It brings a kind of despair, a lack of faith in the foundations upon which we have built our lives. For we believe that women should not take the life of a child. Just as Lady Macbeth begged to be unsexed so as to kill the old king, so also a woman who killed a child appeared to be denatured, a being divorced from her sex. Adelaide Modine was like Milton's night hag, "lured with the smell of infant blood."

I cannot countenance the death of children. The killing of a child seems to bring with it the death of hope, the death of the future. I recall how I used to listen to Jennifer breathe, how I used to watch the rise and fall of my infant daughter's chest, how I felt a sense of gratitude, of relief, with every inhalation and exhalation. When she cried, I would lull her to sleep in my arms, waiting for the sobs to fade into the soft rhythms of rest. And when she was at last quiet, I would bend down slowly, carefully, my back aching from the strain of the position, and lay her in her crib. When she was taken from me it was like the death of a world, an infinite number of futures coming to an end.

I felt a weight of despair upon me as the motel drew closer. Hyams had said that he had seen nothing in the Modines that would have indicated the depths of evil that existed within them. Walt Tyler, if what he had said was true, saw that evil only in Adelaide Modine. She had lived among these people, had grown up with them, perhaps even played with them, had sat with them in church, had watched them marry, have children, and then had preyed upon them, and no one had suspected her.

I think that what I wanted was a power I could not have: the power to perceive evil, the ability to look at the faces in a crowded room and see the signs of depravity and corruption. The thought sparked a memory of a killing in New York State some years before, in which a thirteen-year-old boy had killed a younger kid in the woods, beating him to death with rocks. It was the words of the killer's grandfather that had stayed with me. "My God," he said. "I should have been able to see, somehow. There should have been something to see."

"Are there any pictures of Adelaide Modine?" I asked eventually.

Martin's brow furrowed. "There may be one in the files of the original investigation. The library may have some stuff too. There's a kind of town archive stored in its basement, y'know, yearbooks, photos from the paper. There may be something in there. Why d'you ask?"

"Curiosity. She was responsible for so much of what happened to this town but I find it hard to picture her. Maybe I want to see what her eyes looked like."

Martin shot me a puzzled look. "I can get Laurie to look in the library archives. I'll try to get Burns to look through our own files, but it could take a while. They're all packed in boxes and the filing system is pretty obscure. Some of the files aren't even in date order. It's a lot of work to satisfy your idle curiosity."

"I'd appreciate it anyway."

Martin made a sound in his throat but didn't say anything else for a while. Then, as the motel appeared on our right, he pulled over to the side of the road. "About Earl Lee," he said.

"Go on."

"The sheriff's a good man. He held this town together after the Modine killings, from what I hear, him and Doc Hyams and a couple of others. He's a fair man and I've no complaints about him."

"If what Tyler said is true, maybe you should have."

Martin nodded. "That's as may be. If he's right, then the sheriff's got to live with what he's done. He's a troubled man, Mr. Parker, troubled by the past, by himself. I don't envy him anything but his strength." He spread his hands wide and shrugged slightly. "Part of me figures that you should stay here and talk to him when he comes back, but another part of me, the smart part, tells me that it would be better for all of us if you finished up your business as quickly as you can and then got out."

"Have you heard from him?"

"No, I haven't. He had some leave coming to him and maybe he's a little overdue on returning, but I ain't gonna hold that against him. He's a lonely man. A man who likes the company of other men ain't gonna find much comfort here."

"No," I said, as the neon light of the Welcome Inn flickered beyond us. "I guess not."

The call came through almost as soon as Martin pulled away from the curb. There had been a death at the medical center: the unidentified woman who had tried to kill me the previous night.

When we arrived two cruisers were blocking the entrance to the parking lot and I could see the two FBI men talking together at the door. Martin drove us through and as we got out of the car the two agents moved toward me in unison, their guns drawn.

"Easy! Easy!" shouted Martin. "He was with me the whole time. Put them away, boys."

"We're detaining him until Agent Ross arrives," said one of the agents, whose name was Willox.

"You ain't detaining or arresting nobody, not until we find out what's going on here."

"Deputy, I'm warning you, you're out of your league here."

Wallace and Burns came out of the medical center at that point, alerted by the shouts. To their credit, they moved to Martin's side, their hands hanging close by their guns.

"Like I said, let it go," said Martin quietly. The feds looked like they might push the issue but then they holstered their weapons and moved back.

"Agent Ross is going to hear of this," hissed Willox to Martin, but the deputy just walked by.

Wallace and Burns walked with us to the room in which the woman had been kept.

"What happened?" asked Martin.

Wallace turned bright red and started blabbering. "Shit, Alvin, there was a disturbance outside the center and—"

"What kind of disturbance?"

"A fire in the engine of a car, belonged to one of the nurses. I couldn't figure it out. There weren't nobody in it and she hadn't used it since she got in this morning. I only left the door here for maybe five minutes. When I got back, she was like this . . ."

We arrived at the woman's room. Through the open door I could see the pale, waxy pallor of her skin and the blood on the pillow beside her left ear. Something metal, ending in a wooden handle, glinted in the ear. The window through which the killer had entered was still open and the glass had been shattered in order to unhook the latch. A small sheet of sticky brown paper lay on the floor, with glass adhering to it. Whoever had killed the woman had taken the trouble to stick it to the window before breaking the glass, in order to muffle the sound and to ensure that the glass didn't make any noise when it hit the floor.

"Who's been in here, apart from you?"

"The doctor, a nurse, and the two feds," said Wallace. The elderly doctor called Elise appeared behind us. She looked shaken and weary.

"What happened to her?" said Martin.

"A blade of some kind—I think it's an ice pick—was thrust through her ear and into her brain. She was dead when we got to her."

"Left the pick in her," mused Martin.

"Clean and easy," I said. "Nothing to tie the killer to what happened if he—or she—gets picked up."

Martin turned his back on me and began consulting the other deputies. I moved away as they talked and made my way toward the men's washroom. Wallace looked back at me and I made a gagging expression. He looked away with contempt in his eyes. I spent five seconds in the washroom and then slipped out of the center through the rear exit.

Time was running out for me. I knew Martin would try to grill me on the source of the hit. Agent Ross wasn't far behind. At the very least, he'd hold me until he got the information he wanted, and any hope I might have of finding Catherine Demeter would disappear. I made my way back to the motel, where my car was still parked, and drove out of Haven.

25

□

THE ROAD TO THE RUIN of the Dane house was little more than two mud tracks and the car moved along them only with a great effort, as if nature itself was conspiring against my approach. It had started to rain heavily again, and the wind and rain combined to render the wipers almost useless. I strained my eyes for the stone cross and took the turning opposite. I missed the house the first time, realizing my mistake only when the road turned into a mass of mud and fallen, rotting trees, forcing me to reverse slowly back the way I had come, until I spotted two small ruined pillars to my left and, between them, the almost roofless walls of the Dane house briefly silhouetted against the dark sky.

I pulled up outside the empty eyes of the windows and the gaping mouth of what was once the door, pieces of its lintel strewn on the ground like old teeth. I took the heavy Maglite from under my seat and climbed out, the rain painful on my head as I ran for what little shelter the interior of the ruin could offer.

Over half of the roof was gone, and in the flashlight beam what remained still showed blackened and charred. There were three rooms: what had once been a kitchen and eating area, identifiable from the remains of an ancient stove in one corner; the main bedroom, now empty except for a stained mattress around which old prophylactics were scattered like the discarded skins of snakes; and a smaller room, which might have served as a children's bedroom once but was now a mass of old timber and rusting metal bars dotted with paint tins, left there by someone too lazy to haul them to the municipal dump. The rooms smelled of old wood, of long-extinct fires, and human excrement.

An old couch stood in one corner of the kitchen, its springs flowering through the rotting cushions. It formed a triangle with the corners of the wall, upon which the remains of some faded floral wallpaper hung tenaciously. I shined the flashlight over the back of the couch, my hand resting on the edge. It felt damp but not wet, for the remains of part of the roof still sheltered it from the worst of the elements.

Behind the couch and almost flush with the corners of the house was what appeared to be a trapdoor some three feet at each side. It was locked and its edges seemed filthy and choked with dirt. Its hinges were bloodied with rust, and pieces of wood and old metal covered most of its surface.

I pulled back the couch to take a closer look and started as I heard a rat scurry across the floor at my feet. It melted into the darkness in a far corner of the room and then was still. I squatted down to examine the lock and bolt, using my knife to scrape away some of the filth from around the keyhole. New steel shone through beneath the dirt. I ran the blade of the knife along the bolt, exposing a line of steel that shone like molten silver in the darkness. I tried the same experiment with the hinge but only flakes of rust greeted me.

I examined the bolt more closely. What had appeared at first sight to be rust now looked more like varnish, carefully applied so that it would blend in with the door. The bolt's battered look could easily have been achieved by dragging it behind a car for a while. It wasn't a bad job, designed as it was to fool only necking teenagers seeking a thrill in a house of the dead, or children daring each other to tempt the ghosts of other children long gone.

I had a crowbar in the car but I was reluctant to brave the driving rain again. As I shined the flashlight around the room, a steel bar some two feet long was caught in the beam. I picked it up, felt its weight, inserted it in the U of the lock, and jimmied. For a moment it seemed the bar might bend or fracture under the strain, and then there was a sharp crack as the lock broke. I pulled it free, released the bolt, and raised the door on its complaining hinges.

A rich, heady stench of decay rose from the cellar, causing my stomach to churn. I covered my mouth and moved away, but seconds later I was vomiting by the couch, my nostrils filled with my own smell and the odor from the cellar below. When I had recovered and breathed in some fresh air outside the house, I ran to the car and took the window rag from the dashboard. I sprayed it with defogger from the glove compartment and tied it around my mouth. The defogger made my head reel but I stuck it in the pocket of my coat in case I needed it again and re-entered the house.

Even though I breathed through my mouth, tasting the spray, the smell of putrefaction was overpowering. I descended the wooden stairs carefully, my strong left hand on the rail and the Maglite in my right with the beam shining at my feet. I didn't want to trip on a ruined step and plunge into the darkness below.

At the base of the steps the flashlight beam caught a glint of metal and blue-gray material. A heavy-set man in his sixties lay near the steps, his knees curled beneath him and his hands cuffed behind his back. His face was gray-white and there was a wound on his forehead, a ragged hole like a dark, exploding star. For a moment, as I shined the flashlight upon it, I thought it was an exit wound, but moving the light to the back of his head, I saw the hole in his skull gape, saw the decaying matter within and the white totem of his spine.

The gun had probably been pressed right against his head. There was some gunpowder smudging around the forehead wound and the star-shaped rip had been caused by the gases shooting under the skin next to the bone, expanding and tearing open the forehead as they exploded. The bullet had exited messily, taking most of the back of his skull with it. The contact wound also explained the unusual position of the body: he had been shot while kneeling, looking up into the muzzle of the gun as it approached and falling sideways and back when the bullet entered. Inside his jacket was a wallet, with a driver's license identifying him as Earl Lee Granger.

Catherine Demeter lay slumped against the far wall of the basement, nearly opposite the stairs. Granger had probably seen her as he walked or was pushed down. She was slumped like a doll at the wall, her legs spread out before her and her hands resting palms up on the floor. One leg was bent at an unnatural angle, broken below the knee, and I guessed that she had been thrown down the cellar stairs and dragged to the wall.

She had been shot once in the face at close range. Dried blood, brain tissue, and bone fragments surrounded her head like a bloody halo on the wall. Both bodies had begun to decay rapidly in the cellar, which seemed to stretch the length and breadth of the house.

There were blisters on Catherine Demeter's skin, and fluid leaked from her nose and eyes. Spiders and millipedes scuttled across her face and slipped through her hair, hunting the bugs and mites that were already feeding on the body. Flies buzzed. I guessed she had been dead for two or three days. I took a quick look around the cellar but it was empty apart from bundles of rotting newspaper, some cardboard boxes filled with old clothes, and a pile of warped timbers, the detritus of lives lived long before and now no more.

A scuffling noise on the floor above me, the sound of wood shifting despite careful footsteps, made me turn quickly and run for the stairs. Whoever was above me heard me, for the steps now moved quicker with no regard for any noise that might be made. As my feet hit the first stairs the sound of the trapdoor hinges greeted me and I saw the patch of star-studded sky begin to shrink as the door came down. Two shots were fired randomly through the gap and I heard them impact on the wall behind me.

The trapdoor was almost to the floor when I jammed the Maglite into the gap. There was a grunt from above and then I felt the flashlight being kicked repeatedly so that I had to grip it firmly to prevent it being wrenched from my hand. Still the bell-shaped end held firm, but my injured right shoulder ached from the strain of pushing up and holding the flashlight.

Above me, the entire weight of my assailant was on the trapdoor as he continued to aim kicks at the flashlight. Below, I thought I heard the sound of rats scurrying in alarm, but faced with the prospect of being trapped in that cellar, I thought it might be something else. I felt that I might yet hear the sound of Catherine Demeter dragging her shattered leg across the floor and up the wooden steps, that her white fingers might grip my leg and pull me down to her.

I had failed her. I could not protect her from the violent end in this cellar where four young children before her had met muffled, terrified deaths. She had returned to the place where her sister had perished, and in a strange circularity, she had reenacted a death that she had probably replayed many times in her mind before that day. In the moments before she died, she gained an insight into her sister's awful end. And so she would keep me company, console me for my weakness and my helplessness in the face of her passing, and lie beside me as I died.

As I breathed through gritted teeth, the stench of decay felt like a dead hand over my mouth and nostrils. I felt vomit rising once again and forced it down, for if I stopped pushing even for a moment I felt sure I would die in this cellar. Momentarily the pressure above me eased and I pushed upward with all my remaining strength. It was an error that my opponent exploited to the full. The torch was kicked once, hard, and slipped through the enlarged gap. The trapdoor slammed shut like the door of my tomb, its echo mocking me from the walls of the cellar. I groaned in despair and began to press futilely against the door once again, when there was an explosion from above and the pressure eased entirely, the trapdoor shooting upward and coming to rest flat on the floor.

I flung myself out, my hand inside my jacket reaching for my gun and the flashlight beam casting wild shadows on the ceilings and walls as I landed awkwardly and painfully on the floor.

The beam caught the lawyer Connell Hyams leaning against the wall just beyond the rim of the trapdoor, his left hand to his wounded shoulder while his right hand tried to raise his gun. His suit was soaked and his clean white shirt clung to his body like a second skin. I held him in the flashlight beam, my gun outstretched in the other hand.

"Don't," I said, but the gun was rising now and his mouth curled into a snarl of fear and pain as he brought it up to fire. Two shots sounded. Neither of them was from Hyams. He jerked as each bullet hit, and his gaze moved from me to a place over my shoulder. As he fell I was already turning, the gun still following the beam of the flashlight. Through the glassless window I caught a glimpse of a thin besuited figure fading into the dark, its limbs like sheathed blades and a scar running across its narrow, cadaverous features.

Maybe I should have called Martin then and let the police and the FBI handle the rest. I was sick and weary inside, and an almost overpowering sense of loss tore through me and threatened to unman me. The death of Catherine Demeter was like a physical pain, so that I lay for a moment on the ground, the body of Connell Hyams slumped opposite, and clutched my stomach in agony. I could hear the sound of a car as Bobby Sciorra drove away.

It was that sound that caused me to scramble to my feet. It had been Sciorra who had killed the assassin in the medical center, probably under orders from the old man in case she implicated Sonny in the hit. Yet I couldn't understand why he had killed Hyams and why he had let me live. I staggered to my car, my shoulder aching, and started to drive toward Hyams's house.

26

□

As I DROVE, I tried to piece together what had taken place. Catherine Demeter had returned to Haven in an effort to contact Granger, and Hyams had intervened. Maybe he had learned of Catherine's presence here by chance; the other possibility was that someone had informed him that she was coming and had urged him to ensure that she never spoke to anyone when she got here.

Hyams had killed Catherine and Granger, that much seemed certain. At a guess, I reckoned that he had watched for the sheriff's return and followed him into his house. If Hyams had a key to the sheriff's house—which, since he was a neighbor and a trusted citizen, was a likely possibility—Hyams could have listened to the messages on the sheriff's machine himself and, through that, could have learned of Catherine Demeter's location. Catherine Demeter had been dead before the sheriff returned. The proof: Granger's body had not decayed to the same extent as Demeter's.

Hyams might even have erased the messages, but he couldn't be certain that Granger had not picked them up by remote contact through a Touch-Tone phone. Either way, Hyams couldn't take any chances and acted, probably knocking the sheriff unconscious before cuffing him and then taking him to the Dane house, where he had already killed Catherine Demeter. The sheriff's car, his own Dodge, had probably been dumped or driven to another town and left somewhere it wouldn't attract undue attention, at least for the time being.

The use of the Dane house pointed to another part of the

puzzle: Connell Hyams was almost certainly Adelaide Modine's accomplice in the killings, the man for whom William Modine had been hanged. That raised the question of why he had been forced to act now, and I believed that I was close to an answer to that too, although it was a possibility that made me sick to my stomach.

Hyams's house was dark when I arrived. There was no other car parked nearby, but I kept my gun in my hand as I approached the door. The thought of facing Bobby Sciorra in the darkness made my skin crawl, and my hands shook as I used the keys I had taken from Hyams's body to open the door.

Inside, the house was silent. I went from room to room, my heart pounding, my finger on the trigger of the gun. The house was empty. There was no sign of Bobby Sciorra.

I went through to Hyams's office, pulled the curtains, and turned on the desk light. His computer was password protected but a man like Hyams would have to keep hard copies of all his documents. I wasn't even sure what I was looking for, except that it was something that would connect Hyams to the Ferrera family. The connection seemed almost absurd and I was tempted to give up the search and return to Haven and explain it all to Martin and Agent Ross. The Ferreras were many things, but they were not the consorts of child killers.

The key to Hyams's filing cabinets was also on the set I had taken from his body. I worked fast, ignoring local files and others that seemed irrelevant or unrelated. There were no files for the trust, which seemed extraordinary until I remembered his office in town and my heart sank. If the trust files were not kept in the house, there was a possibility that other files were not here either. If that was the case, the search could prove fruitless.

In the end, I almost passed over the link and only some half-remembered Italian phrases caused me to stop and consider it. It was a rental agreement for a warehouse property in Flushing, Queens, signed by Hyams on behalf of a company called Circe. The agreement was over five years old and had been made with a firm called Mancino Inc. *Mancino*, I remembered, meant "left-handed" in Italian. It derived from another word, meaning "deceitful." It was Sonny Ferrera's idea of a joke: Sonny was left-handed and Mancino Inc. was one of a number of paper companies established by Sonny in the early part of the decade when he had not yet been reduced to the level of a sick, dangerous joke in the Ferrera operation.

I left the house and started driving. As I reached the town limits, I saw a pickup by the side of the road. Two figures sat in the back, drinking beer from cans enclosed in brown paper bags, while a third stood leaning against the cab with his hands in his pockets. The headlights identified the standing man as Clete and one of the seated figures as Gabe. The third was a thin, bearded man whose face I didn't recognize. I caught Clete's eye as I passed and saw Gabe lean toward him and start talking, but Clete just raised a hand. As I drove away I could see him staring after me, caught in the headlights of the pickup, a dark shadow against the light. I felt almost sorry for him: Haven's chances of becoming Little Tokyo had just taken a terminal beating.

I didn't call Martin until I reached Charlottesville.

"It's Parker," I said. "Anybody near you?"

"I'm in my office and you're in deep shit. Why'd you run out like that? Ross is here and wants all our asses, but your ass especially. Man, when Earl Lee gets back there's gonna be hell to pay."

"Listen to me. Granger's dead. So is Catherine Demeter. I think Hyams killed them."

"Hyams?" Martin almost shrieked the name. "The lawyer? You're out of your mind."

"Hyams is dead too." It was starting to sound like a sick joke, except I wasn't laughing. "He tried to kill me out at the Dane house. The bodies of Granger and Catherine Demeter were dumped in the cellar there. I found them and Hyams tried to lock me in. There was some shooting and Hyams died. There's another player, the guy who took out the woman in the medical center." I didn't want to bring Sciorra's name into it, not yet.

Martin was silent for a moment. "You gotta come in. Where are you?"

"It's not finished. You've got to hold them off for me."

"I ain't holding anyone off. This town is turning into a morgue because of you and now you're a suspect in I don't know how many murders. Come in. You got enough trouble coming to you already."

"I'm sorry, I can't do that. Listen to me. Hyams killed Demeter to prevent her contacting Granger. I think Hyams was Adelaide Modine's accomplice in the child killings. If that's the case, if he escaped, then she could have escaped too. He could have rigged her death. He had access to her dental records through his father's office. He could have switched a set of records from another woman, maybe a migrant worker, maybe someone snatched from another town, I don't know. But something made Catherine Demeter run. Something sent her back here. I think she saw her. I think she saw Adelaide Modine because there's no other reason why she would have come back here, why she would have contacted Granger after all these years away."

There was silence at the other end of the phone. "Ross looks like a volcano in a linen suit. He's going to be onto you. He got your plates from your motel registration."

"I need your help."

"You say Hyams was involved?"

"Yes. Why?"

"I had Burns check our files. Didn't take as long as I thought it would. Earl Lee has . . . *had* the file relating to the killings. He used to check it out every so often. Hyams came looking for it, day before yesterday."

"My guess is that, if you find it, any photos will be gone. I think Hyams probably searched the sheriff's house for it. I think Hyams had to eliminate any traces of Adelaide Modine, anything that might link her to her new identity."

It is hard to disappear. A trail of paper, of public and private records, follows us from birth. For most of us, they define what we are to the state, the government, the law. But there are ways to disappear. Obtain a new birth certificate, maybe from a death index or by using someone else's birth name and DOB, and age the cert by carrying it around in your shoe for a week. Apply for a library card and, from that, obtain a voter's registration card. Head for the nearest DMV clerk, flash the birth certificate and the VRC, and you now have a driver's license. It's a domino effect, each step based on the validity of the documents obtained in the preceding step.

The easiest way of all is to take on another's identity, someone who won't be missed, someone from the margins. My guess was that, with Hyams's help, Adelaide Modine took on the identity of the girl who burned to death in a Virginia ruin.

"There's more," said Martin. "There was a separate file on the Modines. The photos from that are all gone as well."

"Could Hyams have got access to those files?"

I could hear Martin sigh at the other end of the phone.

"Sure," he said eventually. "He was the town lawyer. He was trusted by everyone."

"Check the motels again. I reckon you'll find Catherine Demeter's belongings in one of them. There might be something there."

"Man, you gotta come back here, sort this out. There's a lot of bodies here and your name is connected with all of them. I can't do any more than I've done already."

"Just do what you can. I'm not coming in."

I hung up and tried another number. "Yeah," answered a voice.

"Angel. It's Bird."

"Where the fuck have you been? Things are going down here. Are you on the cell phone? Call me back on a landline."

I called him back seconds later from a phone outside a convenience store.

"Some of the old man's goons have picked up Pili Pilar. They're holding him until Bobby Sciorra gets back from some trip. It's bad. He's being held in isolation at the Ferrera place—anyone talks to him and they get it in the head. Only Bobby gets access to him."

"Did they get Sonny?"

"No, he's still out there, but he's alone now. He's gonna have to sort whatever it is out with his old man."

"I'm in trouble, Angel." I explained to him briefly what had taken place. "I'm coming back but I need something from you and Louis."

"Just ask, man."

I gave him the address of the warehouse. "Watch the place. I'll meet you there as soon as I can."

I didn't know how long it would take them to start tracking me. I drove as far as Richmond and parked the Mustang in a long-term parking garage. Then I made some calls. For fifteen hundred dollars I bought silence and a flight on a small plane from a private airfield back to the city.

27

□

"YOU SURE you wanna be dropped here?" The cabdriver was a huge man, his hair lank with sweat, which dribbled down his cheeks and over the rolls of fat in his neck, eventually losing itself in the greasy collar of his shirt. He seemed to fill the whole front of the cab. The door looked too small for him to have entered through. He gave the impression that he had lived and eaten in the cab for so long that it was no longer possible for him to leave: the cab was his home, his castle, and his bulk gave the impression that it would be his tomb.

"I'm sure," I replied.

"This is a tough area."

"That's okay. I have tough friends."

The Morelli wine warehouse was one of a number of similar premises that lined one side of a long, ill-lit street west of Northern Boulevard in Flushing. It was a redbrick building, its name reduced to a white, flaking shadow below the edge of its roof. Wire screens covered the windows on both the ground and upper levels. There were no visible lights on the walls; the area between the gate and the main building was in almost total darkness.

On the other side of the street stood the entrance to a large yard filled with storage depots and railroad containers. The ground inside was pitted with ponds of filthy water and discarded pallets. I saw a mongrel dog, its ribs almost bursting through its fur, tearing at something in the dim light of the lot's filthy spotlights.

As I stepped from the cab, headlights flashed briefly from

the alleyway by the warehouse. Seconds later, as the cab
pulled away, Angel and Louis emerged from the black Chevy
van, Angel carrying a heavy-looking training bag, Louis immaculate in a black leather coat, a black suit, and a black
polo shirt.

Angel screwed up his face as he drew nearer. It wasn't
hard to see why. My suit was torn and covered with mud
and dirt from the encounter with Hyams in the Dane house.
My arm had begun to bleed again and the right cuff of my
shirt was a deep red color. I ached all over and I was tired of
death.

"You look good," said Angel. "Where's the dance?"

I looked toward the Morelli warehouse. "In there. Have I
missed anything?"

"Not here. Louis just got back from Ferrera's place,
though."

"Bobby Sciorra arrived there about an hour ago by chop-
per," said Louis. "Reckon him and Pili are having a real
heart-to-heart."

I nodded. "Let's go," I said.

The warehouse was surrounded by a high brick wall
topped with barbed wire and spiked fencing. The gate,
inset slightly as the wall curved inward at the entrance, was
also wire topped and solid except for a gap where a heavy
lock and chain linked its two halves together. While Louis
lounged semidiscreetly nearby, Angel removed a small, cus-
tom-built drill from his bag and inserted the bit into the
lock. He pressed the trigger and a high-pitched grinding
sound seemed to fill the night. Instantly, every dog in the
vicinity started to bark.

"Shit, Angel, you got a fuckin' whistle built into that
thing?" hissed Louis. Angel ignored him and moments later
the lock fell open.

We entered and Angel gingerly removed the lock and
placed it inside the gate. He replaced the chain so that to a
casual observer it would still appear secure if, oddly, locked
from the inside.

The warehouse dated from the thirties but would have
appeared functional even then. Old doors at the right and

left sides had been sealed shut, leaving only one way in at the front. Even the fire exit at the back had been welded in place. The security lights, which might once have lit up the yard, now no longer functioned and the illumination from the streetlights did not penetrate the darkness here.

Angel went to work on the lock with a selection of picks, a small flashlight in his mouth, and less than a minute later we were in, lighting our heavy Mags as we went. A small booth, which was probably once occupied by a security guard or watchman when the building was in use, stood directly inside the door. Empty shelves stretched along the walls of the room, paralleled by similar shelving through the center, creating two aisles. The shelves were separated into alcoves, each sufficient to hold a bottle of wine. The floor was stone. This had originally been the display area where visitors could examine the stock. Below, in the cellars, was where the cases were kept. At the far end of the room stood a raised office, reached by three stairs to the right.

Beside the small flight of stairs up to the office, a larger staircase descended down. There was also an old freight elevator, unlocked. Angel stepped in and pulled the lever, and the lift descended a foot or two. He brought it back to its original level, stepped out again, and raised an eyebrow at me.

We started down the stairs. There were four flights, the equivalent of two stories, but there were no other floors between the shop floor and the cellars. At the base was another locked door, this one wooden with a glass window through which the flashlight beam revealed the cellar's arches. I left Angel to the lock. It took him seconds to open the door. He looked ill at ease entering the cellars. The training bag appeared suddenly heavy in his hand.

"Want me to take that for a while?" asked Louis.

"When I'm that old you'll be feeding me through a straw," replied Angel. Although the cellars were cool, he licked at sweat on his upper lip.

"Practically feeding you through a straw already," muttered the voice from behind us.

In the basement, a series of curved, cavelike alcoves

stretched away before us. Each had bars running vertically
down from ceiling to floor, with a gate set in the middle.
They were the old storage bins for the wine. They were obviously disused, strewn with litter. The flashlight beams
caught the edge of the floor of one bin that differed from
the others. It was the one nearest us on the right, bare earth
showing where the cement floor had been removed. Its gate
stood ajar.

Our footsteps echoed around the stone walls as we approached. Inside, the floor was clean and the dirt neatly
raked. In one corner was a green metal table with two slits
on either side through which ran leather restrainers. In another corner stood a large, industrial-sized roll of what appeared to be plastic sheeting.

Two layers of shelving ran around the walls. They were
empty except for a bundle, tightly wrapped in plastic, that
had been tucked in against the far wall. I walked toward it
and the beam of the flashlight caught denim and a green
check shirt, a pair of small shoes and a mop of hair, a discolored face whose skin had cracked and burst, with a pair of
open eyes, the corneas milky and cloudy. The smell of decay
was strong, but dulled somewhat by the plastic. I recognized
the clothing. I had found Evan Baines, the child who had
disappeared from the Barton estate.

"Sweet Jesus," I heard Angel say. Louis was silent.

I drew closer to the body, checking the fingers and face.
Apart from natural decay, the body was undamaged and the
boy's clothing appeared undisturbed. Evan Baines had not
been tortured before he died but there was some heavier dis-
coloration at his temple and there was dried blood in his
ear.

The fingers of his left hand were splayed against his chest
but his small right hand had formed into a tightly closed
fist.

"Angel, come here. Bring the bag."

He stood beside me and I saw the anger and despair in
his eyes.

"It's Evan Baines," I said. "Did you bring the masks?"

He bent down and took out two dust masks and a bottle

of Aramis aftershave. He sprinkled the aftershave on each mask, handed one to me, and put the other one on himself. Then he handed me a pair of plastic gloves. Louis stood farther back but didn't take a mask. Angel held the flashlight beam on the body.

I took my pocketknife and sliced through the plastic by the child's right hand. Even through the mask the stench grew stronger and there was a hiss of escaping gas.

I took the blunt edge of the knife and pried at the boy's fist. The skin broke and a nail came loose.

"Hold the light steady, dammit," I hissed. I could see something small and blue in the boy's grip. I pried again, heedless now of the damage I was causing. I had to know. I had to find the answer to what had happened here. Eventually, the object came loose and fell to the floor. I bent to pick it up and examined it by the light of my own flashlight. It was a shard of blue china.

Angel had begun scanning the far corners of the room with his flashlight as I examined the shard and then had left the room. As I clutched the piece of china, I heard the sound of his drill and then his voice calling us from above. We went back up the stairs and found him in a small room, little bigger than a closet, almost directly above the room where the boy lay. Three linked videocassette recorders were stacked one above the other on some shelving and a thin cable snaked through a hole at the base of the wall and disappeared into the floor of the warehouse. On one of the VCRs the seconds ticked off inexorably until Angel stilled them.

"In the corner of that cellar there's a tiny hole, not much bigger than my fingernail but big enough to take a fish-eye and a motion sensor," he said. "An ordinary Joe couldn't have found them unless he knew they were there and he knew where to look. I reckon the wire follows the ventilation system. Someone wanted to record what went on in that room anytime it was entered."

Someone, but not whoever went to work on the children in that room. A regular video camera set up in the room would give better-quality pictures. There was no reason for concealment unless the viewer didn't want to be noticed.

There was no monitor in the room, so whoever was responsible either wanted to watch the tapes in the comfort of his or her own home or wanted to be sure that whoever picked them up couldn't sample what was on them before handing them over. I knew a lot of people who could put together a deal like that, and so did Angel, but I had one in particular in mind: Pili Pilar.

We went back down to the basement. I took the folding spade from Angel's bag and began to break the earth. It didn't take long for me to hit something soft. I dug wider and then began to scrape away the earth, Angel beside me using a small garden trowel to help. A film of plastic was revealed, and through it, barely discernible, I could see brown, wrinkled skin. We scraped away the rest of the dirt until the child's body was visible, curled in a fetal position with its head hidden by its left arm. Even in decay, we could see the fingers had been broken, although I couldn't tell if it was a boy or a girl without moving it.

Angel looked slowly around the floor of the cellar and I knew what he was thinking. It was probably worse than that. This child had been buried barely six inches beneath the ground, which meant there were probably others below. This room had been in use for a long time.

Louis slipped into the room, his finger pressed to his lips. He glanced once at the child, then he pointed slowly above us with his right hand. We stayed still, hardly breathing, and I heard the sound of soft steps on the stairs. Angel retreated into the shadows beside the shelves, clicking off the flashlight as he went. Louis was already gone when I stood up. I moved to take up a position at the other side of the door and was reaching for my gun when a flashlight beam hit me in the face. The voice of Bobby Sciorra simply said, "Don't," and I withdrew my hand slowly.

He had moved quickly, surprisingly so. He emerged from the shadows, the ugly Five-seveN in his right hand and his flashlight focused on me as he neared the open gate. He stopped about ten feet away from me and I could see his teeth shining as he smiled.

"Dead man," he said. "Dead as the kids in the room behind you. I was gonna kill you back in that house but the old man wanted you left alive, 'less there was no other option. I just ran out of options."

"Still doing Ferrera's dirty work," I replied. "Even you should have scruples about this."

"We all have our weaknesses." He shrugged. "Sonny's is short-eyes. He likes looking, you know. Can't do nothing else with his limp dick. He's a sick fuck but his daddy loves him and now his daddy wants the mess cleaned up."

And so it was Sonny Ferrera who had recorded the death agonies of these children, who had watched while Hyams and Adelaide Modine tortured them to death, their screams echoing around the walls as the silent unblinking eye of the camera took it all in to spew out again into his living room. He must have known who the killers were, must have watched them kill again and again, yet he did nothing because he liked what he was seeing and didn't want it to end.

"How did the old man find out?" I asked, but I already knew the answer. I knew now what had been in the car with Pili when he crashed, or thought I knew. It turned out that I was as wrong in that as I had been in so much else.

There was a scuffle of movement in the corner of the alcove and Sciorra reacted with the swiftness of a cat. The flashlight beam widened and he stepped back, the gun moving minutely from me to the corner.

The beam caught the bowed head of Angel. He glanced up into Bobby Sciorra's eyes and smiled. Sciorra looked puzzled for a moment and then his mouth opened in slow-dawning realization. He was already turning to try to locate Louis when the darkness seemed to come alive around him and his eyes widened as he realized, too late, that death had come for him too.

Louis's skin gleamed in the light and his eyes were white as his left hand clamped tight over Sciorra's jaw. Sciorra seemed to tighten and spasm, his eyes huge with pain and fear. He rose up on his toes and his arms stretched wide at either side. He shook hard once, twice, then the air seemed to leave him and his arms and body sagged, yet his head remained rigid, his eyes wide and staring. Louis pulled the long, thin blade from the back of Sciorra's head and pushed him forward, and he fell to the ground at my feet, small shudders running through his body until they stopped entirely.

Angel emerged from the darkness of the room behind me.

"I always hated that fucking spook," he said, looking at the small hole at the base of Sciorra's skull.

"Yeah," said Louis. "I like him a whole lot better now." He looked at me. "What do I do with him?"

"Leave him. Give me his car keys."

Louis frisked Sciorra's body and tossed me the keys.

"He's a made guy. Is that gonna be a problem?"

"I don't know. Let me handle it. Stay close to here. At some point, I'm going to call Cole. When you hear the sirens, disappear."

Angel bent down and gingerly lifted the FN from the ground using the end of a screwdriver.

"We gonna leave this here?" he asked. "That's some gun, what you say is true."

"It stays," I said. If I was right, Bobby Sciorra's gun was the link between Ollie Watts, Connell Hyams, and the Ferrera family, the link between a set of child killings that spanned thirty years and a mob dynasty that was more than twice as old again.

I stepped over Sciorra's body and ran from the warehouse. His black Chevy was pulled into the yard, its trunk facing the warehouse, and the gates had been closed behind it. It looked a lot like the car that had taken out Fat Ollie Watts's killer. I reopened the gates and drove away from the Morelli warehouse and Queens itself. Queens, a mass of warehouses and cemeteries.

And sometimes both together.

28

□

I WAS CLOSE now, close to an end, a termination of sorts. I was about to witness the cessation of something that had been happening for over three decades and that had claimed enough young lives to fill the catacombs of an abandoned warehouse. But no matter what the resolution might be, it was insufficient to explain what had taken place. There would be an ending. There would be a closure. There would be no solution.

I wondered how many times each year Hyams had traveled up to the city in his neat lawyer's clothes, clutching an expensive yet understated overnight bag, in order to tear another child apart. As he boarded the train in front of the ticket collector, or smiled at the girl behind the airline check-in desk, or passed the woman at the toll booth in his Cadillac, the interior redolent with the scent of leather, had there been anything in his face that might have caused them to pause, to reconsider their assessment of this polite, reserved man with his trim gray hair and his conservative suit?

And I wondered also at the identity of the woman who had burned to death in Haven all those years ago, for it was not Adelaide Modine.

I remembered Hyams telling me that he had returned to Haven the day before the body was found. It was not difficult to put together a chain of events: the panicked call from Adelaide Modine; the selection of a suitable victim from the files of Doc Hyams; the alteration of the dental files to match the body; the planting of the jewelry and purse beside the corpse; and the flickering of the first flames, the smell like roasting pork, as the body began to burn.

And then she disappeared back into the darkness to hibernate, to find time to reinvent herself so the killing could continue. Adelaide Modine was like a dark spider squatting in the corner of a web, rushing out when a victim wandered into her sphere of influence and cocooning it in plastic. She had moved unhindered through thirty long years, presenting one face to the world and revealing another to the children. She was a figure glimpsed only by the young, a bogeyman, the creature waiting in the darkness when all the world was asleep.

I believed I could see her face now. I believed also that I understood why Sonny Ferrera had been hunted by his own father, why I had been tracked to Haven by Bobby Sciorra, why Fat Ollie Watts had fled in fear of his life and died in the roar of a gun in a street soaked in late summer sunlight.

The streetlights flashed by like pistol flares. There was dirt beneath my fingernails as I clutched the wheel and I had an almost irresistible desire to pull into a gas station and wash them clean, to take a wire brush and to scrub my skin until it bled, scraping away all the layers of filth and death that seemed to have adhered to me in the past twenty-four hours. I could taste bile in my mouth and I swallowed back hard, focusing on the road ahead, on the lights of the car in front, and, just once or twice, on the careless dusting of stars in the black skies above.

When I arrived at the Ferrera house, the gates were open, and there was no sign of the feds who had watched the house earlier in the week. I drove Bobby Sciorra's car up the driveway and parked in the shadows beneath some trees. My shoulder ached badly now and bouts of nauseous sweating racked my body.

The front door of the house was ajar and I could see men moving inside. Beneath one of the front windows a dark-suited figure sat slouched with his head in his hands, his automatic lying discarded beside him. I was almost on top of him when he saw me.

"You ain't Bobby," he said.

"Bobby's dead."

He nodded to himself, as if this was no more than he expected. Then he stood up, frisked me, and took my gun. Inside the house, armed men stood in corners talking in hushed tones. The place had a funereal air, a sense of barely suppressed shock. I followed him to the old man's study. He left me to open the door for myself, standing back to watch me as I did so.

There was blood and gray matter on the floor and a dark, black-red stain on the thick Persian carpet. There was blood also on the tan pants of the old man as he cradled his son's head in his lap. His left hand, its fingers red, toyed with Sonny's lank, thinning hair. A gun hung limply from the right, its barrel pointing at the floor. Sonny's eyes were open and in his dark pupils I could see the light of a lamp reflected.

I guessed that he had shot Sonny as he held his head in his lap, as his son knelt beside him pleading for . . . what? For help, for a reprieve, for forgiveness? Sonny, with his mad-dog eyes, dressed in a cheap cream suit and an open-necked shirt, gaudy with gold even in death. The old man's face was stern and unyielding, but when he turned to look at me, his eyes were huge with guilt and despair, the eyes of a man who has killed himself along with his son.

"Get out," said the old man, softly but distinctly, but he wasn't looking at me now. A slight breeze blew in through the open French windows from the garden beyond, bringing with it some petals and leaves and the sure knowledge of the end of things. A figure had appeared, one of his own men, an older soldier whose face I recognized but whose name I did not know. The old man raised the gun and pointed it at him, his hand shaking now.

"Get out!" he roared, and this time the soldier moved, pulling the windows closed instinctively as he departed. The breeze simply blew them open again and the night air began to make the room its own. Ferrera kept the gun trained there for a few seconds longer and then it wavered and fell. His left hand, stilled by the appearance of his man, returned to its methodical stroking of his dead son's hair with the soothing, insane monotony of a caged animal stalking its pen.

"He's my son," he said, staring into a past that was and a future that might have been. "He's my son but there's something wrong with him. He's sick. He's bad in the head, bad inside."

There was nothing for me to say. I stayed silent.

"Why are you here?" he said. "It's over now. My son is dead."

"A lot of people are dead. The children . . ." For an instant the old man winced. "Ollie Watts . . ."

He shook his head slowly, his eyes unblinking. "Fucking Ollie Watts. He shouldn't have run. When he ran, we knew. Sonny knew."

"What did you know?"

I think that if I had entered the room only minutes later the old man would have had me killed instantly, or would have killed me himself. Instead, he seemed to seek some sort of release through me. He would confess to me, unburden himself to me, and that would be the last time he would bring himself to speak it aloud.

"That he'd looked in the car. He shouldn't have looked. He shoulda just walked away."

"What did he see? What did he find in the car? Videos? Pictures?"

The old man's eyes closed tightly, but he couldn't hide from what he had seen. Tears squeezed themselves from wrinkled corners and ran down the sides of his cheeks. His mouth formed silent words. No. No. More. Worse. When he opened his eyes again, he was dead inside. "Tapes. And a child. There was a child in the trunk of the car. My boy, my Sonny, he killed a child."

He turned to look at me again but this time his face was moving, twitching almost, as if his head could not contain the enormity of what he had seen. This man, who had killed and tortured and who had ordered others to kill and torture in his name, had found in his own son a darkness that was beyond naming, a lightless place where slain children lay, the black heart of every dead thing.

Watching had no longer been enough for Sonny. He had seen the power these people had, the pleasure they took in tearing the life slowly from the children, and wanted to experience it too.

"I told Bobby to bring him to me but he ran, ran as soon as he heard about Pili." His face hardened. "Then I told Bobby to kill them all, all the rest, every one of them." And then he seemed to be talking to Bobby Sciorra again, his face red with fury. "Destroy the tapes. Find the kids, find where they are, and then put them somewhere they'll never be found. Dump them at the bottom of the fucking ocean if you can. I want it like it never happened. It never happened." Then he seemed to remember where he was and what he had done, at least for a time, and his hand returned to its stroking.

"And then you came along, trailing the girl, asking questions. How could the girl know? I let you go after her, to get you away from here, to get you away from Sonny."

But Sonny had come after me through his hired killers and they had failed. Their failure forced his father to act. If the woman lived and was forced to testify, Sonny would be cornered again. And so Sciorra had been dispatched, and the woman had died.

"But why did Sciorra kill Hyams?"

"What?"

"Sciorra killed a lawyer in Virginia, a man who was trying to kill me. Why?"

For a moment, Ferrera's eyes grew wary and the gun rose. "You wearing a wire?" I shook my head wearily and painfully ripped open the front of my shirt. The gun fell again.

"He recognized him from the tapes. That's how he found you, in the old house. Bobby's driving through the town and suddenly he sees this guy driving in the opposite direction and it's the guy in the video, the guy who . . ." He stopped again and rolled his tongue in his mouth, as if to generate enough saliva to keep talking. "All the traces had to be wiped out, all of them."

"But not me?"

"Maybe he should've killed you too, when he had the chance, no matter what your cop friends would have done."

"He should have," I said. "He's dead now."

Ferrera blinked hard.

"Did you kill him?"

"Yes."

"Bobby was a made guy. You know what that means?"

"You know what your son did?"

He was silent then, as the enormity of his son's crime swept over him once more, but when he spoke again there was a barely suppressed fury in his voice and I knew that my time with him was drawing to a close.

"Who are you to judge my son?" he began. "You think because you lost a kid that you're the patron saint of dead children. Fuck. You. I've buried two of my sons and now, now I've killed the last of them. You don't judge me. You don't judge my son." The gun rose again and pointed at my head.

"It's all over," he said.

"No. Who else was on the tapes?"

His eyes flickered. The mention of the tapes was like a hard slap to him.

"A woman. I told Bobby to find her and kill her too."

"And did he?"

"He's dead."

"Do you have the tapes?"

"They're gone, all burned."

He stopped, as he remembered again where he was, as if the questions had briefly taken him away from the reality of what he had done and of the responsibility he bore for his son, for his crimes, for his death.

"Get out," he said. "If I ever see you again, you're a dead man."

No one stood in my way as I left. My gun was on a small table by the front door and I still had the keys to Bobby Sciorra's car. As I drove away from the house it looked silent and peaceful in the rearview, as if nothing had ever happened.

29

□

EACH MORNING after the deaths of Jennifer and Susan, I would wake from my strange, disordered dreams, and for an instant, it seemed that they would still be near me, my wife sleeping softly by my side, my child surrounded by her toys in a room nearby. For a moment they still lived and I experienced their deaths as a fresh loss with each waking, so that I was unsure whether I was a man waking from a dream of death or a dreamer entering a world of loss, a man dreaming of unhappiness or a man waking to grief.

And amid all, there was the constant aching regret that I had never really known Susan until she was gone and that I loved a shadow in death as in life.

The woman and the child were dead, another woman and child in a cycle of violence and dissolution that seemed unbreakable. I was grieving for a young woman and a boy whom I had never encountered when they were alive, about whom I knew almost nothing, and through them I grieved for my own wife and child.

The gates of the Barton estate stood open; either someone had entered and planned to leave quickly or someone had already gone. There were no other cars in sight as I parked on the gravel drive and walked toward the house. Light was visible through the glass above the front door. I rang the bell twice but there was no answer, so I moved to a window and peered in.

The door into the hallway was open, and in the gap I could see a woman's legs, one foot bare, the other with a black shoe still clinging to its toes. The legs were bare to the

tops of the thighs, where the end of a black dress still covered her buttocks. The rest of her body was obscured. I shattered the glass with the butt of my gun, half expecting to
hear an alarm, but there was only the sound of the glass tin-
kling on the floor inside.

I reached in carefully to open the latch and climbed
through the window. The room was illuminated by the hallway lights. I could feel my blood pounding through my
veins, could hear it in my ears as I opened the door wider,
sensed it tingling at the tips of my fingers as I stepped into
the hall and looked at the body of the woman.

Blue veins marbled the skin on her legs, and the flesh at
the thighs was dimpled and slightly flabby. Her face had
been pounded in, and strands of gray hair adhered to the
torn flesh. Her eyes were still open and her mouth was dark
with blood. Only the stumps of teeth remained within; she
was almost unrecognizable. There was only the gold, emer-
ald-studded necklace, the deep red nail varnish, and the
simple yet expensive de la Renta dress to suggest the body
was that of Isobel Barton. I touched the skin at her neck.
There was no pulse—I hardly expected any—but she was
still warm.

I stepped into the study where we had first met and compared the shard of china I had taken from Evan Baines's
hand with the single blue dog on the mantelpiece. The pattern matched. I imagined Evan had died quickly when the
damage was discovered, the victim of a fit of rage at the loss
of one of Adelaide Modine's family heirlooms.

From the kitchen down the hall came a series of uneven
clicking sounds and I could smell a faint odor of burning,
like a pot left on a stove for too long. Above it, almost unno-
ticed until now, was the faint hint of gas. No light showed
around the edge of the closed door as I approached, although the acrid smell grew more definite, more intense,
and the odor of gas was stronger now. I opened the door
carefully and stepped back and to one side. My finger rested
gently on the trigger, but even as I noticed the pressure, I
was aware that the gun was useless if there was gas leaking.

There was no movement from within but the smell was

very strong now. The strange, irregular clicking was loud, with a low drone above it. I took a deep breath and flung myself into the room, my useless gun attempting to draw a bead on anything that moved.

The kitchen was empty. The only illumination came from the windows, the hall, and the three large, industrial microwave ovens side by side in front of me. Through their glass doors I could see blue light dance over a range of metal objects inside: pots, knives, forks, pans, all were alive with tiny flickers of silver-blue lightning. The stench of gas made my head swim as the tempo of the clicks increased. I ran. I had the front door open when there was a dull *whump* from the kitchen, followed by a second, louder bang, and then I was flying through the air as the force of the explosion hurled me to the gravel. There was the sound of glass breaking and the lawn was set aglow as the house burst into flames behind me. As I stumbled toward my car I could feel the heat and see the dancing fire reflected in the windows.

At the gate to the Barton estate, a pair of red brake lights glowed briefly and then a car turned into the road. Adelaide Modine was covering her tracks before disappearing into the shadows once again. The house was ablaze, the flames escaping to scale the outside walls like ardent lovers, as I pulled into the road and followed the rapidly receding lights.

She drove fast down the winding Todt Hill Road and in the silence of the night I could hear the shriek of her brakes as she negotiated the bends. I took her at Ocean Terrace, as she headed for the Staten Island Expressway. To the left, a steep slope dense with trees fell down to Sussex Avenue below. I gained on her, mounted the verge at Ocean and swung hard to the left, the weight of the Chevy forcing the BMW closer and closer to the verge, the tinted windows revealing nothing of the driver within. Ahead of me, I saw Todt Hill Road curve viciously to the right, and I pulled away to stay with the curve just as the BMW's front wheels left the road and the car plunged down the hill.

The BMW rolled on garbage and scree, striking two trees before coming to a stop halfway down the leaf-strewn slope, its progress arrested by the dark mass of a young beech. The roots of the tree were partially yanked from the ground and it arched backward, its branches eventually coming to rest unsteadily against the trunk of another tree farther down the slope.

I pulled my car onto the verge, its headlights still on, and ran down the slope, my feet slipping on the grass so that I was forced to steady myself with my good arm.

As I approached the BMW the driver's door opened and the woman who was Adelaide Modine staggered out. A huge gash had opened in her forehead and her face was streaked with blood so that amid the woods and the leaves, in the bleak reflected light of the heads, she seemed a strange, feral being, her clothes inappropriate trappings to be shed as she returned to her ferocious natural state. She was hunched over slightly, clutching her chest where she had slammed into the steering column, but she straightened painfully as I approached.

Despite her pain, Isobel Barton's eyes were alive with viciousness. Blood flowed from her mouth when she opened it and I saw her test something within with her tongue and then release a small bloodied tooth onto the ground. I could see the cunning in her face, as if, even now, she was seeking a means of escape.

There was evil still in her, a foulness that went far beyond the limited viciousness of a cornered beast. I think concepts of justice, of right, of recompense were beyond her. She lived in a world of pain and violence where the killing of children, their torture and mutilation, were like air and water to her. Without them, without the muffled cries and the futile, despairing twistings, existence had no meaning and would come to an end.

And she looked at me and seemed almost to smile. "Cunt," she said, spitting the word out.

I wondered how much Ms. Christie had known or suspected before she died in that hallway. Not enough, obviously.

I was tempted to kill Adelaide Modine then. To kill her would be to stamp out one part of that terrible evil that had taken my own child along with the lives of the children in the cellars, the same evil that had spawned the Traveling Man and Johnny Friday and a million other individuals like them. I believed in the devil and pain. I believed in torture and rape and vicious, prolonged death. I believed in hurt and agony and the pleasure they gave to those who caused them, and to all these things I gave the name evil. And in Adelaide Modine I saw its red, sputtering spark exploded into bloody flame.

I cocked the pistol. She didn't blink. Instead, she laughed once and then grimaced at the pain. She was now curled over again, almost fetal near the ground. I could smell gasoline on the air as it flowed from the ruptured tank.

I wondered what Catherine Demeter had felt when she saw this woman in De Vries's department store. Had she glimpsed her in a mirror, in the glass of a display case? Had she turned in disbelief, her stomach tightening as if in the grip of a fist? And when their eyes met, when she knew that this was the woman who had killed her sister, did she feel hatred, or anger, or simply fear, fear that this woman could turn on her as she had once turned on her sister? For a brief moment, had Catherine Demeter become a frightened child again?

Adelaide Modine might not have recognized her immediately, but she must have seen the recognition in the eyes of the other woman. Maybe it was that slight overbite that gave it away, or perhaps she looked into the face of Catherine Demeter and was instantly back in that dark cellar in Haven, killing her sister.

And then, when Catherine could not be found, she had set about finding a resolution to the problem. She had hired me on a pretext and had killed her own stepson, not only so that he could not give the lie to her story but as the first step in a process that would lead to the eventual death of Ms. Christie and the destruction of her home as she covered the traces of her existence.

Maybe Stephen Barton bore some blame for what happened, for only he could have provided a link between Sonny Ferrera, Connell Hyams, and his stepmother, when

Hyams was seeking somewhere to take the children, a property owned by someone who wouldn't ask too many questions. I doubt if Barton ever really knew what was taking place, and that lack of understanding killed him in the end.

And I wondered when Adelaide Modine had learned of the death of Hyams and realized that she was now alone, that the time had come to move on, leaving Ms. Christie as a decoy just as she had left an unknown woman to burn in her place in Virginia.

But how would I prove all this? The videos were gone. Sonny Ferrera was dead, Pilar was certainly dead. Hyams, Sciorra, Granger, Catherine Demeter, all gone. Who would remember a child killer from three decades ago? Who would recognize her in the woman before me? Would the word of Walt Tyler be enough? She had killed Christie, true, but even that might never be proved. Would there be enough forensic evidence in the wine cellars to prove her guilt?

Adelaide Modine, curled in a ball, unraveled like a spider that senses a shift in its web and sprang toward me, the nails of her right hand digging into my face, scratching for my eyes, while the left sought the gun. I struck her in the face with the heel of my hand, pushing her back simultaneously with my knee. She came at me again and I shot her, the bullet catching her above the right breast.

She stumbled back against the car, supporting herself on the open door, her hand clutching at the wound in her chest.

And she smiled.

"I know you," she said, forcing the words out through the pain. "I know who you are."

Behind her, the tree shifted slightly as the weight of the car forced its roots up from the ground. The big BMW moved forward a little. Adelaide Modine swayed before me, blood pouring now from the wound in her chest. There was something bright in her eyes, something that made my stomach tighten.

"Who told you?"

"I know," she said, and smiled again. "I know who killed your wife and child."

I moved toward her as she tried to speak again but her words were swallowed by the sound of grinding metal from the car as the tree finally gave way. The BMW shifted on the slope and then plummeted down the hill. As it rolled, impacting on trees and stones, the rending metal sparked and the car burst into flame. And as I watched, I realized that it was always meant to end this way.

Adelaide Modine's world exploded into yellow flame as the gasoline around her ignited; and then she was enveloped, her head back and her mouth wide for an instant before she fell, striking feebly at the flames as she toppled, burning, into the darkness. The car was blazing at the bottom of the slope, thick black smoke ascending in plumes into the air. I watched it from the road, the heat searing my face. Farther down the hill, in the wooded dark, a smaller pyre burned.

30

I SAT in the same police interview room with the same
wooden table with the same wooden heart carved into its
surface. My arm was freshly bandaged and I had showered
and shaved for the first time in over two days. I had even
caught a few hours' sleep stretched across three chairs. Despite Agent Ross's best effort, I was not in a jail cell. I had
been interrogated comprehensively, first by Walter and another detective, then by Walter and the assistant chief, and
finally, by Ross and one of his agents, with Walter in attendance to make sure they didn't beat me to death out of
frustration.

Once or twice I thought I caught glimpses of Philip
Kooper striding around outside, like a corpse that had ex-
humed itself to sue the undertaker. I guessed that the trust's
public profile was about to take a terminal hammering.

I told the cops nearly everything. I told them about
Sciorra, about Hyams, about Adelaide Modine, about Sonny
Ferrera. I did not tell them that I had become involved in
the case at Walter Cole's instigation. The other gaps in my
story I left them to fill in for themselves. I told them simply
that I had taken some leaps of the imagination. Ross almost
had to be forcibly restrained at that point.

Now there was only Walter and me and a pair of coffee
cups.

"Have you been down there?" I asked eventually,
breaking the silence.

Walter nodded. "Briefly. I didn't stay."

"How many?"

"Eight so far, but they're still digging."

And they would continue digging, not just there but in scattered locations across the state and maybe even farther afield. Adelaide Modine and Connell Hyams had been free to kill for thirty years. The Morelli warehouse had been rented for only a portion of that time, which meant that there were probably other warehouses, other deserted basements, old garages, and disused lots that contained the remains of lost children.

"How long had you suspected?" I asked.

He seemed to think I was asking about something else, maybe a dead man in the toilet of a bus station, because he started and turned to me. "Suspected what?"

"That someone in the Barton household was involved in the Baines disappearance?"

He almost relaxed. Almost. "Whoever took him had to know the grounds, the house."

"Assuming he was taken at the house and hadn't wandered."

"Assuming that, yes."

"And you sent me to find out."

"I sent you."

I felt culpable for Catherine Demeter's death, not only because of my failure to find her alive but because, unwittingly, I might have brought Modine and Hyams to her.

"I may have led them to Catherine Demeter," I said to Walter after a while. "I told Ms. Christie I was going to Virginia to follow a lead. It might have been enough to give her away."

Walter shook his head. "She hired you as insurance. She must have alerted Hyams as soon as she was seen. He was probably on the lookout for her already. If she didn't turn up in Haven, then they were relying on you to find her. As soon as you did, I think you'd both have been killed."

I had a vision of Catherine Demeter's body slumped in the basement of the Dane house, her head surrounded by a circle of blood. And I saw Evan Baines wrapped in plastic, and the decayed body of a child half covered in earth, and the other corpses still to be discovered in the Morelli basement, and elsewhere.

And I saw my own wife, my own child in all of them.

"You could have sent someone else," I said.

"No, only you. If Evan Baines's killer was there, I knew you'd find out. I knew you'd find out because you're a killer yourself."

The word hung in the air for a moment, then tore a rift between us, like a knife cutting through our past together. Walter turned away.

I stayed silent for a time and then, as if he had never spoken, I said: "She told me that she knew who killed Jennifer and Susan."

He seemed almost grateful for the break in the silence. "She couldn't have known. She was a sick, evil woman and that was her way of trying to torture you after she died."

"No, she knew. She knew who I was before she died, but I don't think she knew when she hired me. She would have suspected something. She wouldn't have taken the chance."

"You're wrong," he said. "Let it go."

I didn't say anything more but I knew that, somehow, the dark worlds of Adelaide Modine and the Traveling Man had come together.

"I'm considering retirement," said Cole. "I don't want to look at death anymore. I've been reading Sir Thomas Browne. You ever read Thomas Browne?"

"No."

"*Christian Morals:* 'Behold not Death's Heads til thou doest not see them, nor look upon mortifying objects til thou overlook'st them.' " His back was to me but I could see his face reflected in the window and his eyes seemed far away. "I've spent too long looking at death. I don't want to force myself to look any longer."

He sipped his coffee. "You should go away from here, do something to put your ghosts behind you. You're no longer what you once were, but maybe you can still step back, before you lose yourself forever."

A film was forming on my untouched coffee. When I didn't respond, Walter sighed and spoke with a sadness in his voice that I had never heard before. "I'd prefer it if I didn't have to see you again," he said. "I'll talk to some people, see if you can go."

Something had changed within me, that much was true, but I was not sure that Walter could see it for what it was. Maybe only I could really understand what had happened, what Adelaide Modine's death had unlocked within me. The horror of what she had done through the years, the knowledge of the hurt and pain she had inflicted on the most innocent among us, could not be balanced in this world.

And yet it had been brought to an end. I had brought it to an end.

All things decay, all things must end, the evil as well as the good. What Adelaide Modine's death had done, in its brutal, flame-red way, was to show me that this was true. If I could find Adelaide Modine and could bring her to an end, then I could do the same with others. I could do the same with the Traveling Man.

And somewhere, in a dark place, a clock began to tick, counting off the hours, the minutes, the seconds, before it would toll the end for the Traveling Man.

All things decay. All things must end.

And as I thought of what Walter had said, of his doubts about me, I thought too of my father and the legacy he left me. I have only fragmented memories of my father. I remember a large, red-faced man carrying a Christmas tree into the house, his breath rising into the air like the puffs of steam from an old train. I remember walking into the kitchen one evening to find him caressing my mother and her laughter at their shared embarrassment. I remember him reading to me at night, his huge fingers following the words as he spoke them to me so that they might be familiar to me when I returned to them again. And I remember his death.

His uniform was always freshly pressed and he kept his gun oiled and cleaned. He loved being a policeman, or so it seemed. I did not know then what it was that drove him to do what he did. Maybe Walter Cole gained some knowledge of it when he looked upon the bodies of those dead children. Maybe I, too, have knowledge of it. Maybe I have become like my father.

What is clear is that something inside him died and the world appeared to him in different, darker colors. He had looked upon death's heads for too long and become a reflection of what he saw.

The call had been a routine one: two kids fooling around in a car late at night on a patch of urban wasteland, flashing the lights and sounding the horn. My father had responded and found one of the local boys, a petty criminal well on the road to graduating into felonies, and his girlfriend, a middle-class girl who was flirting with danger and enjoying the sexual charge it brought.

My father couldn't recall what the boy said to him as he tried to impress his girl. Words were exchanged and I can imagine my father's voice deepening and hardening in warning. The boy made mocking movements toward the inside pocket of his jacket, enjoying the effect on my father's nerves and bathing in the ripples of laughter from the young woman beside him.

Then my father drew his gun and the laughter stopped. I can see the boy raising his hands, shaking his head, explaining that there was no weapon there, that it was all just fun, that he was sorry. My father shot him in the face, blood streaking the interior of the car, the windows, the face of the girl in the passenger seat, his mouth wide in shock. I don't think she even screamed before my father shot her too. Then he walked away.

Internal Affairs came for him as he stripped in the locker room. They took him before his brother officers, to make an example of him. No one got in their way. By then, they all knew, or thought they knew.

He admitted everything but could not explain it. He simply shrugged his shoulders when they asked. They took his gun and his badge—his backup, the one I now hold, remained back in his bedroom—and then they drove him home under the NYPD rule that prevented a policeman from being questioned about the possible commission of a crime until forty-eight hours had elapsed. He looked dazed when he returned and wouldn't speak to my mother. The two Internal Affairs men sat outside in their car, smoking cigarettes, while I watched from my bedroom window. I think they knew what would happen next. When the gunshot sounded, they didn't leave their car until the echoes of the shot had faded into the cool night air.

I am my father's son, with all that entails.

The door of the interview room opened and Rachel Wolfe entered. She was dressed casually in blue jeans, high-top sneakers, and a black hooded cotton top by Calvin Klein. Her hair was loose, hanging over her ears and resting on her shoulders, and there was a sprinkling of freckles on her nose and at the base of her neck.

She took a seat across from me and gave me a look of concern and sympathy. "I heard about the death of Catherine Demeter. I'm sorry."

I nodded and thought of Catherine Demeter and how she looked in the basement of the Dane house. They weren't good thoughts.

"How do you feel?" she asked. There was curiosity in her voice, but tenderness too.

"I don't know."

"Do you regret killing Adelaide Modine?"

"She called it. There was nothing else I could do." I felt numb about her death, about the killing of the lawyer, about the sight of Bobby Sciorra rising up on his toes as the blade entered the base of his skull. It was the numbness that scared me, the stillness inside me. I think that it might have scared me more, but for the fact that I felt something else too: a deep pain for the innocents who had been lost, and for those who had yet to be found.

"I didn't know you did house calls," I said. "Why did they call you in?"

"They didn't," she said, simply. Then she touched my hand, a strange, faltering gesture in which I felt—I hoped?— that there was something more than professional understanding. I gripped her hand tightly in mine and closed my eyes. I think it was a kind of first step, a faltering attempt to reestablish my place in the world. After all that had taken place over the previous two days, I wanted to touch, however briefly, something positive, to try to awaken something good within myself.

"I couldn't save Catherine Demeter," I said at last. "I tried and maybe something came out of that attempt. I'm still going to find the man who killed Susan and Jennifer."

She nodded slowly and held my gaze. "I know you will."

Rachel had been gone for a short time when the cell phone rang.

"Yes?"

"Mista Parker?" It was a woman's voice.

"This is Charlie Parker."

"My name is Florence Aguillard, Mista Parker. My mother is *Tante* Marie Aguillard. You came to visit us."

"I remember. What can I do for you, Florence?" I felt the tightening in my stomach, but this time it was born of anticipation, born of the feeling that *Tante* Marie might have found something to identify the figure of the girl who was haunting us both.

In the background I could hear the music of a jazz piano and the laughter of men and women, thick and sensual as treacle. "I been tryin' to get you all afternoon. My momma say to call you. She say you gotta come to her now." I could hear something in her voice, something that conspired to trip her words as they tumbled from her mouth. It was fear and it hung like a distorting fog around what she had to say.

"Mista Parker, she say you gotta come now and you gotta tell no one you comin'. No one, Mista Parker."

"I don't understand, Florence. What's happening?"

"*I don't know,*" she said. She was crying now, her voice wracked by sobs. "But she say you gotta come, you gotta come *now.*" She regained control of herself and I could hear her draw a deep breath before she spoke again.

"Mista Parker, she say the Travelin' Man comin'."

There are no coincidences, only patterns we do not see. The call was part of a pattern, linked to the death of Adelaide Modine, which I did not yet understand. I said nothing about the call to anyone. I left the interrogation room, collected my gun from the desk, then headed for the street and took a cab back to my apartment. I booked a first-class ticket to Moisant Field, the only ticket left on any flight leaving for Louisiana that evening, and checked in shortly before departure, declaring my gun at the desk, my bag swallowed up in the general confusion. The plane was full, half of the passengers tourists who didn't know better heading for the stifling August heat of New Orleans. The stewards served ham sandwiches with potato chips and a packet of dried raisins, all tossed in the sort of brown paper bag you got on school trips to the zoo.

There was darkness below us when the pressure began building in my nose. I was already reaching for a cocktail napkin when the first drops came, but quickly the pressure became pain, a ferocious, shooting pain that caused me to jerk back in my seat.

The passenger beside me, a businessman who had earlier been cautioned about using his laptop computer while the plane was still on the runway, stared at me in surprise and then shock as he saw the blood. I watched his finger pressing repeatedly to summon the steward, and then my head was thrown back, as if by the force of a blow. Blood spurted violently from my nose, drenching the back of the seat in front of me, and my hands shook uncontrollably.

Then, just as it seemed that my head was going to explode from the pain and the pressure, I heard a voice, the voice of an old, black woman in the Louisiana swamps.

"Chile," said the voice. "Chile, he's here."

And then she was gone and my world turned black.

III

The concavities of my body are like another hell for their capacity.

Sir Thomas Urquhart,
"Rabelais' Gargantua"

31

□

THERE WAS a loud thud as the insect hit the windshield. It was a large dragonfly, a "mosquito hawk."

"Shit, that thing must have been big as a bird," said the driver, a young FBI agent named O'Neill Brouchard. Outside, it was probably in the high nineties, but the Louisiana humidity made it seem much hotter. My shirt felt cold and uncomfortable where the air-conditioning had dried it against my body.

A smear of blood and wings lay across the glass and the wipers struggled to remove it. The blood matched the drops that still stained my shirt, an unnecessary reminder of what had happened on the plane since my head still ached and the bridge of my nose felt tender to the touch.

Beside Brouchard, Woolrich remained silent, intent upon loading a fresh clip into his SIG Sauer. The assistant SAC was dressed in his usual garb of cheap tan suit and wrinkled tie. Beside me, a dark Windbreaker marked with the agency's letters lay crumpled on the seat.

I had called Woolrich from the satellite phone on the plane but couldn't get a connection. At Moisant Field, I left a number with his message service telling him to contact me immediately, then hired a car and set out toward Lafayette on I-10. Just outside Baton Rouge, the cell phone rang.

"Bird?" said Woolrich's voice. "What the hell are you doing down here?" There was concern in his voice. In the background, I could hear the sound of a car engine.

"You get my message?"

"I got it. Listen, we're already on our way. Someone spotted Florence out by her house, with blood on her dress and a gun in her hand. We're going to meet up with the local cops at exit one-twenty-one. Wait for us there."

"Woolrich, it may be too late . . ."

"Just wait. No hotdogging on this one, Bird. I got a stake in this too. I got Florence to think about."

In front of us I could see the taillights of two other vehicles, patrol cars out of the St. Martin Parish Sheriff's Office. Behind us, its headlights illuminating the inside of the FBI Chevy and the blood on the windshield, was an old Buick driven by two St. Martin detectives. I knew one of them, John Charles Morphy, vaguely, having met him once before with Woolrich in Lafitte's Blacksmith Shop on Bourbon, as he swayed quietly to the sound of Miss Lily Hood's voice.

Morphy was a descendant of Paul Charles Morphy, the world chess champion from New Orleans who retired in 1859 at the grand old age of twenty-two. It was said that he could play three or four games simultaneously while blindfolded. By contrast, John Charles, with his hard bodybuilder's frame, never struck me as a man much given to chess. Power lifting competitions, maybe, but not chess. He was a man with a past, according to Woolrich: a former detective in the NOPD who had left the force in the shadow of an investigation by the Public Integrity Division over the killing of a young black man named Luther Bordelon near Chartres two years earlier.

I looked over my shoulder and saw Morphy staring back at me, his shaven head glowing in the Buick's interior light, his hands tight on the wheel as he negotiated the rutted track through the bayou. Beside him, his partner, Toussaint, held the Winchester Model 12 pump upright between his legs. The stock was pitted and scratched, the barrel worn, and I guessed that it wasn't regulation issue but Toussaint's own. It had smelled strongly of oil when I spoke to Morphy through the window of the car back where the Bayou Courtableau intersected with I-10.

The lights of the car caught the branches of palmetto, tupelo, and overhanging willows, huge cypress heavy with

Spanish moss, and, occasionally, the stumps of ancient trees in the swamps beyond. We turned into a road that was dark as a tunnel, the branches of the cypress trees above us like a roof against the starlight, and then we were rattling over the bridge that led to the house of *Tante* Marie Aguillard.

Before us, the two sheriff's office cars turned in opposing directions and parked diagonally, the lights of one shining out into the dark undergrowth that led down to the swamp banks. The lights of the second hit the house, casting shadows over the tree trunks that raised it from the ground, the building's overlapping boards, the steps leading up the screen door, which now stood open on the porch, allowing the night creatures easy access to the interior of the house.

Woolrich turned around as we pulled up. "You ready for this?"

I nodded. I had my Smith & Wesson in my hand as we stepped from the car into the warm air. I could smell rotting vegetation and a faint trace of smoke. Something rustled through the vegetation to my right and then splashed lightly into the water. Morphy and his partner came up beside us. I could hear the sound of a shell being jacked into the pump.

Two of the deputies stood uncertainly beside their car. The second pair advanced slowly across the neat garden, their guns drawn.

"What's the deal?" said Morphy. He was six feet tall with the V shape of a lifter, his head hairless and a circle of mustache and beard around his mouth.

"No one enters before us," said Woolrich. "Send those two jokers around the back but tell them to stay out of the house. The other two stay at the front. You two back us up. Brouchard, stay by the car and watch the bridge."

We moved across the grass, stepping carefully around the discarded children's toys on the lawn. There were no lights on in the house, no sign of any occupants. I could hear the blood pumping in my head and the palms of my hands were slick with sweat. We were ten feet from the porch steps when I heard a pistol cock and the voice of the deputy to our right.

"Ah, sweet Jesus," he said. "Sweet Jesus Lord, this can't be . . ."

A dead tree, little more than an extended trunk, stood about ten yards from the water's edge. Branches, some no more than twigs, others as thick as a man's arm, commenced some three feet up the trunk and continued to a height of eight or nine feet.

Against the tree trunk stood Tee Jean Aguillard, the old woman's youngest son, his naked body glistening in the flashlight beam. His left arm was hooked around a thick branch so that his forearm and empty hand hung vertically. His head rested in the crook of another branch, his ruined eyes like dark chasms against the exposed flesh and tendons of his flayed face.

Tee Jean's right arm was also wrapped around a branch but this time his hand was not empty. In his fingers he grasped a flap of his own skin, a flap that hung like an opened veil and revealed the interior of his body from his exposed ribs to the area above his penis. His stomach and most of the organs in his abdomen had been removed. They lay on a stone by his left foot, a pile of white, blue, and red body parts in which coils of intestine curled like snakes.

Beside me, I heard one of the deputies begin to retch. I turned to see Woolrich grabbing him by the collar and hauling him to the water's edge some distance away. "Not here," he said. "Not here." He left the deputy on his knees by the water and turned toward the house.

"We've got to find Florence," he said. His face looked sickly and pale in the flashlight beam. "We gotta find her."

Florence Aguillard had been seen standing at the bridge to her house by the owner of a local bait shop. She had been covered in blood and held a Colt Service revolver in her hand. When the bait shop owner stopped, Florence raised the gun and fired a single shot through the driver's window, missing the bait shop owner by a fraction of an inch. He had called the St. Martin cops from a gas station and they, in turn, had called Woolrich, acting on his notice to the local police that any incident involving *Tante* Marie should be reported immediately to him.

Woolrich took the steps up the porch at a run and was almost at the door when I reached him. I put my hand on his shoulder and he spun toward me, his eyes wide.

"Easy," I said. The wild look disappeared from his eyes and he nodded slowly. I turned back to Morphy and motioned him to follow us into the house. Morphy took the Winchester pump from Toussaint and indicated that he should hang back with the deputy, now that his partner was indisposed.

A long central hallway led, shotgun style, to a large kitchen at the rear of the house. Six rooms radiated off the central artery, three on either side. I knew that *Tante* Marie's was the last door on the right and I was tempted to make straight for it. Instead we progressed carefully, taking a room at a time, the flashlight beams cutting a swath through the darkness, dust motes and moths bobbing in the beams.

The first room on the right, a bedroom, was empty. There were two beds, one made and the second, a child's bed, unmade, the blanket lying half on the floor. The living room opposite was also empty. Morphy and Woolrich each took a room as we progressed to the second set of doors. Both were bedrooms. Both were empty.

"Where are all the children, the adults?" I said to Woolrich.

"Eighteenth birthday party at a house two miles away," he replied. "Only Tee Jean and the old lady supposed to be here. And Florence."

The door opposite *Tante* Marie's room stood wide open and I could see a jumble of furniture, boxes of clothes, and piles of children's toys. A window was open and the curtains stirred slightly in the night air. We turned to face the door of *Tante* Marie's bedroom. It was slightly ajar and I could see moonlight within, disturbed and distorted by the shadows of the trees. Behind me, Morphy had the shotgun raised and Woolrich had the SIG held double-handed close to his cheek. I put my finger on the trigger of the Smith & Wesson, flicked open the door with the side of my foot, and dived low into the room.

A bloody handprint lay on the wall by the door and I could hear the sound of night creatures in the darkness beyond the window. The moonlight cast drifting shadows across a long sideboard, a huge closet filled with almost identically patterned dresses, and a long, dark chest on the floor near the door. But the room was dominated by the giant bed that stood against the far wall, and by its occupant, *Tante* Marie Aguillard.

Tante Marie: the old woman who had reached out to a dying girl as the blade began to cut her face; the old woman who had called out to me in my wife's voice when I last stood in this room, offering me some kind of comfort in my sorrow; the old woman who had, in turn, reached out to me in her final torment.

She sat naked on the bed, a huge woman undiminished by death. Her head and upper body rested against a mountain of pillows, stained dark by her blood. Her face was a red-and-purple mass. Her jaw hung open, revealing long teeth stained yellow with tobacco. The flashlight caught her thighs, her thick arms, and the hands that reached towards the center of her body.

"God have mercy," said Morphy.

Tante Marie had been split from sternum to groin and the skin pulled back to be held in place by her own hands. As with her son, most of her internal organs had been removed and her stomach was a hollow cavern, framed by ribs, through which a section of her spine gleamed dully in the light. Woolrich's flashlight moved lower, toward her groin. I stopped it with my hand.

"No," I said. "No more."

Then a shout came from outside, startling in the silence, and we were running together toward the front of the house.

Florence Aguillard stood swaying on the grass in front of her brother's body. Her mouth was curled down at either side, the bottom lip turned in on itself in grief. She held the long-barreled Colt in her right hand, the muzzle pointing toward the ground. Her white dress was patterned with blue flowers, obscured in places by her mother's blood. She made no noise, although her body was racked by silent cries.

Woolrich and I came down the steps slowly; Morphy and a deputy stayed on the porch. The second pair of deputies had come from the back of the house and stood facing Florence, Toussaint slightly to the right of them. To Florence's left, I could see the figure of Tee Jean hanging on the tree and, beside him, Brouchard with his unholstered SIG.

"Florence," said Woolrich softly, putting his gun back in his shoulder holster. "Florence, put the gun down."

Her body shook and her left hand wrapped itself tightly around her waist. She bent over slightly and shook her head slowly from side to side.

"Florence," repeated Woolrich. "It's me."

She turned her head toward us. There was misery in her eyes, misery and hurt and guilt and rage all vying for supremacy in her troubled mind.

She raised the gun slowly and pointed it in our direction. I saw the deputies bring their weapons up quickly. Toussaint had already assumed a sharpshooter's stance, his arms in front of his body, his gun unwavering.

"No!" shouted Woolrich, his right hand raised. I saw the cops look toward him in doubt and then toward Morphy. He nodded and they relaxed slightly, still keeping their weapons trained on Florence.

The Colt moved from Woolrich to me, and still Florence Aguillard shook her head slowly. I could hear her voice, soft in the night, repeating Woolrich's word like a mantra—"No no no no no"—and then she turned the gun toward herself, placed the barrel in her mouth, and pulled the trigger.

The explosion sounded like a cannon's roar in the night air. I could hear the sound of birds' wings flapping and small animals hurtling through the undergrowth as Florence's body crumpled to the ground. Woolrich stumbled to his knees beside her and reached out to touch her face with his left hand, his right reaching instinctively, futilely, for the pulse in her neck. Then he lifted her and buried her face in his sweat-stained shirt, his mouth open in pain.

In the distance, red lights shone. Farther away, I could hear the sound of a helicopter's blades scything at the darkness.

32

□

THE DAY DAWNED heavy and humid in New Orleans, the smell of the Mississippi strong in the morning air. I left my guest house and skirted the Quarter, trying to clear the tiredness from my head and my bones. I eventually ended up on Loyola, the traffic adding to the oppressive warmth. The sky overhead was gray and overcast with the threat of rain, and dark clouds hung over the city, seeming to lock in the heat. I bought a copy of the *Times-Picayune* from a vending machine and read it as I stood before City Hall. The newspaper was so heavy with corruption that it was a wonder the paper didn't rot: two policemen arrested on drug trafficking charges, a federal investigation into the conduct of the last Senate elections, suspicions about a former governor. New Orleans itself, with its run-down buildings, the grim shopping precinct of Poydras, the Woolworth store with its *Closing Down* notices, seemed to embody this corruption, so it was impossible to tell whether the city had infected the populace or if some of its people were dragging down the city with them.

Chep Morrison had built the imposing City Hall shortly after he returned from the Second World War to dethrone the millionaire Mayor Maestri and drag New Orleans into the twentieth century. Some of Woolrich's cronies still remembered Morrison with fondness, albeit a fondness arising from the fact that police corruption had flourished under him, along with numbers rackets, prostitution, and gambling. More than three decades later, the police department in New Orleans was still trying to deal with his legacy.

For almost two decades, the Big Sleazy had been top of the league table of complaints about police misconduct, numbering over one thousand complaints per year.

The NOPD had been founded on the principal of "the cut": like the police forces in other southern cities—Savannah, Richmond, Mobile—it had been formed in the eighteenth century to control and monitor the slave population, with the police receiving a portion of the reward for capturing runaways. In the nineteenth century, members of the force were accused of rapes and murders, lynchings and robberies, of taking graft to allow gambling and prostitution to continue. The fact that police had to stand for election annually meant that they were forced to sell their allegiance to the two main political parties. The force manipulated government elections, intimidated voters, even participated in the massacre of moderates at the Mechanics Institute in 1866.

New Orleans's first black mayor, Dutch Morial, tried to clean up the department at the start of the nineteen eighties. If the independent Metropolitan Crime Commission, which had a quarter of a century's start on Morial, couldn't clean up the department, what hope did a black mayor have? The predominantly white police union went on strike and the Mardi Gras was cancelled. The national guard had to be called out to maintain order. I didn't know if the situation had improved since then. I hoped that it had.

New Orleans is also homicide central, with about four hundred Code 30s—NOPD code for a homicide—each year. Maybe half get solved, leaving a lot of people walking the streets of New Orleans with blood on their hands. That's something the city fathers prefer not to tell the tourists, although maybe a lot of the tourists would still come anyway. After all, when a city is so hot that it offers riverboat gambling, twenty-four-hour bars, strippers, prostitution, and a ready supply of drugs, all within a few blocks of one another, there's got to be some kind of downside to it all.

I walked on, eventually stopping to sit on the edge of a potted tree outside the pink New Orleans Center, the tower of the Hyatt rising behind it, while I waited for Woolrich to

show. In the midst of the previous night's confusion, we
had arranged a meeting for breakfast. I had considered staying in Lafayette or Baton Rouge, but Woolrich indicated
that the local cops might not like having me so close to the
investigation, and as he pointed out, he himself was based
in New Orleans.

I gave him twenty minutes, and when he didn't arrive, I
began to walk down Poydras Street, its canyon of office
buildings already thronged with businesspeople and tourists
heading for the Mississippi.

At Jackson Square, La Madeleine was packed with break-
fasters. The smell of baking bread from its ovens seemed to
draw people in like cartoon characters pulled along by a visible, snakelike scent. I ordered a pastry and coffee and finished reading the *Times-Picayune*. It's next to impossible to
get the *New York Times* in New Orleans. I read somewhere
that the New Orleans citizenry bought fewer copies of the
New York Times than any other city in the United States, although they made up for it by buying more formal wear
than anywhere else. If you're going out to formal dinners
every evening, you don't get much time to read the *New
York Times*.

Amid the magnolia and banana trees of the square,
tourists watched tap dancers and mimes and a slim black
man who maintained a steady, sensual rhythm by hitting
his knees with a pair of plastic bottles. There was a light
breeze blowing from the river, but it was fighting a losing
battle with the morning heat and contented itself with tossing the hair of the artists hanging their paintings on the
square's black iron fence and threatening the cards of the
fortune-tellers outside the cathedral.

I felt strangely distant from what I had seen at *Tante*
Marie's house. I had expected it to bring back memories of
what I had seen in my own kitchen, the sight of my own
wife and child reduced to flesh, sinew, and bone. Instead,
I felt only a heaviness, like a dark, wet blanket over my
consciousness.

I flicked through the newspaper once again. The killings
had made the bottom of the front page, but the details of

the mutilations had been kept from the press. It was hard to tell how long that would last; rumors would probably begin to circulate at the funerals.

Inside, there were pictures of two bodies, those of Florence and Tee Jean, being taken across the bridge toward waiting ambulances. The bridge had been weakened by the traffic and there were fears that it might collapse if the ambulances tried to cross. Mercifully, there were no pictures of *Tante* Marie being transported on a special gurney to her ambulance, her huge bulk seeming to mock mortality even as it lay shrouded in black.

I looked up to see Woolrich approaching the table. He had changed his tan suit for a light gray linen; the tan had been covered in Florence Aguillard's blood. He was unshaven and there were black bags beneath his eyes. I ordered him coffee and a plate of pastries and stayed quiet as he ate.

He had changed a great deal in the years I had known him, I thought. There was less fat on his face, and when the light caught him a certain way, his cheekbones were like blades beneath his skin. It struck me for the first time that he might be ill, but I didn't raise the topic. When Woolrich wanted to talk about it, he would.

While he ate, I recalled the first time that I had met him, over the body of Jenny Ohrbach. She had been pretty once, a thirty-year-old woman who had kept her figure through regular exercise and a careful diet and who had, it emerged, lived a life of considerable luxury without any obvious means of support.

I had stood over her in an Upper West Side apartment on a cold January night. Two large bay windows opened out on to a small balcony overlooking Seventy-ninth Street and the river, two blocks from Zabar's deli on Broadway. It wasn't our territory, but Walter Cole and I were there because the initial MO looked like it might have matched two aggravated burglaries we were investigating, one of which had led to the death of a young account executive, Deborah Moran.

All of the cops in the apartment wore coats, some with mufflers dangling around their necks. The apartment was warm and nobody was in any great hurry to head back out into the cold, least of all Cole and I, despite the fact that this seemed to be a deliberate homicide rather than an aggravated burglary. Nothing in the apartment appeared to have been touched and a purse containing three credit cards and over seven hundred dollars in cash was found undisturbed in a drawer under the television set. Someone had brought coffee from Zabar's and we sipped from the containers, our hands cupped around them, enjoying the unaccustomed feeling of warmth on our fingers.

The coroner had almost finished his work and an ambulance team was standing by to remove the body when an untidy figure shambled into the apartment. He wore a long brown overcoat the color of beef gravy, and the sole of one of his shoes had come adrift from the upper. Through the gap, a red sock and an exposed big toe revealed themselves. His tan pants were as wrinkled as a two-day-old newspaper and his white shirt had given up the struggle to keep its natural tones, settling instead for the unhealthy yellow pallor of a jaundice victim. A fedora was jammed on his head. I hadn't seen anyone wear a fedora at a crime scene since the last film noir revival at the Angelika.

But it was the eyes that attracted the most attention. They were bright and amused and cynical, trailing lines like a jellyfish moving through water. Despite his ramshackle appearance, he was clean shaven and his hands were spotless as he took a pair of plastic gloves from his pocket and pulled them on.

"Cold as a whore's heart out there," he remarked, squatting down and placing a finger gently beneath Jenny Ohrbach's chin. "Cold as death."

I felt a figure brush my arm and turned to see Cole standing beside me.

"Who the hell are you?" he asked.

"I'm one of the good guys," responded the figure. "Well, I'm FBI, so whatever that makes me in your eyes." He flicked his ID at us. "Special Agent Woolrich."

He rose, sighed, and pulled the gloves from his hands, then thrust both gloves and hands deep into the pockets of his coat.

"What brings you out on a night like this, Agent Woolrich?" I asked. "Lose the keys to the Federal Building?"

"Oh, the witty NYPD," said Woolrich, with a half smile. "Lucky there's an ambulance standing by in case my sides split." He turned his head to one side as he took in the body again. "You know who she is?" he asked.

"We know her name, but that's it," said a detective I didn't recognize. I didn't even know her name at that point. I knew only that she had been pretty once and now she was pretty no longer. She had been beaten around the face and head with a piece of hollow-centered coaxial cable, which had been dumped beside her body. The cream carpet around her head was stained a deep, dark red and blood had splashed on the walls and the expensive, and probably uncomfortable, white leather furniture.

"She's Tommy Logan's woman," said Woolrich.

"The garbage collection guy," I said.

"The very same."

Tommy Logan's company had clinched a number of valuable garbage collection contracts in the city over the previous two years. Tommy had also expanded into the window cleaning business. Tommy's boys cleaned the windows in your building or you didn't have any windows left to clean, and possibly no building either. Anyone with those kinds of contacts had to be connected.

"Racketeering interested in Tommy?" It was Cole.

"Lots of people interested in Tommy. Lot more than usual, if his girlfriend is lying dead on the carpet."

"You think maybe someone's sending him a message?" I asked.

Woolrich shrugged. "Maybe. Maybe someone should have sent him a message telling him to hire a decorator whose eyesight didn't give out the year Elvis died."

He was right. Jenny Ohrbach's apartment was so retro it should have been wearing flares and a goatee. Not that it mattered to Jenny Ohrbach any more.

No one ever found out who killed her. Tommy Logan seemed genuinely shocked when he was told that his girlfriend was dead, so shocked he even stopped worrying that his wife might find out about her. Maybe Tommy decided to be more generous to his business partners as a result of Jenny Ohrbach's death, but if he did, their arrangement still didn't last much longer. One year later, Tommy Logan was dead, his throat cut and his body dumped by the Borden Bridge in Queens.

But Woolrich I saw more of. Our paths crossed on occasion; we went for a drink once or twice before I returned home and he went back to his empty apartment in Tribeca. He produced tickets to a Knicks game; he came to the house for dinner; he gave Jennifer an enormous stuffed elephant as a birthday present; he watched, but did not judge or interfere, as I drank myself away shot by shot.

I have a memory of him at Jenny's third birthday party, a cardboard clown's hat jammed on his head and a bowl of Ben & Jerry's Cherry Garcia ice cream in his hand. He looked embarrassed, sitting there in his crumpled suit surrounded by three- and four-year-olds and their adoring parents, but also strangely happy as he helped small children blow up balloons or drew quarters from behind their ears. He did farmyard impressions and taught them how to balance spoons on their noses. When he left, there was a sadness in his eyes. I think he was recalling other birthdays, when his child was the center of attention, before he lost his way.

When Susan and Jennifer died, he followed me to the station and waited outside for four hours until they had finished questioning me. I couldn't go back to the house, and after that first night when I found myself crying in a hospital lobby, I couldn't stay with Walter Cole, not only because of his involvement in the investigation but because I did not want to be surrounded by a family, not then. Instead, I went to Woolrich's small, neat apartment, the walls lined with books of poetry: Marvell, Vaughan, Richard Crashaw, Herbert, Jonson, and Ralegh, whose "Passionate Man's Pilgrimage" he sometimes quoted. He gave me his bed. On the day of the funeral, he had stood behind me in the rain and let the water wash over him, the drops falling from the brim of his hat like tears.

□

"How you doing?" I asked eventually.

He puffed his cheeks and breathed out, his head moving slightly from side to side like a nodding-dog figure on the backseat of a car. Gray was seeping through his hair from silver pools over his ears. There were lines like the cracks in fine china spreading from his eyes and the corners of his mouth.

"Not so good," he said. "I got three hours' sleep, if you can call waking up every twenty minutes to flashes of red 'sleep.' I keep thinking of Florence and the gun and the way it looked as it slid into her mouth."

"Were you still seeing her?"

"Not so much. On and off. We got together a coupla times and I was out at the house a few days back to see if everything was okay. Jesus, what a mess."

He pulled the newspaper toward him and scanned its coverage of the killings, his finger moving along the sides of each paragraph so that it became dark with print. When he had finished reading, he looked at his blackened fingertip, rubbed his thumb lightly across it, then wiped them both on a paper napkin.

"We got a fingerprint, a partial print," he said, as if the sight of his own lines and whorls had only just reminded him of it.

Outside, the tourists and the noise seemed to recede into the distance and there was only Woolrich and his soft eyes. He drained the last of his coffee then dabbed at his mouth with the napkin.

"That's why I was delayed. Confirmed it just an hour ago. We've compared it against Florence's prints, but it's not her. There are traces of the old woman's blood in it."

"Where did you find it?"

"Underside of the bed. He may have tried to steady himself as he cut, or maybe he slipped. Doesn't look like there was an attempt to erase it. We're comparing it against local files and our master fingerprint identification records. If he's in the system, we'll find him." As well as criminals, the files covered federal employees, aliens, military personnel, and those individuals who had requested that their prints be retained for identification purposes. Over the next twenty-four hours, the print found at the scene would be checked against about two hundred million others on record.

If it turned out to be the Traveling Man's print, then it would be the first real break since the deaths of Susan and Jennifer, but I wasn't holding my breath. A man who took the time to clean my wife's fingernails after he killed her was unlikely to be so careless as to leave his own fingerprint at a crime scene. I looked at Woolrich and knew he thought the same thing. He raised his hand for more coffee as he looked out at the crowds on Jackson Square and listened to the snorting of the ponies hitched to the touring carriages pulled up on Decatur.

"Florence'd been shopping in Baton Rouge earlier in the day, then returned home to change for some birthday party, one of her second cousins. She called you from some juke joint in Breaux Bridge, then went back to the house. She stayed there until maybe eight-thirty, then went to a cousin's birthday party at Breaux Bridge at about nine. According to witness statements taken by the local cops, she was distracted and didn't stay for long—seems that her momma insisted that she go, that Tee Jean could take care of her. She stayed one hour, maybe ninety minutes, then came back. Brennan, the bait shop owner, spotted her maybe thirty minutes after that. So we're looking at a window of one to two hours, no more, for the killings."

"Who's dealing with the case?"

"Morphy's bunch, in theory. In practice, a lot of it is likely to devolve mainly to us, since it matches the MO on Susan and Jennifer, and because I want it. Brillaud is going to hook up your phone, in case our man calls. It'll mean hanging around your hotel room for a while, but I don't see what else we can do." He avoided my eyes.

"You're cutting me out."

"You can't be too involved in this, Bird. You know that. I've told you before and I'm telling you again: we'll decide the extent of your involvement."

"Limited."

"Damn yes, limited. Look, Bird, you're the link to this guy. He's called once, he *will* call again. We wait, we see." He spread his hands wide.

"She was killed because of the girl. Are you going to look for the girl?"

Woolrich rolled his eyes in frustration. "Look where, Bird? The whole fucking bayou? We don't even know that she existed. We have a print, we'll run with that and see where it takes us. Now pay the check and let's get out of here. We've got things to do."

I was staying in a restored Greek Revival house, the Flaisance House, on Esplanade, a white mansion filled with dead men's furniture. I had opted for a room in the converted carriage house at the rear, partly for the seclusion but also because it contained a natural alarm in the form of two large dogs who prowled the courtyard beneath and growled at anyone who wasn't a guest, according to the guy manning the night desk. In fact, the dogs just seemed to sleep a lot in the shade of an old fountain. My large room had a balcony, a brass ceiling fan, two heavy leather armchairs, and a small refrigerator, which I filled with bottled water.

When we reached the Flaisance, Woolrich turned on an early morning game show and we waited, unspeaking, for Brillaud to arrive. He knocked on the door about twenty minutes later, long enough for a woman from Tulsa to win a trip to Maui. Brillaud was a small, neatly dressed man with receding hair, through which he ran his fingers every few minutes as if to reassure himself that there was still some there. Behind him, two men in shirtsleeves awkwardly carried an array of monitoring equipment on a metal trolley, carefully negotiating the wooden external stairway that led up to the four carriage house rooms.

"Get cooking, Brillaud," said Woolrich. "I hope you brought something to read." One of the men in shirtsleeves waved a sheaf of magazines and some battered paperbacks that he had removed from the base of the trolley.

"Where will you be if we need you?" asked Brillaud.

"The usual place," said Woolrich. "Around." And then he was gone.

I had once visited, through Woolrich, an anonymous room in the FBI's New York office. This was the tech room, where the squads engaged in long-term investigations—organized crime, foreign counterintelligence—monitored their wiretaps. Six agents sat before a row of reel-to-reel voice-activated tape recorders, logging the calls whenever the recorders kicked in, carefully noting the time, the date, the subject of the conversation. The room was almost silent, save for the click and whir of the machines and the sound of pens scratching on paper.

The feds do love their wiretaps. Back in 1928, when the FBI was called the Bureau of Investigation, the Supreme Court allowed almost unrestricted access to wiretaps of targets. In 1940, when the attorney general, Andrew Jackson, tried to end wiretapping, Roosevelt twisted his arm and extended taps to cover "subversive activities." Under Hoover's interpretation, "subversive activities" covered anything from running a Chinese laundry to screwing someone else's wife. Hoover was the god of wiretaps.

Now the feds no longer have to squat by junction boxes in the rain trying to protect their notebooks from the elements. Judicial approval, followed by a call to the telephone company in order to have the signal diverted, is usually enough. It's even easier when the subject is willing to cooperate. In my case, Brillaud and his men didn't even have to sit in a surveillance van, smelling one another's sweat.

I excused myself for five minutes while Brillaud worked to hook up both my own cell phone and the room phone, telling him that I was just heading for the kitchen of the main house. I left the Flaisance and strolled through the courtyard, attracting a bored glance from one of the dogs huddled in the shadows. I walked down to a telephone by a grocery store one block away. From there, I called Angel's number. The machine was on. I left a message telling him the situation and advising him not to call me on the cell phone.

Technically, the feds are supposed to engage in minimization on wiretapping or surveillance duties. In theory, this means that the agents hit the pause button on the recorder and tune out of the conversation, apart from occasional checks, if it becomes apparent that it's a private call unconnected with the business at hand. In practice, only a moron would assume that his private business would remain private on a tapped line and it seemed unwise for me to have conversations with a burglar and an assassin while the FBI was listening. When I had left the message, I picked up four coffees in the grocery store, reentered the Flaisance, and went up to my room, where an anxious-looking Brillaud was waiting by the door.

"We can order coffee up, Mr. Parker," he said disapprovingly.

"It never tastes the same," I replied.

"Get used to it," he concluded, closing the door behind me.

The first call came at 4 P.M., after hours of watching bad TV and reading the problem pages in back issues of *Cosmo*. Brillaud rose quickly from the bed and clicked his fingers at the technicians, one of whom was already tugging at his headphones. He counted down from three with his fingers and then signaled me to pick up the cell phone.

"Charlie Parker?" It was a woman's voice.

"Yes?"

"It's Rachel Wolfe."

I looked up at the FBI men and shook my head. There was the sound of breath being released. I put my hand over the mouthpiece. "Hey, minimization, remember?" There was a click as the recorder was turned off. Brillaud went back to lying on my clean sheets, his fingers laced behind his head and his eyes closed.

Rachel seemed to sense that there was something happening at the other end of the line.

"Can you talk?"

"I have company. Can I call you back?"

She gave me her home number and told me she planned

to be out until 7:30 P.M. I could call her then. I thanked her and hung up.

"Lady friend?" asked Brillaud.

"My doctor," I replied. "I have a low tolerance syndrome. She hopes that within a few years I'll be able to cope with idle curiosity."

Brillaud sniffed noisily but his eyes stayed closed.

The second call came at six. The humidity and the sound of the tourists had forced us to close the balcony window, and the air was sour with male scent. This time, there was no doubt about the caller.

"Welcome to New Orleans, Bird," said the synthesized voice, in deep tones that seemed to shift and shimmer like mist.

I paused for a moment and nodded at the FBI men. Brillaud was already paging Woolrich. On a computer screen by the balcony, I could see maps shifting and I could hear the Traveling Man's voice coming thinly through the headphones of the FBI men.

"No point in welcoming your FBI friends," said the voice, this time in the high, lilting cadences of a young girl's voice. "Is Agent Woolrich with you?"

I paused again before responding, conscious of the seconds ticking by and the "number withheld" message on the cell phone display.

"Don't fuck with me, Bird!" Still the child's voice, but this time in the petulant tones of one who has been told that she can't go out and play with her friends, the swearing rendering the effect even more obscene than it already was.

"No, he's not here."

"Thirty minutes." Then the connection ended.

Brillaud shrugged. "He knows. He won't stay on long enough to get a fix." He lay back down on the bed to wait for Woolrich.

Woolrich looked exhausted. His eyes were red rimmed from lack of sleep and his breath smelled foul. He shifted his feet constantly, as if they were too big for his shoes. Five minutes after he arrived, the phone rang again. Brillaud counted down and I picked up the phone.

"Yes."

"Don't interrupt, just listen." It sounded like a woman's voice, the voice of someone who was about to tell her lover one of her secret fantasies, but distorted, inhuman. "I'm sorry about Agent Woolrich's lover, but only because I missed her. She was supposed to be there. I had something special planned for her, but I suppose she had ideas of her own."

Woolrich blinked hard once, but gave no other indication that he was disturbed by what he heard.

"I hope you liked my presentation," continued the voice. "Maybe you're even beginning to understand. If you're not, don't worry. There's plenty more to come. Poor Bird. Poor Woolrich. United in grief. I'll try to find you some company."

Then the voice changed again. This time it was deep and menacing.

"I won't be calling again. It's rude to listen in on private conversations. The next message you get from me will have blood on it." The call ended.

"Fuck," said Woolrich. "Tell me you got something."

"We got nothing," said Brillaud, tossing his headphones on the bed. "Number keeps changing. He knows."

I left the FBI men to pack away their equipment in a white Ford van and walked down through the Quarter to the Napoleon House to call Rachel Wolfe. I didn't want to use the cellular. For some reason, it seemed soiled by its role as the means of contact with a killer. I also wanted the exercise, after being cooped up in my room for so long.

She picked up on the third ring.

"It's Charlie Parker."

"Hi . . ." She seemed to struggle for a time as she tried to decide what to call me.

"You can call me Bird."

"Well spotted."

There was an awkward pause, then: "Where are you? It sounds incredibly noisy."

"It is. It's New Orleans." And then I filled her in as best I could on what had taken place. She listened in silence, and once or twice, I heard a pen tapping rhythmically against the phone at the other end of the line.

"Any of those details mean anything to you?" I asked, when I had finished.

"I'm not sure. I seem to recall something from my time as a student but it's buried so far back that I'm not sure that I can find it. I think I may have something for you arising out of your previous conversation with this man. It's a little obscure, though." She was silent for a moment. "Where are you staying?"

I gave her the number of the Flaisance. She repeated the name and the number to herself as she wrote them down.

"Are you going to call me back?"

"No," she said. "I'm going to make a reservation. I'm coming down."

I looked around the Napoleon after I hung up. It was packed with locals and vaguely bohemian looking visitors, some of them tourists staying in the rooms above the dimly lit bar. A classical piece I couldn't identify was playing over the speakers and smoke hung thick in the air.

Something about the Traveling Man's calls bothered me, although I wasn't sure what. He knew I was in New Orleans when he made his calls. He knew where I was staying, too, since he was aware of the presence of the feds, and that awareness meant that he was familiar with police procedures and was monitoring the investigation, which matched Rachel's profile.

He had to have been watching the crime scene as we arrived, or shortly after. His reluctance to stay on the line was understandable, given the feds' surveillance, but that second call . . . I played it back in my mind, trying to discern the source of my unease, but it yielded nothing.

I was tempted to stay in the Napoleon House, to breathe in the sense of life and gaiety in the old bar, but instead I returned to the Flaisance. Despite the heat I walked to the large windows, opened them, and stepped out onto the balcony. I looked out at the faded buildings and wrought iron balconies of the upper Quarter and breathed deeply of the smells of cooking coming from a restaurant nearby, mingled with smoke and exhaust fumes. I listened to the strains of jazz music coming from a bar on Governor Nicholls, the shouts and laughter of those heading for the rip-off joints on Bourbon Street, the singsong accents of the locals blending with the voices of the out-of-towners, the sound of human life passing beneath my window.

And I thought of Rachel Wolfe, and the way her hair rested on her shoulders, and the sprinkling of freckles across her white neck.

33

THAT NIGHT, I dreamed of an amphitheater, with rising aisles filled with old men. Its walls were hung with damask, and two high torches illuminated its central rectangular table, with its curved edges and legs carved like bones. Florence Aguillard lay on the table, the exterior of her womb exposed while a bearded man in dark robes tore at it with an ivory-handled scalpel. Around her neck and behind her ears was the mark of a rope burn. Her head lay at an impossible angle on the tabletop.

When the surgeon cut her, eels slithered from her uterus and tumbled to the floor and the dead woman opened her eyes and tried to cry out. The surgeon stifled her mouth with a burlap sack, then continued to cut until the light went from her eyes.

Figures watched from a twilight corner of the amphitheater. They came to me from the shadows, my wife and child, but now they were joined by a third, one who stayed farther back in the dimness, one who was barely a silhouette. She came from a cold, wet place and brought with her a dense, loamy smell of rotting vegetation, of flesh bloated and disfigured by gas and decay. The place where she lay was small and cramped, its sides unyielding, and sometimes the fish bumped against it as she waited. I seemed to smell her in my nostrils when I woke and could still hear her voice . . .

help me

as the blood rushed in my ears

I'm cold, help me

and I knew that I had to find her.

□

I was awakened by the sound of the telephone in my room. Dim light lanced through the curtains and my watch glowed the time at 8:35 A.M. I picked up the phone.

"Parker? It's Morphy. Get your ass in gear. I'll see you at La Marquise in an hour."

I showered, dressed, and walked down to Jackson Square, following the early morning worshipers into St. Louis Cathedral. Outside the cathedral, a huckster tried to attract worshipers to his fire-eating act while a group of black nuns crowded beneath a yellow-and-green parasol.

Susan and I had attended mass here once, beneath the cathedral's ornately decorated ceiling depicting Christ among the shepherds and, above the small sanctuary, the figure of the Crusader king Louis IX, Roi De France, announcing the Seventh Crusade.

The cathedral had effectively been rebuilt twice since the original wooden structure, designed in 1724, burned down during the Good Friday fire of 1788, when over eight hundred buildings went up in flames. The present cathedral was less than one hundred and fifty years old, its stained-glass windows, overlooking the Place Jean-Paul Deux, a gift from the Spanish government.

It was strange that I should have remembered the details so clearly after so many years. Yet I remembered them less for their own intrinsic interest than for their connections to Susan. I remembered them because she had been with me when I learned them, her hand clasped in mine, her hair pulled back and tied with an aquamarine bow.

For a brief moment it seemed that, by standing in the same place and remembering the same words spoken, I could reach back to that time and feel her close beside me, her hand in my hand, her taste still on my lips, her scent on my neck. If I closed my eyes, I could imagine her sauntering down the aisle, her hand in mine, breathing in the mingled smells of incense and flowers, passing beneath the windows, moving from darkness to light, light to darkness.

I knelt at the back of the cathedral, by the statue of a

cherub with a font in its hands and its feet upon a vision of evil, and I prayed for my wife and child.

Morphy was already at La Marquise, a French-style patisserie on Chartres. He was sitting in the rear courtyard, his head freshly shaved. He wore a pair of gray sweatpants, Nike sneakers, and a Timberland fleece top. A plate of croissants and two cups of coffee stood on the table before him. He was carefully applying grape jelly to one half of a croissant as I sat down across from him.

"I ordered coffee for you. Take a croissant."

"Coffee's fine, thanks. Day off?"

"Nah, just avoided the dawn patrol." He took the half croissant and stuffed it into his mouth, using his finger to cram in the last part. He smiled, his cheeks bulging. "My wife won't let me do this at home. Says it reminds her of a kid hogging food at a birthday party."

He swallowed and set to work on the remaining half of the croissant. "St. Martin's been frozen out of the picture, 'part from running around looking under rocks for bloody clothes," he said. "Woolrich and his boys have pretty much taken over the investigation. We don't have a helluva lot to do with it anymore, legwork excepted."

I knew what Woolrich would be doing. The killings of *Tante* Marie and Tee Jean now confirmed the existence of a serial killer. The details would be passed on to the FBI's Investigative Support Unit, the hard-pressed section responsible for advising on interrogation techniques and hostage negotiation, as well as dealing with VICAP, ABIS—the arson and bombing program—and, crucially for this case, criminal profiling. Of the thirty-six agents in the unit, only ten worked on profiling, buried in a warren of offices sixty feet below ground in what used to be the FBI director's fallout shelter at Quantico.

And while the feds sifted through the evidence, trying to build up their picture of the Traveling Man, the police on the ground continued to search for physical traces of the killer in the area around *Tante* Marie's house. I could picture them already, the lines of cops moving through the undergrowth, warm green light shedding down upon them from the trees above. Their feet would be catching in the mud, their uniforms snagging on briars, as they searched the ground before them. Others would be working through the green waters of Atchafalaya, swatting at no-see-ums and sweating heavily through their shirts.

There had been a lot of blood at the Aguillard house. The Traveling Man must have been awash with it by the time his work was done. He must have worn overalls, and it would be too risky for him to hold on to them. They had either been dumped in the swamp, or buried, or destroyed. My guess was that he had destroyed them, but the search had to go on.

"I don't have a helluva lot to do with it anymore, either," I said.

"I hear that." He ate some more croissant and finished off his coffee. "You finished, we'll get going." He left some money on the table and I followed him outside. The same battered Buick that had followed us to *Tante* Marie's was parked half a block away, a hand-lettered cop-on-duty sign taped to the dashboard with duct tape. A parking ticket flapped beneath the wiper.

"Shit," said Morphy, tossing the ticket in a trash can. "Nobody got respect for the law no more."

We drove to the Desire projects, a harsh urban landscape where young blacks lounged by rubbish-strewn lots or shot hoops desultorily in wire-rimmed courts. The two-story blocks were like barracks, lining streets with bad-joke names like Piety, Abundance, and Humanity. We pulled in near a liquor store, which was barricaded like a fortress, causing young men to skip away from us at the smell of cop. Even here, Morphy's trademark bald head appeared to be instantly recognizable.

"You know much about New Orleans?" said Morphy after a time.

"Nope," I replied. Beneath his fleece top, I could see the trademark bulge of his gun. The palms of his hands were callused from gripping dumbbells and barbells, and even his fingers were thickly muscled. When he moved his head, muscles and tendons stood out on his neck like snakes moving beneath his skin.

Unlike most bodybuilders, there was an air of suppressed danger about Morphy, a sense that the muscle wasn't just for show. I knew that he had killed a man once in a bar in Monroe, a pimp who had shot up one of his girls and the john she was with in a hotel room in Lafayette. The pimp, a two-hundred-and-twenty-pound Creole who called himself Le Mort Rouge, had stabbed Morphy in the chest with a broken bottle and then tried to choke him on the ground. Morphy, after trying punches to the face and body, had eventually settled for a grip on Le Mort's neck, and the two men had remained like that, locked in each other's grip, until something burst in Le Mort's head and he fell sideways against the bar. He was dead by the time the ambulance arrived.

It had been a fair fight, but sitting beside Morphy in the car, I wondered about Luther Bordelon. He had been a thug, that much was certain. He had a string of assaults stretching back to his years as a juvenile and he was suspected of the rape of a young Australian tourist. The girl had failed to identify Bordelon in a lineup and no physical evidence of the rapist had been left on the girl's body because her assailant had used a condom and then made her wash her pubic region with a bottle of mineral water, but the NOPD cops knew it was Bordelon. Sometimes, that's just the way things are.

On the night he died, Bordelon had been drinking in an Irish bar in the Quarter. He was wearing a white T-shirt and white Nike shorts, and three customers in the bar, with whom he had been playing pool, later swore statements that Bordelon had not been armed. Yet Morphy and his partner, Ray Garza, reported that Bordelon had fired on them when they attempted to routinely question him and that he had been killed in their return of fire. A gun, an old S&W Model 60 that was at least twenty years old, was found by his side with two shots fired. The serial number of the gun had been filed away from the frame under the cylinder crane, making the gun difficult to identify, and Ballistics reported that it was clean and had not been previously used in the commission of a crime in the city of New Orleans.

The gun looked like a throwdown and the NOPD's Police Integrity Division clearly felt that was the case, but Garza and Morphy stuck by their story. One year later Garza was dead, stabbed to death while trying to break up a brawl in the Irish Channel, and Morphy had transferred to St. Martin, where he had bought a house. That was it. That was how it ended.

Morphy gestured toward a group of young blacks, the asses of their jeans around their knees and oversized trainers slapping the sidewalk as they walked. They returned our gaze unflinchingly, as if daring us to make a move on them. From a boom box they carried came the sound of the Wu-Tang Clan, music to kick start the revolution. I felt a kind of perverse pleasure from recognizing the music. Charlie Parker, honorary homeboy.

Morphy grimaced. "That is the worst goddamn racket I ever heard. Shit, these people invented the blues. Robert Johnson heard that crap, he'd know for sure that he'd sold his soul to the devil and gone straight to hell." He turned on his car radio and flicked through the channels with an unhappy look. Resignedly, he pushed in a tape and the warm sound of Little Willie John filled the car.

"I grew up in Metairie, before the projects really took hold in this city," he began. "I can't say any of my best friends were black or nothing—most of the blacks went to public schools, I didn't—but we got along together.

"But when the projects went up, that was the end. Desire, Iberville, Lafitte, those were places you didn't want to end up, 'less you were armed to the teeth. Then fucking Reagan came along and the place got worse. You know, they say there's more syphilis now than there was fifty years ago. Most of these kids ain't even been immunized against measles. If ya have a house in the inner city, might as well abandon it and let it rot. It ain't worth shit." He shook his head and slapped the steering wheel.

"When you got that kind of poverty, a man can make a

lot of money from it if he puts his mind to it. Lot of people fighting for a slice of the projects, fighting for a slice of other things too: land, property, booze, gambling."

"Like who?"

"Like Joe Bonanno. His crew's been running things down here for the past decade or so, controlling the supply of crack, smack, whatever. They been trying to expand into other areas too. There's talk that they want to open a big leisure center between Lafayette and Baton Rouge, maybe build a hotel. Maybe they just want to dump some bricks and mortar there and write it off as a tax loss, launder money through it."

He cast an appraising eye around the projects. "And this is where Joe Bones grew up." He said this with a sigh, as if he could not understand how a man would set out to undermine the place in which he had grown and matured. He started the car again, and as he drove, he told me about Joe Bones.

Salvatore Bonanno, Joe's father, had owned a bar in the Irish Channel, standing up against the local gangs who didn't believe that an Italian had any place in an area where people named their children after Irish saints and an "oul sod" mentality still prevailed. There was nothing particularly honorable about Sal's stance; it was simply born out of pragmatism. There was a lot of money to be made in Chep Morrison's postwar New Orleans, if a man was prepared to take the knocks and grease the right palms.

Sal's bar was to be the first in a string of bars and clubs that he acquired. He had loans to pay off, and the income from a single bar in the Irish Channel wasn't going to satisfy his creditors. He saved and bought a second bar, this time in Chartres, and from there his little empire grew. In some cases, only a simple financial transaction was required to obtain the premises he wanted. In others, some more forceful encouragement had to be used. When that didn't work, the Atchafalaya Basin had enough water to hide a multitude of sins. Gradually, he built up his own crew to take care of business, to make sure the city authorities, the police, the mayor's office were all kept happy, and to deal with the consequences when those lower down the food chain tried to better themselves at Sal's expense.

Sal Bonanno married Maria Cuffaro, a native of Gretna, east of New Orleans, whose brother was one of Sal's right-hand men. She bore him one daughter, who died of TB at the age of seven, and a son, who died in Vietnam. She died herself in '58, of breast cancer.

But Sal's real weakness was a woman named Rochelle Hines. Rochelle was what they called a high yellow woman, a Negress whose skin was almost white following generations of interbreeding. She had, as Morphy put it, a complexion like butter oil, although her birth certificate bore the words "black, illegitimate." She was tall, with long dark hair framing almond eyes and lips that were soft and wide and welcoming. She had a figure that would stop a clock and there were rumors that she might once have been a prostitute, although, if that was the case, Sal Bonanno quickly put an end to those activities.

Bonanno bought her a place in the Garden District and began introducing her as his wife after Maria died. It probably wasn't a wise thing to do. In the Louisiana of the late 1950s, racial segregation was a day-to-day reality. Even Louis Armstrong, who grew up in the city, could not perform with white musicians in New Orleans because the state of Louisiana prohibited racially integrated bands from playing in the city.

And so, while white men could keep black mistresses and consort with black prostitutes, a man who introduced a black woman, no matter how pale her skin, as his wife was just asking for trouble. When she gave birth to a son, Sal insisted that he bear his name and he took the child and his mother to band recitals in Jackson Square, pushing the huge white baby carriage across the grass and gurgling at his son.

Maybe Sal thought that his money would protect him; maybe he just didn't care. He made sure that Rochelle was always protected, that she didn't walk out alone, so that no one could come at her. But in the end, they didn't come at Rochelle.

One hot July night in 1964, when his son was five years old, Sal Bonanno disappeared. He was found three days later, tied to a tree by the shore of Lake Cataouatche, his head almost severed from his body. It seems likely that someone decided to use his relationship with Rochelle Hines as an excuse to move in on his operation. Ownership of his clubs and bars was transferred to a business consortium with interests in Reno and Vegas.

As soon as her "husband" was found, Rochelle Hines vanished with her son and a small quantity of jewelry and cash before anyone could come after them. She resurfaced one year later in the area that would come to be called Desire, where a half sister rented a property. The death of Sal had destroyed her: she was an alcoholic and had become addicted to morphine.

It was here, among the rising projects, that Joe Bones grew up, paler yet than his mother, and made his stand against both blacks and whites since neither group would accept him as its own. There was a rage inside Joe Bones and he turned it on the world around him. By 1990, ten years after his mother's death in a filthy cot in the projects, Joe Bones owned more bars than his father had thirty years before, and each month, planeloads of cocaine flew in from Mexico, bound for the streets of New Orleans and points north, east, and west.

"Now Joe Bones calls himself a white man, and don't nobody differ with him," said Morphy. "Anyway, how's a man gonna talk with his balls in his mouth? Joe got no time for the brothers now." He laughed quietly. "Ain't nothin' worse than a man who can't get on with his in-laws."

We stopped at a gas station and Morphy filled the tank, then came back with two sodas. We sipped them by the pumps, watching the cars go by.

"Now there's another crew, the Fontenots, and they got their eyes on the projects too. Two brothers, David and Lionel. Family was out of Lafayette originally, I think—still got ties there—but came to New Orleans in the twenties. The Fontenots are ambitious, violent, and they think maybe Bonanno's time has come. All of this has been coming to a head for about a year now, and maybe the Fontenots have a piece of work planned for Joe Bones."

The Fontenots were not young men—they were both in their forties—but they had gradually established themselves in Louisiana and now operated out of a compound in Delacroix guarded by wire and dogs and armed men, including a hardcore of Cajuns from back in Acadiana. They were into gambling, prostitution, some drugs. They owned bars in Baton Rouge, one or two others in Lafayette. If they could take out Joe Bones, it was likely that they would muscle in on the drugs market in a big way.

"You know anything about the Cajuns?" asked Morphy.

"No, not beyond their music."

"They're a persecuted minority in this state and in Texas. During the oil boom, they couldn't get any work because the Texans refused to employ coon asses. Most of them did what we all do when times are tough: they knuckled down and made the best of things. There were clashes with the blacks, because the blacks and the Cajuns were competing for the same few jobs, and some bad things went down, but most people just did what they could to keep body and soul together without breaking too many laws.

"Roland Fontenot—that's the grandfather—he left all that behind when he came to New Orleans, following some other obscure branch of the family. But the boys, they never forgot their roots. When things were bad in the seventies, they gathered a pretty disaffected bunch around them—a lot of young Cajuns, some blacks—and somehow kept the mixture from blowing up in their faces." Morphy drummed his fingers on the dashboard. "Sometimes I think maybe we're all responsible for the Fontenots. They're a visitation on us, because of the way their people were treated. I think maybe Joe Bones is a visitation too, a reminder of what happens when you grind a section of the population into the dirt."

Joe Bones had a vicious streak, said Morphy. He once killed a man by slowly burning him with acid over the space of an afternoon and was thought by some to be missing part of his brain, the part that controlled unreasonable actions in most men. The Fontenots were different. They killed, but they killed like businessmen closing down an unprofitable or unsatisfactory operation. They killed joylessly, but professionally. In Morphy's view, the Fontenots and Joe Bones were all bad. They just had different ways of expressing it.

I finished my soda and trashed the can. Morphy wasn't the type to spin a yarn for its own sake. All of this was leading up to something.

"What's the point, Morphy?" I asked.

"The point is, the fingerprint that was found at *Tante* Marie's belongs to Tony Remarr. He's one of Joe Bones's men." I thought about that as he started the car and pulled into the street, trying to match the name to any incident that might have occurred back in New York, anything that might connect me to Remarr. I found nothing.

"You think he did it?" Morphy asked.

"Do you?"

"No, no way. At first I thought, yeah, maybe. You know, the old woman, she owned that land. Wouldn't have taken much drainage work to make something of it."

"If a man was considering opening a big hotel and building a leisure center."

"Exactly, or if he wanted to convince someone he was serious enough about it to dump some bricks there. I mean, swamp's swamp. Assuming he could get permission to build, who wants to share the warm evening air with critters even God regrets making?

"Anyway, the old woman wouldn't sell. She was shrewd. Her people have been buried out there for generations. The original landowner, an old Southern type who traced his ancestry back to the Bourbons, died in sixty-nine. He stipulated in his will that the land should be offered for sale at a reasonable rate to the existing tenants.

"Now most of the tenants were Aguillards and they bought that land with all the money they had. The old woman, she made all the decisions for them. Their ancestors are there and they have a history with that land going back to the time when they wore chains around their ankles and dug channels through the dirt with their bare hands."

"So Bonanno had been putting pressure on her to sell up, but she wouldn't, so he decided to take things a step further," I said.

Morphy nodded. "I figure maybe Remarr was sent out to put more than pressure on her—maybe he's going to threaten the girl or some of the children, maybe even kill one of them—but when he arrives she's already dead. And maybe Remarr gets careless from the shock, thinks he hasn't left any traces, and heads off into the night."

"Does Woolrich know all this?"

"Most of it, yeah."

"You bringing Bonanno in?"

"Brought him in last night and let him go an hour later, accompanied by a fancy lawyer called Rufus Thibodeaux. He ain't movin', says he ain't seen Remarr for three or four days. Says he wants to find Remarr as much as anyone, something about money from some deal out in West Baton Rouge. It's bullshit, but he's sticking with the story. I think Woolrich is going to try to put some pressure on his operations through Anti-Racketeering and Narcotics, put the squeeze on him to see if he can change his mind."

"That could take time."

"You got a better idea?"

I shrugged. "Maybe."

Morphy's eyes narrowed. "You don't be fuckin' with Joe Bones, now, y'hear? Joe ain't like your boys back in New York, sittin' in social clubs in Little Italy with their fingers curled around the handles of espresso cups, dreaming about the days when everyone respected them. Joe don't got no time for that. Joe don't want folks to respect him; Joe wants folks to be scared to death of him."

We turned onto Esplanade. Morphy signaled and pulled in about two blocks from the Flaisance. He stared out the window, tapping the index finger of his right hand against the steering wheel to some internal rhythm in his head. I sensed he had something more to say. I decided to let him say it in his own time.

"You've spoken to this guy, the guy who took your wife and kid, right?"

I nodded.

"It's the same guy? The same guy who did Tee Jean and the old woman?"

"He called me yesterday. It's him."

"He say anything?"

"The feds have it on tape. He says he's going to do more."

Morphy rubbed the back of his neck with his hand and squeezed his eyes shut tightly. I knew he was seeing *Tante* Marie in his head again.

"You going to stay here?"

"For a while, yes."

"Could be the feds ain't gonna like it."

I smiled. "I know."

Morphy smiled back. He reached beneath his seat and handed me a long brown envelope. "I'll be in touch," he said. I slipped the envelope under my jacket and stepped from the car. He gave a small wave as he drove away through the midday crowd.

I opened the envelope in my hotel room. Inside were a set of crime scene pictures and photocopied extracts of the police reports, all stapled together. Stapled separately was a copy of the coroner's report. One section had been emphasized with a luminous yellow felt tip.

The coroner had found traces of ketamine hydrochloride in the bodies of *Tante* Marie and Tee Jean, equivalent to a dosage of one milligram per two pounds of weight. According to the report, ketamine was an unusual drug, a special type of anesthetic used for some minor surgical procedures. No one was too clear on its precise mode of action apart from the fact that it was a PCP analogue and worked on sites in the brain, affecting the central nervous system.

It was becoming the drug of choice in the clubs of New York and L.A. while I was still on the force, usually in capsules or tabs made by heating the liquid anesthetic to evaporate the water, leaving ketamine crystals. Users described a ketamine trip as "swimming in the K pool" since it distorted the perception of the body, creating a feeling that the user was floating in a soft yet supportive medium. Other side effects included hallucinations, distortions in the perception of space and time, and out-of-body experiences.

What the coroner did note was that ketamine could be used as a chemical restrainer on animals, since it induced paralysis and dulled pain while allowing the normal pharyngeal-laryngeal reflexes to continue. It was for this purpose, he surmised, that the killer had injected both *Tante* Marie and Tee Jean Aguillard with the drug.

When they were flayed and anatomized, the report concluded, *Tante* Marie and her son had been fully conscious.

34

WHEN I HAD FINISHED reading the coroner's report, I put on my sweats and running shoes and did about four miles on Riverfront Park, back and forth past the crowds lining up to take a trip on the Natchez paddle steamer, the sound of its wheezing calliope sending tunes like messengers across the Mississippi. I was thick with sweat when I was done, and my knees ached. Even three years ago, four miles wouldn't have troubled me to such a degree. I was getting old. Soon, I'd be looking at wheelchairs and feeling impending rain in my joints.

Back at the Flaisance, Rachel Wolfe had left a message to say that she would be flying in later that evening. The flight number and the arrival time were listed at the bottom of the message slip. I thought about Joe Bones and decided then that Rachel Wolfe might like some company on the flight down to New Orleans.

I called Angel and Louis.

The Aguillard family collected the bodies of *Tante* Marie, Tee Jean, and Florence later that day. A firm of Lafayette undertakers placed *Tante* Marie's coffin into a wide-back hearse. Tee Jean and Florence lay side by side in a second.

The Aguillards, led by the eldest son, Raymond, and accompanied by a small group of family friends, followed the hearses in a trio of pickup trucks, dark-skinned men and women seated on pieces of sackcloth amid machine parts and farm tools. I stayed behind them as they slipped from the highway and made their way down the rutted track, past *Tante* Marie's, where the police tape fluttered lightly in the breeze, and on to the house of Raymond Aguillard.

He was a tall, large-boned man in his late forties or early fifties, running to fat now but still an imposing figure. He wore a dark cotton suit, a white shirt, and a slim black tie. His eyes were red rimmed from crying. I had seen him briefly at *Tante* Marie's the night the bodies were found, a strong man trying to hold his family together in the face of violent loss.

He spotted me as the coffins were unloaded and carried toward the house, a small group of men struggling with *Tante* Marie. I stood out, since I was the only white face in the crowd. A woman, probably one of *Tante* Marie's daughters, shot me a cold look as she passed by, a pair of older women at each shoulder. When the bodies had been carried into the house, a raised, slatted-wood building not unlike the home of *Tante* Marie herself, Raymond kissed a small cross around his neck and walked slowly toward me.

"I know who you are," he said, as I extended my hand. He paused for a moment before taking it in a short, firm grip.

"I'm sorry," I said, "sorry about it all."

He nodded. "I know that." He walked on, past the white fence at the boundary of the house, and stood by the side of the road, staring out at the empty stretch of track. A pair of mallards flew overhead, their wing beats slowing as they approached the water below. Raymond watched them with a kind of envy, the envy that a man deeply grieving feels for anything untouched by his sorrow.

"Some of my sisters, they think maybe you brought this man with you. They think you got no right to be here."

"Is that what you think?"

He didn't answer. Then: "She felt him comin'. Maybe that's why she sent Florence to the party, to get her away from him. And that's why she sent for you: she felt him comin' and I think she knowed who he was. Deep down, I think she knowed." His voice sounded thick in his throat.

He fingered the cross gently, rubbing his thumb back and forth along its length. I could see that it had originally been ornately carved—it was still possible to discern some details of spirals at its edges—but for the most part it had been rubbed smooth by the action of this man's hand over many years.

"I don't blame you for what happened to my momma and my brother and sister. My momma, she always done what she believed was right. She wanted to find that girl and to stop the man that killed her. And that Tee Jean . . ." He smiled sadly. "The policeman said that he'd been hit three, maybe four times from behind, and there were still bruises on his knuckles where he tried to fight this man."

Raymond coughed and then breathed deeply through his mouth, his head tipped back slightly like a man who has run a great distance in pain.

"He took your woman, your child?" he said. It was as much a statement as a question, but I answered it anyway.

"Yes, he took them. Like you said, *Tante* Marie believed that he took another girl too."

He dug the thumb and forefinger of his right hand into the corners of his eyes and blinked out a tear.

"I know. I seen her."

The world around me seemed to grow silent as I shut out the noise of the birds, the wind in the trees, the distant sound of water splashing on the banks. All I wanted to hear was Raymond Aguillard's voice.

"You saw the girl?"

"That's what I said. Down by a slough in Honey Island, three nights ago. Night before my momma died. Seen her other times too. My sister's husband, he got hisself some traps down there." He shrugged. Honey Island was a nature reserve. "You a superstitious man, Mista Parker?"

"I'm getting there," I replied. "You think that's where she is, down in Honey Island?"

"Could be. My momma'd say she didn't know where she was, just *that* she was. She knew the girl was out there somewhere. I just don't know how, Mista Parker. I never did understand my momma's gift. But then I seen her, a figure out by a cypress grove and a kinda darkness over her face, like a hand was coverin' it, and I knowed it was her."

He looked down and, with the toe of his shoe, began picking at a stone embedded in the dirt. When he eventually freed it, sending it skidding into the grass, tiny black ants scurried and crawled from the hole, the entrance to their nest now fully exposed.

"Other people seen her too, I hear, folks out fishin' or checking the hooch they got distillin' in a shack somewheres." He watched as the ants swarmed around his foot, some of them climbing onto the rim of his sole. Gently, he lifted his foot, shook it, and moved it away.

There were seventy thousand acres of Honey Island, Raymond explained. It was the second-biggest swamp in Louisiana, forty miles long and eight miles wide. It was part of the floodplain of the Pearl River, which acts as a boundary line between Louisiana and Mississippi. Honey Island was better preserved than the Florida Everglades: there was no dredging allowed, no draining or timber farming, no development and no dams, and parts of Honey Island weren't even navigable. Half of it was state owned; some was the responsibility of the Nature Conservancy. If someone was trying to dump a body in a place where it was unlikely to be discovered, then, tourist boats apart, Honey Island sounded like a good place to do it.

Raymond gave me directions to the slough and drew a rough map on the back of an opened-out Marlboro pack.

"Mista Parker, I know you're a good man and that you're sorry for what happened, but I'd be grateful to you if you didn't come out here no more." He spoke softly, but there was no mistaking the force in his voice. "And maybe you'd be kind enough not to turn up at the burial. My family, it's gonna take us a long time to get over this."

Then he lit the last cigarette from the pack, nodded a good-bye, and walked back to his house trailing smoke behind him.

I watched him as he walked away. A woman with steel-gray hair came out to the porch and placed her arm around his waist when he reached her. He put a big arm around her shoulders and held her to him as they walked into the house, the screen door closing gently behind them. And I thought of Honey Island and the secrets that it held beneath its green waters as I drove away from the Aguillard house, the dust rising behind me.

As I drove, the swamp was already preparing to reveal its secrets. Honey Island would yield a body within twenty-four hours, but it would not be the body of a girl.

35

□

I ARRIVED EARLY at Moisant Field so I browsed around the bookstore for a while, taking care to avoid tripping over the piles of Anne Rice novels. I had been sitting in the arrivals terminal for about an hour when Rachel Wolfe walked through the gates. She was wearing dark blue jeans, white sneakers, and a red-and-white Polo Sport top. Her red hair hung loose on her shoulders and her makeup had been so carefully applied that it was almost indiscernable.

The only luggage she carried herself was a brown leather shoulder bag. The rest of what I took to be her belongings was being toted by Angel and Louis, who walked slightly self-consciously at either side of her, Louis in a cream double-breasted suit with a snow white dress shirt open at the neck, Angel in jeans, battered Reebok high-tops, and a green check shirt that had not felt an iron since it left the factory many years before.

"Well, well," I said, as they stood before me. "All human life is here."

Angel raised his right hand, from which dangled three thick piles of books, tied together by string. The ends of his fingers were turning purple. "We brought half the New York Public Library with us as well," he groaned. "Tied with string. I ain't seen books tied with string since *Little House on the Prairie* stopped reruns."

Louis, I noticed, was carrying a lady's pink umbrella and a cosmetics case. He had the look of a man who is trying to pretend that a dog isn't screwing his leg. "Don't say a word, man," he warned. "Not a word."

Between them, the two men also carried two suitcases, two leather traveling bags, and a suit carrier. "Car's parked outside," I said as I walked with Rachel to the exit. "Might be just enough room for the bags."

"They paged me at the airport," whispered Rachel. "They were very helpful." She giggled and glanced over her shoulder. Behind us, I heard the unmistakable sound of Angel tripping on a bag and swearing loudly.

We ditched the luggage at the Flaisance, despite Louis's stated preference for the Fairmont at University Place. The Fairmont was where the Republicans usually stayed when they hit New Orleans, which was part of its appeal for Louis. He was the only gay, black, Republican criminal I knew.

"Gerald Ford stayed at the Fairmont," he lamented as he surveyed the small suite he was to share with Angel.

"So?" I countered. "Paul McCartney stayed at the Richelieu and you don't hear me demanding to stay there." I left the door open and headed back to my own room for a shower.

"Paul *who?*" said Louis.

We ate in the Grill Room of the Windsor Court on Gravier Street, in deference to Louis's wishes, its marbled floors and heavy Austrian drapes strangely uncomfortable for me after the informal setting of the smaller eateries in the Quarter. Rachel had changed into dark pants and a black jacket over a red top. It looked fine but the hot night air had taken its toll on her and she was still pulling the damp cloth of her top away from her body as we waited for the main courses.

As we ate, I explained to them about Joe Bones and the Fontenots. They would be a matter for Angel, Louis, and me. Rachel remained silent for much of our conversation, interjecting occasionally to clarify things that had been said by Woolrich or Morphy. She scribbled notes in a small, wirebound notebook, her handwriting neat and even. At one point her hand brushed my bare arm lightly and she left it there for an instant, her skin warm against mine.

I watched Angel pulling at his lip as he considered what I had said. "This Remarr must be pretty dumb, dumber than our guy at least," he said eventually.

"Because of the print?" I said.

He nodded. "Careless, very careless." He wore the dissatisfied look of a respected theologian who has seen someone bring his calling into disrepute by identifying Jesus as an alien.

Rachel spotted the look. "It seems to bother you a lot," she commented. I glanced at her. She had an amused expression on her face, but her eyes were calculating and slightly distant. She was playing over in her mind what I had told her, even as she engaged Angel in a conversation that he would usually have avoided. I waited to see how he would respond.

He smiled at her and tilted his head. "I have a certain professional interest in these things," he admitted. He cleared a space in front of him and held up his hands before us.

"Anyone doing a B&E job—that's breaking and entering, for the benefit of our more respectable listener—needs to take certain precautions," began Angel. "The first and most obvious is to make sure that he—or she, B&E being an equal opportunity profession—doesn't leave any fingerprints. So what do you do?"

"You wear gloves," said Rachel. She leaned forward now, enjoying the lesson and putting aside any other thoughts.

"Right. Nobody, no matter how dumb, enters a place he shouldn't be without wearing gloves. Otherwise, you leave visuals, you leave latents, you pretty much sign your name and confess to the crime."

Visuals are the visible marks left on surfaces by a dirty or bloody hand, latents the invisible marks left by natural secretions of the skin. Visuals can be photographed or lifted using adhesive tape, but latents need to be dusted, typically with a chemical reagent like iodine vapor or ninhydrin solution. Electrostatic and fluorescence techniques are also useful, and in the search for latents on human skin, specialized X-ray photography can be used.

But if what Angel had said was correct, Remarr was too much of a professional to risk a job without gloves and then to leave not merely a latent, but a visual. He must have been wearing gloves, but something had gone wrong.

"You working it through in your head, Bird?" smirked Angel.

"Go on, Sherlock, baffle us with your brilliance," I responded.

His smirk widened to a grin, and he continued. "It's possible to get a fingerprint from *inside* a glove, assuming you have the glove. Rubber or plastic gloves are best for obtaining prints: your hands get sweaty under them.

"But what most people don't know is that the exterior surface of a glove can act like a fingerprint as well. Say it's a leather glove, then you got wrinkles, you got holes, you got scars, you got tears, and no two leather gloves are gonna be the same. Now, in the case of this guy Remarr, what we have is a print and no gloves. Unless Remarr can't tie his shoelaces without falling over, we know that he was probably wearing gloves, but he still manages to leave a print. It's a mystery." He made a small, exploding gesture with his hands, like a magician making a rabbit disappear in a puff of smoke, then his face became serious.

"My guess is that Remarr was wearing only a single pair of gloves, probably latex. He imagined this was going to be an easy job: either he was gonna off the old lady and her son, or he was gonna put the frighteners on her, maybe leave a calling card in the house. Since the son, from what I hear, wasn't the kind of guy to let anyone frighten his momma, I'd say Remarr went in there thinking that he might have to kill someone.

"But when he arrives, they're either dead or they're in the process of being killed. Again, my guess is they were already dead: if Remarr stumbled in on the killer, Remarr would be dead as well.

"So Remarr is going in, his one pair of gloves on, and maybe he spots the kid and it throws him. He probably starts to sweat. He goes into the house and finds the old lady. Bam! Second shock, but he goes to take a closer look, steadying himself as he leans over her. He touches blood and maybe considers wiping it away, but he figures wiping it away will only attract more attention to it and, anyway, he's got his gloves.

"But the problem with latex gloves is that one pair isn't enough. You wear them for too long and your prints start coming through. You get thrown, you start to sweat, the prints are gonna come through faster. Could be Remarr has been eating before he came out, maybe some fruit or some kind of pasta with vinegar. That causes extra moisture on the skin, so now Remarr is in real trouble. He's left a print he doesn't even know about, and now the cops, the feds, and difficult people like our good selves want to ask him about it. Ta-da!" He gave a small bow from the waist. Rachel gave him a round of applause. Louis just raised an eyebrow in resignation.

"Fascinating," said Rachel. "You must read a lot of books." Her tone was heavily ironic.

"He does, then Barnes and Noble gonna be grateful that their stolen stock being put to good use," remarked Louis.

Angel ignored him. "Maybe I dabbled in these things, in my younger days."

"Did you learn anything else, in your 'younger' days?" Rachel smiled.

"Lot of things, some of them hard lessons," said Angel with feeling. "Best thing I ever learned: don't hold on to nothin'. If you don't have it, can't nobody prove you took it.

"And I *have* been tempted. There was this figure of a knight on a horse once. French, seventeenth century. Gold inlaid with diamonds and rubies. About this tall." He held the palm of his hand flat about six inches above the table. "It was the most beautiful thing I ever saw." His eyes lit up at the memory. He looked like a child.

He sat back in his chair. "But I let it go. In the end, you have to let things go. The things you regret are the things you hold on to."

"So is nothing worth holding on to?" asked Rachel.

Angel looked at Louis for a while. "Some things are, yeah, but they ain't made of gold."

"That's so romantic," I said. Louis made choking noises as he tried to swallow his water.

Before us, the remains of our coffee lay cold in the cups. "Do you have anything to add?" I asked Rachel when Angel had finished playing to the gallery.

She glanced back through her notes. Her brow furrowed slightly. She held a glass of red wine in one hand and the light caught it, reflecting a streak of red across her breast like a wound.

"You said you had pictures, crime scene pictures?" she asked.

I nodded.

"Then I'd like to hold off until I've had a chance to see them. I have an idea based on what you told me over the phone, but I'd prefer to keep it to myself until I've seen the pictures and done a little more research. I do have one thing, though." She took a second notebook from her bag and flicked through the pages to where a yellow Post-it note stuck out. " 'I lusted for her, but that has always been a weakness of my kind,' " she read. " 'Our sin was not pride, but lust for humanity.' "

She turned to me, but I already recognized the words. "They were the words this Traveling Man said to you when he called," she said. I was aware of Angel and Louis moving forward in their chairs.

"It took a theologian in the archbishop's residence to track down the reference. It's pretty obscure, at least if you're not a theologian." She paused, then asked, "Why was the devil banished from heaven?"

"Pride," said Angel. "I remember Sister Agnes telling us that."

"It was pride," said Louis. He glanced at Angel. "I remember *Milton* telling us that."

"*Anyway*," said Rachel pointedly, "you're right, or partially right. From Augustine onward, the devil's sin is pride. But before Augustine, there was a different viewpoint. Up until the fourth century, the Book of Enoch was considered to be part of the biblical canon. Its origins are a matter of dispute—it may have been written in Hebrew or Aramaic, or a combination of both—but it does seem to have provided a basis for some concepts that are still found in the Bible today. The Last Judgment may have been based on the Similitudes of Enoch. The fiery hell ruled by Satan also appears for the first time in Enoch.

"What is interesting for us is that Enoch takes a different view of the devil's sin." She turned a page of her notebook and began to read again.

" 'And it came to pass, when men began to multiply on the face of the earth, and daughters were born unto them, that the sons of God saw the daughters of men that they were fair; and they took them wives of all which they chose . . .' "

She looked up again. "Now that's from Genesis, which derives from a similar source as Enoch. The 'sons of God' were the angels, who gave in to sexual lust against the will of God. The leader of the sinning angels, the devil, was cast into a dark hole in the desert and his accomplices were thrown into the fire for their punishment. Their offspring, 'evil spirits upon the earth,' went with them. The martyr Justin believed that the children of the union between angels and human women were responsible for all evil on the earth, including murder.

"In other words, lust was the sin of the devil. Lust for humanity, the 'weakness of our kind.' " She closed the notebook and permitted herself a small smile of triumph.

"So this guy believes he's a demon," said Angel eventually.

"Or the offspring of an angel," added Louis. "Depends on how you look at it."

"Whatever he is, or thinks he is, the Book of Enoch is hardly likely to turn up on Oprah's book choice," I said. "Any idea what his source might have been?"

Rachel reopened the notebook. "The most recent reference I could find is a nineteen eighty-three New York edition: *The Old Testament Pseudepigrapha: Enoch,* edited by a guy called Isaac, appropriately enough," she said. "There's also an older translation from Oxford, published in nineteen thirteen by R. H. Charles."

I noted the names. "Maybe Morphy or Woolrich can check with the University of New Orleans, see if anyone local has been expressing an interest in the obscure end of biblical studies. Woolrich might be able to extend the search to the other universities. It's a start."

We paid the bill and left. Angel and Louis headed off toward the lower Quarter to check out the gay night life while Rachel and I walked back to the Flaisance. We didn't speak for a time, both of us conscious that we were on the verge of some intimacy.

"I get the feeling that I shouldn't ask what those two currently do for a living," said Rachel, as we paused at a crossing.

"Probably not. It's best to view them as independent operators and leave it at that."

She smiled. "They seem to have a certain loyalty to you. It's unusual. I'm not sure that I understand it."

"I've done things for them in the past, but if there ever was a debt, it was paid a long time ago. I owe them a lot."

"But they're still here. They still help when they're asked."

"I don't think that's entirely because of me. They do what they do because they like it. It appeals to their sense of adventure, of danger. In their own separate ways, they're both dangerous men. I think that's why they came: they sensed danger and they wanted to be part of it."

"Maybe they see something of that in you."

"I don't know. Maybe they do."

We walked through the courtyard of the Flaisance, stopping only to pat the dogs. Her room was three doors down from mine. Between our rooms were the room shared by Angel and Louis and one unoccupied single room. She opened the door and stood at the threshold. From inside, I could feel the coolness of the air-conditioning and could hear it pumping at full power.

"I'm still not sure why you're here," I said. My throat felt dry and part of me was not certain that it wanted to hear an answer.

"I'm still not sure either," she said. She stood on her toes and kissed me gently, softly on the lips, and then she was gone.

I went to my room, took a book of Sir Walter Ralegh's writings from my bag, and headed back out to the Napoleon House, where I took a seat by the portrait of the Little Corporal. I didn't want to lie on my bed, conscious of the presence of Rachel Wolfe so near to me. I was excited and troubled by her kiss, and by the thought of what might follow.

Almost until the very end, Susan and I had enjoyed an incredible intimacy together. When my drinking truly began to take its toll on us, that intimacy had disintegrated. When we made love it was no longer totally giving. Instead, we seemed to circle each other warily in our lovemaking, always holding something back, always expecting trouble to rear its head and cause us to spring back into the security of our own selves.

But I had loved her. I had loved her until the end and I still loved her now. When the Traveling Man had taken her he had severed the physical and emotional ties between us, but I could still feel the remains of those ties, raw and pulsing at the very extremity of my senses.

Maybe this is common to all those who lose someone whom they have loved deeply. Making contact with another potential partner, another lover, becomes an act of reconstruction, a building not only of a relationship but also of oneself.

But I felt myself haunted by my wife and child. I felt them, not only as an emptiness or a loss, but as an actual presence in my life. I seemed to catch glimpses of them at the edges of my existence, as I drifted from consciousness to sleep, from sleep to waking. Sometimes, I tried to convince myself that they were simply phantoms of my guilt, creations born of some psychological imbalance.

Yet I had heard Susan speak through *Tante* Marie, and once, like a memory from a delirium, I had awakened in the darkness to feel her hand on my face and I had caught a trace of her scent beside me in the bed. More than that, I saw traces of Susan and Jennifer in every young wife, in each female child. In a young woman's laughter, I heard the voice of my wife. In the footsteps of a little girl, I heard the echo of my daughter's shoes.

I felt something for Rachel Wolfe, a mixture of attraction and gratitude and desire. I wanted to be with her but only, I thought, when my wife and child were at peace.

36

DAVID FONTENOT died that night. His car, a vintage Jensen Interceptor, was found on 190, the road that skirts Honey Island and leads down to the shores of the Pearl. The front tires of the car were flat and the doors were hanging open. The windshield had been shattered and the interior was peppered with 9 millimeter holes.

The two St. Tammany cops followed a trail of broken branches and flattened scrub to an old trapper's shack made of bits of salvaged wood, its tin roof almost obscured by overhanging Spanish moss. It overlooked a bayou lined with gum trees, its waters thick with lime green duckweed and ringing with the sound of mallards and wood ducks.

The shack had been abandoned for a long time. Few people now trapped in Honey Island. Most had moved farther out into the bayous, hunting beaver, deer, and in some cases, alligators.

There were noises coming from the shack as the party approached, sounds of scuffling and thudding and heavy snorting drifting through the open door.

"Hog," said one of the deputies.

Beside him, the local bank official who had called them in flicked the safety on his Ruger rifle.

"Shit, that won't do no good against no hog," said the second deputy. The local, a thick-set, balding man in a Tulane Green Wave T-shirt and an almost unused hunting jacket, reddened. He was carrying a 77V with a telescopic sight, what they used to call in Maine a "varmint rifle." It was good for small game and some police forces even used it as a sniper rifle, but it wouldn't stop a feral hog first time unless the shot was perfect.

They were only a few feet away from the shack when the hog sensed them. It erupted from the open door, its tiny, vicious eyes wild and blood dripping from its snout. The man with the Ruger dived into the bayou waters to avoid it as it came at him. The hog spun, cornered at the water's edge by the party of armed men, then lowered its head and charged again.

There was an explosion in the bayou, then a second, and the hog went down. Most of the top of its head was gone and it twitched briefly on the ground, pawing at the dirt, until eventually it ceased to move. The deputy blew smoke theatrically from the long barrel of a Colt Anaconda, ejected the spent .44 Magnum cartridges with the ejector rod, then reloaded.

"Jesus," said the voice of his partner. He was standing in the open doorway of the shack, his gun by his side. "Hog sure got at him, but it's Dave Fontenot all right."

The hog had ruined most of Fontenot's face and part of his right arm was gnawed away, but even the damage caused by the hog couldn't disguise the fact that someone had forced David Fontenot from his car, hunted him through the trees, and then cornered him in the shack, where he was shot in the groin, the knees, the elbows, and the head.

"Mon," said the hog killer, exhaling deeply. "When Lionel hears about this, there's gonna be hell to pay."

I learned most of what had taken place during a hurried telephone conversation with Morphy and a little more from WDSU, the local NBC affiliate. Afterward, Angel, Louis, and I breakfasted at Mother's on Poydras Street. Rachel had barely worked up the energy to answer the phone when we called her room, and had decided to sleep on and eat later in the morning.

Louis, dressed in an ivory-colored linen suit and a white T-shirt, shared my bacon and homemade biscuits, washed down with strong coffee. Angel opted for ham, eggs, and grits.

"Old folks eat grits, Angel," said Louis. "Old folks and the insane."

Angel wiped a white grit trail from his chin and gave Louis the finger.

"He's not so eloquent first thing in the morning," said Louis. "Rest of the day, he don't have no excuse."

Angel gave Louis the finger again, scraped the last of the grits from the bowl, and pushed it away.

"So, you figure Joe Bones took a preemptive strike against the Fontenots?" he said.

"Looks that way," I replied. "Morphy figures he used Remarr to do the job—pulled him out of hiding, then squirreled him away again. He wouldn't entrust a job like that to anyone else. But I don't understand what David Fontenot was doing out by Honey Island without any backup. He must have known that Joe Bones would take a crack at him if the opportunity arose."

"Could be one of his own people set him up, hauled him out there on some dead-end pretext, and let Joe Bones know he was coming?" said Angel.

It sounded plausible. If someone had drawn Fontenot out to Honey Island, then it must have been someone he trusted enough to make the trip. More to the point, that someone must have been offering something that Fontenot wanted, something to make him risk the drive to the reserve late at night.

I said nothing to Angel or Louis, but I was troubled that both Raymond Aguillard and David Fontenot had, in their own different ways, drawn my attention to Honey Island in a period of less than one day. I thought that, after I had spoken to Joe Bones, I might have to disturb Lionel Fontenot in his time of grief.

My cell phone rang. It was the desk clerk from the Flaisance, informing us that a delivery addressed to a Mr. Louis had arrived and a courier was waiting for us to sign. We took a taxi back to the hotel. Outside, a black transit van was parked with two wheels on the curb.

"Courier," said Louis, but there were no markings on the van, nothing to identify it as a commercial vehicle.

In the lobby, the desk clerk sat nervously watching a huge black man who was squeezed into an easy chair. He was shaven-headed and wearing a black T-shirt with *Klan Killer* written in jagged white writing across the chest. His black combat trousers were tucked into nine-hole army boots. At his feet lay a long steel container, locked and bolted.

"Brother Louis," he said, rising. Louis took out his wallet and handed over three hundred-dollar bills. The man tucked the money into the thigh pocket of his combats, removed a pair of Ray-Ban sunglasses from the same pocket, and put them on before strolling out into the sunlight.

Louis motioned to the container. "If you gentlemen would like to take that up to the room," he said. Angel and I took an end each and followed him up to the suite. The case was heavy and something inside rattled as we walked.

"Those UPS couriers are sure getting bigger," I said, as I waited for him to open the door.

"It's a specialized service," said Louis. "There are some things the airlines just wouldn't understand."

When he had closed and locked the door behind us, he took a set of keys from the pocket of his suit and opened the case. It was separated into three layers, which opened up like those in a tool kit. On the first layer were the constituent parts of a Mauser SP66, a three-round heavy-barreled sniper rifle with a combined muzzle brake and flash hider. The parts were packed in a removable case. Beside it, a SIG P226 pistol and a shoulder holster lay in a fitted compartment.

In the second compartment sat two Calico M-960A minisubs, made in the good old U.S. of A., each handheld sub fitted with a short barrel that extended less than an inch and a half beyond the fore end. With the stock retracted, each gun measured a little over two feet in length and, empty, weighed just under five pounds. They were exceptionally lethal little guns, with a rate of fire of seven hundred and fifty rounds per minute. The third compartment contained an array of ammunition, including four one-hundred-round magazines of 9 millimeter Parabellum for the subs.

"Christmas present?" I asked.

"Yup," said Louis, loading a fifteen-round magazine into the butt of the SIG. "I'm hoping to get a rail gun for my birthday."

He handed Angel the case containing the Mauser, slipped on the holster, and inserted the SIG. He then relocked the case and went into the bathroom. As we watched, he removed the paneling from beneath the sink with a screwdriver and shoved the case into the gap before replacing the panel. When he was satisfied that it was back in place, we left.

"You think Joe Bones will be pleased to see a bunch of strangers show up on his doorstep?" asked Angel, as we walked to my rental.

"We ain't strangers," said Louis. "We're just friends he ain't met yet."

Joe Bones owned three properties in Louisiana, including a weekend house at Cypremort Point, where his presence must have made the more respectable weekenders, with their expensive holiday houses bearing jokey names like Eaux-Asis and End of the Trail, distinctly uneasy.

His city residence lay across from Audubon Park, almost opposite the bus stop for the shuttle bus that took tourists to the New Orleans Zoo. I had taken a trip on the St. Charles streetcar to inspect the house, a brilliantly white confection adorned with black wrought iron balconies and a cupola topped with a gold weather vane. Finding Joe Bones inside a place like that was like finding a cockroach in a wedding cake. In the carefully maintained garden, a flower I couldn't identify bloomed lushly. Its scent was sickly and heavy, its flower so large and red that it seemed more rotten than blooming, as if the flowers themselves might suddenly burst and send thick fluid down the branches of the plant, poisoning the aphids.

Joe Bones had deserted the house for the summer in favor of a restored plantation house out in West Feliciana Parish, over one hundred miles north of New Orleans. As impending hostilities with the Fontenots grew more and more likely, the decision to remain in West Feliciana allowed him to defend the country house with more force than he could in the city.

It was a white, eight-columned mansion set on about forty acres, bordered at two sides by an expanse of river flowing south toward the Mississippi. Four large windows looked out on a wide gallery, and the house was topped by two dormer windows set into its roof. An avenue of oaks led from a black iron gate through grounds set with camellias and azaleas until the trees stopped before a wide expanse of lawn. On the lawn, a small group of people stood around a barbecue or lounged on iron lawn furniture.

I spotted three security cameras within ten feet of the gate when we drew up, side-on. We had dropped Angel about half a mile back after cruising by the house once, and I knew he was already making for the stand of cypress that stood opposite the gate. In the event of anything going down with Joe Bones, I decided that I had a better chance of dealing with it with Louis rather than Angel by my side.

A fourth camera overlooked the gate itself. There was no intercom and the gate remained resolutely closed, even when Louis and I leaned against the car and waved.

After two or three minutes a converted golf cart came from behind the house and hummed down the oak-lined avenue toward us. Three men in chinos and sports shirts stepped from it. They made no attempt to hide their Steyr machine pistols.

"Hi," I said. "We're here to see Joe Bones."

"There ain't no Joe Bones here," said one of the men. He was tanned and short, no more than five-six. His hair was braided tightly against his scalp, giving him a reptilian appearance.

"How about Mr. Joseph Bonanno, is he there?"

"What are you, cops?"

"We're concerned citizens. We were hoping Mr. Bones would make a donation to the David Fontenot funeral fund."

"He already gave," said the guy by the golf cart, a fatter

version of the Lizard Man. His colleagues at the gate laughed fit to burst a gut.

I moved closer to the gate. Lizard Man's gun came up quickly.

"Tell Joe Bones that Charlie Parker is here, that I was in the Aguillard house on Sunday night, and that I'm looking for Remarr. You think funny man back there can remember all that?"

He stepped back from the gate and, without taking his eyes off us, relayed what I had said to the guy by the golf cart. He took a walkie-talkie from the rear seat, spoke into it for a moment, and then nodded at Lizard Man. "He says let 'em through, Ricky."

"Okay," said Ricky, taking a remote signaler from his pocket, "step back from the gate, turn around, and put your hands against the car. You packing, then tell me now. I find anything you haven't told me about, I put a bullet in your head and feed you to the 'gators."

We owned up to a Smith & Wesson and a SIG between us. Louis threw in an ankle knife for good measure. We left the car at the gate and walked behind the golf cart toward the house. One man sat in the back with his pistol pointing at us while Ricky walked behind us.

As we neared the lawn I could smell shrimp and chicken cooking on the barbecue. An iron table held an assortment of spirits and glasses. Abita and Heineken lay in a steel cooler packed with ice.

From the side of the house came a low growl, deep with viciousness and menace. At the end of a strong chain, which was anchored to a bolt set in concrete, was a huge animal. It had the thick coat of a wolf, flecked with the coloring of an Alsatian. Its eyes were bright and intelligent, which rendered its obvious savagery all the more threatening. It looked like it weighed at least one hundred and eighty pounds. Each time it tugged at its chain, it threatened to wrench the bolt from the ground.

I noticed that it seemed to be directing most of its attention at Louis. Its eyes focused on him intently and at one point it raised itself up on its hind legs in its efforts to strike at him. Louis looked at it with the detached interest of a scientist finding a curious new type of bacteria growing in his Petri dish.

Joe Bones speared a piece of spiced chicken with a fork and placed it on a china plate. He was only slightly taller than Ricky, with long dark hair swept back from his forehead. His nose had been broken at least once and a small scar twisted his upper lip on the left side. His white shirt was open to the waist and hung over a pair of Lycra running shorts. His stomach was hard and muscular, his chest and arms slightly overdeveloped for a man of his height. He looked mean and intelligent, like the animal on the chain, which probably explained how he had lasted for ten years at the top of the heap in New Orleans.

He placed some tomatoes, lettuce, and cold rice mixed with peppers beside the chicken and handed the plate to a woman seated nearby. She was older than Joe, I guessed, probably in her early or mid-forties. There was no darkness at her blond roots and she wore little or no makeup, although her eyes were obscured by a pair of Wayfarers. She wore a short-sleeved silk robe over a white blouse and white shorts. Like Joe Bones, she was barefoot. To one side of them stood two more men in shirts and chinos, each armed with a machine pistol. I counted two more on the balcony and one sitting beside the main door to the house.

"You want something to eat?" asked Joe Bones. His voice was low, with only a faint trace of Louisiana in it. He looked at me until I responded.

"No, thanks," I said. I noticed that he didn't offer any to Louis. I think Louis noticed too.

Joe Bones helped himself to some shrimp and salad, then motioned to the two guards to help themselves to what was left. They took turns to do so, each eating a breast of chicken with his fingers.

"Those Aguillard murders. A terrible thing," said Joe Bones. He waved me toward the only empty seat left after he sat down. I exchanged a look with Louis, shrugged, and sat.

"Excuse me for presuming on an intimacy with you," he

continued, "but I hear that the same man may have been responsible for the deaths of your family." He smiled almost sympathetically. "A terrible thing," he repeated. "A terrible thing."

I held his gaze. "You're well informed about my past."

"When someone new comes to town and starts finding bodies in trees, I like to make it my business to find out about them. They might be good company." He picked a piece of shrimp from his plate and examined it briefly before starting to eat.

"I understand you had an interest in purchasing the Aguillards' land," I said.

Joe Bones sucked at the shrimp and placed the tail carefully to one side of his plate before responding. "I have a lot of interests, and that wasn't Aguillard land. Just because some senile fuck decides to make up for a bad life by slipping land to the niggers doesn't make it nigger land." He spat the word "nigger" each time. His shell of courtesy had proved remarkably fragile and he seemed intent upon deliberately provoking Louis. It was an unwise course of action, even with guns around him.

"It seems that one of your men, Tony Remarr, may have been in the house the night that the Aguillards died. We'd be interested in talking to him."

"Tony Remarr is no longer part of my operation," said Joe Bones, returning to his formal mode of speech after the burst of profanity. "We agreed a mutual parting of the ways and I haven't seen him in weeks. I had no idea he was in the Aguillard house until the police told me."

He smiled at me. I smiled back.

"Did Remarr have anything to do with David Fontenot's death?"

Joe Bones's jaw tensed but he kept smiling. "I have no idea. I heard about David Fontenot on the news this morning."

"Another terrible thing?" I suggested.

"The loss of a young life is always terrible," he responded. "Look, I'm sorry about your wife and kid, I truly am, but I can't help you. And frankly, now you're getting rude, so I'd like you to take your nigger and get the fuck off my property."

The muscles in Louis's neck rippled, the only sign he gave that he had heard Joe Bones. Joe Bones leered at him, picked up a piece of chicken, and tossed it toward the beast on the chain. It ignored the tidbit until its owner snapped his fingers, when it fell on the chicken and devoured it in a single bite.

"You know what that is?" asked Joe Bones. He spoke to me, but his body language was directed at Louis. It expressed utter contempt. When I didn't respond, he continued.

"It's called a *boerbul*. A man named Peter Geertschen, a German, developed it for the army and antiriot squads in South Africa by crossing a Russian wolf with an Alsatian. It's a white man's watchdog. It sniffs out niggers." He turned his gaze on Louis and smiled.

"Careful," I said. "He might get confused and turn on you." Joe Bones jerked in his chair as if he had been hit by a jolt of electricity. His eyes narrowed and searched my face for any indication that I was aware of a double meaning in what I had said. I stared right back at him.

"You better leave now," said Joe Bones, with quiet, obvious menace. I shrugged and stood up, Louis moving close to me as I did so. We exchanged a look.

"Man got us on the run," said Louis.

"Maybe, but if we leave like this he won't respect us."

"Without respect, a man got nothing," agreed Louis.

He picked a plate from the stack on the table and held it above his head. It exploded in a shower of china fragments as the .300 Winchester cartridge impacted and buried itself in the wood of the house behind. The woman in the chair dived to the grass, the two goons moved to cover Joe Bones, and three men appeared running from the side of the house as the shot echoed in the air.

Ricky, the Lizard Man, was the first to reach us. He raised the pistol and his finger tightened on the trigger, but Joe Bones struck out at his gun arm, pushing it upward.

"No! You dumb fuck, you want to get me killed?" He

scanned the treeline beyond his property, then turned back to me.

"You come in here, you shoot at me, you scare my woman. The fuck do you think you're dealing with here?"

"You said the N-word," said Louis quietly.

"He's right," I agreed. "You did say it."

"I hear you got friends in New Orleans," said Joe Bones, his voice threatening. "I got enough troubles without the feds crawling on me, but I see you or your"—he paused, swallowing the word—"friend anywhere near me again and I'll take my chances. You hear?"

"I hear you," I said. "I'm going to find Remarr, Joe. If it turns out that you've been holding out on us and this man gets away because of it, I'll come back."

"You make us come back, Joe, and we gonna have to hurt your puppy," said Louis, almost sorrowfully.

"You come back and I'll stake you out on the grass and let him feed on you," snarled Joe Bones.

We backed away toward the oak-lined avenue, watching Joe Bones and his men carefully. The woman moved toward him to comfort him, her white clothes stained with grass. She kneaded gently at his trapezius with her carefully manicured hands, but he pushed her away with a hard shove to the chest. There was spittle on his chin.

Behind us, I heard the gate open as we retreated beneath the oaks. I hadn't expected much from Joe Bones, and had got less, but we had succeeded in rattling his cage. My guess was that he would contact Remarr and that might be enough to flush him from wherever he was holed up. It seemed like a good idea. The trouble with good ideas is that nine times out of ten someone has had the same idea before you.

"I didn't know Angel was such a good shot," I said to Louis as we reached the car. "You been giving him lessons?"

"Uh-huh," said Louis. He sounded genuinely shocked.

"Could he have hit Joe Bones?"

"Uh-uh. I'm surprised he didn't hit me."

Behind us, I heard the door open as Angel slid into the back seat, the Mauser already back in its case.

"So, we gonna start hangin' out with Joe Bones, maybe shoot some pool, whistle at girls?"

"When did you ever whistle at girls?" asked Louis, bemused, as we pulled away from the gate and headed toward St. Francisville.

"It's a guy thing," said Angel. "I can do guy things."

37

□

I WAS LATE afternoon when we got back to the Flaisance, where there was a message waiting from Morphy. I called him at the Sheriff's Office and got passed on to a cell phone.

"Where you been?" he asked.

"Visiting Joe Bones."

"Shit, why'd you do a thing like that?"

"Making trouble, I guess."

"I warned you, man. Don't be screwing with Joe Bones. You go alone?"

"I brought a friend. Joe didn't like him."

"What'd your friend do?"

"He got born to black parents."

Morphy laughed. "I guess Joe is kind of sensitive about his heritage, but it's good to remind him of it now and then."

"He threatened to feed my friend to his dog."

"Yeah," said Morphy, "Joe sure does love that dog."

"You got something?"

"Maybe. You like seafood?"

"No."

"Good, then we'll head out to Bucktown. Great seafood there, best shrimp around. I'll pick you up in two hours."

"Any other reason for seeing Bucktown other than seafood?"

"Remarr. One of his exes has a pad there. Might be worth a visit."

□

Bucktown was pretty in a quaint sort of way, as long as you liked the smell of fish. I kept the window up to try to limit the damage but Morphy had his rolled right down and was taking deep, sinful breaths. All in all, Bucktown seemed an unlikely place for a man like Remarr to hole up, but that in itself was probably reason enough for him to choose it.

Carole Stern lived in a small camelback house, a single-story at the front against a two-story rear, set in a small garden a few blocks off Bucktown's main street. According to Morphy, Stern worked in a bar on St. Charles but was currently serving time for possession of coke with intent to supply. Remarr was rumored to be keeping up the rental payments until she got out. We parked around the corner from the house and we clicked off the safeties of our guns in unison as we stepped from the car.

"You're a little out of your territory here, aren't you?" I asked Morphy.

"Hey, we just came out here for a bite to eat and decided to check on the off chance," he said, with an injured look. "I ain't steppin' on no toes."

He motioned me toward the front of the house while he took the back. I walked to the front door, which stood on a small raised porch, and peered carefully through the glass. It was caked with dirt, in keeping with the slightly run-down feel of the house itself. I counted five and then tried the door. It opened with a gentle creak and I stepped carefully into the hall. At the far end, I heard the tinkle of glass breaking and saw Morphy's hand reach in to open the rear door.

The smell was faint, but obvious, like meat that has been left in the sunlight on a warm day. The downstairs rooms were empty and consisted only of a kitchen, a small room with a sofa and an old TV, and a bedroom with a single bed and a closet. The closet contained women's clothes and shoes. The bed was covered only by a worn mattress.

Morphy took the stairs first. I stayed close behind, both of us with our guns pointing toward the second floor. The smell was stronger here now. We passed a bathroom with a dripping showerhead, which had stained the ceramic bath brown. On a sink unit beneath a small mirror stood some shaving foam, blades, and a bottle of Boss aftershave.

Three other doors stood partially open. On the right was a woman's bedroom. It had white sheets on the bed, potted plants, which had begun to wither, and a series of Monet prints on the walls. There were cosmetics on a long dressing table and a white fitted closet ran the length of one wall. A window opposite looked out on a small, overgrown garden. There were more women's clothes in the closet, and more shoes. Carole Stern was obviously funding some kind of shopping addiction by selling drugs.

The second door provided the source of the smell. A large open pot sat on a camper stove by a window facing on to the street. It contained scummy water in which a stew of some kind was cooking on a low heat. From the stench, the meat had been allowed to simmer for some time, probably most of the day. It smelled foul, like offal. Two easy chairs stood in the room on a new red carpet. A portable TV with a coat-hanger aerial sat blankly on a small table.

The third room was also at the front of the house facing onto the street, but its door was almost closed. Morphy took one side of the door. I took the other. He counted three and then nudged the door open with his foot and went in fast to the right-hand wall. I moved in low to the left, my gun level with my chest, my finger resting on the trigger.

The setting sun cast a golden glow over the contents of the room: an unmade bed, a suitcase open on the floor, a dressing table, a poster on the wall advertising a concert by the Neville Brothers in Tipitina's, with the brothers' signatures scrawled loosely across their images. The carpeted floor felt damp beneath my feet.

Most of the plaster had been removed from the ceiling and the roof beams lay exposed. I guessed Carole Stern had been considering some sort of remodeling before her prison sentence put her plans temporarily on hold. At the far end of the room, a series of what looked like climbing ropes had been strung over the beams and used to hold Tony Remarr in position.

His remains glowed with a strange fire in the dying sunlight. I could see the muscles and veins in his legs, the tendons in his neck, the yellow mounds of fatty deposits seeping at his waist, the muscles in his stomach, the shriveled husk of his penis. Huge masonry nails had been driven into the far wall of the room and he hung partially on them, one beneath each arm, while the ropes took the main weight of his body.

As I moved to the right I could see a third nail in the wall behind his neck, holding his head in place. The head faced to the right, in profile, supported by another nail beneath his chin. In places, his skull gleamed whitely through the blood. His eye sockets were almost empty and his gritted teeth were white against his gums.

Remarr had been totally flayed, carefully posed, and hung against the wall. His left hand stretched diagonally outward and down from his body. A long-bladed knife, like a butcher's filleting tool but wider, heavier, hung from his hand. It looked like it had been glued in place.

But the viewer's gaze was drawn, like Tony Remarr's own blind stare, to the figure's right hand. It stood at a right angle to his body until it reached the elbow. From there, the forearm was raised vertically, pulled upward by a rope around the wrist. In the fingers of his right hand and draped over his right arm, Tony Remarr held his own flayed skin. I could see the shape of the arms, the legs, the hair of his scalp, the nipples on his chest. Beneath the scalp, which hung almost at his knees, there were bloody edges where the face had been removed. The bed, the floor, the wall, all were shaded in red.

I looked to my left to see Morphy cross himself and softly say a prayer for the soul of Tony Remarr.

We sat against Morphy's car drinking coffee from paper cups as the feds and the New Orleans police milled around the Stern house. A crowd of people, some local, some on their way to eat in Bucktown's seafood joints, hung around the edges of the police cordon waiting to see the body being removed. They were likely to be disappointed: the crime scene was highly organized by the killer, and both the police

and the feds were anxious to document it fully before allowing the body to be taken away.

Woolrich, his tan suit now restored to its former tar-
nished glory, came over to us and offered us the remains of
a bag of donuts from his suit pocket. Behind the cordon, I
could see his own Chevy, a red '96 model that shone like
new.

"Here, you must be hungry." Both Morphy and I declined the offer. I still had visions of Remarr in my head and
Morphy looked pale and ill.

"You speak to the locals?" asked Woolrich.

We both nodded. We had given lengthy statements to a
pair of Homicide detectives from Orleans Parish, one of
whom was Morphy's brother-in-law.

"Then I guess you can go," said Woolrich. "I'll want to
talk to both of you again, though." Morphy wandered
around to the driver's side of his car. I moved to open the
passenger door but Woolrich held my arm.

"You okay?" he asked.

"I think so."

"It was a good hunch that Morphy followed, but he
shouldn't have brought you along. Durand's gonna be on
my back when he finds out that you were first on another
crime scene." Durand was the FBI's special agent in charge
in New Orleans. I had never met him but I knew what most
SACs were like. They ruled their field offices like kingdoms,
assigning agents to squads and giving the go-ahead to operations. The competition for SAC posts was intense. If nothing else, Durand was a tough customer.

"You're still at the Flaisance?"

"Still there."

"I'll drop by. There's something I want to bounce off
you."

He turned and walked back toward the Stern house. On
his way through the gate, he handed the bag of crushed
donuts to a pair of patrolmen sitting in their car. They took
the bag reluctantly, holding it like it was a bomb. When
Woolrich had entered the house, one of them climbed out
of the car and threw the donuts in a trash can.

Morphy dropped me at the Flaisance. Before he left, I gave him my cell phone number. He wrote it in a small black notebook, bound tightly with a rubber band. "If you're free tomorrow, Angie's cooking dinner. It's worth the trip. You taste her cooking and you won't regret it." The tone of his voice changed. "Besides, there's some things I think we need to discuss."

I told him it sounded okay, although part of me wanted never to see Morphy, Woolrich, or another cop again. He was about to pull away when I patted the roof of the car with my palm. Morphy leaned over and rolled down the window.

"Why are you doing this?" I asked. Morphy had gone to considerable lengths to involve me, to keep me posted on what was happening. I needed to know why. I think I also needed to know if I could trust him.

He shrugged. "The Aguillards died on my beat. I want to get the guy who killed them. You know something about him. He's come at you, at your family. The feds are conducting their own investigation and are telling us as little as they can. You're all I got."

"Is that it?" I could see something more in his face, something that was almost familiar.

"No. I got a wife. I'm starting a family. You know what I'm sayin'?"

I nodded and let it go, but there was something else in his eyes, something that resonated inside me. I patted the roof of the car once again in farewell and watched as he drove away, wondering how badly Morphy wanted absolution for what he might have done.

38

□

As I RETURNED to my room at the Flaisance I felt an overpowering sense of decay, which seemed to creep into my nostrils, almost stopping my breathing. It lodged itself beneath my nails and stained my skin. I felt it in the sweat on my back and saw it in the weeds breaking through the cracks in the pavement beneath my feet. It was as if the city were corroding around me. I went to my room and showered under a hot jet until my skin was red and raw, then changed into a sweater and chinos, called Angel and Louis in their room, and arranged to meet them in Rachel's room in five minutes.

She answered the door with an ink-stained hand. She had a pencil tucked behind her ear, and a pair of pencils held her red hair back in a bun. There were dark rims under her eyes, which were red from reading.

Her room had been transformed. A Macintosh Power-Book stood open on the room's only table, surrounded by a mass of paper, books, and notes. On the wall above it were diagrams, yellow Post-it notes, and a series of what appeared to be anatomy sketches. A pile of faxes lay on the floor by her chair, beside a tray of half-eaten sandwiches, a pot of coffee, and a stained cup.

I heard a knock on the door behind me. I opened it to admit Angel and Louis. Angel looked at the wall in disbelief. "Guy on the desk already thinks you're crazy, with all the shit that's been comin' in on his fax. He sees this, he's gonna call the cops."

Rachel sat back in her chair and pulled the pencils from

her bun, releasing her hair. She shook her tresses out with her left hand and then twisted her neck to ease her knotted muscles.

"So," she said, "who wants to start?"

I told them about Remarr, and instantly, the tiredness went from Rachel's face. She made me detail the position of the body twice and then spent a couple of minutes shuffling papers on her desk.

"There!" she said, handing me a sheet of paper with a flourish. "Is that it?"

It was a black-and-white illustration, marked at the top of the page, in old lettering: TAB. PRIMERA DEL LIB. SEGVNDO. At the bottom of the page, in Rachel's handwriting, was written "Valverde 1556."

The illustration depicted a flayed man, his left foot on a stone, his left hand holding a long knife with a hooked hilt, his right holding his own flayed skin. The outline of his face was visible on the skin and his eyes remained in his sockets, but with those exceptions, the illustration was profoundly similar to the position in which Remarr had been found. The various parts of the body were each marked with Greek letters.

"That's it," I said quietly as Angel and Louis peered silently over my shoulder. "That's what we found."

"The *Historia de la composición del cuerpo humano*," said Rachel. "It was written by the Spaniard Juan de Valverde de Hamusco in 1556 as a medical textbook. This drawing"—she took the page and held it up so we could all see it—"is an illustration of the Marsyas myth. Marsyas was a satyr, a follower of the goddess Cybele. He was cursed when he picked up a bone flute discarded by Athene. The flute played itself, because it was still inspired by Athene, and its music was so beautiful that the peasants said it was greater even than that of Apollo himself.

"Apollo challenged Marsyas to a competition to be judged by the Muses, and Marsyas lost because he couldn't play the flute upside down and sing at the same time.

"And so Apollo took his revenge on Marsyas. He flayed him alive and nailed his skin to a pine. According to the poet Ovid, at his moment of death Marsyas cried out, *"Quid me mihi detrahis?"*—which can be roughly translated as: "Who is it that tears me from myself?" The artist Titian painted a version of the myth. So did Raphael. My guess is that Remarr's body will reveal traces of ketamine. To fulfill the myth, the flaying would have to be carried out while the victim was still alive—it's hard to create a work of art if the subject keeps moving."

Louis interrupted. "But in this picture he looks like he flayed himself. He's holding the knife *and* the skin. Why did the killer choose this depiction?"

"This is just a guess, but maybe it's because, in a sense, Remarr did flay himself," I said. "He was at the Aguillard house when he shouldn't have been. I think the Traveling Man was concerned at what he might have seen. Remarr was somewhere he shouldn't have been, so he was responsible for what happened to him."

Rachel nodded. "It's an interesting point, but there may be something more to it, given what happened to Tee Jean Aguillard." She handed me a pair of papers. The first was a photocopy of the crime scene photo of Tee Jean. The second was another illustration, this time marked DE DISSECT. PARTIVM. At the bottom of the page, the date "1545" had been handwritten by Rachel.

The illustration depicted a man crucified against a tree, with a stone wall behind it. His head was cradled by the branches of the tree, his arms spread by further branches. The skin below his chest had been flayed, revealing his lungs, kidneys, and heart. Some unidentified organ, probably his stomach, lay on a raised platform beside him. His face was intact, but once again, the illustration matched the posture of Tee Jean Aguillard's body.

"Marsyas again," said Rachel. "Or at least an adaptation of the myth. That's from Estienne's *De dissectione partium corporis humani,* another early textbook."

"Are you saying that this guy is killing according to a Greek myth?" asked Angel.

Rachel sighed. "It's not that simple. I think the myth has resonances for him, for the basic reason that he's used it twice. But the Marsyas theory breaks down with *Tante* Marie, and Bird's wife and child. I found the Marsyas illustrations almost by accident, but I haven't found a match yet for the other deaths. I'm still looking. The likelihood is that they are also based on early medical textbooks. If that's the case, then I'll find them."

"It raises the possibility that we're looking for someone with a medical background," I said.

"Or a knowledge of obscure texts," said Rachel. "We already know that he has read the Book of Enoch, or some derivative of it. It wouldn't take a great deal of medical knowledge to carry out the kind of mutilation we've found on the bodies so far, but an assumption of some surgical skills, or even some mild familiarity with medical procedures, might not be totally amiss."

"What about the blinding and the removal of the faces?" I asked. I pushed a flashing image of Susan and Jennifer to the back of my mind. "Any idea where they fit in?"

Rachel shook her head. "I'm still working on it. The face appears to be some form of token for him. Jennifer's was returned because she died before he could start working on her, I'd guess, but also because he wanted to shock you personally. The removal could also indicate the killer's disregard for them as individuals, a sign of his disregard for their own status as people. After all, when you remove a person's face, you take away the most immediate representation of their individuality, their main physical distinguisher.

"As for the eyes, there is a myth that the image of the killer stays on the retina of the victim. There were lots of myths like that attached to the body. Even at the start of the last century, some scientists were still examining the theory that a murder victim's body bled when it was in the same room as its killer. I need to do more work on it, then we'll see."

She stood up and stretched. "I don't mean to sound callous, but now I want to take a shower. Then I want to go out and get something decent to eat. After that, I want to sleep for twelve hours."

Angel, Louis, and I started to leave but she held up her

hand to stop us. "There's just one more thing. I don't want to give the impression that this is just some freak copying violent images. I don't know enough about this to make that kind of judgment and I want to consult some people who are more experienced in this area than I am. But I can't help feeling that there's some underlying philosophy behind what he's doing, some pattern that he's following. Until we find out what that is, I don't think we're going to catch him."

I had my hand on the door handle when there was a knock at the door. I opened it slowly and blocked the view of the room with my body while Rachel cleared away her papers. Woolrich stood before me. In the light from the room, I noticed a thin growth of beard was forming on his face. "Clerk told me you might be here if you weren't in your own room. Can I come in?"

I paused for a moment, then stepped aside. I noticed that Rachel was standing in front of the material on the wall, obscuring it from view, but Woolrich wasn't interested in her. His eyes had fixed on Louis.

"I know you," he said.

"I don't think so," said Louis. His eyes were cold.

Woolrich turned to me. "You bringing your hired killers to my town, Bird?"

I didn't reply.

"Like I said, man, I think you're making a mistake," said Louis. "I'm a businessman."

"Really? And what kind of business would you be in?"

"Pest control," said Louis.

The air seemed to crackle with tension, until Woolrich turned around and walked from the room. He stopped in the hall and gestured to me. "I need to talk to you. I'll wait for you in the Café du Monde."

I watched him go, then looked at Louis. He raised an eyebrow. "Guess I'm more famous than I thought."

"Guess you are," I said, and went after Woolrich.

I caught up with him on the street but he said nothing until we were seated and he had a beignet in front of him.

He tore off a piece, sprinkling powdered sugar on his suit, then took a long gulp of coffee, which half drained the cup and left a brown stain along its sides. "C'mon, Bird," he said. "What are you trying to do here?" He sounded weary and disappointed. "That guy, I know his face. I know what he is." He chewed another piece of beignet.

I didn't reply. We stared at each other until Woolrich looked away. He dusted sugar from his fingers and ordered another coffee. I had hardly touched mine.

"Does the name Edward Byron mean anything to you?" he said eventually, when he realized that Louis was not going to be a topic of discussion.

"It doesn't ring any bells. Why?"

"He was a janitor in Park Rise. That's where Susan had Jennifer, right?"

"Right." Park Rise was a private hospital on Long Island. Susan's father had insisted that we use it, arguing that its staff were among the best in the world. They were certainly among the best paid. The doctor who delivered Jennifer earned more in a month than I made in a year.

"Where's this leading?" I asked.

"Byron was let go—quietly—following the mutilation of a corpse earlier this year. Someone performed an unauthorized autopsy on a female body. Her abdomen was opened and her ovaries and Fallopian tubes removed."

"No charges were pressed?"

"The hospital authorities considered it, then decided against it. Surgical gloves with traces of the dead woman's blood and tissue on them were found in a bag in Byron's locker. He argued that someone was trying to frame him. The evidence wasn't conclusive—theoretically, someone could have planted that stuff in his locker—but the hospital let him go anyway. No court case, no police investigation, nothing. The only reason we have any record of it is because the local cops were investigating the theft of drugs from the hospital around the same time, and Byron's name was noted on the report. Byron was dismissed after the thefts began and they pretty much ceased, but he had an alibi each time there were found to be drugs missing.

"That was the last anyone heard of Byron. We have his Social Security number, but he hasn't claimed unemployment, paid tax, dealt with state government, or visited a hospital since he was dismissed. His credit cards haven't been used since October nineteenth, ninety-six."

"What brings his name up now?"

"Edward Byron is a native of Baton Rouge. His wife—his ex-wife, Stacey—still lives there."

"Have you spoken to her?"

"We interviewed her yesterday. She says she hasn't seen him since last April, that he owes her six months' alimony. The last check was drawn on a bank in East Texas but his old lady thinks he may be living in the Baton Rouge area, or somewhere nearby. She says he always wanted to come back here, that he hated New York. We've also put out photos of him, taken from his employee record at Park Rise."

He handed me a blown-up picture of Byron. He was a handsome man, his features marred only by a slightly receding chin. His mouth and nose were thin, his eyes narrow and dark. He had dark brown hair, swept from left to right. He looked younger than thirty-five, his age when the picture was taken.

"It's the best lead we've got," said Woolrich. "Maybe I'm telling you because I figure you have a right to know. But I'm telling you something else as well: you keep away from Mrs. Byron. We've told her not to talk to anyone in case the press get wind of it. Secondly, stay away from Joe Bones. His guy Ricky was caught on one of our taps swearing blue hell about some stunt you pulled today, but you won't get away with it a second time."

He laid some money on the table. "Your little team back there got anything that might help us?"

"Not yet. We figure a medical background, maybe a sexual pathology. If I get anything more, I'll let you know. I've got a question for you, though. What drugs were taken from Park Rise?"

He tilted his head to one side and twisted his mouth slightly, as if debating with himself whether or not to tell me.

"Ketamine hydrochloride. It's related to PCP." I gave no indication that I already knew about the drug. The feds would tear Morphy a new asshole if they knew he had been feeding me details like that, although they must have already had their suspicions. Woolrich paused for a moment and then went on. "It was found in the bodies of *Tante* Marie Aguillard and her son. The killer used it as a form of anesthetic."

He spun his coffee cup on its saucer, waiting until it came to rest with the handle pointing in my direction.

"Are you scared of this guy, Bird?" he asked quietly. "Because I sure am. You remember that conversation we had about serial killers, when I brought you to meet *Tante* Marie?"

I nodded.

"Back then, I thought I'd seen it all. These killers were abusers and rapists and dysfunctionals who had crossed some line, but they were so pathetic that they were still recognizably human. But this one . . ."

He watched a family pass by in a carriage, the driver urging the horse on with the reins while he gave them his own history of Jackson Square. A child, a small, dark-haired boy, was seated at the edge of the family group. He watched us silently as they passed by, his chin resting on his bare forearm.

"We were always afraid that one would come who was different from the others, who was motivated by something more than a twisted, frustrated sexuality or wretched sadism. We live in a culture of pain and death, Bird, and most of us go through life without ever really understanding that. Maybe it was only a matter of time before we produced someone who understood that better than we did, someone who saw the world as just one big altar on which to sacrifice humanity, someone who believed he had to make an example of us all."

"And do you believe that this is him?"

" 'I am become Death, the destroyer of worlds.' Isn't that what the Bhagavadgita says? 'I am become Death.' Maybe that's what he is: pure Death."

He moved toward the street. I followed him, then remembered my slip of paper from the previous night. "Woolrich, there is one more thing." He looked testy as I gave him the references for the Book of Enoch.

"What the fuck is the Book of Enoch?"

"It's part of the Apocrypha. I think he may have some knowledge of it."

Woolrich folded the paper and put it in the pocket of his pants.

"Bird," he said, and he almost smiled, "sometimes I'm torn between keeping you in touch with what's happening and not telling you anything." He grimaced, then sighed as if to indicate that this was something that just wasn't worth arguing about. "Stay out of trouble, Bird, and tell your friends the same." He walked away, to be swallowed up by the evening crowds.

I knocked on Rachel's door, but there was no reply. I knocked a second time, harder, and I heard some noises from inside the room. She answered the door with a towel wrapped around her body and her hair hidden by a second, smaller towel. Her face was red from the heat of the shower and her skin glowed.

"Sorry," I said. "I forgot that you'd be showering."

She smiled and waved me in.

"Take a seat. I'll get dressed and let you buy me dinner." She took a pair of gray pants and a white cotton shirt from the bed, picked some matching white underwear from her case, and stepped back into the bathroom. She didn't close the door fully behind her so that we could talk while she dressed.

"Should I ask what that exchange was about?" she said.

I walked to her balcony window and looked out on the street below.

"What Woolrich said about Louis is true. It's not as simple as that, maybe, but he has killed people in the past. Now, I'm not so sure. I don't ask, and I'm not in a position to pass judgment on him. But I trust both Angel and Louis. I asked them to come because I know what they're good at."

She came out of the bathroom buttoning her shirt, her damp hair hanging. She dried her hair with a travel dryer, then applied a little makeup. I had seen Susan do the same things a thousand times, but there was a strange intimacy in watching Rachel perform them in front of me. I felt something stir inside me, a tiny yet significant shift in my feelings toward her. She sat on the edge of the bed and slipped her bare feet into a pair of black slingbacks, her finger moving inside each one to ease the progress of her heel. As she leaned foward, moisture glistened on the small of her back. She caught me looking at her and smiled cautiously, as if afraid of misinterpreting what she had seen. "Shall we go?" she said.

I held the door open for her as we left, her shirt brushing my hand with a sound like water sizzling on hot metal.

We ate in Mr. B's on Royal Street, the big mahogany room cool and dark. I had steak, tender and luscious, while Rachel ate blackened redfish, the spices causing her to gasp at the first bite. We talked of little things, of plays and films, of music and reading. It emerged that we had both attended the same performance of *The Magic Flute* at the Met in '91, both of us alone. I watched her as she sipped her wine, the reflected light playing on her face and dancing in the darkness of her pupils like moonlight seen from a lakeshore.

"So, you often follow strange men to distant lands?"

She smiled. "I bet you've been waiting to use that line all your life."

"Maybe I use it all the time."

"Oh *puh*-lease. Next thing you'll be wielding a club and asking the waiter to step outside."

"Okay, guilty as charged. It's been a while."

I felt myself redden and caught something playful but uncertain in her glance—a kind of sadness, a fear of hurting and being hurt. Inside me, something twisted and stretched its claws, and I felt a little tear in my heart.

"I'm sorry. I know almost nothing about you," I said quietly.

She reached out gently and brushed along the length of

my left hand, from the wrist to the end of the little finger. She followed the curves of my fingers, delicately tracing the lines and whorls of my fingerprints, her touch soft as a leaf. At last, she let her hand rest on the table, the tips of her fingers resting on top of my own, and began to speak.

She was born in Chilson, near the foothills of the Adirondacks. Her father was a lawyer, her mother taught kindergarten. She liked basketball and running, and her prom date got the mumps two days before the prom, so her best friend's brother went with her instead and tried to feel her breast during "Only the Lonely." She had one brother of her own, Curtis, ten years her elder. For five of his twenty-eight years, Curtis had been a cop. He was two weeks short of his twenty-ninth birthday when he died. "He was a detective with the State Police, newly promoted. He wasn't even on duty the day he was killed." She spoke without hesitation, not too slowly, not too quickly, as if she had gone over the story a thousand times, examining it for flaws, tracing its beginning, its resolution, cutting all extraneous detail from it until she was left with the gleaming core of her brother's murder, the hollow heart of his absence.

"It was a quarter after two, a Tuesday afternoon. Curtis was visiting some girl in Moriah—he always had two or three girls trailing him at any one time. He just broke their hearts. He was carrying a bunch of flowers, pink lilies bought in a store five doors from the bank. He heard some shouting and saw two people come running from the bank, both armed, both masked, a man and a woman. There was another man sitting in a car, waiting for them to come out.

"Curtis was drawing his gun when they saw him. They both had sawed-offs and they didn't hesitate. The man emptied both barrels into him and then, while he lay dying on the ground, the woman finished him off. She shot him in the face, and he was so handsome, so lovely."

She stopped talking and I knew that this was a story she had told only in her mind, that it was something not to be shared, but to be safeguarded. Sometimes, we need our pain. We need it to call our own.

"When they caught them, they had three thousand dollars. That was all they got from the bank, all that my brother was worth to them. The woman had been released from an institution the week before. Someone decided that she no longer posed a threat to the community."

She lifted her glass and drained the last of her wine. I signaled for more and she remained silent as the waiter refilled her glass.

"And here I am," she said at last. "Now I try to understand, and sometimes I get close. And sometimes, if I'm lucky, I can stop things from happening to other people. Sometimes."

I found that her hand was now gripped tightly in mine, and I could not recall how that had happened. Holding her hand, I spoke for the first time in many years about leaving New York and the move to Maine with my mother.

"Is she still alive?"

I shook my head. "I got in trouble with a local big shot named Daddy Helms," I said. "My grandfather and my mother agreed that I should go away to work for the summer, until things quieted down. A friend of his ran a store in Philly, so I worked there for a while, stocking shelves, cleaning up at night. I slept in a room above the store.

"My mother began taking physiotherapy for a trapped nerve in her shoulder, except it turned out that she had been misdiagnosed. She had cancer. I think she knew, but she chose not to say anything. Maybe she thought that if she didn't admit it to herself, she could fool her system into giving her more time. Instead, one of her lungs collapsed as she left the therapist's office.

"I came back two days later on a bus. I hadn't seen her in two months and when I tried to find her in the hospital ward, I couldn't. I had to check the names on the ends of the beds because she had changed so much. She lasted six weeks after that. Toward the end, she became lucid, even with the painkillers. It happens a lot, I believe. It can fool you into thinking they're getting better. It's like the cancer's small joke. She was trying to draw a picture of the hospital the night before she died, so she would know where she was going when it was time to leave."

I sipped some water. "I'm sorry," I said. "I don't know why all those things should have come back to me."

Rachel smiled and I felt her hand tighten again on mine. "And your grandfather?"

"He died eight years ago. He left me his house in Maine, the one I'm trying to fix up." I noticed that she didn't ask me about my father. I guessed that she knew all there was to know.

Later, we walked slowly back through the crowds, the music from the bars blending together into one blast of sound in which familiar tunes could sometimes be identified. When we came to the door of her room we held each other for a while, then kissed softly, her hand on my cheek, before we said good night.

Despite Remarr and Joe Bones and my exchanges with Woolrich, I slept peacefully that night, my hand still holding the specter of her own.

39

It was a cool, clear morning and the sound of the St. Charles streetcar carried on the air as I ran. A wedding limousine passed me on its way to the cathedral, white ribbons rippling on its hood. I jogged west along North Rampart as far as Perdido, then back through the Quarter along Chartres. The heat was intense, like running with my face in a warm, damp towel. My lungs struggled to pull in the air and my system rebelled, struggling to reject it, but still I ran.

I was used to training three or four times each week, alternating circuits for a month or so with a split bodybuilding workout. After a few days outside my training regimen I felt bloated and out of condition, as if my system was full of toxins. Given the choice between exercise and colon cleansers, I opted for exercise as the less uncomfortable option.

Back at the Flaisance I showered and changed the dressing on my wounded shoulder; it still ached a little, but the wounds were closing. Finally, I left a batch of clothes at the local laundry, since I hadn't figured on staying quite so long in New Orleans and my underwear selection was becoming pretty limited.

Stacey Byron's number was in the phone book—she hadn't reverted to her maiden name, at least not as far as the phone company was concerned—so Angel and Louis volunteered to take a trip to Baton Rouge and see what they could find out from her, or about her. Woolrich wouldn't be pleased, but if he wanted her left in peace then he shouldn't have said anything at all.

Rachel e-mailed details of the kind of illustrations she was seeking to two of her research students at Columbia and Father Eric Ward, a retired professor in Boston who had lectured at Loyola in New Orleans on Renaissance culture. Instead of hanging around waiting for a response, she decided to come with me to Metairie, where David Fontenot was due to be buried that morning.

We were silent as we drove. The subject of our growing intimacy and what it might imply had not come up between us, but it seemed that we were both acutely aware of it. I could see something of it in Rachel's eyes when she looked at me. I thought that she could probably see the same in mine.

"So what else do you want to know about me?" she asked.

"I guess I don't know too much about your personal life."

"Apart from the fact that I'm beautiful and brilliant."

"Apart from that," I admitted.

"By personal, do you mean sexual?"

"It's a euphemism. I don't want to seem pushy. If it makes you happier you can start with your age, since you didn't tell me last night. The rest will seem easy by comparison."

She gave me a twisted grin and the finger. I chose to ignore the finger.

"I'm thirty-three but I admit to thirty, if the lighting is right. I have a cat and a two-bedroom apartment on the Upper West Side, but no one to share it with currently. I do step aerobics three times a week and I like Chinese food, soul music, and cream ale. My last relationship ended six months ago and I think my hymen may be growing back."

I arched an eyebrow at her and she laughed. "You do look shocked," she said. "You need to get out more."

"Sounds like you do, too. Who was the guy?"

"A stockbroker. We'd been seeing each other for over a year and we agreed to live together on a test basis. He had a one-bed, I had a two-bed, so he moved in with me and we used the second bedroom as a shared study."

"Sounds idyllic."

"It was. For about a week. It turned out that he couldn't stand the cat, he hated sharing a bed with me because he said I kept him awake by turning over all the time, and all my clothes started to smell of his cigarettes. That clinched it. Everything stank: the furniture, the bed, the walls, the food, the toilet paper, even the cat. Then he came home one evening, told me he was in love with his secretary, and moved to Seattle with her three months later."

"Seattle's nice, I hear."

"Fuck Seattle. I hope it falls into the sea."

"At least you're not bitter."

"Very funny." She looked out of her window for a while and I felt an urge to reach out and touch her, an urge enhanced by what she said next. "I still feel reluctant to ask you too many questions," she said, gently. "After what happened."

"I know." Slowly, I extended my right hand and touched her lightly on the cheek. Her skin was smooth and slightly moist. She leaned her head toward me, increasing the pressure against my hand, and then we were pulling up outside the entrance to the cemetery and the moment was gone.

Branches of the Fontenots had lived in New Orleans since the late nineteenth century, long before the family of Lionel and David had moved to the city, and the Fontenots had a large vault in Metairie Cemetery, the largest of the city's cemeteries, at Metairie Road and Pontchartrain Boulevard. The cemetery covered one hundred and fifty acres and was built on the old Metairie racecourse. If you were a gambling man, it was an appropriate final resting place, even though it proved that, in the end, the odds are always stacked in favor of the house.

New Orleans cemeteries are strange places. While most cemeteries in big cities are carefully manicured and encourage discreet headstones, the dead citizens of New Orleans rested in ornate tombs and spectacular mausoleums. They reminded me of Père Lachaise in Paris, or the Cities of the Dead in Cairo, where people still lived among the bodies. The resemblance was echoed by the Brunswig tomb at

Metairie, which was shaped like a pyramid and guarded by a sphinx.

It was not simply the funerary architecture of Spain and France that had caused the cemeteries to develop the way they did. Most of the city was below sea level, and until the development of modern drainage systems, graves dug in the ground had rapidly filled with water. Aboveground tombs were the natural solution.

The Fontenot funeral had already entered the cemetery when we arrived. I parked away from the main body of vehicles and we walked past the two police cruisers at the gate, their occupants' eyes masked by shades. We followed the stragglers past the four statues representing Faith, Hope, Charity, and Memory, at the base of the long Moriarity tomb, until we came to a Greek Revival tomb marked with a pair of Doric columns. FONTENOT was inscribed on the lintel above the door.

It was impossible to tell how many Fontenots had come to rest in the family vault. The tradition in New Orleans was to leave the body for a year and a day, after which the vault was reopened, the remains moved to the back, and the rotting casket removed to make way for the next occupant. A lot of the vaults in Metairie were pretty crowded by this point.

The wrought iron gate, inlaid with the heads of angels, stood open and the small party of mourners had surrounded the vault in a semicircle. A man I guessed to be Lionel Fontenot towered above them. He was wearing a black, single-breasted suit and a thick black tie. His face had been weathered to a reddish brown, and deep lines etched his forehead and snaked out from the corners of his eyes. His hair was dark but streaked with gray at the temples. He was a big man, certainly six-three at least and weighing close to two hundred and forty pounds, maybe two-fifty. His suit seemed to struggle to contain him.

Beyond the mourners, ranged at intervals around the vaults and tombs, or standing beneath trees scanning the cemetery, were four hard-faced men in dark jackets and trousers. Their pistols caused the jackets to bulge slightly. A fifth man, a dark overcoat hanging loosely on his shoulders, turned at an old cypress and I caught a glimpse of the tell-tale sights of an M16-based submachine gun concealed beneath its folds. Two others stood at either side of Lionel Fontenot. The big man wasn't taking any chances.

The mourners, both black and white, young white men in snappy black suits, old black women wearing black dresses gilded with lace at the neckline, grew silent as the priest began to read the rites of the dead from a tattered prayer book with gold-edged pages. There was no wind to carry away his words and they hung in the air around us, reverberating from the surrounding tombs like the voices of the dead themselves.

"Our Father, who art in heaven . . ."

The pallbearers moved forward, struggling awkwardly to fit the casket through the narrow entrance to the vault. As it was placed inside, a pair of New Orleans policemen appeared between two round vaults about eighty feet west of the funeral party. Two more emerged from the east and a third pair moved slowly down past a tree to the north. Rachel followed my glance.

"An escort?"

"Maybe."

"Thy kingdom come, thy will be done on earth . . ."

I felt uneasy. They could have been sent to ensure that Joe Bones wasn't tempted to disturb the mourners, but something was wrong. I didn't like the way they moved. They looked uncomfortable in the uniforms, as if their shirt collars were too tight and their shoes pinched.

"Forgive us our trespasses . . ."

Fontenot's men had spotted them too, but they didn't look too concerned. The policemen's arms hung loosely by their sides and their guns remained in their holsters. They were about thirty feet away from us when something warm splashed my face. An elderly moonfaced woman in a tight black dress, who had been sobbing quietly beside me, spun sideways and tumbled to the ground, a dark hole in her temple and a damp glistening in her hair. A chip of marble flew from the vault, the area around it stained a vivid red.

The sound of the shot came almost simultaneously, a dull subdued noise like a fist hitting a punching bag.

"But deliver us from evil . . ."

It took the mourners a few seconds to realize what was happening. They looked dumbly at the fallen woman, a pool of blood already forming around her head as I pushed Rachel into the space between two vaults, shielding her with my body. Someone screamed and the crowd began to scatter as more bullets came, whining off the marble and stone. I could see Lionel Fontenot's bodyguards rush to protect him, pushing him to the ground as the bullets bounced from the tomb and rattled its iron gate.

Rachel covered her head with her arms and crouched to try to make herself a smaller target. Over my shoulder, I saw the two cops to the north separate and pick up machine pistols concealed in the bushes at either side of the avenue. They were Steyrs, fitted with sound suppressors: Joe Bones's men. I saw a woman try to run for the cover of the outspread wings of a stone angel, her dark coat whipping around her bare legs. The coat puffed twice at the shoulder and she sprawled face forward on the ground, her hands outstretched. She tried to drag herself forward but her coat puffed again and she was gone.

Now there were pistol shots and the rattle of a semiautomatic as Fontenot's men returned fire. I drew my own Smith & Wesson and joined Rachel as a uniformed figure appeared in the gap between the tombs, the Steyr held in a two-handed grip. I shot him in the face and he crumpled to the ground.

"But they're cops!" said Rachel, her voice almost drowned by the exchange of fire around us.

I reached out and pushed her down further. "They're Joe Bones's men. They're here to take out Lionel Fontenot." But it was more than that: Joe Bones wanted to sow chaos and to reap blood and fear and death from the consequences. He didn't simply want Lionel Fontenot dead. He also wanted others to die—women, children, Lionel's family, his associates—and for those left alive to remember what had taken place and to fear Joe Bones more because of it. He wanted to break the Fontenots and he would do it here, beside the vault where they had buried generations of their dead. This was the action of a man who had moved beyond reason and passed into a dark, flame-lit place, a place that blinded his vision with blood.

Behind me, there was a scuffling, tumbling sound and one of Fontenot's men, the overcoated man with the semi-automatic, fell to his knees beside Rachel. Blood bubbled from his mouth and I heard her scream as he fell forward, his head coming to rest by her feet. The M16 lay on the grass beside him. I reached for it but Rachel got to it first, a deep, unquenchable instinct for survival now guiding her actions. Her mouth and eyes were wide as she fired a burst over the prone frame of the bodyguard.

I flung myself to the end of the tomb and aimed in the same direction, but Joe Bones's man was already down. He lay on his back, his left leg spasming and a bloody pattern etched across his chest. Rachel's hands were shaking as the adrenaline coursed through her system. The M16 began to fall from her fingers. Its strap became entangled in her arm and she shook herself furiously to release it. Behind her, I could see mourners running low through the avenues of tombs. Two white women dragged a young black man by his arms over the grass. The belly of his white shirt was smeared with blood.

I figured that there must have been a fourth set of Joe Bones's men who approached from the south and fired the first shots. At least three were down: the two killed by Rachel and me and a third who lay sprawled by the old cypress. Fontenot's man had taken one of them out before he was hit himself.

I helped Rachel to her feet and moved her quickly to a grimy vault with a corroded gate. I struck at the lock with the butt of the M16 and it gave instantly. She slipped inside and I handed her my Smith & Wesson and told her to stay there until I came back for her. Then, gripping the M16, I ran east past the back of the Fontenot tomb, using the other vaults as cover. I didn't know how many shots were left in the M16. The selector switch was set for three-round bursts.

Depending on the magazine capacity, I might have anything between ten and twenty rounds left.

I had almost reached a monument topped by the figure of a sleeping child when something hit me on the back of the head and I stumbled forward, the M16 slipping from my grasp. Someone kicked me hard in the kidneys, the pain lancing through my body as far as the shoulder. I was kicked again in the stomach, which forced me on to my back. I looked up to see Ricky standing above me, the reptilian coils of his hair and his small stature at odds with the NOPD uniform. He had lost his hat and the side of his face was cut slightly where he had been hit by splinters of stone. The muzzle of his Steyr pointed at my chest.

I tried to swallow but my throat seemed to have constricted. I was conscious of the feel of the grass beneath my hands and the glorious pain in my side, sensations of life and existence and survival. Ricky raised the Steyr to point it at my head.

"Joe Bones says hello," he said. His finger tightened on the trigger in the same instant as his head jerked back, his stomach thrusting forward and his back arching. A burst of fire from the Steyr raked the grass beside my head as Ricky fell to his knees and then toppled sideways, his body lying prone across my left leg. There was a jagged red hole in the back of his shirt.

Behind him, Lionel Fontenot stood in a marksman's stance, the pistol in his hand slowly coming down. There was blood on his left hand and a bullet hole in the upper left arm of his suit. The two bodyguards who had stood beside him at the cemetery walked quickly from the direction of the Fontenot tomb. They glanced at me, then turned their attention back to Fontenot. I could hear the sound of sirens approaching from the west.

"One got away, Lionel," said one. "The rest are dead."

"What about our people?"

"Three dead, at least. More injured."

Beside me, Ricky stirred slightly and his hand moved feebly. I could feel his body move against my leg. Lionel Fontenot walked over and stood above him for a moment before shooting him once in the back of the head. He looked at me curiously once more, then picked up the M16 and tossed it to one of his men.

"Now go help the wounded," he said. He cradled his injured left arm with his right hand and walked back toward the Fontenot tomb.

My rib ached as I returned to where I had left Rachel, after kicking Ricky's corpse from my leg. I approached carefully, conscious of the Smith & Wesson I had left with her. When I reached the tomb, Rachel was gone.

I found her about fifty yards away, crouching beside the body of a young girl who was barely beyond her teens. As I approached, Rachel reached for the gun by her side and spun toward me.

"Hey, it's me. You okay?"

She nodded and returned the gun to its resting place. I noticed that she had kept her hand pressed on the young girl's stomach for the entire exchange.

"How is she?" I asked, but as I looked over her shoulder, I knew the answer. The blood oozing from the gunshot wound was almost black. Liver shot. The girl, shivering uncontrollably, her teeth gritted in agony, was not going to live. Around us, mourners were emerging from hiding, some sobbing, some trembling with shock. I saw two of Lionel Fontenot's men running toward us, both with pistols, and I took hold of Rachel's arm.

"We have to go. We can't afford to wait for the cops to arrive."

"I'm staying. I'm not leaving her."

"Rachel." She looked at me. I held her gaze and we shared our knowledge of the girl's impending death. "We can't stay."

The two Fontenots were beside us now. One of them, younger than the other, dropped to his knee beside the girl and took her hand. She gripped it tightly and he whispered her name. "Clara," he said. "Hold on, Clara, hold on."

"Please, Rachel," I repeated.

She took the younger man's hand and pressed it against

Clara's stomach. The girl cried out as the pressure was reapplied.

"Keep your hand there," hissed Rachel. "Don't take it away until the medics get here."

She picked up the gun and handed it to me. I took it from her, slipped the safety, and put it back in my holster. We made our way from the focus of the mayhem, until the shouting had diminished, then I stopped and she reached out and held me tightly. I cradled her in my arms and kissed the top of her head and breathed in the scent of her. She squeezed me and I gasped as the pain in my ribs increased dramatically.

Rachel pulled back quickly. "Are you hurt?"

"I took a kick, nothing else." I held her face in my hands. "You did all that you could for her."

She nodded but her mouth trembled. The girl had an importance to her that went beyond the simple duty to save her life. "I killed that man," she said.

"He would have killed us both. You had no choice. If you hadn't done it, you'd be dead. Maybe I'd be dead too." It was true, but it wasn't enough, not yet. I held her tightly as she cried, the pain in my side inconsequential beside her own suffering.

40

I HAD NOT THOUGHT of Daddy Helms in many years, not until I spoke of him to Rachel the previous night and recalled the part he played in my absence during my mother's lingering death.

Daddy Helms was the ugliest man I had ever seen. He ran most of Portland from the late sixties to the early eighties, building up a modest empire that had started with Daddy Helms boosting liquor warehouses and moved on to take in the sale of drugs over three states.

Daddy Helms weighed over three hundred pounds and suffered from a skin ailment that had left him with raised bumps all over his body, but most visible on his face and hands. They were a deep red color and formed a kind of scaly skin over his features, blurring them so that the observer always seemed to be seeing Daddy Helms through a red mist. He wore three-piece suits and Panama hats and always smoked Winston Churchill cigars, so you smelled Daddy Helms before you saw him. If you were smart enough, this usually gave you just enough time to be somewhere else before he arrived.

Daddy Helms was mean, but he was also a freak. If he had been less intelligent, less bitter, and less inclined toward violence, he would probably have ended up living in a little house in the woods of Maine and selling Christmas trees door-to-door to sympathetic citizens. Instead, his ugliness seemed to be an outward manifestation of some deeper spiritual and moral blight within himself, a corruption that made you think that Daddy Helms's skin might not be the worst thing about him. There was a rage inside him, a fury at the world and its ways.

My grandfather, who had known Daddy Helms since he was a young boy and was generally a man who empathized with those around him, even the criminals he was forced to arrest when he served as a sheriff's deputy, could see nothing but evil in Daddy Helms. "I used to think maybe it was his ugliness that made him what he is," he said once, "that the way he behaves is because of the way he looks, that he's finding a way to strike back at the world he sees around him." He was sitting on the porch of the house that he shared with my grandmother, my mother, and me, the house in which we had all lived since my father's death. My grandfather's basset hound, Doc—named after the country singer Doc Watson for no reason other than that my grandfather liked his rendition of the song "Alberta"—lay curled at his feet, his ribs expanding in deep sleep and small yelps occasionally erupting from his jowls as he enjoyed dog dreams.

My grandfather took a sip of coffee from a blue tin mug and then laid it down by his feet. Doc stirred slightly, opened one bleary eye to make sure he wasn't missing anything interesting, and then went back to his dreams.

"But Daddy Helms isn't like that," he continued. "Daddy Helms just has something wrong with him, something I can't figure. Only thing I wonder is what he might have made of himself if he weren't so damn ugly. I reckon he could have been the president of the United States, if he'd wanted to be and if people could have beared to look at him, 'cept he would've been more like Joe Stalin than John Kennedy. You oughta have stayed outta his way, boy. You learned a hard lesson yesterday, a hard lesson at the hands of a hard man."

I had come from New York with the idea that I was a tough guy, that I was smarter and faster and, if it came down to it, harder than those I would come up against in the Maine boondocks. I was wrong. Daddy Helms taught me that.

Clarence Johns, a kid who lived with his drunk father

near Maine Mall Road, learned that lesson too. Clarence was amiable but dumb, a natural sidekick. We had been hanging out together for about a year, firing off his air rifle on lazy summer afternoons, drinking beers stolen from his old man's stash. We were bored and we let everybody know it, even Daddy Helms.

He had bought an old, run-down bar on Congress Street and was slowly working to transform it into what he imagined would be a pretty high-class establishment. This was before the refurbishment of the port area, before the arrival of the T-shirt stores, the craft shops, the art house cinema, and the bars that serve free nibbles to the tourist crowd between five and seven. Maybe Daddy Helms had a vision of what was to come, for he replaced all of the old windows in the bar, put a new roof on the place, and bought up furnishings from some old Belfast church that had been deconsecrated.

One Sunday afternoon, when Clarence and I were feeling particularly at odds with the world, we sat on the wall at the back of Daddy Helms's half-finished bar and broke just about every goddamned window in the place, flinging stones with pinpoint accuracy at the new panes. Eventually, we found an old abandoned septic tank, and, in a final act of vandalism, we hoisted it through the large arched window at the back of the premises, which Daddy Helms had intended would span the bar itself like a fan.

I didn't see Clarence for a few days after that and thought nothing of the consequences until one night, as we walked down St. John with an illicitly bought six-pack of beer, three of Daddy Helms's men caught us and dragged us toward a black Cadillac Eldorado. They cuffed our hands and put duct tape over our mouths and tied dirty rags over our eyes, then dumped us in the trunk and closed it. Clarence Johns and I lay side by side as we were carried away and I was conscious of the sour, unwashed smell from him, until I realized that I probably smelled the same.

But there were other smells in that trunk beyond oil and rags and the sweat of two teenage boys. It smelled of human excrement and urine, of vomit and bile. It smelled of the fear of impending death and I knew, even then, that a lot of people had been brought for rides in that Cadillac.

Time seemed to fade away in the blackness of the car, so that I couldn't tell how far we had traveled until it ground to a halt. The trunk was opened and I could hear waves crashing to my left and could taste the salt in the air. We were hauled from the trunk and dragged through bushes and over stones. I could feel sand beneath my feet, and, beside me, I heard Clarence Johns start to whimper, or maybe it was my own whimperings I heard. Then we were thrown facedown on the sand and there were hands at my clothes, my shoes. My shirt was ripped from me and I was stripped from the waist down, kicking frantically at the unseen figures around me until someone punched me hard with his knuckles in the small of the back and I stopped kicking. The rag was pulled away from my eyes and I looked up to see Daddy Helms standing above me. Behind him, I could see the silhouette of a large building: the Black Point Inn. We were on Western Beach at Prouts Neck, part of Scarborough itself. If I had been able to turn, I would have seen the lights of Old Orchard Beach, but I was not able to turn.

Daddy Helms held the butt of his cigar in his deformed hand and smiled at me. It was a smile like light flashing on a blade. He wore a white three-piece suit, a gold watch chain snaking across his vest, and a red-and-white spotted bow tie arranged neatly at the collar of his white cotton shirt. Beside me, Clarence Johns's shoes scuffled in the sand as he tried to gain enough purchase to raise himself up, but one of Daddy Helms's men, a blond-haired savage called Tiger Martin, placed the sole of his foot on Clarence's chest and forced him back on to the sand. Clarence, I noticed, was not naked.

"You Bob Warren's grandson?" Daddy Helms asked after a while. I nodded. I thought I was going to choke. My nostrils were filled with sand and I couldn't seem to get enough air into my lungs.

"You know who I am?" asked Daddy Helms, still looking at me.

I nodded again.

"But you can't know who I am, boy. You knew me, you wouldn'ta done what you did to my place. 'Less you're a fool, that is, and that's worse than not knowin'."

He turned his attention briefly to Clarence, but he didn't say anything to him. I thought I caught a flash of pity in his eyes as he looked at Clarence. Clarence was dumb, there was no doubt about that. For a brief instant, I seemed to be looking at Clarence with new eyes, as if he alone was not part of Daddy Helms's gang and all five of us were about to do something terrible to him. But I was not with Daddy Helms and the thought of what was about to happen brought me back again. I felt the sand beneath my skin and I watched as Tiger Martin came forward, carrying a heavy-looking black garbage bag in his arms. He looked to Daddy Helms, Daddy Helms nodded, and then the bag was tipped upside down and the contents poured over my body.

It was earth, but something else too: I sensed thousands of small legs moving on me, crawling through the hairs on my legs and groin, exploring the crevasses of my body like tiny lovers. I felt them on my tightly closed eyes and shook my head hard to clear them away. Then the biting started, tiny pinpoints of pain on my arms, my eyelids, my legs, even my penis, as the fire ants began to attack. I felt them crawling into my nostrils, and then the biting started there as well. I twisted and writhed, rubbing myself on the sand in an effort to kill as many of them as I could, but it was like trying to remove the sand itself, grain by grain. I kicked and spun and felt tears running down my cheeks and then, just as it seemed that I couldn't take any more, I felt a gloved hand on my ankle and I was dragged through the sand toward the surf. My wrists were freed and I plunged into the water, ripping the tape from my mouth, ignoring the pain as it tore my lips in my desire to rub and scratch myself. I submerged my head as the waves crashed above me, and still it seemed that I felt threadlike legs moving on me and felt the final bites of the insects before they drowned. I was shouting in pain and panic and then I was crying too, crying in shame and hurt and anger and fear.

For days afterward, I found the remains of ants in my

hair. Some of them were longer than the nail on my middle finger, with barbed pincers that curved forward to embrace the skin. My body was covered in raised bumps, almost an imitation of those of Daddy Helms himself, and the inside of my nose felt tender and swollen.

I pulled myself from the water and staggered onto the sand. Daddy Helms's men had gone back to the car, leaving only Clarence and me on the beach with Daddy Helms himself. Clarence was untouched. Daddy Helms saw the realization in my face and he smiled as he puffed on his cigar.

"We found your friend last night," he said. He placed a thick, melted-wax hand on Clarence's shoulders. Clarence flinched, but he didn't move. "He told us everything. We didn't even have to hurt him."

The pain of betrayal superseded the bites and the itching, the lingering sensation of movement on my skin. I looked at Clarence Johns with new eyes, adult eyes. He stood on the sand, his arms wrapped around his body, shivering. His eyes were filled with a pain that sang out from the depths of his being. I wanted to hate him for what he had done, and Daddy Helms wanted me to hate him, but instead I felt only a deep emptiness and a kind of pity.

And I felt a kind of pity, too, for Daddy Helms, with his ravaged skin and his mounds and folds of heavy flesh, forced to visit this punishment on two young men because of some broken glass, punishing them not only physically but by severing the bonds of their friendship.

"You learned two lessons here tonight, boy. You learned not to fuck with me, ever, and you learned something about friendship. In the end, the only friend you got is yourself, 'cause all the others, they'll let you down in the end. We all stand alone, in the end." Then he turned and waddled through the marram and dunes, back to his car.

They left us to walk back to Route 1, my clothes torn and soaked through from the seawater. We said nothing to each other, not even when we parted at the gate to my grandfather's property and Clarence headed off into the night, his cheap plastic shoes slapping on the road. We didn't hang out together after that and I largely forgot Clarence until he died in a failed robbery attempt at a computer warehouse on the outskirts of Austin twelve years later. Clarence was working as a security guard. He was shot by the raiders as he tried to defend a consignment of PCs.

When I entered my grandfather's house I took some antiseptic from the medicine cabinet, then stripped and stood in the bath, rubbing the liquid into the bites. It stung. When I had finished, I sat in the empty bath and wept, and that was where my grandfather found me. He said nothing for a while, then disappeared and came back with a red bowl containing a paste made from baking soda and water. He rubbed it painstakingly across my shoulders and chest, my legs and arms, then poured a little into my hand so I could rub it into my groin. He wrapped me in a white cotton sheet and sat me down in a chair in the kitchen, before pouring us each a large glass of brandy. It was Remy Martin, I remember, XO, the good stuff. It took me some time to finish it, but neither of us spoke a word. As I stood to go to bed, he patted me lightly on the head.

"A hard man," repeated my grandfather, draining the last of his coffee. He stood and the dog rose with him.

"You want to walk the dog with me?"

I declined. He shrugged his shoulders and I watched him as he walked down the porch steps, the dog already running ahead of him, barking and sniffing and looking back to make sure the old man was following, then running on farther again.

Daddy Helms died two years later of stomach cancer. When he died, it was estimated that he had been involved, directly or indirectly, with over forty killings, some of them as far south as Florida. There was no more than a handful of people at his funeral.

I thought of Daddy Helms again as Rachel and I made our way from the killings in Metairie. I don't know why.

Maybe I felt there was something of his rage in Joe Bonanno, a hatred of the world that stemmed from something rotten inside him. I remembered my grandfather, I remembered Daddy Helms, and I recalled the lessons they had tried to teach me, lessons that I still had not yet fully learned.

41
□

OUTSIDE THE MAIN cemetery gate, the New Orleans police were corralling witnesses and clearing the way for the injured to be carried to waiting ambulances. TV crews from WWDL and WDSU were trying to talk with survivors. I stayed close to one of Lionel Fontenot's men, the one who had been entrusted with the care of the M16, as we approached the gates at an angle. We followed him until he arrived at a portion of ruptured fencing by the highway, then made his way through it to a waiting Lincoln. As he drove away, Rachel and I climbed over the fence and walked back toward our car, unspeaking, approaching it from the west. It was parked away from the main center of activity and we were able to slip off without attracting any attention.

"How did that happen?" asked Rachel in a quiet voice as we drove back into the city. "There should have been police. There should have been someone to stop them . . ." Her voice trailed away and she remained silent as we drove back to the Quarter, her hands clasped across her upper body. I didn't disturb her.

One of a number of things had happened. Someone in charge could have screwed up by assigning insufficient police to Metairie, believing that Joe Bones would never try to take out Lionel Fontenot at his brother's funeral in front of witnesses. The guns had been stashed either late the previous night or early that morning, and the cemetery had not been searched. It could also have been the case that Lionel warned off the cops, just as he had warned off the media, anxious not to turn his brother's funeral into a circus. The other possibility was that Joe Bones had paid off or threatened some or all of the cops at Metairie and they had turned their backs while his men went about their business.

When we reached the hotel, I took Rachel to my room—I didn't want her surrounded by the images she had pinned to the walls of her own room. She went straight to the bathroom and closed the door behind her. I could hear the sound of the shower starting up. She stayed there for a long time.

When she eventually emerged, she had a big white bath towel draped around her from her breasts to her knees and was drying her hair with a smaller towel. Her eyes were red as she looked at me, then her chin trembled and she began to cry again. I held her, kissing the top of her head, then her forehead, her cheeks, her lips. Her mouth was warm as she responded to the kiss, her tongue darting around my teeth and entwining with my own tongue. I pressed hard against her, pulling the towel from her as I did. Her fingers fumbled at my belt and my zipper, then reached inside and held me tightly. Her other hand worked at the buttons on my shirt as she kissed my neck and ran her tongue across my chest and around my nipples.

I kicked off my shoes and leaned over awkwardly to try to take off my socks. Damn socks. She smiled a little as I almost fell over while removing the left one and then I was on top of her as she pushed down my pants and shorts.

Her breasts were small, her hips slightly wide, the small triangle of hair at their center a deep, fiery red. She tasted sweet. When she came, her back arched high and her legs wrapped around my thighs, I felt like I had never been held so tightly, or loved so hard.

Afterward, she slept. I slipped from the bed, put on a T-shirt and jeans, and took the key to her room from her bag. I walked barefoot down the gallery to the room, closed the door behind me, and stood for a time before the pictures on the wall. Rachel had bought a large draftsman's pad on which to work out patterns and ideas. I took two sheets from it, taped them together, and added them to the images on the wall. Then, surrounded by pictures of the anatomized Marsyas and photocopies of the crime-scene photos of *Tante* Marie and Tee Jean, I took a felt-tip and began to write.

In one corner I wrote the names of Jennifer and Susan, a kind of pang of regret and guilt hitting me as I wrote Susan's name. I tried to put it from my mind and continued writing. In another corner I put the names of *Tante* Marie, Tee Jean, and slightly to one side, Florence. In the third corner I wrote Remarr's name and in the fourth I placed a question mark and the word "girl" beside it. In the center I wrote "Trav Man" and then, like a child drawing a star, I added a series of lines emanating from the center and tried to write down all that I knew, or thought I knew, about the killer.

When I had finished, the list included a voice synthesis program or unit; the Book of Enoch; a knowledge of Greek myths / early medical texts; a knowledge of police proce-dures and activities, based on what Rachel had said follow-ing the deaths of Jennifer and Susan, the fact that he had known that the feds were monitoring my cell phone, and the killing of Remarr. Initially I thought that if he had seen Remarr at the Aguillard house, then Remarr would have died there and then, but I reconsidered on the basis that the Traveling Man would have been reluctant to remain at the scene or to engage an alert Remarr, and had decided to wait for another chance. The other option was that the killer had found out about the fingerprint and, somehow, the killer had also later found Remarr.

I added other elements based on standard assumptions: white, male killer, probably somewhere between his twen-ties and forties; a Louisiana base from which to strike at Re-marr and the Aguillards; a change of clothing, or coveralls worn over his own clothes, to protect him from the blood; and access to and knowledge of ketamine.

I drew another line from Trav Man to the Aguillards, since the killer knew that *Tante* Marie had been talking, and a second line connecting him to Remarr. I added a dotted line to Jennifer and Susan, and wrote Edward Byron's name with a question mark beside it. Then, on impulse, I added a third dotted line and wrote David Fontenot's name between

those of the Aguillards and Remarr, based only on the
Honey Island connection and the possibility that, if the
Traveling Man had lured him to Honey Island and tipped
off Joe Bones that David Fontenot would be there, then the
killer was someone known to the Fontenot family. Finally, I
wrote Edward Byron's name on a separate sheet and pinned
it beside the main diagram.

I sat on the edge of Rachel's bed and breathed in the
scent of her in the room as I looked at what I had written,
shifting the pieces around in my head to see if they would
match up anywhere. They didn't, but I made one more addition before I returned to my own room to wait for Angel
and Louis to return from Baton Rouge: I drew a light line between David Fontenot's name and the question mark representing the girl in the swamp. I didn't know it then, but by
drawing that line I had made the first significant leap into
the world of the Traveling Man.

I returned to my own room and sat by the balcony,
watching Rachel in her uneasy sleep. Her eyelids moved
rapidly and once or twice she let out small groans and made
pushing movements with her hands, her feet scrambling beneath the blankets. I heard Angel and Louis before I saw
them, Angel's voice raised in what seemed to be anger, Louis
responding in measured tones with a hint of mockery beneath them.

Before they could knock, I opened the door and indicated that we should talk in their room. They hadn't heard
about the shootings at Metairie since, according to Angel,
they hadn't been listening to the radio in the rental car. His
face was red as he spoke and his lips were pale. I don't think
that I had ever seen him so angry.

In their room, the bickering started again. Stacey Byron, a
bottle blonde in her early forties who had kept her figure remarkably well for a woman of her age, had apparently come
on to Louis in the course of their interrogation of her. Louis
had, in a manner, responded.

"I was pumping her for information," he explained, his
mouth twitching in amusement as he looked sideways at
Angel. Angel was unimpressed.

"Sure you wanted to pump her, but the only information you were after was her bra size and the dimensions of her ass," he spat. Louis rolled his eyes in exaggerated bafflement and I thought, for a moment, that Angel was going to strike him. His fists bunched and he moved forward slightly before he managed to restrain himself.

I felt sorry for Angel. While I didn't believe there was anything in Louis's courting of Edward Byron's wife, beyond the natural response of any individual to the favorable attentions of another and Louis's belief that, by leading her on, she might give away something about her ex-husband, I knew how much Louis mattered to Angel. Angel's history was murky, Louis's more so, but I remembered things about Angel, things that I sometimes felt Louis forgot.

When Angel was sent down to Rikers Island, he attracted the attentions of a man named William Vance. Vance had killed a Korean shopkeeper in the course of a botched robbery in Brooklyn and that was how he ended up in Rikers, but there were other things suspected of him: that he had raped and killed an elderly woman in Utica, mutilating her before she died; that he may have been linked to a similar killing in Delaware. There was no proof, other than rumor and conjecture, but when the opportunity came to put Vance away for the killing of the Korean, the DA, to his credit, seized it.

And for some reason, Vance decided that he wanted Angel dead. I heard that Angel had dissed him when Vance had tried to get it on with him, that he had knocked out one of Vance's teeth in the showers. But there was no telling with a man like Vance: the workings of his mind were obscure and confused by hatred and strange, bitter longing. Now Vance didn't just want to rape Angel: he wanted to kill him, and kill him slowly. Angel had pulled three to five. After one week in Rikers, the odds of him surviving his first month had plummeted.

Angel had no friends on the inside and fewer still outside, so he called me. I knew that it pained him to do so. He was proud and I think that, under ordinary circumstances, he would have tried to work out his problems for himself. But William Vance, with his tattoos of bloodied knives on his arms and a spider's web over his chest, was far from ordinary.

I did what I could. I pulled Vance's files and copied the transcripts of his interrogation over the Utica killing and a number of similar incidents. I copied details of the evidence assembled against him and the account of an eyewitness who later retracted after Vance made a call and threatened to fuck her and her children to death if she gave evidence against him. Then I took a trip to Rikers.

I spoke to Vance through a transparent screen. He had added an india ink tattoo of a tear below his left eye, bringing the total number of tattooed tears to three, each one representing a life taken. A spider's silhouette was visible at the base of his neck. I spoke to him softly for about ten minutes. I warned him that if anything happened to Angel, anything at all, I would make sure that every con in the place knew that he was only a hair's breadth away from sexual homicide charges involving old, defenseless women. Vance had five years left to serve before he became eligible for parole. If his fellow inmates found out what he was suspected of doing, there were men who could ensure that he would have to spend those five years in solitary to avoid death. Even then, he would have to check his food every day for powdered glass, would have to pray that a guard's attention didn't wander for an instant while he was being escorted to the yard for his hour's recreation, or while he was being brought to the prison doctor when the stress began to take its toll on his health.

Vance knew all this and yet, two days after we spoke, he tried to castrate Angel with a shank. Only the force of Angel's heel connecting with Vance's knee saved him, although Angel still needed twenty stitches across his stomach and thigh after Vance slashed wildly at him as he fell to the ground.

Vance was taken in the shower the next morning. Persons unknown held him down, used a wrench to hold his mouth open, and then pumped water mixed with detergent into his body. The poison destroyed his insides, tearing apart his stomach and almost costing him his life. For the remainder of his life in prison he was a shell of a man, racked by pains in his gut that made him howl in the night. It had taken one telephone call. I live with that too.

After he was released, Angel hooked up with Louis. I'm not even sure how these two solitary creatures met, exactly, but they had now been together for six years. Angel needed Louis, and in his way, Louis needed Angel too, but I sometimes thought that the balance of the relationship hinged on Angel. Men and men, men and women, whatever the permutation, in the end one partner always feels more than the other and that partner usually suffers for it.

It emerged that they hadn't learned much from Stacey Byron. The cops had been watching the house from the front but Louis and Angel, dressed in the only suit he owned, had come in from the back. Louis had flashed his fitness club membership and his smile as he told Mrs. Byron that they were just conducting a routine search of her garden and they spent the next hour talking to her about her ex-husband, about how often Louis worked out, and in the end, whether or not he'd ever had a white woman. It was at that point that Angel had really started to get annoyed.

"She says she hasn't seen him in four months," said Louis. "Says that last time she saw him, he didn't say much, just asked after her and the kids and took some old clothes from the attic. Seems he had a carrier bag from some drugstore in Opelousas and the feds are concentrating their search there."

"Does she know why the feds are looking for him?"

"Nope. They told her that he might be able to assist them with information on some unsolved crimes. She ain't dumb, though, and I fed her a little more to see if she'd bite. She said that he always had an interest in medical affairs; seems he might have had ambitions to be a doctor at one time, although he didn't have the education to be a tree surgeon."

"Did you ask her if she thought he could kill?"

"I didn't have to. Seems he threatened to kill her once, while they were arguing over the terms of the divorce."

"Did she remember what he said?"

Louis nodded deeply, once.

"Uh-huh. He said he'd tear her fucking face off."

Angel and Louis parted on bad terms, with Angel retiring to Rachel's room while Louis sat on the balcony of their room and took in the sounds and smells of New Orleans, not all of them pleasant.

"I was thinking of getting a bite to eat," he said. "You interested?"

I was surprised. I guessed that he wanted to talk but I had never spent time with Louis without Angel being present as well.

I checked on Rachel. The bed was empty and I could hear the shower running. I knocked gently on the door.

"It's open," she said.

When I entered, she had the shower curtain wrapped around her. "Suits you," I said. "Clear plastic is in this season."

The sleep hadn't done her any good. There were dark rings under her eyes and she still looked shaky. She made a halfhearted effort to smile, but it was more like a grimace of pain than anything else.

"You want to go out and eat?"

"I'm not hungry. I'm going to do some work, then take two sleeping pills and try to sleep without dreaming."

I told her that Louis and I were heading out, then went to tell Angel. I found him flicking through the notes Rachel had made. He motioned to my chart on the bedroom wall. "Lot of blank spaces on that."

"I still have one or two details to work out."

"Like who did it and why." He gave me a twisted grin.

"Yeah, but I'm trying not to get too hung up on minor problems. You okay?"

He nodded. "I think this whole thing is gettin' to me, all this . . ." He waved an arm at the illustrations on the wall.

"Louis and I are heading out to eat. You wanna come?"

"Nah, I'd only be the lemon. You can have him."

"Thanks. I'll break the bad news of my sexual awakening

to the *Swimsuit Illustrated* models tomorrow. They'll be heartbroken. Look after Rachel, will you? This hasn't been one of her better days."

"I'll be right along the hall."

Louis and I sat in Felix's Restaurant and Oyster Bar on the corner of Bourbon and Iberville. There weren't too many tourists there; they tended to gravitate toward the Acme Oyster House across the street, where they served red beans and savory rice in a hollowed-out boat of French bread, or a classier French Quarter joint like Nola. Felix's was plainer. Tourists don't care much for plain. After all, they can get plain at home.

Louis ordered an oyster po'boy and doused it in hot sauce, sipping an Abita beer between bites. I had fries and a chicken po'boy, washed down with mineral water.

"Waiter thinks you're a sissy," commented Louis as I sipped my water. "The ballet was in town, he'd hit on you for tickets."

"Shows what he knows," I replied. "You're confusing things by not conforming to the stereotype. Maybe you should mince more."

His mouth twitched and he raised his hand for another Abita. It came quickly. The waiter performed the neat trick of making sure we weren't left waiting for anything while trying to spend as little time as possible in the vicinity of our table. Other diners chose to take the scenic route to their tables rather than pass too close to us and those forced to sit near us seemed to eat at a slightly faster pace than the rest. Louis had that effect on people. It was as if there was a shell of potential violence around him, and something more: the sense that, if that violence erupted, it would not be the first time that it had done so.

"Your friend Woolrich," he said as he drained the Abita halfway with one mouthful. "You trust him?"

"I don't know. He has his own agenda."

"He's a fed. They only got their own agendas." He eyed me over the top of the bottle. "I think, if you were climbing a rock with your friend and you slipped, found yourself dan-

gling on the end of the rope with him at the other end, he'd
cut the rope."

"You're a cynic."

His mouth twitched again. "If the dead could speak,
they'd call all cynics realists."

"If the dead could speak, they'd tell us to have more sex
while we can." I picked at my fries. "The feds have anything
on you?"

"Suspicions, maybe; nothing more. That's not really
what I'm getting at."

His eyes were unblinking and there was no warmth in
them now. I think that, if he had believed Woolrich was
close to him, he would have killed him and it would not
have cost him another thought afterward.

"Why is Woolrich helping us?" he asked, eventually.

"I've thought about that too," I said. "I'm not sure. Part
of it could be that he empathizes with the need to stay in
touch with what's going on. If he feeds me information,
then he can control the extent of my involvement."

But I knew that wasn't all. Louis was right. Woolrich had
his own agenda. He had depths to him that I only occasionally glimpsed, as when the different shifting colors on the
surface of the sea hint at the sharp declivities and deep
spaces that lie beneath. He was a hard man to be with in
some ways: he conducted his friendship with me on his
own terms, and in the time I had known him, months had
gone by without any contact from him. He made up for this
with a strange loyalty, a sense that, even when he was absent from their lives, he never forgot those closest to him.

But as a fed, Woolrich played hardball. He had progressed to assistant SAC by making collars, by attaching
his name to high-profile operations, and by fixing other
agents' wagons when they got in his way. He was intensely
ambitious and maybe he saw the Traveling Man as a way
of reaching greater heights: SAC, assistant director, a
deputy directorship, maybe even to eventually becoming
the first agent to be appointed directly to the post of director. The pressure on him was intense, but if Woolrich were
to be responsible for bringing an end to the Traveling Man,

he would be assured a bright, powerful future within the Bureau.

I had a part to play in this, and Woolrich knew it and felt it strongly enough that he would use whatever friendship existed between us to bring about an end to what was taking place. "I think he's using me as bait," I said at last. "And he's holding the line."

"How much you think he's holding back?" Louis finished his beer and smacked his lips appreciatively.

"He's like an iceberg," I replied. "We're only seeing the ten percent above the surface. Whatever the feds know, they're not sharing it with the local cops and Woolrich sure isn't sharing it with us. There's something more going on here, and only Woolrich and maybe a handful of feds are privy to it. You play chess?"

"In my way," he replied dryly. Somehow, I couldn't see that way including a standard board.

"This whole thing is like a chess game," I continued. "Except we only get to see the other player's move when one of our pieces is taken. The rest of the time, it's like playing in the dark."

Louis raised a finger for the check. The waiter looked relieved.

"And our Mr. Byron?"

I shrugged. I felt strangely distant from what was happening. Part of it was because we were players on the periphery of the investigation, but part of it was also because I needed that distance to think. In one way, what had taken place with Rachel that afternoon, and what it meant to my feelings of grief and loss about Susan, had given me some of that distance.

"I don't know." We were only beginning to construct a picture of Byron, like a figure at the center of a jigsaw puzzle around which other pieces might interlock. "We'll work our way toward him. First, I want to find out what Remarr saw the night *Tante* Marie and Tee Jean were killed. And I want to know why David Fontenot was out at Honey Island alone."

It was clear now that Lionel Fontenot would move

against Joe Bones. Joe Bones knew that too, which was why he had risked an assault at Metairie. Once Lionel was back in his compound, he would be out of the reach of Joe Bones's men. The next move was Lionel's.

The check arrived. I paid and Louis left a deliberately overgenerous twenty-dollar tip. The waiter looked at the bill like Andrew Jackson was going to bite his finger when he tried to lift it.

"I think we're going to have to talk to Lionel Fontenot," I said as we left. "And Joe Bones."

Louis actually smiled. "Joe ain't gonna be too keen on talking to you, seeing as how his boy tried to put you in the ground."

"I kinda figured that," I replied. "Could be that Lionel Fontenot might help us out there."

We walked back to the Flaisance. The streets of New Orleans aren't the safest in the world but I didn't think that anyone would bother us.

I was right.

42

□

I SLEPT LATE the next morning. Rachel had returned to her own room to sleep. When I knocked, her voice sounded harsh with tiredness. She told me she wanted to stay in bed for a while, and when she felt better, she would go out to Loyola again. I asked Angel and Louis to watch out for her, then drove from the Flaisance.

The incident at Metairie had left me shaken, and the prospect of facing Joe Bones again was unappealing. I also felt a crushing sense of guilt for what had happened to Rachel, for what I had drawn her into and for what I had forced her to do. I needed to get out of New Orleans, at least for a short time. I wanted to clear my head, to try to see things from a different angle. I ate a bowl of chicken soup in the Gumbo Shop on St. Peter and then headed out of the city.

Morphy lived about four miles from Cecilia, a few miles northwest of Lafayette. He had bought and was refurbishing a raised plantation home by a small river, a budget version of the classic old Louisiana houses that had been built at the end of the nineteenth century, a blend of French Colonial, West Indian, and European architectural influences.

The house presented a strange spectacle. Its main living quarters were on top of an aboveground basement area, which had once been used for storage and as protection from flooding. This section of the house was brick and Morphy had reworked the arched openings with what looked like hand-carved frames. The living quarters above, which would usually have been weatherboard or plaster-covered, had been replaced with timber slats. A double-pitched roof, which had been partially reslated, extended over the gallery.

I had called ahead and told Angie I was on my way. Morphy had just got home when I arrived. I found him in the yard at the rear of the house, benching two hundred in the evening air.

"What do you think of the house?" he asked as I approached, not even pausing in his reps as he spoke.

"It's great. Looks like you still have some way to go before it's finished."

He grunted with the effort of the final rep as I acted as spotter, slotting the bar back onto its rest. He stood up and stretched, then looked at the back of his house with barely concealed admiration.

"It was built by a Frenchman in eighteen eighty-eight," he said. "He knew what he was doing. It's built on an east-west axis, with principal exposure to the south." He pointed out the lines of the building as he spoke. "He designed it the way the Europeans designed their houses, so that the low angle of the sun in winter would heat the building. Then, in the summer, the sun would only shine on it in the morning and evening. Most American houses aren't built that way, they just put 'em up whatever way suits 'em, throw a stick in the air and see where it lands. We were spoiled by cheap energy. Then the Arabs came along and hiked up their prices and people had to start thinking again about the layout of their houses."

He smiled. "Don't know how much good an east-west house does around here, though. Sun shines all the goddamn time anyway."

When he had showered, we sat at a table in the kitchen with Angie and talked as she cooked. Angie was almost a foot smaller than her husband, a slim, dark-skinned woman with auburn hair that flowed down her back. She was a junior school teacher, but she did some painting in her spare time. Her canvases, dark, impressionistic pieces set around water and sky, adorned the walls of the house.

Morphy drank a bottle of Breaux Bridge and I had a soda. Angie sipped a glass of white wine as she cooked. She cut four chicken breasts into about sixteen pieces and set them to one side as she set about preparing the roux.

Cajun gumbo is made with roux, a glutinous thickener, as a base. Angie poured peanut oil into a cast iron skillet over a high flame, added in an equal amount of flour, and beat it with a whisk continuously so it wouldn't burn, gradually turning the roux from blond to beige and through mahogany until it reached a dark chocolate color. Then she took it off the heat and allowed it to cool, still stirring.

While Morphy looked on, I helped her chop the trinity of onion, green pepper, and celery and watched as she sweated them in oil. She added a seasoning of thyme and oregano, paprika and cayenne, onion and garlic salt, then dropped in thick pieces of chorizo. She added the chicken and more spices, until their scent filled the room. After about half an hour, she spooned white rice onto plates and poured the thick rich gumbo over it. We ate in silence, savoring the flavors in our mouths.

When we had washed and dried the dishes, Angie left us and went to bed. Morphy and I sat in the kitchen and I told him about Raymond Aguillard and his belief that he had seen the figure of a girl at Honey Island. I told him of *Tante* Marie's dreams and my feeling that, somehow, David Fontenot's death at Honey Island could be linked to the girl.

Morphy didn't say anything for a long time. He didn't sneer at visions of ghosts, or at an old woman's belief that the voices she heard were real. Instead, all he said was: "You sure you know where this place is?"

I nodded.

"Then we'll give it a try. I'm free tomorrow, so you better stay here tonight. We got a spare room you can use." I called Rachel at the Flaisance and told her what I intended to do the next day and where in Honey Island we were likely to be. She said that she would tell Angel and Louis, and that she felt a little better for her sleep. It would take her a long time to get over the death of Joe Bones's man.

It was early morning, barely ten before seven, when we prepared to leave. Morphy wore heavy steel-toed Caterpillar

work boots, old jeans, and a sleeveless sweatshirt over a
long-sleeved T-shirt. The sweat was dappled with paint and
there were patches of tar on the jeans. His head was freshly
shaved and smelled of witch hazel.

While we drank coffee and ate toast on the gallery, Angie
came out in a white robe and rubbed her husband's clean
scalp, smirking at him as she took a seat beside him. Morphy acted like it annoyed the hell out of him, but he doted
on her every touch. When we rose to go, he kissed her
deeply with the fingers of his right hand entwined in her
hair. Her body instinctively rose from the chair to meet him,
but he pulled away laughing and she reddened. It was only
then that I noticed the swelling at her belly: she was no
more than five months gone, I guessed. As we walked across
the grass at the front of the house, she stood on the gallery,
her weight on one hip and a light breeze tugging at her
robe, and watched her husband depart.

"Been married long?" I asked, as we walked toward a cypress glade that obscured the view of the house from the
road.

"Two years in January. I'm a contented man. Never
thought I would be, but that girl changed my life." There
was no embarrassment as he spoke and he acknowledged it
with a smile.

"When is the baby due?"

He smiled again. "Late December. Guys held a party for
me when they found out, to celebrate the fact that I was
shooting live ones."

An old Ford truck was parked in the glade, with a trailer
attached on which a wide, flat-bottomed aluminum boat lay
covered in tarpaulin, its engine tilted forward so that it
rested on the bed. "Toussaint's brother dropped it over late
last night," he explained. "Does some hauling on the side."

"Where's Toussaint?"

"In bed with food poisoning. He ate some bad shrimp,
least that's how he tells it. Personally, I think he's just too
damn lazy to give up his morning in bed."

In the back of the truck, beneath some more tarpaulin,
were an axe, a chain saw, two lengths of chain, some strong

nylon rope, and a cooler. There was also a dry suit and mask, a pair of waterproof flashlights, and two air tanks. Morphy added a flask of coffee, some water, two sticks of French bread, and four chicken breasts coated in K-Paul's Cajun spices, all contained in a waterproof bag, then climbed into the driver's seat of the truck and started her up. She belched smoke and rattled a bit, but the engine sounded good and strong. I climbed in beside him and we drove toward Honey Island, a Clifton Chenier tape on the truck's battered stereo.

We entered the reserve at Slidell, a collection of shopping malls, fast food joints, and Chinese buffets on the north shore of Lake Pontchartrain named for the Democratic senator John Slidell. In the 1844 federal election, Slidell arranged for two steamboats to carry a bunch of Irish and German voters from New Orleans to Plaquemines Parish to vote. There was nothing illegal about that; what was illegal was letting them vote at all the other polling stations along the route.

A mist still hung over the water and the trees as we unloaded the boat at the Pearl River ranger station, beside a collection of run-down fishing shacks that floated near the bank. We loaded the chains, rope, chain saw, the diving gear, and the food. In a tree beside us, the early morning sun caught the threads of a huge, intricate web, at the center of which lay, unmoving, a golden orb spider. Then, with the sound of the motor blending with the noise of insects and birds, we moved onto the Pearl.

The banks of the river were lined with high tupelo gum, water birch, willows, and some tall cypress with trumpet creeper vines, their red flowers in bloom, winding up their trunks. Here and there trees were marked with plastic bottles, signs that catfish lines had been sunk. We passed a village of riverside homes, most of them down-at-the-heel, with flat-bottomed pirogues tied up outside them. A blue heron watched us calmly from the branches of a cypress; on a log beneath him, a yellow-bellied turtle lay soaking up the sun.

I still had Raymond Aguillard's map but it took us two attempts to find the trevasse, the trappers' channel that he had marked. There was a stand of gum trees at its entrance, their swollen buttresses like the bulbs of flowers, with a sole green ash leaning almost across the gap. Further in, branches weighed down with Spanish moss hung almost to the surface of the water and the air was redolent with the mingled scents of growth and decay. Misshapen tree trunks surrounded by duckweed stood like monuments in the early morning sun. East, I could see the gray dome of a beaver lodge, and as we watched, a snake slithered into the water not five feet from us.

"Diamondback," said Morphy.

Around us, water dripped from cypress and tupelo, and birdsong echoed in the trees.

"Any chance of 'gators here?" I asked.

He shrugged. "Maybe. Don't bother people much, though, unless people bother them. There's easier pickings in the swamps. If you see any while I'm down there, fire a shot to let me know what's happening."

The bayou started to narrow until it was barely wide enough to allow the boat passage. I felt the bottom scrape on a tree trunk resting below us. Morphy killed the engine and we used our hands and a pair of wooden paddles to pull ourselves through.

It seemed then that we might somehow have made a mistake in our map reading, because we were faced with a wall of wild rice, the tall, green stalks like blades in the water. There was only one narrow gap visible, big enough for a child to pass through. Morphy shrugged and restarted the engine, aiming us for the gap. I used the paddle to beat back the rice stalks as we moved forward. Something splashed close by us and a dark shape, like a large rat, sliced through the water.

"Nutria," said Morphy. I could see the big rodent's nose and whiskers now as it stopped beside a tree trunk and sniffed the air inquisitively. "Taste worse than 'gators. I hear we're trying to sell their meat to the Chinese since no one else wants to eat it."

The rice blended into sharp-edged grass that cut at my hands as I worked the paddle, and then the boat was free and we were in a kind of lagoon formed by a gradual accumulation of silt, its banks surrounded mainly by gum and willows that dragged the fingers of their branches in the water. There was some almost firm ground at the eastern edge, near some arrowroot lilies, with wild pig tracks in the dirt, the animals attracted by the promise of the arrowroot at the lilies' base. Further in, I could see the rotting remains of a T-cutter, probably one of the craft that had originally cut the channel. Its big V-8 engine was gone, and there were holes in its hull.

We tied the boat up at a sole red swamp maple that was almost covered with resurrection fern, waiting for the rains to bring it back to life. Morphy stripped down to a pair of Nike cycling shorts, rubbed himself down with grease, and put the dry suit on. He added the flippers, then strapped on the tank and tested it. "Most of the waters around here are no more than ten, maybe fifteen feet deep, but this place is different," he said. "You can see it in the way the light reflects on the water. It's deeper, twenty feet or more." Leaves, sticks, and logs floated on the water, and insects flitted above the surface. The water looked dark and green.

He washed the mask in the swamp water then turned to me. "Never thought I'd be looking for swamp ghosts on my day off," he said.

"Raymond Aguillard says he saw the girl here," I replied. "David Fontenot died up the river. There's something here. You know what you're looking for?"

He nodded. "Probably a container of some sort, heavy, sealed."

Morphy flicked on the flashlight, slipped on his mask, and began sucking bottled air. I tied one end of the climbing rope to his belt and another to the trunk of the maple, yanked it firm, then patted him on the back. He raised a thumb and waded into the water. Two or three yards out, he began to dive and I started to feed the rope out through my hands.

I had had little experience of diving, beyond a few basic lessons taken during a holiday with Susan on the Florida Keys. I didn't envy Morphy, swimming around in that swamp. During my teens, we went swimming in the Saco River, south of the Portland city limits, during the summer. Long, lean pike dwelt in those waters, vicious things that brought a hint of the primeval with them. When they brushed your bare legs, it made you think of stories you had heard about them biting small children or dragging swimming dogs down to the bottom of the river.

The waters of Honey Island swamp were like another world compared to the Saco. With its glittering snakes and its cowens, the name the Cajuns give to the swamp's snapping turtles, Honey Island seemed so much more feral than the backwaters of Maine. But there were alligator gar here too, and scaled shortnoses, as well as perch and bass and bowfins. And 'gators.

I thought of these things as Morphy disappeared below the surface of the bayou, but I also thought of the young girl who might have been dumped in these waters, where creatures she couldn't name bumped and clicked against the side of her tomb while others searched for rust holes through which to get at the rotting meat inside.

Morphy surfaced after five minutes, indicated the short, northeastern bank, and shook his head. Then he submerged again and the line on the ground snaked south as he swam. After another five minutes the rope began to pull out quickly. Morphy broke the surface again, but this time some distance from where the rope entered the water. He swam back to the bank, removed the mask and mouthpiece, and breathed in short gasps as he gestured back toward the southern end of the bayou.

"We got a couple of metal boxes, maybe four feet long, two feet wide, and eighteen inches deep, dumped down there," he said. "One's empty, the other's locked and bolted. Maybe a hundred yards away there's a bunch of oil barrels marked with red fleurs-de-lys. They belong to the old Brevis Chemical Company, used to operate out of West Baton Rouge until a big fire in eighty-nine put it out of business. That's it. Nothing else down there."

I looked out toward the edge of the bayou, where thick roots lay obscured beneath the water.

"Could we pull in the box using the rope?" I asked.

"Could do, but that box is heavy and if we bust it open while hauling it in we'll destroy whatever's inside. We'll have to bring the boat out and try to haul it up."

It was getting very warm now, although the trees on the bank provided some shade from the sun. Morphy took two bottles of still mineral water from the cooler and we drank them sitting on the bank. Then Morphy and I got into the boat and took it out to his marker.

Twice the box caught on some obstacle on the bottom as I tried to pull it up, and I had to wait for Morphy to signal before I could start hauling it in again. Eventually, the gray metal box broke the surface of the water, Morphy pushing up from beneath before he went back down to tie the marker rope to one of the oil barrels in case we had to search them.

I brought the boat back to the landing and dragged the box up onto the shore. The chain and lock securing it were old and rusted, probably too old to yield anything of any use to us. I took the axe and struck at the rusty lock that held the chain in place. It broke as Morphy walked onto the bank. He knelt beside me, the air tank still on his back and the mask pushed up on his forehead as I pulled at the lid of the box. It was stuck fast. I took the blunt head of the axe and struck upward along the edges until the lid lifted.

Inside was a consignment of breech-loading Springfield .50 caliber rifles and the bones of what seemed to be a small dog. The butts of the rifles had almost rotted but I could still see the letters *LNG* on the metal butt plates.

"Stolen rifles," said Morphy, pulling one free and examining it. "Maybe eighteen seventy or eighteen eighty. The authorities probably issued a stolen arms proclamation after these were taken and the thief dumped them or left them there with the intention of coming back."

He prodded at the dog's skull with his fingers. "The bones are an indicator of some kind. Pity nobody been seein' the Hound of the Baskervilles out here, else we'd have the whole mystery cleared up." He looked at the rifles, then back out toward the oil drums. He sighed, then began to swim out to the marker.

Hauling in the drums was a laborious process. The chain slipped off three times as we tried to pull in the first drum. Morphy came back for a second chain and wrapped it, parcel style, around the drum. The boat almost overturned when I tried to open the barrel while I was still on the water, so we were forced to bring it back to dry land. When we eventually got it to the bank, brown and rusting, it contained only stale oil. The drums had a hole for loading and pouring the oil, but the entire lid could also be pried off. When we opened the second drum it didn't even contain oil, just some stones that had been used to weigh the barrel down.

By now, Morphy was exhausted. We stopped for a time to eat some of the chicken and bread, and drink some of the coffee. It was now past midday and the heat in the bayou was heavy and draining. After we had rested, I offered to do some of the diving. Morphy didn't refuse, so I handed him my shoulder holster, then suited up and strapped on the spare tank.

The water was surprisingly cool as I slipped into it. As it reached my chest, it almost took my breath away. The chains were heavy across my shoulder as I guided myself along the marker rope with one hand. When I reached the spot where the rope entered the water, I slipped the flashlight from my belt and dived.

The water was deeper than I expected and very dark, the duckweed above me blocking out the sunlight in patches. At the periphery of my vision, fish twisted and spun. The barrels, of which five remained, all piled in a heap, were gathered around the submerged trunk of an ancient tree, its roots buried deep in the bottom of the bayou. Any boat that might have been using the bayou bank to land on would have avoided the tree, which meant that the barrels were in no danger of being disturbed. The water at the base of the tree was darker than the rest, so that without the flashlight the barrels would have been invisible.

I wrapped the top barrel in chains and yanked once to

test its weight. It tumbled from the top of the pile, yanking the rope from my grasp as it headed for the bottom. The water muddied, and dirt and vegetation obscured my vision, and then everything went black as oil began to leak from the drum. I was kicking back to get into clearer water when I heard the dull, echoing sound of a gunshot from above me. For a moment, I thought that Morphy might be in trouble until I remembered what the gunshot was supposed to signal and realized that it was I, not Morphy, who was in trouble.

I was breaking for the surface when I saw the 'gator. It was small, maybe only six feet long, but the flashlight beam caught the wicked-looking teeth jutting out along its jaws and its light-colored underbelly. It was as disoriented by the oil and dirt as I was, but it seemed to be angling toward my flashlight. I clicked it off and instantly lost sight of the 'gator as I made a final kick for the surface.

When I broke the water the marker rope was fifteen feet in front of me, Morphy beside it.

"Come on!" he shouted. "There's no other landing around you."

I splashed hard as I swam to him, all the time aware of the reptile cruising beneath me. As I splashed, I spotted it on the surface to my left, about twenty feet away from me. I could see the scales of its back, its hungry eyes and the line of its jaw pointed in my direction. I turned on my back so I could keep the 'gator in my sight and kicked out, sometimes using the rope to pull myself along, at other times using my hands.

I was still five feet from the boat when the 'gator moved, working its way swiftly through the water in my direction. I spat the mouthpiece out.

"Shoot it, goddammit," I shouted. I heard the boom of a gun and a spume of water kicked up in front of the 'gator, then a second. The creature stopped short and then a sprinkling of pink and white fell to my right and it turned in that direction. It reached the objects just as a second shower fell, farther away to the right, and I felt the boat against my back and Morphy's hands helping me to haul myself up. We turned for the bank as Morphy sent a third handful of marshmallows into the air. When I looked at him, he was grinning as he popped a last marshmallow into his mouth. Out on the bayou, the 'gator was snapping at the last of the candy.

"Scared you, huh?" Morphy smiled as I shrugged off the air tank and lay flat on the bottom of the boat.

I nodded and kicked off a flipper.

"I think you're going to have to get your dry suit cleaned," I said.

We sat on a log and watched the 'gator for a while. It cruised the bayou looking for more marshmallows, eventually settling for a wait-and-see policy, which consisted of it lying partially submerged near the marker rope. We sipped coffee from tin cups and finished off the last of the chicken.

"You should have shot it," I said.

"This *is* a nature reserve and there are laws about killing 'gators," responded Morphy testily. "Not much point in having a nature reserve if people can come in when they please and shoot all the wildlife."

We sipped the coffee some more, until I heard the sound of a boat coming our way through the rice and grass.

"Shit," said a familiar Brooklyn drawl as the prow of the boat broke the grass, "it's the Donner Party."

Angel emerged first, then Louis behind him, controlling the rudder. They moved steadily toward us and tied up at the maple. Angel splashed into the water, then followed our gaze out to the 'gator. He caught one sight of the partially submerged reptile and ran awkwardly onto the bank, his knees high and his elbows pumping.

"Man, what is this, Jurassic Park?" he said. He turned to Louis, who jumped from his boat to ours and then onto the bank. "Hey, didn't you tell your sister not to be swimmin' in no strange ponds?"

Angel was dressed in his usual jeans and battered sneakers, with a denim jacket over a Doonesbury T-shirt that depicted Duke and the motto *Death Before Unconsciousness*. Louis was wearing crocodile-skin boots, black Levi's, and a white collarless Liz Claiborne shirt.

"We dropped by to see how you were," said Angel, casting anxious glances out at the 'gator after I had introduced him to Morphy. He held a bag of donuts in his hand.

"Our friend's gonna be real upset if he sees you wearing one of his relatives, Louis," I said.

Louis sniffed and approached the water's edge. "Is there a problem?" he asked at last.

"We were diving and then Wally Gator appeared and we weren't diving anymore," I explained.

Louis sniffed again. "Hmm," he said. Then he drew his SIG and blew the tip of the 'gator's tail off. The reptile thrashed in pain and the water around it turned bright red. Then it turned and headed off into the bayou, trailing blood behind it. "You should have shot it," he said.

"Let's not get into it," I responded. "Roll up your sleeves, gentlemen, we're going to need some help."

I still had the dry suit on so I offered to keep diving.

"Trying to prove to me that you ain't chicken?" grinned Morphy.

"Nope," I said, as we untied the boat. "Trying to prove it to myself."

We rowed out to the marker rope and then I dived down with the hook and chains, leaving Angel topside with Morphy and his gun in case the 'gator showed up again. Louis joined us in the second boat A thick black film of oil had formed on the surface of the water and hung in the depths below. The barrels had scattered when the topmost drum fell. I checked the ruptured barrel with the flashlight but it appeared to contain nothing except the oil that remained.

It was laborious work, tying the barrel and hauling it up each time, but with two boats it meant that we could transport two barrels at a time to the bank. There was probably an easier way to do it, but we hadn't figured it out.

The sun was growing low and the waters were bathed in gold when we found her.

43

□

It seems to me now that when I touched the barrel for the first time to attach the chains, something coursed through my system and tightened in my stomach like a fist. I felt a jolt. A blade flashed before my eyes and the depths were colored by a fountain of blood, or perhaps it was simply the dying sun on the water above reflected on my mask. I closed my eyes for a moment and felt movement around me, not just the water of the bayou or the fish in its depths but another swimmer who twisted around my body and legs. I thought I felt her hair brush my cheek but when I reached out I caught only swamp weed in my hand.

This barrel was heavier than the others, weighed down, as we would discover, with masonry bricks that had been split neatly in half. It would need the combined efforts of Morphy and Angel to pull it up.

"It's her," I said to Morphy. "We've found her." And then I swam down to the barrel and maneuvered it slowly over the rocks and tree trunks at the bottom as we brought it up. We all seemed to handle this barrel more gently than the rest, as if the girl inside was merely sleeping and we didn't want to disturb her, as if she was not long decayed but had been laid within it only yesterday. On the bank, Angel took the crowbar and carefully applied it to the rim of the lid, but it refused to move. He examined it more closely.

"It's been sealed," he said. He scraped the crowbar over the surface of the barrel and checked the mark left. "The barrel's been treated with something as well. That's why it's in better condition than the others."

It was true. The barrel had hardly rusted and the fleur-de-lys on its side was as clear and bright as if it had been painted only days before.

I thought for a moment. We could use the chain saw to cut it, but if I was right and the girl was inside, I didn't want to damage the remains. We could also have called for assistance from the local cops, or even the feds. I suggested it, more out of duty than desire, but even Morphy declined. He might have been concerned at the embarrassment that would be caused if the barrel was empty, but when I looked in his eyes I could see that wasn't the case. He wanted us to take it as far as we could.

In the end, we tested the barrel by gently tapping along its length with the axe. From the difference in sound, we judged as best we could where we could safely cut. Morphy carefully made an incision near the sealed end of the barrel, and using a combination of chain saw and crowbar, we cut an area that was roughly half the circumference, then pushed it up with the crowbar and shined a flashlight inside.

The body was little more than bones and shreds of material, the skin and flesh entirely rotted away. She had been dumped in headfirst and her legs had been broken to fit her into the space. When I shined the beam to the far end of the barrel, I glimpsed bared teeth and strands of hair. We stood silently beside her, surrounded by the lapping water and the sounds of the swamp.

It was late that night when I got back to the Flaisance. While we waited for the Slidell police and the rangers, Angel and Louis departed, with Morphy's agreement. I stayed on to give my statement and back up Morphy's version of what had taken place. On Morphy's advice, the locals called the FBI. I didn't wait around. If Woolrich wanted to talk, he knew where to find me.

The light was still on in Rachel's room as I passed, so I stopped and knocked. She opened the door wearing a pink Calvin Klein nightshirt, which stopped at mid-thigh level.

"Angel told me what happened," she said, opening the door wider to let me enter. "That poor girl." She hugged me and then ran the shower in the bathroom. I stayed in there for a long time, my hands against the tiles, letting the water roll over my head and back.

After I had dried myself, I wrapped the towel around my waist and found Rachel sitting on the bed, leafing through her papers. She cocked an eyebrow at me.

"Such modesty," she said, with a little smile.

I sat on the edge of the bed and she wrapped her arms around me from behind. I felt her cheek and her warm breath against my back. "How are you feeling?" I asked.

Her grip tightened a little. "Okay, I think."

She turned me around so that I was facing her. She knelt on the bed before me, her hands clasped between her legs, and bit her lip. Then she reached out and gently, almost tentatively, ran her hand through my hair.

"I thought you psychology types were supposed to be good at all this," I said.

She shrugged. "I get just as confused as everybody else, except I know all the terminology for my confusion." She sighed. "Listen, what happened yesterday . . . I don't want to put pressure on you. I know how hard all this is for you, because of Susan and—"

I held my hand against her cheek and rubbed her lips gently with my thumb. Then I kissed her and felt her mouth open beneath mine. I wanted to hold her, to love her, to drive away the vision of the dead girl.

"Thanks," I said, my mouth still against her, "but I know what I'm doing."

"Well," she said, as she eased back slowly on the bed, "at least one of us does."

The following morning, the remains of the girl lay on a metal table, curled fetally by the constriction of the barrel as if to protect herself for eternity. On the instructions of the FBI, she had been brought to New Orleans, weighed and measured, X-rayed, and fingerprinted. The body bag in which she had been removed from Honey Island had been examined for debris that might have fallen from her while she was being transported.

The clean tiles, the shining metal tables, the glinting medical instruments, the white lights hanging above them all seemed too harsh, too relentless in their mission to expose, to examine, to reveal. It seemed a final indignity, after the terrors of her final moments, to display her here in the sterility of this room, with these men looking upon her. A part of me wanted to cover her with a shroud and carry her carefully, gently, to a dark hole beside flowing water, where green trees would shade the ground under which she lay and where no one would disturb her again.

But another part of me, the rational part, knew that she deserved a name, that she needed an identity to put an end to the anonymity of her sufferings and, perhaps, to close in on the man who had reduced her to this. And so we stood back as the gowned coroner and his assistants moved in with their tapes and their blades and their white-gloved hands.

The pelvis is the most easily recognizable distinguishing feature between the male and female skeletons. The greater sciatic notch, situated behind the inominate bone—which itself consists of the hip, the ischium, the ilium, and the pubis—is wider in the female, with a subpubic angle roughly the size of that between the thumb and forefinger. The pelvic outlet is also larger in the female but the thigh sockets are smaller, the sacrum wider.

Even the female skull is different from that of the male, a reflection in miniature of the physical differences between the two sexes. The female skull is as smooth and rounded as the female breast, yet smaller than the male skull; the forehead is higher and more rounded; the eye sockets, too, are higher and the edges less sharply defined; the female jaw, palate, and teeth are smaller.

The skeletal remains before us conformed to the general pelvic and skull rules governing the female body. In estimating the age of the body at the time of death, the ossification centers, or areas of bone formation, were examined, as were the teeth. The femur of the girl's body was almost completely fused at the head, although there was only partial joining of the collarbone to the top of the breastbone. After an examination of the sutures on her skull, the coroner estimated her age at twenty-one or twenty-two. There were marks on her forehead, the base of her jaw, and on her left cheekbone, where the killer had cut through to the bone as he removed her face.

Her dental features were recorded, a process known as forensic odontology, to be checked against missing persons files, while samples of bone marrow and hair were removed for possible use in DNA profiling. Then Woolrich, Morphy, and I watched as the remains were wheeled away, covered in a plastic wrap. We exchanged a few words before we each went our separate way, but to be honest, I don't recall what they were. All I could see was the girl. All I could hear was the sound of water in my ears.

If the DNA profiling and the dental records failed to reveal her identity, Woolrich had decided that facial reconstruction might prove valuable, using a laser reflected from the skull to establish the contours, which could then be compared against a known skull of similar dimensions. He decided to contact Quantico to make the initial arrangements as soon as he had had time to wash and grab a cup of coffee.

But facial reconstruction proved unnecessary. It took less than two hours to identify the body of the young woman in the swamp. Although she had been lying in the dark waters for almost seven months, she had been reported missing only three months before.

Her name was Lutice Fontenot. She was Lionel Fontenot's half sister.

44

□

THE FONTENOT COMPOUND lay five miles east of Delacroix. It was approached via a raised private road, newly built, which wound through swamps and decaying trees until it reached an area that had been cleared of all vegetation and was now only dark earth. High fencing, topped with razor wire, enclosed two or three acres, at the center of which lay a low, single-story, horseshoe-shaped concrete building. A black convertible and three black Explorers were parked in a line in the concrete lot created by the arms of the building. To the rear was an older house, a standard single-story wooden dwelling with a porch and what looked like a series of parallel linked rooms. No one seemed to be around as I pulled the rented Taurus up to the compound gate, Louis in the passenger seat beside me. Rachel had taken the other rental with her on a final visit to Loyola University.

"Maybe we should have called ahead," I said as I looked at the silent compound.

Beside me, Louis raised his hands slowly above his head and gestured in front of him with his chin. Two men, dressed in jeans and faded shirts, stood before us pointing Heckler & Koch HK53s with retracted stocks. I caught two more in the rearview mirror and a fifth, wearing an axe in his belt, opposite the passenger window. They were hard, weathered-looking men, some of them with beards already tinged with gray. Their boots were muddy and their hands were the hands of manual laborers, scarred in places.

I watched as a man of medium height, dressed in a blue denim shirt, jeans, and work boots, walked toward the gate from the main compound building. When he reached the gate he didn't open it but stood watching us through the fencing. He had been burned at some point: the skin on the right of his face was heavily scarred, the right eye useless, and the hair hadn't grown back on that side of his scalp. A fold of skin hung over his dead eye, and when he spoke, he did so out of the left side of his mouth.

"What you want here?" The voice was heavily accented: Cajun stock.

"My name's Charlie Parker," I replied through the open window. "I'm here to see Lionel Fontenot."

"Who this?" He motioned at Louis with a finger.

"Count Basie," I said. "The rest of the band couldn't make it."

Pretty Boy didn't crack a smile, or even a half smile. "Lionel don't see no one. Get yo' ass outta here 'fo you get hurt." He turned and walked back toward the compound.

"Hey," I said. "You accounted for all of Joe Bones's goons at Metairie yet?"

He stopped and turned back to us.

"What you say?" He looked like I'd just insulted his sister.

"I figure you have two bodies at Metairie that no one can account for. If there's a prize, I'd like to claim it."

He seemed to consider this for a moment, then: "You a joker? You are, I don't think you funny."

"You don't think I'm funny?" I said. There was an edge to my voice now. His left eyelid flickered and an H&K ended up two inches from my nose. It smelled like it had been used recently. "Try this for funny: I'm the guy who hauled Lutice Fontenot from the bottom of Honey Island swamp. You want to tell Lionel that, see if he laughs?"

He didn't reply, but pointed an infrared signaler at the compound gate. It opened almost noiselessly.

"Get outta the car," he said. Two of the men kept our hands in view and their guns trained on us as we opened the car doors, then two others came forward and frisked us against the car, looking for wires and weapons. They handed Louis's SIG and knife and my S&W to the scarred guy, then checked the interior of the car for concealed weapons. They opened the hood and trunk and checked under the car.

"Man, you like the Peace Corps," whispered Louis. "Make friends wherever you go."

"Thanks," I replied. "It's a gift."

When they were satisfied that it was clean, we were allowed to drive slowly up to the compound with one of Fontenot's men, the axe man, in the back. Two men walked alongside the car. We parked beside the jeeps and were escorted up to the older house.

On the porch, waiting for us with a china cup of coffee in his hand, was Lionel Fontenot. The burn victim went up to him and spoke a few words in his ear, but Lionel stopped him with a raised hand and turned the hard stare on us. I felt a raindrop fall on my head and within seconds we were standing in a downpour. Lionel left us in the rain. I was wearing my blue linen Liz Claiborne suit and a white shirt with a blue silk-knit tie. I wondered if the dye would run. The rain was heavy and the dirt around the house was already turning to mud when Lionel ordered his men to leave, took a seat on the porch, and indicated with a nod of his head that we should come up. We sat on a pair of wooden chairs with woven seats while Lionel took a wooden recliner. The burn victim stood behind us. Louis and I moved our chairs slightly as we sat so that we could keep him in view.

An elderly black maid, with a face that I recognized from the Metairie funeral party, emerged from the house with a silver coffeepot and sugar and cream in a matching set, all on an ornate silver tray. There were three china cups and saucers on the tray. Multicolored birds chased one another's tails around the rim of the cups, and a heavy silver spoon with a sailing ship at the end lay neatly positioned beneath the handle of each one. The maid placed the tray on a small wicker table and then left us.

Lionel Fontenot was wearing a pair of black cotton pants and a white shirt with an open collar. A matching black jacket lay over the back of his chair and his brogues were newly polished. He leaned over the table and poured three cups of coffee, added two sugars to one, and then handed it wordlessly to the burn victim.

"Cream and sugar?" he asked, looking to Louis and me in turn.

"Black's fine," I said.

"Likewise," said Louis.

Lionel handed us each a cup. It was all very polite. Above us, the rain hammered on the porch roof.

"You want to tell me how you came to be looking for my sister?" Lionel said at last. He looked like someone who finds a strange guy cleaning the windshield of his car and can't decide whether to tip him a buck or hit him with a tire iron. He held his cup with his little finger cocked while he sipped his coffee. I noticed that the burn victim did the same.

I told Lionel some of what I knew then. I told him about *Tante* Marie's visions and her death and about the stories of the ghost of a girl at a Honey Island slough. "I think the man who killed your sister killed *Tante* Marie Aguillard and her son. He also killed my wife and my little girl," I said. "That's how I came to be looking for your sister."

I didn't say that I was sorry for his pain. He probably knew that anyway. If he didn't, then it wasn't worth saying.

"You take out two men at Metairie?"

"One," I answered. "Someone else killed the other."

Lionel turned to Louis. "You?"

Louis didn't reply.

"Someone else," I repeated.

Lionel put his cup down and spread his hands. "So why are you here now? You want my gratitude? I'm going to New Orleans now to take away my sister's body. I don't know that I want to thank you for that." He turned his face away. There was pain in his eyes, but no tears. Lionel Fontenot didn't look like a man with well-developed tear ducts.

"That's not why I'm here," I said quietly. "I want to know why Lutice was reported missing only in the last three months. I want to know what your brother was doing out at Honey Island on the night he was killed."

"My brother," he said. Love and frustration and guilt

chased one another in his voice like the birds on his pretty cups. Then he seemed to catch himself. I think he was about to tell me to go to hell, to keep out of his family's business if I wanted to stay alive, but I held his gaze and for a while he said nothing.

"I got no reason to trust you," he said.

"I can find the man who did this," I said. My voice was low and even. Lionel nodded, more to himself than to me, and appeared to make his decision.

"My sister left at the end of January, start of February," he began. "She didn't like"—he waved his left hand gently at the compound—"all this. There was trouble with Joe Bones, some people got hurt." He paused and chose his next words carefully. "One day she closed her bank account, packed a bag, and left a note. She didn't tell us to our faces. David wouldn't have let her leave anyways.

"We tried to trace her. We looked up friends in the city, even people she knew in Seattle and Florida. There was nothing, not a trace. David was real cut up about her. She was our half sister. When my momma died, my father married again. Lutice came out of that marriage. When my father and her momma died—that was in nineteen eighty-three, in an automobile accident—we took care of her, David especially. They were real close.

"Few months back, David started having dreams about Lutice. He didn't say nothing at first, but he got thinner and paler and his nerves started to play at him. When he told me, I thought he was going crazy and told him so, but the dreams just kept comin'. He dreamed of her underwater, he said, heard her banging against metal in the night. He was sure that something had happened to her.

"But what could we do? We had searched half of Louisiana. I'd even made approaches to some of Joe Bones's men, to see if there was something that maybe needed to be sorted out. There was nothing. She was gone.

"Next thing I knew, he reported her missing and we had the cops crawling over the compound. Mon, I nearly killed him that day, but he insisted. He said something had happened to Lutice. He was beyond reason by then, and I had to take care of things on my own, with Joe Bones hangin' over me like a sword 'bout to fall."

He looked to the burn victim.

"Leon here was with him when the call came. He wouldn't say nothin' about where he was goin', just took off in his damned yellow car. When Leon tried to stop him, he pulled a gun on him." I glanced at Leon. If he felt any guilt about what had happened to David Fontenot, he kept it well hidden.

"Any idea who made the call?" I asked.

Lionel shook his head.

I put my cup on the tray. The coffee was cold and untasted.

"When are you going to hit Joe Bones?" I asked. Lionel blinked like he had just been slapped, and out of the corner of my eye, I saw Leon step forward.

"The hell you talkin' about?" said Lionel.

"You've got a second funeral coming up, at least as soon as the police release your sister's body. Either you won't have too many mourners or the funeral will be overrun with police and media. Whatever happens, I figure you'll try to take out Joe Bones before then, probably at his place in West Feliciana. You owe him for David, and anyway, Joe won't rest easy until you're dead. One of you will try to finish it."

Lionel looked at Leon. "They clean?" Leon nodded.

Lionel leaned forward. There was menace in his voice. "The fuck does any of this have to do with you?"

I wasn't fazed by him. The threat of violence was in his face, but I needed Lionel Fontenot.

"You heard about Tony Remarr's death?"

Lionel nodded.

"Remarr was killed because he was out at the Aguillard place after *Tante* Marie and her son were murdered," I explained. "His fingerprints were found in *Tante* Marie's blood, Joe Bones heard about it, and told Remarr to lie low. But the killer found out—I don't know how yet—and I think he used your brother to lure Remarr into making the hit so he could take him out. I want to know what Remarr told Joe Bones."

Lionel considered what I had said. "And you can't get to Joe Bones without me."

Beside me, Louis's mouth twitched. Lionel caught the movement.

"That's not entirely true," I said. "But if you're going to be calling on him anyway, we might tag along."

"I go calling on Joe Bones, his fucking place is gonna be real fucking quiet by the time I leave," said Lionel softly.

"You do what you have to do," I replied. "But I need Joe Bones alive. For a while."

Lionel stood and buttoned the top of his shirt. He took a wide black silk tie from the inside pocket of his jacket and began to put it on, using his reflection in the window to check the knot.

"Where you staying?" he asked. I told him, and gave Leon the number of my phone. "We'll be in touch," said Lionel. "Maybe. Don't come out here again."

Our discussions appeared to be at an end. Louis and I were almost at the car when Lionel spoke again. He pulled on his jacket and adjusted the collar, then smoothed down the lapels.

"One thing," he said. "I know Morphy out of St. Martin was there when Lutice was found. You got cop friends?"

"Yeah. I got federal friends too. That a problem?"

He turned away. "Not as long as you don't make it one. If you do, the crabs gonna be feeding on you and your buddy."

Louis fooled around with the car radio until he found a station that seemed to be playing back-to-back Dr. John. "This is music, right?" he said.

The music segued uneasily from "Makin' Whoopee" to "Gris Gris Gumbo Ya-Ya" and John's throaty rumble filled the car. Louis flicked the presets again, until he found a country station playing three in a row from Garth Brooks.

"This be the devil's music," mumbled Louis. He turned the radio off and tapped his fingers on the dash.

"You know," I said, "you don't have to hang around if you don't want to. Things could get difficult, or Woolrich and the feds could decide to make them difficult for you." I knew that Louis was what Angel diplomatically referred to as semiretired. Money, it appeared, was no longer an issue. The "semi" indicated that it might have been replaced by something else, although I wasn't sure yet what that was.

He looked out the window, not at me. "You know why we're here?"

"Not entirely. I asked, but I wasn't sure that you'd come."

"We came because we owe you, because you'd look out for us if we needed it, and because someone has to look out for you after what happened to your woman and your little girl. More than that, Angel thinks that you're a good man. Maybe I think so too and maybe I think that what you brought to an end with the Modine bitch, what you're trying to bring to an end here, they're things that should be brought to an end. You understand me?"

It was strange to hear him talk this way, strange and affecting. "I think I understand," I replied quietly. "Thank you."

"You *are* going to end this thing here?" he said.

"I think so, but we're missing something, a detail, a pattern, something." I kept catching glimpses of it, like a rat passing under streetlights. I needed to find out more about Edward Byron. I needed to talk to Woolrich.

Rachel met us in the main hall of the Flaisance House. I guessed that she had been watching for the car. Angel lounged beside her eating a Lucky Dog, which looked like the business end of a baseball bat topped with onion, chili, and mustard.

"The FBI came," said Rachel. "Your friend Woolrich was with them. They had a warrant. They took everything: my notes, the illustrations, everything they could find." She led the way to her room. The walls had been stripped of their notes. Even the diagram I had drawn was gone.

"They searched our room too," remarked Angel to Louis. "And Bird's." My head jerked up as I thought of the case of guns. Angel spotted the move. "We ditched them soon as your FBI friend put the stare on Louis. They're in a storage depot on Bayonne. We both have keys."

I noticed that Rachel seemed more irritated than upset as we followed her to her room. "Am I missing something here?"

She smiled. "I said they took everything they could *find*. Angel saw them coming. I hid some of the notes in the waistband of my jeans, under my shirt. Angel took care of most of the rest."

She took a small pile of papers from under her bed and waved them with a small flourish. She kept one separate in her hand. It was folded over once.

"I think you might want to see this," she said, handing the paper to me. I unfolded it and felt a pain in my chest.

It was an illustration of a woman seated naked on a chair. She had been split from neck to groin and the skin on each side had been pulled back so that it hung over her arms like the folds of a gown. Across her lap lay a young man, similarly opened but with a space where his stomach and other internal organs had been removed. Apart from the detail of the anatomization and the alteration in the sex of one of the victims, it resembled in its essence what had been done to Jennifer and Susan.

"It's Estienne's *Pietà*," said Rachel. "It's very obscure, which is why it took so long to track down. Even in its day, it was regarded as excessively explicit and, more to the point, blasphemous. It bore too much of a resemblance to the figure of the dead Christ and Mary for the liking of the church authorities. Estienne nearly burned for it."

She took the illustration from me and looked at it sadly, then placed it on her bed with the other papers. "I know what he's doing," she said. "He's creating memento mori, death's-heads." She sat on the edge of the bed and put her hands together beneath her chin, as if in prayer.

"He's giving us lessons in mortality."

IV

He had a mind to be acquainted with your inside, Crispin.

Edward Ravenscroft
The Anatomist

45

□

In the medical school of the Complutense University of Madrid there is an anatomical museum, founded by King Carlos III. Much of its collection derives from the efforts of Dr. Julián de Velasco in the early to mid-nineteenth century. Dr. Velasco was a man who took his work seriously. He was reputed to have mummified the corpse of his own daughter, just as William Harvey was assisted in his discovery of circulation by his decision to autopsy the bodies of his own father and sister.

The long rectangular hall is arrayed with glass cases of exhibits: two giant skeletons, the wax model of a fetal head, and at one point, two figures labeled *despellejados*. They are the "flayed men," who stand in dramatic poses, displaying the movement of the muscles and the tendons without the white veil of the skin to hide it from the eye of the beholder. Vesalius, Valverde, Estienne, their forebears, their peers, their successors, worked in the knowledge of this tradition. Artists such as Michelangelo and Leonardo da Vinci created their own *écorchés*, as they termed their drawings of flayed figures, basing their work on their own participation in dissections.

And the figures they created were more than merely anatomical specimens: they served, in their way, as reminders of the flawed nature of our humanity, a reminder of the body's capacity for pain and, eventually, mortality. They warned of the futility of the pursuits of the flesh, the reality of disease and pain and death in this life, and the promise of something better in the next.

In eighteenth-century Florence, the practice of anatomical modeling reached its peak. Under the patronage of the Abbot Felice Fontana, anatomists and artists worked side by side to create natural sculptures from beeswax. Anatomists exposed the cadavers, the artists poured the liquid plaster, and molds were created. Layers of wax were placed into them, with pig fat used to alter the temperature of the wax where necessary, allowing a process of layering that reproduced the transparency of human tissue.

Then, with threads and brushes and fine point, the lineaments and striations of the body were reproduced. Eyebrows and eyelashes were added, one by one. In the case of the Bolognese artist Lelli, real skeletons were used as a frame for his wax creations. The emperor of Austria, Joseph II, was so impressed by the collection that he ordered 1,192 models, to promote medical teaching in his own country. By contrast, Frederik Ruysch, professor of anatomy at the Atheneum Illustre in Amsterdam, used chemical fixatives and dyes to preserve his specimens. His house contained an exhibition of the skeletons of infants and children in various poses, reminders of the transience of life.

Yet nothing could compare to the reality of the actual human body exposed to view. Public demonstrations of anatomization and dissection attracted huge crowds, some of them in carnival disguise. Ostensibly, they were there to learn. In reality, the dissection was little more than an extension of the public execution. In England, the Murder Act of 1752 provided a direct link between the two events by permitting the bodies of murderers to be anatomically dissected, and postmortem penal dissection became a form of further punishment for the criminal, who would now be denied a proper burial. In 1832, the Anatomy Act extended the deprivation of the poor into the next life by allowing the confiscation of the bodies of dead paupers for dissection.

So death and dissection walked hand in hand with the extension of scientific knowledge. But what of pain? What of the Renaissance disgust with the workings of the female body, which led to a particularly morbid fascination with the uterus? In the acts of flaying and anatomization, the realities of suffering, sex, and death were not far away.

The interior of the body, when revealed, speaks to us of mortality. But how many of us can ever bear witness to our own interiors? We see our own mortality only through the prism of the mortality of others. Even then, it is only in exceptional circumstances, in cases of war, or violent accidental death, or murder, when the viewer is a witness to the act itself or its immediate consequences, that mortality in all its deep red reality is made clear to us.

In his violent, pain-filled way, Rachel believed, the Traveling Man was trying to break down these barriers. In killing his victims in this way, he was making them aware of their own mortality, exposing to them their own interiors, introducing them to the meaning of true pain; but they also served as a reminder to others of their own mortality and the final, dreadful pain that would someday find them.

The Traveling Man crisscrossed the boundaries between torture and execution, between intellectual and physical curiosity and sadism. He was part of the secret history of mankind, the history recorded in the thirteenth-century *Anatomia Magistri Nicolai Physici,* which observed that the ancients practiced dissection upon both the living and the dead, binding condemned criminals hand and foot and gradually dissecting them, beginning with their legs and arms and moving on to their internal organs. Celsus and Augustine made similar allegations about live dissections, still contested by medical historians.

And now the Traveling Man had come to write his own history, to offer his own blending of science and art, to make his own notes on mortality and to create a Hell within the human heart.

All this Rachel explained as we sat in her room. Outside, it had grown dark and the strains of music floated on the air.

"I think the blinding may be related to ignorance, a physical representation of a failure to understand the reality of pain and death," she said. "But it indicates just how far the killer himself is removed from ordinary humanity. We all suffer, we all experience death in various ways before we die ourselves. He believes that only he can teach us this."

"That, or he believes we've lost sight of it and need to be reminded, that it's his role to tell us just how inconsequential we are," I added. Rachel nodded her assent.

"If what you say is true, then why was Lutice Fontenot dumped in a barrel?" It was Angel. He sat by the balcony, staring out on to the street below.

" 'Prentice work," said Rachel. Louis cocked an eyebrow but stayed silent.

"This Traveling Man believes he's creating works of art: the care he takes in displaying the bodies, their relation to old medical texts, the links with mythology and artistic representations of the body all point in that direction. But even artists have to start somewhere. Poets, painters, sculptors all serve an apprenticeship of sorts, formal or otherwise. The work they create during their apprenticeships may go on to influence their later work, but it's usually not for public display. It's a chance to make mistakes without criticism, to see what you can and cannot achieve. Maybe that's what Lutice Fontenot was to him: 'prentice work."

"But she died after Susan and Jennifer," I added softly.

"He took Susan and Jennifer because he wanted to, but the results were unsatisfactory. I think he used Lutice to practice again before he returned to the public arena," she answered, not looking at me. "He took *Tante* Marie and her son for a combination of reasons, out of both desire and necessity, and this time he had the time he needed to achieve the effect for which he was searching. He then had to kill Remarr, either because of what he actually saw or the mere possibility that he might have seen something, but again he created a memento mori out of him. He's practical, in his way: he's not afraid to make a virtue out of necessity."

Angel looked unhappy with the thrust of Rachel's words. "But what about the way most of us react to death?" he began. "It makes us want to live. It even makes us want to *screw.*"

Rachel glanced at me, then returned to her notes.

"I mean," continued Angel, "what does this guy want us to do? Stop eating, stop loving, because he's got a thing about death and he thinks the next world is going to be something better?"

I picked up the illustration of the *Pietà* again and examined the detail of the bodies, the carefully labeled interiors, and the placid expressions on the faces of the woman and the man. The faces of the Traveling Man's victims had looked nothing like this. They were contorted in their final agonies.

"He doesn't give a damn about the next world," I said. "He's only concerned with the damage he can do in this one."

I stood and joined Angel at the window. Beneath us, the dogs scampered and sniffed in the courtyard. I could smell cooking and beer and imagined that, beneath it all, I could smell the mass of humanity itself, passing us by.

"Why hasn't he come after us? Or you?" It was Angel. His words were directed at me, but it was Rachel who answered.

"Because he wants us to understand," she said. "Everything he's done is an attempt to lead us to something. All of this is an effort to communicate, and we're the audience. He doesn't want to kill us."

"Yet," said Louis softly.

Rachel nodded once, her eyes locked on mine. "Yet," she agreed quietly.

I arranged to meet Rachel and the others later in Vaughan's. Back in my room, I called Woolrich and left a message on his machine. He returned the call within five minutes and told me he'd meet me at the Napoleon House within the hour.

He was as good as his word. Shortly before ten he appeared, dressed in off-white chinos and carrying a matching jacket over his arm, which he put on as soon as he entered the bar.

"Is it chilly in here, or is it just the reception?" There was sleep caked at the corners of his eyes and he smelled sour and unwashed. He was no longer the assured figure I recalled from Jenny Orbach's apartment, wresting control of the room from a group of vaguely hostile cops. Instead he looked older, more uncertain. Taking Rachel's papers in the way he did was out of character for him; the old Woolrich would have taken them anyway, but he would have asked for them first.

He ordered an Abita for himself and another mineral water for me.

"You want to tell me why you seized materials from the hotel?"

"Don't look on it as a seizure, Bird. Consider it as borrowing." He sipped at his beer and looked at himself in the mirror. He didn't seem to like what he saw.

"You could just have asked," I said.

"Would you have given it to me?"

"No, but I'd have discussed what was there."

"I don't think that Durand would have been too impressed with that. Frankly, I wouldn't have been too impressed either."

"Durand called it? Why? You have your own profilers, your own agents on it. Why were you so sure that we could add something?"

He spun around on his stool and leaned close to me, close enough that I could smell his breath. "Bird, I know you want this guy. I know you want him for what he did to Susan and Jennifer, to the old woman and her son, to Florence, to Lutice Fontenot, maybe even to that fuck Remarr. I've tried to keep you in touch with what's been going down and you've walked all over this case like a fucking child in new boots. You've got an assassin staying in the room next door, God alone knows what his pal does, and your lady friend is collecting graphic medical imagery like box tops. You ain't given me shit, so I did what I had to do. You think I'm holding back on you? With the shit you're pulling, you're lucky I don't put you back on a plane to Noo Yawk."

"I need to know what you know," I said. "What are you holding back about this guy?"

We were now head to head now. Then Woolrich grimaced and leaned back.

"Holding back? Jesus, Bird, you're unbelievable. Here's something: Byron's wife? You want to know what she majored in when she was at college? Art. Her thesis was on Renaissance art and depictions of the body. You think that might have included medical representations, that maybe that was where her ex got some of his ideas?"

He took a deep breath and a long swig of beer. "You're bait, Bird. You know it, and I know it. And I know something else too." His voice was cold and hard. "I know you were at Metairie. There's a guy in the morgue with a bullet hole in his head and the cops have the remains of a ten millimeter Smith & Wesson bullet that was dug out of the marble behind him. You want to tell me about that, Bird? You want to tell me if you were alone in Metairie when the killing started?"

I didn't reply.

Then: "You screwing her, Bird?"

I looked at him. There was no mirth in his eyes and he wasn't smiling. Instead, there was hostility and distrust. Whatever I needed to know about Edward Byron and his ex-wife, I would have to find out myself. If I had hit him then, we would have hurt each other badly. I didn't waste any more words on him and I didn't look back as I left the bar.

I took a cab to Bywater and stopped off right outside Vaughan's Lounge on the corner of Dauphine and Lesseps. I paid the five-dollar cover at the door. Inside, Kermit Ruffins and the Barbecue Swingers were lost in a rhapsody of New Orleans brass and there were plates of red beans scattered on the tables. Rachel and Angel were dancing around chairs and tables while Louis looked on with a long-suffering expression. As I approached, the tempo of the music slowed a little and Rachel made a grab for me. I moved with her for a while as she stroked my face, and I closed my eyes and let her. Then I sipped a soda and thought my own thoughts until Louis moved from his seat and sat beside me.

"You didn't have much to say back in Rachel's room," I said.

He nodded. "It's bullshit. All this stuff, the religion, the medical drawings, they're all just trappings. And maybe he believes them and maybe he don't. Sometimes it's nothing to do with mortality, it's to do with the beauty of the color of meat."

He took a sip of beer.

"And this guy just likes red."

Back at the Flaisance, I lay beside Rachel and listened to her breathing in the dark.

"I've been thinking," she said. "About our killer."

"And?"

"I think the killer may not be male."

I raised myself up on my elbows and looked at her. I could see the whites of her eyes, wide and bright.

"Why?"

"I'm not sure, exactly. There just seems to be something almost feminine about the sensibility of whoever is committing these crimes, a . . . *sensitivity* to the interconnectedness of things, to their potential for symbolism. I don't know. I guess I'm thinking out loud, but it's not a sensibility typical of a modern male. Maybe "female" is wrong—I mean, the hallmarks, the cruelty, the capacity to overpower, all point to a male—but it's as close as I can get, at least for now."

She shook her head and then was silent again.

"Are we becoming a couple?" she asked at last.

"I don't know. Are we?"

"You're avoiding the question."

"No, not really. It's not one that I'm used to answering, or that I ever thought that I'd have to answer again. If you're asking if I want us to stay together, then the answer is yes, I do. It worries me a little, and I'm bringing in more baggage than the handlers at JFK, but I want to be with you."

She kissed me softly.

"Why did you stop drinking?" she asked, adding: "Since we're having this heart-to-heart."

I started at the question. "Because if I took one drink now, I'd wake up in Singapore with a beard a week later," I replied.

"It doesn't answer the question."

"I hated myself and that made me hate others, even the people closest to me. I was drinking the night Susan and Jennifer were killed. I'd been drinking a lot, not just that night but other nights too. I drank because of a lot of things, because of the pressure of the job, because of my failings as a husband, as a father, and maybe other things as well, things from way back. If I hadn't been a drunk, Susan and Jennifer might not have died. So I stopped. Too late, but I stopped."

She didn't say anything else. She didn't say, "It wasn't your fault," or, "You can't blame yourself." She knew better than that.

I think I wanted to say more, to try to explain to her what it was like without alcohol, about how I was afraid that, without alcohol, each day would now leave me with nothing to look forward to. Each day would simply be another day without a drink. Sometimes, when I was at my lowest ebb, I wondered if my search for the Traveling Man was just a way to fill my days, a way to keep me from going off the rails.

Later, as she slept, I lay on the bed, on top of the sheets, and thought about Lutice Fontenot and bodies turned into art, before I, too, faded into sleep.

46

□

I SLEPT BADLY that night, wound up by my conversation with Woolrich and troubled by dreams of dark water. The next morning, I had breakfast alone after tracking down what seemed to be the only copy of the *New York Times* in Orleans Parish, over at Riverside News, by the Jax Brewery. Later, I met Rachel at Café du Monde and we walked through the French Market, wandering between the stalls of T-shirts and CDs and cheap wallets, and on to the fresh produce at the Farmers' Market. There were pecans like dark eyes, pale, shrunken heads of garlic, melons with dark red flesh that held the gaze like a wound. White-eyed fish lay packed in ice beside crawfish tails; headless shrimp rested by racks of " 'gator on a stick" and murky tanks in which baby alligators lay on display. There were stalls loaded with eggplants and militones, sweet onions and elephant toe garlic, fresh Roma tomatoes and ripe avocadoes.

Over a century before, this had been a two-block stretch of Gallatin Street on the riverfront docks between Barracks and Ursuline. Outside of maybe Shanghai and the Bowery, it was one of the toughest places in the world, a strip of brothels and lowlife gin mills where hard-faced men mixed with harder women and anyone without a weapon had taken a wrong turning somewhere that he was bound to regret.

Gallatin is gone now, erased from the map, and instead tourists mix with Cajun fishermen from Lafayette and beyond, come to sell their wares surrounded by the thick, heady smell of the Mississippi. The city was like that, it seemed: streets disappeared; bars opened and, a century later, were gone; buildings were torn down or burned to the ground and others rose to take their place. There was change, but the spirit of the city remained the same. On this muggy summer morning, it seemed to brood beneath the clouds, feeling the people as a passing infection that it would cleanse from itself with rain.

The door of my room was slightly ajar when we returned through the courtyard. I motioned Rachel against the wall and drew my Smith & Wesson, keeping to the sides of the wooden stairway so that the steps wouldn't creak. The noise of Ricky's Steyr sending bullets raking past my ear had stayed with me. *"Joe Bones says hello."* I figured that if Joe Bones tried to say hello again, I could spare enough powder to blow him back to Hell.

I listened at the door but no sounds came from inside. If it had been the maid in my room, she'd have been whistling and bumping, maybe listening to a blues station on her tinny portable radio. If there was a maid in my room now, she was either asleep or levitating.

I hit the door hard with my shoulder and entered fast, my gun at arm's length, scanning the room with the sight. It came to rest on the figure of Leon sitting in a chair by the balcony, flicking through a copy of *GQ* that Louis had passed on to me. Leon didn't look like the kind of guy who bought much on *GQ*'s recommendation, unless the *Q* had made a big play for the JCPenney contract. Leon glanced at me with even less interest than he gave to *GQ*. His damaged eye glistened beneath its fold of skin like a crab peering out of a shell.

"When you're finished, there are hairs in the shower and the closet door sticks," I said.

"Room falls down around your ears, I could give a fuck," he replied. That Leon, what a kidder.

He threw the magazine on the floor and looked past me to Rachel, who had followed me into the room. His eyes didn't register any interest there either. Maybe Leon was dead and no one had worked up the guts to tell him.

"She's with me," I said. Leon looked like he could have keeled over from apathy.

"Ten tonight, at the nine-sixty-six junction at Starhill. You *et ton ami noir*. Anyone else, Lionel cornhole you both with a shotgun."

He stood to leave. As I moved aside to let him pass, I made a pistol of my finger and thumb and fired it at him. There was a flash of steel in each of his hands and two barb-edged knives appeared inches from each of my eyes. I could see the tops of the spring loaders in his sleeves. That explained why Leon didn't seem to feel the need to carry a gun.

"Impressive," I said, "but it's only funny until someone loses an eye." Leon's dead right eye seemed to gaze into my soul, as if to rot it and turn it to dust, then he left. I couldn't hear his footsteps as he walked down the gallery.

"A friend of yours?" asked Rachel.

I walked out of the room and looked down at the already empty courtyard. "If he is, I'm lonelier than I thought."

When Louis and Angel returned from a late breakfast, I went to their door and knocked. A couple of seconds went by before there was a response.

"Yeah?" shouted Angel.

"It's Bird. You two decent?"

"Jeez, I hope not. C'mon in."

Louis sat upright in bed, reading the *Times-Picayune*. Angel sat beside him outside the sheets, naked but for a towel across his lap.

"The towel for my benefit?"

"I'm afraid you might become confused about your sexuality."

"Might take away what little I have."

"Very witty for a man screwing a psychologist. Why don't you just pay your eighty bucks an hour like everyone else?"

Louis gave us both bored looks over the top of his newspaper. Maybe Leon and Louis were related way back.

"Lionel Fontenot's boy just paid me a visit," I said.

"The beauty queen?" asked Louis.

"None other."

"We on?"

"Tonight at ten. Better get your stuff out of hock."

"I'll send my boy." He kicked Angel in the leg from beneath the sheets.

"The ugly queen?"

"None other," said Louis.

Angel continued to watch his game show. "It's beneath my dignity to comment."

Louis returned to his paper. "You got a lot of dignity for a guy with a towel on his dick."

"It's a big towel," sniffed Angel.

"Waste of a lot of good towel space, you ask me."

I left them to it. Back in my room, Rachel was standing by the wall, her arms folded and a fierce expression on her face.

"What happens now?" she asked.

"We go back to Joe Bones," I said.

"And Lionel Fontenot kills him," she spat. "He's no better than Joe Bones. You're only siding with him out of expediency. What will happen when Fontenot kills him? Will things be any better?"

I didn't answer. I knew what would happen. There would be a brief disturbance in the drug trade, as Fontenot renegotiated existing deals or ended them entirely. Prices would go up and there would be some killing, as those who felt strong enough to challenge him for Joe Bones's turf made their play. Lionel Fontenot would kill them; of that I had no doubt.

Rachel was right. It was only expediency that made me side with Lionel. Joe Bones knew something about what had happened the night *Tante* Marie died, something that could bring me a step closer to the man who had killed my wife and child. If it took Lionel Fontenot's guns to find out what that was, then I would side with the Fontenots.

"And Louis will stand beside you," said Rachel quietly. "My God, what have you become?"

Later, I drove to Baton Rouge, Rachel accompanying me at my insistence. We were uneasy together, and no words were exchanged. Rachel contented herself with looking out of the window, her elbow resting against the door, her right hand supporting her cheek. The silence between us remained unbroken until we reached exit 166, heading for LSU and the home of Stacey Byron. Then I spoke, anxious that we should at least try to clear the air between us.

"Rachel, I'll do what I have to do to find whoever killed Susan and Jennifer," I said. "I need this, else I'm dead inside."

She did not reply immediately. For a while, I thought she was not going to reply at all.

"You're already dying inside," she said at last, still staring out the window. I could see her eyes, reflected in the glass, following the landscape. "The fact that you're prepared to do these things is an indication of that."

She looked at me for the first time. "I'm not your moral arbiter, Bird, and I'm not the voice of your conscience. But I am someone who cares about you, and I'm not sure how to deal with these feelings right now. Part of me wants to walk away and never look back, but another part of me wants, needs, to stay with you. I want to stop this thing, all of it. I want it all to end, for everybody's sake." Then she turned away again and left me to deal with what she had said.

Stacey Byron lived in a small white clapboard house with a red door and peeling paint, close to a small mall with a big supermarket, a photo shop, and a twenty-four-hour pizzeria. This area by the LSU campus was populated mainly by students, and some of the houses now had stores on their first floor, selling used CDs and books or long hippie dresses and overwide straw hats. As we drove by Stacey Byron's house and pulled into a parking space in front of the photo shop, I spotted a blue Probe parked close by. The two guys sitting in the front seats looked bored beyond belief. The driver had a newspaper folded in four resting on the wheel and was sucking on a pencil as he tried to do the crossword. His partner tapped a rhythm on the dashboard as he watched the front door of Stacey Byron's house.

"Feds?" asked Rachel.

"Maybe. Could be locals. This is donkey work."

We watched them for a while. Rachel turned on the radio and we listened to an AOR station: Rush, Styx, Richard Marx. Suddenly, the middle of the road seemed to be running straight through the car, musically speaking.

"Are you going in?" asked Rachel.

"May not have to," I replied, nodding at the house.

Stacey Byron, her blond hair tied back in a ponytail and her body encased in a short white cotton dress, emerged from the house and walked straight toward us, a straw shopping basket over her left arm. She nodded at the two guys in the car. They tossed a coin and the one in the passenger seat, a medium-sized man with a small belly protruding through his jacket, got out of the car, stretched his legs, and followed her toward the mall.

She was a good-looking woman, although the short dress was a little too tight at the thighs and dug slightly into the fat below her buttocks. Her arms were strong and lean, her skin tanned. There was a grace to her as she walked: when an elderly man almost collided with her as she entered the supermarket, she spun lightly on her right foot to avoid him.

I felt something soft on my cheek and turned to find Rachel blowing on it.

"Hey," she said, and for the first time since we left New Orleans there was a tiny smile on her lips. "It's rude to lech when you're with another woman."

"It's not leching," I said, as we climbed from the car, "it's surveillance."

I wasn't sure why I had come here, but Woolrich's remarks about Stacey Byron and her interest in art made me want to see her for myself, and I wanted Rachel to see her as well. I didn't know how we might get to talk to her but I figured that these things had a habit of working themselves out.

Stacey took her time browsing in the aisles. There was an aimlessness about her shopping as she picked up items, glanced at the labels, and then discarded them. The cop followed about ten feet behind her, then fifteen, before his attention was distracted by some magazines. He moved to the checkout and took up a position where he could see down two aisles at once, limiting his care of Stacey Byron to the occasional glance in her direction.

I watched a young black man in a white coat and a white hat with a green band stacking prepackaged meat. When he had emptied the tray and marked off its contents on a clipboard, he left the shop floor through a door marked *Staff Only*. I left Rachel to watch Byron and followed him. I almost hit him with the door as I went through, since he was squatting to pick up another plastic tray of meat. He looked at me curiously.

"Hey, man," he said, "you can't come in here."

"How much do you earn an hour?" I asked.

"Five twenty-five. What's it to you?"

"I'll give you fifty bucks if you lend me your coat and that clipboard for ten minutes."

He thought it over for a few seconds, then said: "Sixty, and anyone asks I'll say you stole it."

"Done," I said, and counted out three twenties as he took off the coat. It fitted a bit tightly across the shoulders, but no one would notice as long as I left it unbuttoned. I was stepping back onto the shop floor when the young guy called me.

"Hey, man, 'nother twenty, you can have the hat."

"For twenty bucks, I could go into the hat business myself," I replied. "Go hide in the men's room."

I found Stacey Byron by the toiletries, Rachel close by.

"Excuse me, ma'am," I said, as I approached, "can I ask you some questions?"

Up close, she looked older. There was a network of broken veins beneath her cheekbones and a fine tracery of lines surrounded her eyes. There were tight lines, too, around her mouth, and her cheeks were sunken and stretched. She looked tired and something else: she looked threatened, maybe even scared.

"I don't think so," she said, with a false smile, and started to step around me.

"It's about your ex-husband."

She stopped then and turned back, her eyes searching for her police escort. "Who are you?"

"An investigator. What do you know about Renaissance art, Mrs. Byron?"

"What? What do you mean?"

"You studied it in college, didn't you? Does the name Valverde mean anything to you? Did your husband ever use it? Did you?"

"I don't know what you're talking about. Please, leave me alone." She backed away, knocking some cans of deodorant to the floor.

"Mrs. Byron, have you ever heard of the Traveling Man?"

Something flashed in her eyes and behind me I heard a low whistle. I turned to see the fat cop moving down the aisle in my direction. He passed Rachel without noticing her and she began moving toward the door and the safety of the car, but by then I was already heading back to the staff area. I dumped the coat and walked straight through and on to the back lot, which was crowded with trucks making deliveries, before slipping around the side of the mall where Rachel already had the car started. I stayed low as we drove off, turning right instead of passing Stacey Byron's house again. In the side mirror I could see the fat cop looking around and talking into his radio, Byron beside him.

"And what did we achieve there?" asked Rachel.

"Did you see her eyes when I mentioned the Traveling Man? She knew the name."

"She knows something," agreed Rachel. "But she could have heard it from the cops. She looked scared, Bird."

"Maybe," I said. "But scared of what?"

That evening, Angel removed the door panels of the Taurus and we strapped the Calicos and the magazines into the space behind them, then replaced the panels. I cleaned and loaded my Smith & Wesson in the hotel room while Rachel watched.

I put the gun in my shoulder holster and wore a black Alpha Industries bomber jacket over my black T-shirt and black jeans. With my black Timberlands, I looked like the doorman at a nightclub.

"Joe Bones is living on borrowed time. I couldn't save him if I wanted to," I told her. "He was dead from the moment the Metairie hit went wrong."

Rachel spoke. "I've decided. I'm leaving in a day or two. I don't think I can be part of this any longer, the things you're doing, the things I've done." She wouldn't look at me and there was nothing that I could say. She was right, but she wasn't simply preaching. I could see her own pain in her eyes. I could feel it every time we made love.

Louis was waiting by the car, dressed in a black sweat top and black denim jacket over dark jeans and Ecco boots. Angel checked the door panels one last time to make sure they slipped off without any trouble, then stood beside Louis.

"You don't hear anything from us by three A.M., you take Rachel and clear out of the hotel. Book into the Pontchartrain and get the first plane out in the morning," I said. "I don't want Joe Bones trying to even up scores if this turns bad. Handle the cops whatever way you think is best."

He nodded, exchanged a look with Louis, and went back into the Flaisance. Louis put an Isaac Hayes tape into the stereo and we rolled out of New Orleans to the strains of "Walk On By."

"Dramatic," I said.

He nodded. "We the men."

Leon lounged by a gnarled oak, its trunk knotted and worn, as we reached the Starhill intersection. Louis's left hand was hanging loosely by his side, the butt of the SIG jutting from beneath the passenger seat. I had slipped the Smith & Wesson into the map compartment on the driver's door as we approached the meeting place. Seeing Leon alone against the tree didn't make me feel any better.

We slowed and turned onto a small side road that ran past the oak tree. Leon didn't seem to register our presence. I killed the engine and we sat in the car, waiting for him to make a move. Louis had his hand on the SIG now and drew it up so that it lay along his thigh.

We looked at each other. I shrugged and got out of the car, leaning against the open door with the Smith & Wesson within reach. Louis climbed from the passenger side, stretched slightly to show Leon that his hands were empty, and then rested against the side of the car, the SIG now on the seat beside him.

Leon hauled himself from the tree and walked toward us. Other figures emerged from the trees around us. Five men, H&Ks hanging from their shoulders, long-bladed hunting knives at their belts, surrounded the car.

"Up against the car," said Leon. I didn't move. From around us came the sound of safeties clicking.

"Don't move, you die now," he said. I held his gaze, then turned and put my hands on the roof of the car. Louis did the same. As he stood behind me, Leon must have seen the SIG on the passenger seat but he didn't seem concerned. He patted my chest, beneath my arms, and checked my ankles and thighs. When he was satisfied that I wasn't wearing a wire, he did a similar check on Louis, then stepped back.

"Leave the car," he instructed. Headlights shone as engines started up around us. A brown Dodge sedan and a green Nissan Patrol burst through from behind the treeline, followed by a flatbed Ford pickup with three pirogues lashed down on the bed. If the Fontenot compound was under surveillance, then whoever was responsible needed his eyesight tested.

"We got some stuff in the car," I said to Leon. "We're gonna take it out." He nodded and watched as I removed the minisubs from behind the door panels. Louis took two magazines and handed one to me. The long cylinder stretched over the rear end of the receiver as I checked the safety at the front edge of the trigger guard. Louis placed a second magazine inside his jacket and tossed me a spare.

As we climbed into the back of the Dodge, two men drove our car out of sight and then jumped into the Nissan. Leon sat in the passenger seat of the Dodge beside the driver, a man in his fifties with long gray hair tied back in a ponytail, and indicated to him to move off. The other vehicles followed at a distance, so that we wouldn't look like a convoy to any passing cops.

We drove along the border of East and West Feliciana, Thompson Creek to our right, until we came to a turnoff that led down to the riverbank. Two more cars, an ancient Plymouth and what looked like an even older Volkswagen Beetle, were pulled up at the bank, and two more pirogues lay beside them. Lionel Fontenot, dressed in blue jeans and a blue work shirt, stood by the Edsel. He cast an eye over the Calicos but didn't say anything.

There were fourteen of us in all, most armed with H&Ks, two carrying M16 rifles, and we split three to a pirogue, with Lionel and the driver of the Dodge taking the lead in a smaller boat. Louis and I were separated and each handed a paddle, then we moved off upriver.

We rowed for twenty minutes, staying close to the western bank, before a darker shape appeared against the night sky. I could see lights flickering in windows and then, through a stand of trees, a small jetty against which a motorboat lay moored. The grounds of Joe Bones's house were dark.

There was a low whistle from in front of us and hands were raised in the pirogues to indicate that we should stop rowing. Sheltered by the trees, which hung out over the water, we waited in silence. A light flashed on the jetty, and briefly, the face of a guard was illuminated as he lit a cigarette. I heard a low splash somewhere in front of me, and high on the bank, an owl hooted. I could see the guard moving against the moon-haunted water, could hear the sound of his boots scuffing against the wooden jetty. Then a dark shape rose up beside him and the pattern of the moonlight on the water was disturbed. A knife flashed and the red ember of the cigarette tumbled through the night air like a signal of distress as the guard crumpled to the ground. He made hardly a sound as he was lowered into the water.

The ponytailed man stood waiting at the jetty as we paddled by, moving as close as we could to the grass bank beyond before we climbed from the pirogues and dragged them onto dry land. The bank rose up to join an expanse of green lawn, undisturbed by flowers or trees. It rolled uphill to the back of the house, where steps led up to a patio overlooked by two French windows at ground level and a gallery on the second floor, which mirrored the one on the front of the house. I caught a movement on the gallery and heard voices from the patio. Three guards at least, probably more at the front.

Lionel raised two fingers and singled out two men to my left. They moved forward cautiously, keeping low against the ground as they moved toward the house. They were about twenty yards in front of us when the house and grounds were suddenly illuminated with bright white light. The two men were caught like rabbits in headlights as shouts came from the house and automatic fire burst from the gallery. One of them spun like an ice skater who has missed his jump, blood bursting forth from his shirt like red flowers opening. He fell to the ground, his legs twisting, as his partner dived for the cover of a metal table, part of a lawn set that stood, semiobscured, by the riverbank.

The French windows opened and dark figures spilled out onto the patio. On the gallery, the guard was joined by two or three others, who raked the grass in front of us with heavy fire. From the sides of the house, muzzles flashed as more of Joe Bones's men inched their way around.

Close to where I lay, Lionel Fontenot swore. We were partly protected by the slope of the lawn as it curved down to meet the river, but the guards on the gallery were angling for clear shots at us. Some of Fontenot's men returned fire, but each time they did so, they exposed themselves to the guards at the house. One, a sharp-faced man in his forties with a mouth like a paper cut, grunted as a bullet hit him in the shoulder. He kept firing, even as the blood turned his shirt red.

"It's fifty yards from here to the house," I said. "There are guards moving in from the sides to cut us off. We don't move now, we're dead." A spray of earth kicked up by Fontenot's left hand. One of Joe Bones's men had progressed almost to the bank by approaching from the front of the house. Two bursts of M16 fire came from behind the metal lawn table and he tumbled sideways, rolling along the grass into the river.

"Tell your men to get ready," I hissed. "We'll cover you." The message was passed down the line.

"Louis!" I shouted. "You ready to try these things out?" A figure two men down from me responded with a wave and then the Calicos burst into life. One of the guards on the gallery bucked and danced as the 9 millimeter bullets from Louis's gun tore into him. I pushed the selector on the trigger guard fully forward and sent a burst of automatic fire across the patio. The French windows exploded in a shower of glass and a guard tumbled down the steps and lay unmoving on the lawn. Lionel Fontenot's men sprang from their cover and raced across the lawn, firing as they did so. I switched to single shot firing and concentrated on the eastern end of the house, sending wood splinters shooting into the air as I forced the men there to take cover.

Fontenot's men were almost at the patio when two fell, hit by fire from behind the ruined French windows. Louis sent a burst into the room beyond and Fontenot's men moved to the patio and entered the house. Exchanges of fire were coming from within as Louis and I rose and ran across the lawn.

To my left, the guy behind the lawn table abandoned his cover to join us. As he did so, something huge and dark appeared out of the shadows and launched itself from the grass with a deep, ferocious growl. The *boerbul* struck him on the chest, knocking him to the ground with its enormous weight. He shouted once, his hands pounding at the creature's head, and then the huge jaws closed on his neck and the *boerbul*'s head shook as he tore the man's throat apart.

The animal lifted its head and its eyes gleamed in the darkness as it found Louis. He was turning the Calico in its direction when it bounded from the dead body and sprang into the air. Its speed was astonishing. As it moved toward us, its dark form blotted out the stars in the sky above. It was at the apex of its jump when Louis's Calico sang and bullets ripped into it, causing it to spasm in midair and land with a crunch on the grass not two feet from us. Its paws scrambled for purchase and its mouth worked in biting motions, even as blood and froth spilled from between its teeth. Louis pumped more rounds into it until it lay still.

My eye caught movement at the western corner of the house as we neared the steps. A muzzle flashed and Louis yelled in pain. The Calico dropped to the ground as he leaped for the steps, cradling his injured hand. I fired three shots and the guard dropped. Behind me, one of Fontenot's men fired single shots from his M16 as he advanced toward the house, then let the gun hang from its shoulder strap as he reached the corner. I saw moonlight catch the blade of his knife as he stood waiting. The short muzzle of a Steyr appeared, followed by the face of one of Joe Bones's men. I recognized him as the one who had driven the golf cart to the plantation gates on our first visit here, but the flash of recognition became one with the flash of the knife as it struck across his neck. A crimson jet flew into the air from his severed artery, but even as he fell Fontenot's man raised the M16 once again and fired past him as he moved toward the front of the house.

Louis was examining his right hand as I reached him. The bullet had torn across the back of the hand, leaving a bad gash and damaging the knuckle of his forefinger. I tore a strip from the shirt of a dead guard who lay sprawled across the patio and wrapped it around Louis's hand. I handed him the Calico and he worked the strap over his head, then fitted his middle finger into the trigger guard. With his left hand he freed his SIG, then nodded to me as he rose. "We better find Joe Bones."

Through the patio doors lay a formal dining room. The dining table, which could seat at least eighteen people comfortably, was splintered and pitted by shots. On the wall, a portrait of a Southern gentleman standing by his horse had sustained a large hole through the horse's belly and a selection of antique china plates lay shattered in the remains of their glass-fronted display cabinet. There were two bodies in the room. One of them was the ponytailed man who had driven the Dodge.

The dining room led out into a large carpeted hallway and a white chandeliered reception area, from which a staircase wound up to the next floor. The other doors at ground level stood open, but there were no sounds coming from inside. There was sustained firing on the upper levels as we made our way to the stairs. At their base, one of Joe Bones's men lay in a pair of striped pajama bottoms, blood pooling from an ugly head wound.

From the top of the stairs, a series of doors stretched left and right. Fontenot's men seemed to have cleared most of the rooms, but they had been pinned down in the alcoves and doorways by gunfire from the rooms at the western end of the house, one on the river side to the right, its panels already pockmarked by bullets, and the other facing out to the front of the house. As we watched, a man in blue overalls carrying a short-handled axe in one hand and a captured Steyr in the other moved quickly from his hiding place to within one doorway of the front-facing room. Shots came through the door on the right and he fell to the ground, clutching his leg.

I leaned into an alcove in which the remains of long-stemmed roses lay in a pool of water and shattered pottery and fired a sustained burst at the door on the front-facing side. Two of Fontenot's men moved forward at the same time, keeping low on the ground as they did so. Across from me, Louis fired shots at the semiclosed river-side door. I stopped firing as Fontenot's men reached the room and rushed the occupant. There were two more shots, then one of them emerged wiping his knife on his trousers. It was Lionel Fontenot. Behind him was Leon.

The two men took up positions at either side of the last room. Six more of his men moved forward to join him.

"Joe, it's over now," said Lionel. "We gon' finish this thing."

Two shots burst through the door. Leon raised his H&K and appeared to be about to fire, but Lionel raised his hand, looking past Leon to where I stood. I advanced forward and waited behind Leon's back as Lionel pushed open the door with his foot, then pressed himself flat against the wall as two more shots rang out, followed by the click of a hammer on an empty chamber, a sound as final as the closing of a tomb.

Leon entered the room first, the H&K now replaced by his knives. I followed him, with Lionel behind me. The walls of Joe Bones's bedroom were marked with holes and the night air entered through the shattered window and sent the white curtains swirling in the air like angry ghosts. The blonde who had lunched with Joe on his lawn earlier in the week lay dead against the far wall, a red stain on the left breast of her silk nightgown.

Joe Bones stood before the window in a red silk dressing gown. The Colt in his hand hung uselessly at his side but his eyes glowed with anger and the scar on his lip seemed painfully pinched and white against his skin. He dropped the gun.

"Do it, you fuck," he hissed at Lionel. "Kill me, you got the fucking guts."

Lionel closed the bedroom door behind us as Joe Bones turned to look at the woman.

"Ask him," said Lionel.

Joe Bones didn't seem to hear. His face seemed consumed with a look of terrible grief as his eyes traced the contours of the dead woman's face. "Eight years," he said softly. "Eight years she was with me."

"Ask him," repeated Lionel Fontenot.

I stepped forward and Joe Bones sneered as he turned, that look of sadness now gone. "The fucking grieving widower. You bring your trained nigger with you?"

I slapped him hard and he took a step back.

"I can't save you, Joe, but if you help me maybe I can make it quicker for you. Tell me what Remarr saw the night the Aguillards died."

He wiped blood from the corner of his mouth, smearing it across his cheek. "You have no idea what you're dealing with, no fucking idea in the world. You're so out of your fucking depth, the fucking pressure should be making your nose bleed."

"He kills women and children, Joe. He's going to kill again."

Joe Bones twisted his mouth into the semblance of a grin, the scar distorting his full lips like a crack in a mirror. "You killed my woman and now you're gonna kill me, no matter what I say. You got nothing to bargain with," he said.

I glanced at Lionel Fontenot. He shook his head almost imperceptibly, but Joe Bones caught it. "See, nothing. All you can offer is a little less pain, and pain don't hold no surprises for me."

"He killed one of your own men. He killed Tony Remarr."

"Tony left a print at the nigger's house. He was careless and he paid the price. Your guy, he saved me the trouble of killing the old bitch and her brood myself. I meet him, I'll shake his hand."

Joe Bones smiled a broad smile like a flash of sunshine through dark, acrid smoke. Haunted by visions of tainted blood flowing through his veins, he had moved beyond ordinary notions of humanity and empathy, love and grief. In his shimmering red robe, he looked like a wound in the fabric of space and time.

"You'll meet him in Hell," I said.

"I see your bitch there, I'll fuck her for you." His eyes were bland and cold now. The smell of death hung around him like old cigar fumes. Behind me, Lionel Fontenot opened the door and the rest of his men walked quietly into the room. It was only now, seeing them all together in the ruined bedroom, that the resemblance between them became clear. Lionel held the door open for me.

"It's a family thing," he said as I left. Behind me, the door closed with a soft click like the knocking of bones.

After Joe Bones died, we gathered the bodies of the Fontenot dead on the lawn in front of the house. The five men lay side by side, crumpled and torn as only the dead can be. The gates to the plantation were opened and the Dodge, the VW and the pickup sped in. The bodies were loaded gently but quickly into the trunks of the cars, the injured helped into the rear seats. The pirogues were doused in gasoline, set on fire, and left to float down the river.

We drove from the plantation and kept driving until we reached the rendezvous point at Starhill. The three black Explorers I had seen at the Delacroix compound stood waiting, their motors idling, their lights dimmed. As Leon sprayed gasoline into the cars and the pickup, the bodies of the dead were removed, wrapped in tarps, and placed in the backs of two of the jeeps. Louis and I watched it all in silence.

As the jeeps roared into life and Leon threw lighted rags into the discarded vehicles, Lionel Fontenot walked over to us and stood with us as they burned. He took a small green notebook from his pocket, scribbled a number on a sheet, and tore it out.

"This guy will look after your friend's hand. He's discreet."

"He knew who killed Lutice, Lionel," I said.

He nodded. "Maybe. He wouldn't tell, not even at the end." He rubbed his index finger along a raw cut on the palm of his right hand, picking dirt from the wound. "I hear the feds are looking for someone around Baton Rouge, used to work in a hospital in New York."

I stayed silent and he smiled. "We know his name. Man could hide out in the bayou for a long time, he knew his way around. Feds might not find him, but we will." He gestured with his hand, like a king displaying his finest troops to his worried subjects. "We're looking. We find him, it'll end there."

Then he turned and climbed into the driver's seat of the lead jeep, Leon beside him, and they disappeared into the night, the red taillights like falling cigarettes in the darkness, like burning boats floating on black water.

I called Angel as we drove back to New Orleans. At an all-night drugstore I picked up antiseptic and a first-aid kit so we could work on Louis's hand. There was a sheen of sweat on his face as I drove and the white rags binding his fingers were stained a deep red. When we arrived back at the Flaisance, Angel cleansed the wound with the antiseptic and tried to stitch it with some surgical thread. The knuckle looked bad and Louis's mouth was stretched tight with pain. Despite his protests, I called the number we had been given.

The bleary voice that answered the phone on the fourth ring shook the sleep from its tones when I mentioned Lionel's name.

Angel drove Louis to the doctor's office. When they had gone, I stood outside Rachel's door and debated whether or not to knock. I knew she wasn't asleep: Angel had spoken to her after I called, and I could sense her wakefulness. Still, I didn't knock, but as I walked back toward my own room her door opened. She stood in the gap, a white T-shirt reaching almost to her knees, and waited for me. She stood carefully aside to let me enter.

"You're still in one piece, I see," she said. She didn't sound particularly pleased.

I felt tired and sick from the sight of blood. I wanted to plunge my face into a sink of ice-cold water. I wanted a drink so badly my tongue felt swollen inside my mouth and only a bottle of Abita, ice frosting on its rim, and a shot of Redbreast whiskey could restore it to its normal size. My voice sounded like the croak of an old man on his deathbed when I spoke.

"I'm in one piece," I said. "A lot of others aren't. Louis took a bullet across the hand and too many people died out at the house. Joe Bones, most of his crew, his woman."

Rachel turned her back and walked to the balcony window. Only the bedside lamp lit the room, casting shadows over the illustrations that she had kept from Woolrich and that were now restored to their places on the walls. Flayed arms and the face of a woman and a young man emerged from the semidarkness.

"What did you find out, for all that killing?"

It was a good question. As usual with good questions, the answer didn't live up to it.

"Nothing, except that Joe Bones was happier to die painfully than to tell us what he knew."

She turned then. "What are you going to do now?"

I was getting tired of questions, especially questions as difficult as these. I knew she was right and I felt disgusted at myself. It felt as if Rachel had become tainted through her contact with me. Maybe I should have told her all of those things then, but I was too tired and too sick and I could smell blood in my nostrils; and, anyway, I think she already knew most of it.

"I'm going to bed," I said. "After that, I'm winging it." Then I left her.

47

THE NEXT MORNING I awoke with an ache in my arms from toting the Calico, exacerbated by the lingering pain of the gunshot wound inflicted in Haven. I could smell powder on my fingers, in my hair, and on my discarded clothes. The room stank like the scene of a gunfight, so I opened the window and let the hot New Orleans air slip heavily into the room like a clumsy burglar.

I checked on Louis and Angel. Louis's hand had been expertly bound after the doctor picked the shards of bone from the wound and padded the knuckle. Louis barely opened his eyes as I exchanged a few quiet words with Angel at the door. I felt guilty for what had happened, although I knew that neither of them blamed me.

I sensed, too, that Angel was anxious now to return to New York. Joe Bones was dead, and the police and the feds were probably closing in on Edward Byron, despite Lionel Fontenot's doubts. Besides, I didn't believe that it would take long for Woolrich to connect us to what had happened to Joe Bones, especially if Louis was walking around with a bullet crease on his hand. I told Angel all of this and he agreed that they would leave as soon as I returned, so that Rachel would not be left alone. The whole case seemed to have ground to a kind of halt for me. Elsewhere, the feds and the Fontenots were hunting Edward Byron, a man who still seemed as distant from me as the last emperor of China.

I left a message for Morphy. I wanted to see what his people had on Byron; I wanted to add flesh to the figure. As things stood, he was as shorn of identity as the faceless figures of the slain that the feds believed he had left behind. The feds might well have been right. With the local police, they could conduct a better search than a bunch of visitors from New York with delusions of adequacy. I had hoped to work my way toward him from a different direction, but with the death of Joe Bones that path seemed to have come to an end in a tangle of dark undergrowth.

I took my phone and my book of Ralegh's writings and headed for Mother's on Poydras Street, where I drank too many cups of coffee and picked at some bacon and brown toast. When you reach one of life's dead ends, Ralegh is good company. *"Go soul . . . since I needs must die / And give the world the lie."* Ralegh knew enough to take a stoical attitude to adversity, although he didn't know enough to avoid getting his head cut off.

Beside me, a man ate ham and eggs with the concentrated effort of a bad lover, yellow egg yolk tingeing his chin like sunlight reflected from a buttercup. Someone whistled a snatch of "What's New?" then lost his thread in the complicated chord changes of the song. The air was filled with the buzz of late morning conversation, a radio station easing into neutral with a bland rock song and the low, aggravated hum of distant, slow-moving traffic. Outside, it was another humid New Orleans day, the kind of day that leads lovers to fight and makes children sullen and grim.

An hour passed. I rang the detective squad in St. Martin and was told that Morphy had taken a day's leave to work on his house. I had nothing better to do now, so I paid my bill, put some gas in the car, and started out once again toward Baton Rouge. I found a Lafayette station playing some scratchy Cheese Read, followed by Buckwheat Zydeco and Clifton Chenier, an hour of classic Cajun and zydeco, as the DJ put it. I let it play until the city fell away and the sound and the landscape became one.

A sheet of plastic slapped dryly in the early afternoon wind as I pulled up outside Morphy's place. He was replacing part of the exterior wall on the west side of the house, and the lines holding the plastic in place over the exposed joints sang as the wind tried to yank them from their moorings. It tugged at one of the windows, which had not been fastened properly, and made the screen door knock at its frame like a tired visitor.

I called his name but there was no reply. I walked to the rear of the house, where the back door stood open, held in place by a piece of brick. I called again but my voice seemed to echo emptily through the central hallway. The rooms on the ground level were all unoccupied and no sounds came from upstairs. I drew my gun and climbed the stairs, newly planed in preparation for treating. The bedrooms were empty and the bathroom door stood wide open, toiletries neatly arranged by the sink. I checked the gallery and then went back downstairs. As I turned back toward the rear door, cold metal touched the base of my neck.

"Drop it," said a voice.

I let the gun slip from my fingers.

"Turn around. Slowly."

The pressure was removed from my neck and I turned to find Morphy standing before me, a nail gun held inches from my face. He let out a deep breath of relief and lowered the gun.

"Shit, you scared the hell out of me," he said.

I could feel my heart thumping wildly in my chest. "Thanks," I said. "I really needed that kind of adrenaline rush on top of five cups of coffee." I sat down heavily on the bottom step.

"You look terrible, mon. You up late last night?"

I looked up to see if there was an edge to what he had said, but he had turned his back.

"Kind of."

"You hear the news? Joe Bones and his crew were taken out last night. Someone cut Joe up pretty bad before he died, too. Police weren't even sure it was him until they checked the prints." He walked down to the kitchen and came back with a beer for himself and a soda for me. I noticed it was caffeine-free cola. Under his arm he held a copy of the *Times-Picayune*.

"You see this today?"

I took the paper from him. It was folded into quarter size,

the bottom of the front page facing up. The headline read: POLICE HUNT SERIAL KILLER IN RITUAL MURDERS. The story below contained details of the deaths of *Tante* Marie Aguillard and Tee Jean that could only have come from the investigation team itself: the display of the bodies, the manner of their discovery, the nature of some of the wounds. It went on to speculate on a possible link between the discovery of Lutice Fontenot's body and the death of a man in Bucktown, known to have links with a leading crime figure. Worst of all, it said that police were also investigating a connection to a similar pair of murders in New York earlier this year. Susan and Jennifer were not named, but it was clear that the writer—anonymous beneath a *"Times-Picayune* Journalists" byline—knew enough about the murders to be able to put a name on the victims.

I put the paper down wearily. "Did the leak come from your guys?" I asked.

"Could have done, but I don't think so. The feds are blaming us: they're all over us, accusing us of sabotaging the investigation." He sipped his beer before saying what was on his mind.

"One or two people maybe felt that it could have been you who leaked the stuff." He was obviously uncomfortable saying it, but he didn't look away.

"I didn't do it. If they've got as far as Jennifer and Susan, it won't be too long before they connect me to what's happening. The last thing I need is the press crawling all over me."

He considered what I said, then nodded. "I guess you're right."

"You speak to the editor?"

"He was contacted at home when the first edition came out. We got freedom of the press and the protection of sources coming out our ass. We can't force him to tell but"— he rubbed at the tendons on the back of his neck—"it's unusual for something like this to happen. The papers are real careful about jeopardizing investigations. I think it had to come from someone close to all this."

I thought about it. "If they felt okay about using this

stuff, then it must be cast iron and the source impeccable," I said. "It could be that the feds are playing their own game on this." It seemed to reaffirm our belief that Woolrich and his team were holding back, not only from me but probably from the police investigating team as well.

"It wouldn't be anything new," said Morphy. "Feds wouldn't tell us what day it is, they thought they could get away with it. You think they might have planted the story?"

"Somebody did."

Morphy finished his beer and crushed the can beneath his foot. A small stain of beer spread itself on the bare wood. He picked up a tool belt from where it hung on a hat stand near the door and strapped it on.

"You need any help?"

He looked at me. "Can you carry planks without falling over?"

"No."

"Then you're perfect for the job. There's a spare pair of work gloves in the kitchen."

For the rest of the afternoon I worked with my hands, hoisting and carrying, hammering and sawing. We replaced most of the wood on the west side, a gentle breeze spraying sawdust and shavings around us as we worked. Later, Angie returned from a shopping trip to Baton Rouge, carrying groceries and boutique bags. While Morphy and I cleaned up, she grilled steaks with sweet potatoes, carrots, and Creole rice, and we ate them in the kitchen as the evening drew in and the wind wrapped the house in its arms.

Morphy walked me out to my car. As I put the key in the ignition, he leaned in the window and said softly: "Someone tried to get to Stacey Byron yesterday. Know anything about it?"

"Maybe."

"You were there, weren't you? You were there when they took Joe Bones?"

"You don't want to know the answer to that," I replied. "Just like I don't want to know about Luther Bordelon."

As I drove away, I could see him standing before his uncompleted house. Then he turned away and returned to his wife.

When I arrived back at the Flaisance, Angel and Louis were packed and ready to go. They wished me luck and told me that Rachel had gone to bed early. She had booked a flight for the next day. I decided not to disturb her and went to my own room. I don't even remember falling asleep.

The luminous dial on my watch read 8:30 A.M. when the pounding came at my door. I had been in deep sleep and I pulled myself slowly into wakefulness like a diver struggling for the surface. I had got as far as the edge of the bed when the door exploded inward and there were lights shining in my face and strong arms hauled me to my feet and pushed me hard against the wall. A gun was held to my head as the main light came on in the room. I could see NOPD uniforms, a couple of plainclothesmen, and directly to my right, Morphy's partner Toussaint. Around me, men were tearing the room apart.

And I knew then that something had gone terribly, terribly wrong.

They allowed me to pull on a tracksuit and a pair of sneakers before cuffing me. I was marched through the hotel, past guests peering anxiously from their rooms, to a waiting police car. In a second car, her face pale and her hair matted from sleep, sat Rachel. I shrugged helplessly at her before we were driven in convoy from the Quarter.

I was questioned for three hours, then given a cup of coffee and grilled again for another hour. The room was small and brightly lit. It smelled of cigarette smoke and stale sweat. In one corner, where the plaster was broken and worn, I could see what looked like a bloodstain. Two detectives, Dale and Klein, did most of the questioning, Dale assuming the role of aggressive interrogator, threatening to dump me in the swamp with a bullet in the head for killing a Louisiana cop, Klein taking the part of the reasonable, sensitive man trying to protect me while ensuring that the truth was told. Even with other cops as the object of their attentions, the good cop—bad cop thing never went out of fashion.

I told them all I could, again and again and again. I told them of my visit to Morphy, the work on the house, the dinner, the departure, all of the reasons why my prints were all over the house. No, Morphy hadn't given me the police files found in my room. No, I couldn't say who did. No, only the night porter saw me re-enter the hotel; I didn't speak to anyone else. No, I didn't leave my room again that night. No, there was no one to confirm that fact. No. No. No. No. No.

Then Woolrich arrived and the merry-go-round started all over again. More questions, this time with the feds in attendance. And still, no one told me why I was there or what had happened to Morphy and his wife. In the end, Klein returned and told me I could go. Behind a slatted-rail divider, which separated the detective squadroom from the main corridor, Rachel sat with a mug of tea while the detectives around her studiously ignored her. In a cage ten feet behind her, a skinny white man with tattooed arms whispered obscenely to her.

Toussaint appeared. He was an overweight, balding man in his early fifties, with straggly white curls around his pate like the top of a hill erupting from out of a mist. He looked red eyed and nauseous and was as out of place here as I was.

A patrolman motioned to Rachel. "We'll take you back to your hotel now, ma'am." She stood. Behind her, the guy in the cage made sucking noises and grabbed his crotch in his hand.

"You okay?" I asked as she passed by.

She nodded dumbly, then: "Are you coming with me?"

Toussaint was at my left hand. "He'll follow later," he said. Rachel looked over her shoulder at me as the patrolman led her away. I gave her a smile and tried to make it look reassuring, but my heart wasn't in it.

"Come on, I'll drive you back and buy you a coffee on the way," said Toussaint, and I followed him from the building.

We ended up in Mother's, where less than twenty-four

hours before I had sat waiting for Morphy's call and where Toussaint would tell me how John Charles Morphy and his wife, Angela, had died.

Morphy had been due to work a special early duty that morning and Toussaint had dropped by to pick him up. They alternated pickup duties as it suited. That day, it happened to be Toussaint's turn.

The screen door was closed, but the front door behind stood open. Toussaint called Morphy's name, just as I had the afternoon before. He followed in my footsteps through the central hallway, checking the kitchen and the rooms to the right and left. He thought Morphy might have slept in, although he had never been late before, so he called up the stairs to the bedroom. There was no reply. He recalled that his stomach was already tightening as he worked his way up the stairs, calling Morphy's name, then Angie's, as he advanced. The door of their bedroom was partially open, but the angle obscured their bed.

He knocked once, then slowly opened the door. For a moment, the merest flashing splinter of a second, he thought he had disturbed their lovemaking, until the blood registered and he knew that this was a parody of all that love stood for, of all that it meant, and he wept then for his friend and his wife.

Even now, I seem to recall only snatches of what he said, but I can picture the bodies in my head. They were naked, facing each other on what had once been white sheets, their bodies locked together at the hips, their legs intertwined. From the waist, they leaned backward at arm's length from each other. Both had been cut from neck to stomach. Their rib cages had been split and pulled back, and each had a hand buried in the breast of the other. As he neared, Toussaint saw that each was holding the other's heart in the palm of a hand. Their heads hung back so that their hair almost touched their backs. Their eyes were gone, their faces removed, their mouths open in their final agony, their moment of death like an ecstasy. In them, love was reduced to an example to other lovers of the futility of love itself.

As Toussaint spoke, a wave of guilt swept over me and broke across my heart. I had brought this thing to their house. By helping me, Morphy and his wife had been marked for a terrible death, just as the Aguillards too seemed to have been tainted by their contact with me. I stank of mortality.

And in the midst of it all, some lines of verse seemed to float into my head and I could not recall how I had resurrected them, or who had given them to me in the first place. And it seemed to me that their source was important, although I could not tell why, except that in the lines there seemed to be echoes of what Toussaint had seen. But as I tried to remember a voice speaking them to me, it slipped away, and try as I might, I could not bring it back. Only the lines remained. Some metaphysical poet, I thought. Donne, perhaps. Yes, almost certainly Donne.

> If th'unborne
> Must learne, by my being cut up, and torne:
> Kill, and dissect me, Love; for this
> Torture against thine owne end is,
> Rack't carcasses make ill Anatomies.

Remedium amoris, wasn't that the term? The torture and death of lovers as a remedy for love.

"He helped me," I said. "I involved him in this."

"He involved himself," Toussaint said. "He wanted to do it. He wanted to bring this guy to an end."

I held his gaze.

"For Luther Bordelon?"

Toussaint looked away. "What does it matter now?"

But I couldn't explain that in Morphy I saw something of myself, that I had felt for his pain, that I wanted to believe he was better than me. I wanted to know.

"Garza called the Bordelon thing," said Toussaint at last. "Garza killed him and then Morphy supplied the throwdown. That's what he said. Morphy was young. Garza shouldn't have put him in that situation, but he did, and Morphy's been paying for it ever since." And then he caught himself using the present tense and went silent.

Outside, people were living another day: working, touring, eating, flirting still continued despite all that had taken place, all that was happening. It seemed, somehow, that it should all have come to a halt, that the clocks should have been stopped and the mirrors covered, the doorbells silenced and the voices reduced to a respectful, hushed volume. Maybe if they had seen the pictures of Susan and Jennifer, of *Tante* Marie and Tee Jean, of Morphy and Angie, then they would have stopped and considered. And that was what the Traveling Man wanted: to provide, in the deaths of others, a reminder of the deaths of us all and the worthlessness of love and loyalty, of parenthood and friendship, of sex and need and joy, in the face of the emptiness to come.

As I stood to leave, something else came to me, something awful that I had almost forgotten, and I felt a deep, violent ache in my gut, which spread through my body until I was forced to lean against the wall, my hand scrabbling for purchase.

"Ah, God, she was pregnant."

I looked at Toussaint and his eyes briefly fluttered closed.

"He knew, didn't he?"

Toussaint said nothing, but there was despair in his eyes. I didn't ask what the Traveling Man had done to the unborn child, but in that instant, I saw a terrible progression over the last months of my life. It seemed that I had moved from the death of my own child, my Jennifer, to the deaths of many children, the victims of Adelaide Modine and her partner, Hyams, and now, finally, to the deaths of all children. Everything this Traveling Man did signified something beyond itself: in the death of Morphy's unborn child, I saw all hope for the future reduced to tattered flesh.

"I'm supposed to bring you back to your hotel," said Toussaint at last. "The New Orleans PD will make sure you get on the evening flight back to New York."

But I hardly heard him. All I could think was that the

Traveling Man had been watching us all along and that his game was still going on around us. We were all participants, whether we wanted to be or not.

And I recalled something that a con man named Saul Mann had once told me back in Portland, something that seemed important to me yet I couldn't recall why.

You can't bluff someone who isn't paying attention.

48
□

TOUSSAINT DROPPED ME at the Flaisance. Rachel's door was half open when I reached the carriage house. I knocked gently and entered. Her clothes had been thrown across the bedroom floor and the sheets from her bed were tossed in an untidy pile in the corner. All of her papers were gone. Her suitcase sat open on the bare mattress. I heard movement from the bathroom and she emerged carrying her cosmetics case. It was stained with powder and foundation and I guessed that the cops had broken some of its contents during their search.

She was wearing a faded blue Knicks sweat top, which hung down over her dark blue denims. She had washed and showered and her damp hair clung to her face. Her feet were bare. I had not noticed before how small they were.

"I'm sorry," I said.

"I know." She didn't look at me. Instead, she started to pick up her clothes and fold them as neatly as she could into her suitcase. I bent down to pick up a pair of socks, which lay in a ball by my feet.

"Leave it," she said. "I can do it."

There was another knock at the door and a patrolman appeared. He was polite, but he made it clear that we were to stay in the hotel until someone arrived to take us to the airport.

I went back to my room and showered. A maid came and made up the room and I sat on my clean sheets and listened to the sounds from the street. I thought about how badly I had screwed up, and how many people had been killed because of it. I felt like the Angel of Death; if I stood on a lawn, the grass would die.

I must have dozed for a while, because the light in the room had changed when I awoke. It seemed that it was dusk, yet that could not have been the case. There was a smell in the room, an odor of rotting vegetation and water filled with algae and dead fish. When I tried to take a breath, the air felt warm and humid in my mouth. I was conscious of movement around me, shapes shifting in the shadows at the corners of the room. I heard whispered voices and a sound like silk brushing against wood and, faintly, a child's footsteps running through leaves. Trees rustled and there came a flapping of wings from above me, beating unevenly as if the bird was in distress or pain.

The room grew darker, turning the wall facing me to black. The light through the window frame was tinged with blue and green and shimmered as seen through a heat haze.

Or through water.

They came from out of the dark wall, black shapes against green light. They brought with them the coppery scent of blood, so strong that I could taste it on my tongue. I opened my mouth to call out something—even now, I am not sure what I could have called, or who would have heard—but the dank humidity stilled my tongue like a sponge soaked in warm, filthy water. It seemed that a weight was on my chest, preventing me from rising, and I had trouble taking air into my lungs. My hands clasped and unclasped until they too were still and I knew then how it felt to have ketamine coursing through one's veins, stilling the body in preparation for the anatomist's knife.

The figures stopped at the edge of the darkness, just beyond the reach of the window's dim light. They were indistinct, their edges forming and reforming like figures seen through frosted glass, or a projection losing and then regaining its focus.

And then the voices came,
birdman
soft and insistent,
birdman

fading and then strong again,

birdman

voices that I had never heard and others that had called out to me in passion,

bird

in anger, in fear, in love.

daddy

She was the smallest of them all, linked hand in hand with another who stood beside her. Around them, the others fanned out. I counted eight in all and, behind them, other figures, more indistinct, women, men, young girls. As the pressure built on my chest and I struggled to draw the shallowest of breaths, it came to me that the figure that had haunted *Tante* Marie Aguillard, that Raymond believed he had seen at Honey Island, the girl who seemed to call out to me through dark waters, might not have been Lutice Fontenot.

chile

Each breath felt like my last, none getting farther than the back of my throat before it was choked in a gasp.

chile

The voice was old and dark as the ebony keys on an ancient piano singing out from a distant room.

wake up, chile, his world is unraveling

And then my last breath sounded in my ears and all was stillness and quiet.

I woke to the sound of a tapping on my door. Outside, daylight had passed its height and was ebbing toward evening. When I opened the door, Toussaint stood before me. Behind him, I could see Rachel waiting. "It's time to go," he said.

"I thought the New Orleans cops were taking care of that."

"I volunteered," he replied. He followed me into the room as I threw my shaving gear loosely into my suit carrier, folded it over, and attached the clasps. It was London Fog, a present from Susan.

Toussaint nodded to the NOPD patrolman.

"You sure this is okay?" said the cop. He looked distracted and uncertain.

"Look, New Orleans cops got better things to be doing than baby-sitting," replied Toussaint. "I'll get these people to their plane; you go out and catch some bad guys, okay?"

We drove in silence to Moisant Field. I sat in the passenger seat, Rachel sat in the back. I waited for Toussaint to take the turn to the airport but he continued straight on 10.

"You missed your turn," I said.

"No," said Toussaint. "No, I didn't."

When things start to unravel, they unravel fast. We got lucky that day. Everybody gets lucky some time.

On a junction of the Upper Grand River, southeast of 10 on the road to Lafayette, a dredging operation to remove silt and junk from the bottom of the river got some of its machinery caught up on a batch of discarded barbed wire that was rusting away on the riverbed. They eventually freed it and tried to haul it up, but there were other things caught in the wire as well: an old iron bedstead; a set of slave irons, more than a century and a half old; and, holding the wire to the bottom, an oil drum marked with a fleur-de-lys.

It was almost a joke to the dredging crew as they worked to free the drum. The report of the discovery of a girl's body in a fleur-de-lys drum had been all over the news bulletins and it had taken up ninety lines below the fold on the *Times-Picayune* on the day of its discovery.

Maybe the crew joshed one another morbidly as they worked the barrel out of the water in order to get at the wire. Perhaps they went a little quieter, barring the odd nervous laugh, as one of them worked at the lid. The drum had rusted in places and the lid had not been welded shut. When it came off, dirty water, dead fish, and weeds flowed out.

The legs of the girl, partially decayed but surrounded by a strange, waxy membrane, emerged from the open lid as well, although her body remained jammed, half in, half out of the drum. The river life had fed on her but when one man shined his flashlight to the end of the drum he could see the tattered remains of skin at the forehead and her teeth seemed to be smiling at him in the darkness.

Only two cars were at the scene when we arrived. The body had been out of the water for less than three hours. Two uniformed cops stood by with the dredging crew. Around the body stood three men in plain clothes, one of them wearing a slightly more expensive suit than the rest, his silver hair cut short and neat. I recognized him from the aftermath of Morphy's death: Sheriff James Dupree of St. Martin Parish, Toussaint's superior.

Dupree motioned us forward as we stepped from the car. Rachel hung back slightly but still moved toward the body in the drum. It was the quietest crime scene at which I had ever been present. Even when the ME appeared later, it remained restrained.

Dupree pulled a pair of plastic gloves from his hands, making sure that he didn't touch their exterior with his exposed fingers. His nails were very short and very clean, I noticed, although not manicured.

"You want to take a closer look?" he asked.

"No," I said. "I've pretty much seen all I want to see."

There was a rotten, pungent odor coming from the mud and silt dredged up by the crew, stronger even than the smell from the girl's body. Birds hovered over the detritus, trying to target dead or dying fish. One of the crew lodged his cigarette in his mouth, bent to pick up a stone, and hurled it at a huge gray rat that scuttled in the dirt. The stone hit the mud with a wet, thudding sound like a piece of meat dropped on a butcher's slab. The rat scurried away. Around it, other gray objects burst into activity. The whole area was alive with rodents, disturbed from their nests by the actions of the dredging crew. They bumped and snapped at one another, their tails leaving snaking lines in the mud. The rest of the crew now joined in, casting stones in a skimming motion close to the ground. Most of them had better aims than their friend.

Dupree lit a cigarette with a gold Ronson lighter. He smoked Gitanes, the only cop I had ever seen do so. The smoke was acrid and strong and the breeze blew it directly into my face. Dupree apologized and turned so that his body partially shielded me from the smoke. It was a peculiarly sensitive gesture and it made me wonder, once again, why I was not sitting at Moisant Field.

"They tell me you tracked down that child killer in New York, the Modine woman," said Dupree eventually. "After thirty years, that's no mean feat."

"She made a mistake," I said. "In the end, they all do. It's just a matter of being in the right place at the right time to take advantage of the situation."

He tilted his head slightly to one side, as if he didn't entirely agree with what I had said but was prepared to give it a little thought in case he'd missed something. He took another long drag on his cigarette. It was an upmarket brand, but he smoked it the way I had seen longshoremen on the New York docks smoke, the butt held between the thumb and the first two fingers of the hand, the ember shielded by the palm. It was the sort of hold you learned as a kid, when smoking was still a furtive pleasure and being caught with a cigarette was enough to earn you a smack across the back of the head from your old man.

"I guess we all get lucky sometimes," said Dupree. He looked at me closely. "I'm wondering if maybe we've got lucky here."

I waited for him to continue. There seemed to be something fortuitous in the discovery of the girl's body, or perhaps I was still remembering a dream in which shapes came out of my bedroom wall and told me that a thread in the tapestry being woven by the Traveling Man had suddenly come loose.

"When Morphy and his wife died, my first instinct was to take you outside and beat you to within an inch of your life," he said. "He was a good man, a good detective, despite everything. He was also my friend.

"But he trusted you, and Toussaint here seems to trust you too. He thinks maybe you provide a linking factor in all this. If that's true, then putting you on a plane back to New York isn't going to achieve anything. Your FBI friend Woolrich seemed to feel the same way, but there were louder voices than his shouting for you to be sent home."

He took another drag on his cigarette. "I reckon you're like gum caught in someone's hair," he continued. "The more they try to pry you out, the more you get stuck in, and maybe we can use that. I'm risking a storm of shit by keeping you here, but Morphy told me what you felt about this guy, how you believed he was observing us, manipulating us. You want to tell me what you make of this, or do you want to spend the night at Moisant sleeping on a chair?"

I looked at the bare feet and exposed legs of the girl in the drum, the strange yellow accretion like a chrysalis, lying in a pool of filth and water on a rat-infested stretch of a river in western Louisiana. The ME and his men had arrived with a body bag and a stretcher. They positioned a length of plastic on the ground and carefully maneuvered the drum on to it, one of them supporting the girl's legs with a gloved hand. Then slowly, gently, the ME's hands working inside the drum, they began to free her.

"Everything we've done so far has been dogged and predicted by this man," I began. "The Aguillards learned something, and they died. Remarr saw something, and he was killed. Morphy tried to help me, and now he's dead as well. He's closing off the options, forcing us to follow a pattern that he's already set. Now someone's been leaking details of the investigation to the press. Maybe that person has been leaking things to this man as well, possibly unintentionally, possibly not."

Dupree and Toussaint exchanged a look. "We've been considering that possibility as well," said Dupree. "There are too many damn people crawling over this for anything to stay quiet for long."

"On top of all that," I continued, "the feds are keeping something back. You think Woolrich has told you everything he knows?"

Dupree almost laughed. "I know as much about this guy Byron as I know about the poet, and that's sweet FA."

From inside the drum came a scraping sound, the sound of bone rubbing on metal. Gloved hands supported the girl's naked, discolored body as it was freed from the confines of the drum.

"How long can we keep the details quiet?" I asked Dupree.

"Not long. The feds will have to be informed, the press will find out." He spread his hands in a gesture of helplessness. "If you're suggesting that I don't tell the feds . . ." But I could see in his face that he was already moving in that direction, that the reason why the ME was examining the body so soon after its discovery, the reason why there were so few police at the scene, was to keep the details limited to the minimum number of people.

I decided to push him. "I'm suggesting you don't tell *anyone* about this. If you do, the man who did this will be alerted and he'll cut us off again. If you're put in a position where you have to say something, then fudge it. Don't mention the barrel, obscure the location, say you don't believe the discovery is connected to any other investigation. Say nothing until the girl is identified."

"Assuming that we can identify her," said Toussaint mournfully.

"Hey, you want to rain someplace else?" snapped Dupree.

"Sorry," said Toussaint.

"He's right," I said. "We may not be able to identify her. That's a chance we'll have to take."

"Once we exhaust our own records, we'll have to use the feds," said Dupree.

"We'll burn that bridge when we come to it," I responded. "Can we do this?"

Dupree shuffled his feet and finished his cigarette. He leaned through the open window of his car and put the butt into the ashtray.

"Twenty-four hours max," he said. "After that, we'll be accused of incompetence or deliberately impeding the progress of an investigation. I'm not even sure how far we'll get in that time, although"—he looked at Toussaint, then back to me—"it may not come to that."

"You want to tell me," I said, "or do I have to guess?"

It was Toussaint who answered.

"The feds think they've found Byron. They're going to move on him by morning."

"In which case, this is just a backup," said Dupree. "The joker in our pack."

But I was no longer listening. They were moving on Byron, but I would not be there. If I tried to participate, then a sizable portion of the Louisiana law enforcement community would be used to put me on a plane to New York or to lock me in a cell.

The crew were likely to be the weakest link. They were taken aside and given cups of coffee, then Dupree and I were as honest with them as we felt we could be. We told them that if they didn't keep quiet about what they had seen for at least one day, then the man who had killed the girl would probably get away and that he would kill again. It was at least partly true; cut off from the hunt for Byron, we were continuing the investigation as best we could.

The crew was made up of hardworking local men, most of them married with children of their own. They agreed to say nothing until we contacted them and told them that it was okay to do so. They meant what they said, but I knew that some of them would tell their wives and their girlfriends as soon as they got home, and word of what had happened would spread from there. A man who says he tells his wife everything is either a liar or a fool, my first sergeant used to say. Unfortunately, he was divorced.

Dupree had been in his office when the call came through and had picked pairs of deputies and detectives whom he trusted implicitly. With the addition of Toussaint, Rachel, and me, along with the ME's team and the dredging crew, maybe twenty people knew of the discovery of the body. It was nineteen people too many to keep a secret for long, but that couldn't be helped.

After the initial examination and photography, it was decided to bring the body to a private clinic outside Lafayette, where the ME sometimes consulted, and he agreed to commence his work almost immediately. Dupree prepared a statement detailing the discovery of a woman of unspecified age, cause of death unknown, some five miles from the actual location of the discovery. He dated it, timed it, then left it under a sheaf of files on his desk.

By the time we both arrived at the autopsy room, the remains had been X-rayed and measured. The mobile cart that had brought the body in had been pushed into a corner, away from the autopsy table on its cylindrical tank, which delivered water to the table and collected the fluids that drained through the holes on the table itself. A scale for the weighing of organs hung from a metal frame, and beside it, a small-parts dissection table on its own base stood ready for use.

Only three people, apart from the ME and his assistant, attended the autopsy. Dupree and Toussaint were two. I was the third. The smell was strong and only partly masked by the antiseptic. Dark hair hung from her skull, and the skin that was left was shrunken and torn. The girl's remains were almost completely covered by the yellow-white substance.

It was Dupree who asked the question. "Doc, what is that stuff on the body?"

The examiner's name was Dr. Emile Huckstetter, a tall, stocky man in his early sixties with a ruddy complexion. He ran a gloved finger over the substance before he responded.

"It's a condition called adipocere," he said. "It's rare—I've seen maybe two or three cases at most, but the combination of silt and water in that canal seems to have resulted in its development here."

His eyes narrowed as he leaned toward the body. "Her body fats broke down in the water and they've hardened to create this substance, the adipocere. She's been in the water for a while. This stuff takes at least six months to form on the trunk, less on the face. I'm taking a stab here, but I figure she's been in the water for less than seven months, certainly no more than that."

Huckstetter detailed the examination into a small microphone attached to his green surgical scrubs. The girl was seventeen or eighteen, he said. She had not been tied or bound. There was evidence of a blade's slash at her neck, indicating a deep cut across her carotid artery as the probable cause of death. There were marks on her skull where her face had been removed and similar marks in her eye sockets.

As the examination drew to a close, Dupree was paged, and minutes later, he arrived back with Rachel. She had checked into a Lafayette motel, storing both her own baggage and mine, then returned. She recoiled initially at the sight of the body, then stood beside me and, without speaking, took my hand.

When the ME was done, he removed his gloves and commenced scrubbing. Dupree took the X rays from the case envelope and held them up to the light, each in turn. "What's this?" he said, after a time.

Huckstetter took the X ray from his hand and examined it himself. "Compound fracture, right tibia," he said, pointing with his finger. "Probably two years old. It's in the report, or it will be as soon as I can compile it."

I felt a falling sensation and an ache spreading across my stomach. I reached out to steady myself and the scales jangled as I glanced against their frame. Then my hand was on the autopsy table and my fingers were touching the girl's remains. I pulled my hand back quickly, but I could still smell her on my fingers.

"Parker?" said Dupree. He reached out and gripped my arm to steady me. I could still feel the girl on my fingers.

"My God," I said. "I think I know who she is."

In the early morning light, near the northern tip of Bayou Courtableau, south of Krotz Springs and maybe twenty miles from Lafayette, a team of federal agents, backed up by St. Landry Parish sheriff's deputies, closed in on a shotgun house that stood with its back to the bayou, its front sheltered by overgrown bushes and trees. Some of the agents wore dark rain gear with *FBI* in large yellow letters on the back, others helmets and body armor. They advanced slowly and quietly, their safeties off. When they spoke, they did so quickly and with the fewest possible words. Radio contact was kept to a minimum. They knew what they were doing. Around them, deputies armed with

pistols and shotguns listened to the sound of their breathing and the pumping of their hearts as they prepared to
move on the house of Edward Byron, the man they believed to be directly responsible for the deaths of their col-
league, John Charles Morphy, his young wife, and at least
five other people.

The house was run down, the slates on the roof damaged
and cracked in places, the roof beams already rotting. Two
of the windows at the front of the house were broken and
had been covered with cardboard held in place by duct tape.
The wood on the gallery was warped and, in places, missing
altogether. On a metal hook to the right of the house hung
the carcass of a wild pig, newly skinned. Blood dripped from
its snout and pooled on the ground below.

On a signal from Woolrich, shortly after 6 A.M., agents in
Kevlar body armor approached the house from the front
and the rear. They checked the windows at either side of the
front door and adjoining the rear entrance. Then, simultaneously, they hit the doors, moving into the central hallway
with maximum noise, their flashlights burning through the
darkness of the interior.

The two teams had almost reached each other when a
shotgun roared from the back of the house and blood
erupted in the dim light. An agent named Thomas Seltz
plunged forward as the shot ripped through the unprotected
area of his armpit, the vulnerable point in upper-body
armor, his finger tightening in a last reflex on the trigger of
his machine pistol as he died. Bullets raked across the wall,
ceiling, and floor as he fell, sending dust and splinters
through the air and injuring two agents, one in the leg and
one in the mouth.

The firing masked the sound of another shell being
pumped into the shotgun. The second shot blasted wood
from the frame of an interior door as agents hit the ground
and began firing through the now empty rear door. A third
shot took out an agent moving fast around the side of the
house. A mass of logs and old furniture, destined for fire-
wood, lay scattered on the ground, dispersed when the
shooter broke from his hiding place beneath it. The sound

of small-arms fire directed into the bayou reached the agents as they knelt to tend to their injured colleagues or ran to join the chase.

A figure in worn blue jeans and a white-and-red check shirt had disappeared into the bayou. The agents followed warily, their legs sinking almost to the knee at times in the muddy swamp water, dead tree trunks forcing them to deviate from a straight advance, before they reached firm ground. Using the trees as cover, they moved slowly, their guns at their shoulders, sighting as they went.

There was the roar of a shotgun from ahead. Birds scattered from the trees and splinters shot out at head height from a huge cypress. An agent screamed in pain and stumbled into view, impaled in the cheek by the shards of wood. A second blast rang out and shattered the femur in his left leg. He collapsed on the dirt and leaves, his back arched in agony.

Automatic fire raked the trees, shattering branches and blasting foliage. After four or five seconds of concentrated firing, the order went out to cease fire and the swamp was quiet once again. The agents and police advanced once more, moving quickly from tree to tree. A shout went up as blood was found by a willow, its broken branches white as bone.

From behind came the sounds of dogs barking as the tracker, who had been kept in reserve three miles away, was brought in to assist. The dogs were allowed to sniff around Byron's clothing and the area of the woodpile. Their handler, a thin, bearded man with his jeans tucked into muddy boots, let them smell the blood by the willow as soon as he caught up with the main party. Then, the dogs straining at their leashes, they moved on cautiously.

But no more shots came at them from Edward Byron, because the lawmen were not the only ones hunting him in the swamp.

While the hunt continued for Byron, Toussaint, two young deputies, and I were in the sheriff's office in St. Martinville, where we continued our trawl through Miami's den-

tists, using emergency numbers from answering machines
where necessary.

Rachel provided the only interruption, when she arrived
with coffee and hot Danishes. She stood behind me and
gently laid a hand on the back of my neck. I reached around
and clasped her fingers, then pulled them forward and
lightly kissed their tips.

"I didn't expect you to stay," I said. I couldn't see her
face.

"It's almost at an end, isn't it?" she asked quietly.

"I think so. I feel it coming."

"Then I want to see it out. I want to be there at the end."

She stayed for a little longer, until her exhaustion became almost contagious. Then she returned to the motel to
sleep.

It took thirty-eight calls before the dental assistant at
Erwin Holdman's dental surgery at Brickell Avenue found
the name of Lisa Stott on her records, but she declined even
to confirm if Lisa Stott had attended during the last six
months. Holdman was on the golf course and didn't like
being disturbed, the assistant said. Toussaint told her that
he didn't give a good goddamn what Holdman liked or
didn't like and she gave him a cell phone number.

She was right. Holdman didn't like being disturbed on
the golf course, especially when he was about to make a
birdie on the fifteenth. After some shouting, Toussaint requested Lisa Stott's dental records. The dentist wanted to
seek the permission of her mother and stepfather. Toussaint
handed the phone to Dupree and Dupree told him that, for
the present, that wasn't possible, that they only wanted the
records in order to eliminate the girl from their inquiries
and it would be unwise to disturb the parents unnecessarily.
When Holdman continued to refuse to cooperate, Dupree
warned him that he would ensure that all his records were
seized and his tax affairs subjected to microscopic examination.

Holdman cooperated. The records were kept on computer, he said, along with copies of X rays and dental charts
that had been scanned in. He would send them on as soon

as he returned to his office. His dental assistant was new, he explained, and wouldn't be able to send on the records electronically without his password. He would just finish his round . . .

There was some more shouting and Holdman decided to suspend his golfing activities for that day. It would take him one hour, traffic permitting, to get back to his surgery. We sat back to wait.

Byron had made it about a mile into the swamp. The cops were closing and his arm was bleeding badly. The bullet had shattered the elbow of his left arm and a steady current of pain was coursing through his body. He paused in a small clearing and reloaded the shotgun by tensing the stock against the ground and pumping awkwardly with his good hand. The barking was closer now. He would take the dogs as soon as they came in sight. Once they were gone, he would lose the lawmen in the swamp.

It was probably only when he rose that he first became aware of the movement in front of him. The pack couldn't have got around him already, he reasoned. The waters were deeper to the west. Without boats, they would not have been able to make it into the swamp from the road. Even if they had, he would have heard them coming. His senses had become attuned to the sounds of the swamp. Only the hallucinations threatened to undo him, but they came and went.

Byron crooked the shotgun awkwardly beneath his right arm and moved forward, his eyes moving constantly. He advanced slowly toward the treeline, but the movement seemed to have stopped. Maybe he shook his head then to clear his sight, fearing the onset of the visions, but they didn't come. Instead, death came for Edward Byron as the woods came alive around him and he was surrounded by dark figures. He loosed off one shot before the gun was wrenched from his grip and he felt a pain shoot across his chest as the blade opened his skin from shoulder to shoulder.

The figures surrounded him—hard-faced men, one with

an M16 slung over his shoulder, the others armed with knives and axes, all led by a huge man with reddish brown skin and dark hair streaked with gray. Byron fell to his knees as blows rained down on his back and arms and shoulders. Dazed with pain and exhaustion, he looked up in time to see the big man's axe scything through the air above him.

Then all was darkness.

We were using Dupree's office, where a new PC sat ready to receive the dental records Holdman was sending. I sat in a red vinyl chair that had been repaired so often with tape that it was like sitting on cracking ice. The chair squeaked as I shifted in it, my feet on the windowsill. Across from me was the couch on which I had earlier caught three hours of uncomfortable sleep.

Toussaint had gone off to get coffee thirty minutes before. He still hadn't come back. I was starting to get restless when I heard the sound of voices raised from the squad room beyond. I passed through the open door of Dupree's office and into the squad room, with its rows of gray metal desks, its swivel chairs, and hat stands, its bulletin boards and coffee cups, its half-eaten bagels and donuts.

Toussaint appeared, talking excitedly to a black detective in a blue suit and open-collar shirt. Behind him, Dupree was talking to a uniformed patrolman. Toussaint saw me, patted the black detective on the shoulder, and walked over to me.

"Byron's dead," he said. "It was messy. The feds lost two men, couple more injured. Byron broke for the swamp. When they found him, someone had cut him up and split his skull with an axe. They've got the axe and a lot of boot prints." He fingered his chin. "They think maybe Lionel Fontenot decided to finish things his way."

Dupree ushered us into his office, but didn't close the door. He stood close to me and touched my arm gently.

"It's him. Things are still confused, but they've got sample jars matching the one in which your daughter's"—he paused, then rephrased it—"the jar that you received. They've got a laptop computer, the remains of some kind of homemade speaker attachment, and scalpels with tissue remains, most of it found in a shed at the back of the property. I talked to Woolrich, briefly. He mentioned something about old medical texts. Said to tell you that you were right. They're still searching for the faces of the victims, but that could take some time. They're going to start digging around the house later today."

I wasn't sure what I felt. There was relief, a sense of a weight being lifted and taken away, a sense that it had all come to a close. But there was also something more: I felt disappointment that I had not been there at the end. After all that I had done, after all the people who had died, both at my hands and the hands of others, the Traveling Man had eluded me right until the end.

Dupree left and I sat down heavily in the chair, the sunlight filtering through the shades on the window. Toussaint sat on the edge of Dupree's desk and watched me. I thought of Susan and Jennifer and of days spent in the park together. And I remembered the voice of *Tante* Marie Aguillard, and I hoped that she was now at peace.

A low, two-note signal beeped from Dupree's PC at regular intervals. Toussaint hauled himself from the desk and walked around to where he could see the screen of the PC. He tapped some keys and read what was on-screen.

"It's Holdman's stuff coming through," he said.

I joined him at the screen and watched as Lisa Stott's dental records appeared, detailed in words, then as a kind of two-dimensional map of her mouth with fillings and extractions marked, and then in the form of a mouth X ray.

Toussaint called up the coroner's X ray from a separate file and set the two images side by side.

"They look the same," he said.

I nodded. I didn't want to think of the implications if they were.

Toussaint called up Huckstetter, told him what we had, and asked him to come over. Thirty minutes later, Dr. Emile Huckstetter was running through Holdman's file, comparing it with his own notes and the X-ray images he had taken from the dead girl. At last, he pushed his glasses up on his forehead and pinched the corners of his eyes.

"It's her," he said.

Toussaint let out a long, jagged breath and shook his head in sorrow. It was the Traveling Man's last jest, it seemed, the old jest. The dead girl was Lisa Stott, or, as she once was known, Lisa Woolrich, a young girl who had become an emotional casualty of her parents' bitter divorce, who had been abandoned by a mother anxious to start a new life without the complication of an angry, hurt teenage daughter, and whose father was unable to provide her with the stability and support she needed.

She was Woolrich's daughter.

49

THE VOICE on the telephone was heavy with tiredness and tension.

"Woolrich, it's Bird." I spoke as I drove; a St. Martin's deputy had retrieved the rented car from the Flaisance.

"Hey." There was no life to the word. "What have you heard?"

"That Byron's dead, some of your men too. I'm sorry."

"Yeah, it was a mess. They call you in New York?"

"No." I debated whether or not to tell him the truth and decided not to. "I missed the flight. I'm heading toward Lafayette."

"*Lafayette?* Shit, what you doin' in Lafayette?"

"Hanging around." With Toussaint and Dupree, it had been decided that I should talk to Woolrich. Someone had to tell him that his daughter had been found. "Can you meet me?"

"Shit, Bird, I'm on my last legs here." Then, resignedly: "Sure, I'll meet you. We can talk about what happened today. Give me an hour. I'll meet you in the Jazzy Cajun, off the highway. Anyone will tell you where it is." I could hear him coughing at the other end of the phone.

"Your lady friend go home?"

"No, she's still here."

"That's good," he said. "It's good to have someone with you at times like this." Then he hung up.

The Jazzy Cajun was a small dark bar annexed to a motel, with pool tables and a country music jukebox. Behind the bar, a woman restocked the beer while Willie Nelson played over the speakers.

Woolrich arrived shortly after I began drinking my second coffee. He was carrying a canary yellow jacket and the armpits of his shirt were stained with sweat. The shirt itself was marked with dirt on the back and sleeves, and one elbow was torn. His tan trousers were dark with mud at the cuffs and hung over mud-encrusted, ankle-high boots. He ordered a bourbon and a coffee, then took a seat beside me near the door. We didn't say anything for a time, until Woolrich drained half of his bourbon and began sipping at his coffee.

"Listen, Bird," he began. "I'm sorry for what went down between us this last week or so. We were both trying to bring this to an end our own way. Now that it's done, well . . ." He shrugged and tipped his glass at me before draining it and signaling for another. There were black stains beneath his eyes and I could see the beginnings of a painful boil at the base of his neck. His lips were dry and cracked and he winced as the bourbon hit the inside of his mouth. He noticed my look. "Mouth ulcers," he explained. "They're a bitch." He took another sip of coffee. "I guess you want to hear what happened."

I shook my head. I wanted to put off the moment, but not like that.

"What are you going to do now?" I asked.

"Sleep," he said. "Then maybe take some time off, go down to Mexico and see if I can't rescue Lisa from these goddamn religious freaks."

I felt a pain in my heart and stood suddenly. I wanted a drink as badly as I had ever wanted anything before in my life. Woolrich didn't seem to notice my lack of composure, or even register that I was walking toward the men's room. I could feel sweat on my forehead and my skin felt hypersensitive, as if I was about to come down with a fever.

"She's been asking after you, Birdman," I heard him say, and I stopped dead.

"What did you say?" I didn't turn around.

"She asks after you," he repeated.

I turned then. "When did you hear from her last?"

He waved the glass. "Couple of months back, I suppose. Two or three."

"You sure?"

He stopped and stared at me. I hung by a thread over a dark place and watched as something small and bright separated from the whole and disappeared into the blackness, never to be found again. The surroundings of the bar fell away and there was only Woolrich and me, alone, with nothing to distract either of us from the other's words. There was no ground beneath my feet, no air above me. I heard a howling in my head as images and memories coursed through my mind.

Woolrich standing on the porch, his finger on the cheek of Florence Aguillard.

"I call this my metaphysical tie, my George Herbert tie."

A couplet from Ralegh, from "The Passionate Man's Pilgrimage," the poem from which Woolrich so loved to quote: *"Blood must be my bodies balmer/No other balme will there be given."*

The second phone call I had received in the Flaisance, the one during which the Traveling Man had allowed no questions, the one during which Woolrich was in attendance.

"They have no vision. They have no larger view of what they're doing. There's no purpose to it."

Woolrich and his men seizing Rachel's notes.

"I'm torn between keeping you in touch and telling you nothing."

Cops throwing a bag of donuts he had touched into a trash can.

"Are you fucking her, Bird?"

You can't bluff someone who isn't paying attention.

Adelaide Modine. *"They can sniff each other out."*

And a figure in a New York bar, fingering a Penguin volume of metaphysical verse and quoting verses from Donne.

"Rack't carcasses make ill Anatomies."

A metaphysical sensibility: that was what the Traveling Man had, what Rachel had tried to pinpoint only days before, what united the poets whose works had lined the shelves of Woolrich's East Village apartment on the night he took me back there to sleep, on the night after he killed my wife and child.

"Bird, you okay?" His pupils were tiny, like little black holes sucking the light from the room.

I turned away. "Yeah, just a moment of weakness, that's all. I'll be back."

"Where are you going, Birdman?" There was doubt in his voice, and something else: a note of warning, of violence, and I wondered if my wife had heard it as she tried to escape, as he came after her, as he broke her nose against the wall.

"I have to go to the john," I said.

I am still not certain why I turned away. Bile was rising in my throat, threatening to make me gag and vomit on the floor. A fierce, burning pain dug at my stomach and clawed at my heart. It was as if a veil had been pulled aside at the moment of my death, revealing only a cold, black emptiness beyond. I wanted to turn away. I wanted to turn away from it all, and when I returned, everything would be normal again. I would have a wife and a child who looked like her mother. I would have a small, peaceful home and a patch of lawn to tend and someone who would stand by me, even to the end.

The toilet was dark and smelled of stale urine from the unflushed bowl, but the tap worked. I splashed cold water on my face, then reached into my jacket pocket for my phone.

It wasn't there. I had left it on the table with Woolrich. I wrenched the door open and moved around the bar, my right hand drawing my pistol, but Woolrich was already gone.

I called Toussaint but he had left the office. Dupree had gone home. I convinced the switchboard operator to ring Dupree's home number and to ask him to call me back. Five minutes later he did. His voice was bleary.

"This had better be good," he said.

"Byron isn't the killer," I said.

"What?" He was wide awake instantly.

"He didn't kill them," I repeated. I was outside the bar, gun in hand, but there was no sign of Woolrich. I stopped two black women passing with a child between them, but they backed off as soon as they saw the gun. "Byron wasn't the Traveling Man. Woolrich was. He's running. I caught him out with a lie about his daughter. He said he had spoken to her two or three months back. You and I both know that's not possible."

"You could have made a mistake."

"Dupree, listen to me. Woolrich set Byron up. He killed my wife and daughter. He killed Morphy and his wife, *Tante* Marie, Tee Jean, Lutice Fontenot, Tony Remarr, and he killed his own daughter too. He's running, do you hear me? He's running."

"I hear you," said Dupree. His voice was dry with the realization of how wrong we had been.

One hour later, they hit Woolrich's apartment in Algiers, on the south bank of the Mississippi. It lay on the upper floor of a restored house on Opelousas Avenue, above an old grocery store, approached by a flight of cast iron stairs, girded with gardenias, that led up to a gallery. Woolrich's apartment was the only one in the building, with two arched windows and a solid oak door. The New Orleans police were backed up by six FBI men. The cops led, the feds taking up positions at either side of the door. There was no movement visible in the apartment through the windows. They had not expected any.

Two cops swung an iron battering ram with *Hi, Y'all* painted in white on its flat head. It took one swing to knock the door open. The FBI men poured into the house, the police securing the street and the surrounding yards. They checked the tiny kitchen, the unmade bed, the lounge with the new television, the empty pizza cartons and beer cans, the Penguin poetry editions which sat in a milk crate, the picture of Woolrich and his daughter smiling from on top of a nest of tables.

In the bedroom was a closet, open and containing an array of wrinkled clothes and two pairs of tan shoes, and a metal cabinet sealed with a large steel lock.

"Break it," instructed the agent in charge of the operation, Assistant SAC Cameron Tate. O'Neill Brouchard, the young FBI man who had driven me to *Tante* Marie's house centuries before, struck at the lock with the butt of his machine pistol. It broke on the third attempt and he pulled the doors open.

The explosion blew O'Neill Brouchard backward through the window, almost tearing his head off in the process, and sent a hailstorm of glass shards into the narrow confines of the bedroom. Tate was blinded instantly, glass embedding itself in his face, neck, and his Kevlar vest. Two other FBI men sustained serious injuries to the face and hands as part of Woolrich's store of empty glass jars, his laptop computer, a modified H3000 voice synthesizer, a smaller, portable voice changer with the capacity to alter pitch and tone, and a flesh-colored mask, used to obscure his mouth and nose, were blown to pieces. And amid the flames and the smoke and the shards of glass, burning pages fluttered to the ground like black moths, a mass of biblical apocrypha disintegrating into ash.

As O'Neill Brouchard was dying, I sat in the detective squad room in St. Martinville as men were pulled in from holidays and days off to assist in the search. Woolrich had switched off his cell phone but the phone company had been alerted. If he used it, they would try to pinpoint a location.

Someone handed me a cup of coffee in an alligator cup, and while I drank it, I tried Rachel's room at the motel again. On the tenth ring the desk clerk interrupted.

"Are you . . . Do they call you the Birdman?" he said. He sounded young and uncertain.

"Yes, some people do."

"I'm sorry, sir. Did you call before?"

I told him that this was my third call. I was aware of an edge in my voice.

"I was grabbing lunch. I have a message for you, from the FBI."

He said the three letters with a sort of wonder in his voice. Nausea bubbled in my throat.

"It's from Agent Woolrich, Mr. Birdman. He said to tell you that he and Ms. Wolfe were taking a trip, and that you'd know where to find them. He said he wanted you to keep it to just the three of you. He doesn't want anyone else to spoil the occasion. He told me to tell you that especially, sir."

I closed my eyes and his voice grew further away.

"That's the message, sir. Did I do okay?"

Toussaint, Dupree and I lay the map across Dupree's desk. Dupree took out a red felt-tip and drew a circle around the Crowley-Ramah area, with the two towns acting as the diameters of the circle and Lafayette as its center.

"I figure he's got a place in there somewhere," said Dupree. "If you're right and he needed to be close to Byron, if not to the Aguillards as well, then we're looking at an area as far as Krotz Springs to the north and, damn, maybe as far as Bayou Sorrel to the south. If he took your friend, that probably delayed him a little: he needed time to check motel reservations—not much, but enough if he was unlucky with the places he called—and he needed time to get her out. He won't want to stay on the roads, so he'll hole up, maybe in a motel or, if it's close enough, his own place."

He tapped the pen in the center of the circle. "We've alerted the locals, the feds, and the state troopers. That leaves us—and you."

I had been thinking of what Woolrich had said, that I would know where to find them, but so far nothing had come to me. "I can't pin anything down. The obvious ones, like the Aguillard house and his own place in Algiers, are already being checked, but I don't think he's going to be at either of those places."

I put my head in my hands. My fears for Rachel were obscuring my reasoning. I needed to pull back. I took my jacket and walked to the door.

"I need space to think. I'll stay in touch."

Dupree seemed about to object, but he said nothing. Outside, my car was parked in a police space. I sat in it, rolled down the windows, and took my Louisiana map from the glove compartment. I ran my fingers over the names: Arnaudville, Grand Coteau, Carencro, Broussard, Milton, Catahoula, Coteau Holmes, St. Martinville itself.

The last name seemed familiar from somewhere, but by that point all the towns seemed to resonate with some form of meaning, which left them all meaningless. It was like repeating your name over and over and over again in your head, until the name itself lost its familiarity and you began to doubt your own identity. I started to drive out of town toward Lafayette.

Still, St. Martinville came back to me again. Something about New Iberia and a hospital. A nurse. Nurse Judy Neubolt. Judy the Nut. As I drove, I recalled the conversation that I had had with Woolrich when I'd arrived in New Orleans for the first time after the deaths of Susan and Jennifer. Judy the Nut. *She said I murdered her in a past life.* Was the story true, or did it mean something else? Had Woolrich been toying with me, even then?

The more I thought about it, the more certain I became. He had told me that Judy Neubolt had moved to La Jolla on a one-year contract after their relationship broke up. I doubted that Judy had ever got as far as La Jolla.

Judy Neubolt wasn't in the current directory, or the previous year's directory either. I found her in an old directory in a gas station—her phone had since been disconnected—and figured I could get more directions in St. Martinville. Then I called Huckstetter at home, gave him Judy Neubolt's address, and asked him to contact Dupree in an hour if he hadn't heard from me. He agreed, reluctantly.

As I drove, I thought of David Fontenot and the call from Woolrich that had almost certainly brought him to Honey Island, a promise of an end to the search for his sister. He couldn't have known how close he was to her resting place when he died.

I thought of the deaths I had brought on Morphy and

Angie; the echo of *Tante* Marie's voice in my head as he came for her; and Remarr, gilded in fading sunlight. I think I realized, too, why the details had appeared in the newspaper: it was Woolrich's way of bringing his work to a larger audience, a modern-day equivalent of the public anatomization.

And I thought of Lisa: a small, heavy, dark-eyed girl, who had reacted badly to her parents' separation, who had sought refuge in a strange Christianity in Mexico, and who had returned at last to her father. What had she seen to force him to kill her? Her father washing blood from his hands in a sink? The remains of Lutice Fontenot or some other unfortunate floating in a jar?

Or had he simply killed her because the pleasure he took in disposing of her, in mutilating his own flesh and blood, was as close as he could come to turning the knife on his own body, to enduring his own anatomization and finding at last the deep red darkness within himself?

50

□

NEAT LAWNS mixed with thick growths of cypress as I drove back along the blacktop of 96 to St. Martinville, past a *God Is Pro-Life* sign and the warehouselike structure of Podnuh's nightclub. At Thibodeaux's Café, on the neat town square, I asked for directions to Judy Neubolt's address. They knew the house, even knew that the nurse had moved to La Jolla for a year, maybe longer, and that her boyfriend was maintaining the house.

Perkins Street started almost opposite the entrance to Evangeline State Park. At the end of the street was a T-junction, which disappeared on the right into a rural setting, with houses scattered at distant intervals. Judy Neubolt's house was on this street, a small, two-story dwelling, strangely low despite the two floors, with two windows on either side of a screen door and three much smaller windows on the upper level. At the eastern side, the roof sloped down, reducing it to a single story. The wood of the house had been newly painted a pristine white, and damaged slates on the roof had been replaced, but the yard was overgrown with weeds and the woods beyond had begun to make inroads on the boundaries of the property.

I parked some way from the house and approached it through the woods, stopping at their verge. The sun was already falling from its apex and it cast a red glow across the roof and walls. The rear door was bolted and locked. There seemed to be no option but to enter from the front.

As I moved forward, my senses jangled with a tension I had not felt before. Sounds, smells, and colors were too sharp, too overpowering. I felt as if I could pick out the component parts of every noise that came to me from the surrounding trees. My gun moved jerkily, my hand responding too rapidly to the signals from my brain. I was conscious of the firmness of the trigger against the ball of my finger and every crevice and rise of the grip against the palm of my hand. The sound of the blood pumping in my ears was like an immense hand banging on a heavy oak door, my feet on the leaves and twigs like the crackling of some huge fire.

The drapes were pulled on the windows, top and bottom, and across the inner door. Through a gap in the drapes on the door I could see black material, hung to prevent anyone from peering through the cracks. The screen door opened with a squeak of rusty hinges as I eased it ajar with my right foot, my body shielded by the wall of the house. I could see a thick spider's web at the upper part of the door frame, the brown, drained husks of trapped insects shivering in the vibrations from the opening door.

I reached in and turned the handle on the main door. It opened easily. I let it swing to its fullest expanse, revealing the dimly lit interior of the house. I could see the edge of a sofa, one half of a window at the other side of the house, and to my right, the beginning of a hallway. I took a deep breath, which echoed in my head like the low, pained gasp of a sick animal, then moved quickly to my right, the screen door closing behind me.

I now had a full, uninterrupted view of the main room of the house. The exterior had been deceptive. Judy Neubolt, or whoever had decided on the design of the house's interior, had removed one floor entirely so that the room reached right to the roof, where two skylights, now encrusted with filth and partly obscured by black drapes stretched beneath them, allowed thin shafts of sunlight to penetrate to the bare boards below. The only illumination came from a pair of dim floor lamps, one at each end of the room.

The room was furnished with a long sofa, decorated with a red-and-orange zigzag pattern, which stood facing the front of the house. At either side of it were matching chairs, with a low coffee table in the center and a TV cabinet beneath one of the windows facing the seating area. Behind the sofa was a dining table and six chairs, with a fireplace to their rear. The walls were decorated with samples of Indian art and one or two vaguely mystical paintings of women with flowing white dresses standing on a mountain or beside the sea. It was hard to make out details in the dimness.

At the eastern end was a raised wooden gallery, reached by a flight of steps to my left, which led up to a sleeping area with a pine bed and a matching closet.

Rachel hung upside down from the gallery, a rope attached from her ankles to the rail above. She was naked and her hair stretched to within two feet of the floor. Her arms were free and her hands hung beyond the ends of her hair. Her eyes and mouth were wide open, but she gave no indication that she saw me. A needle, attached to the plastic pipe of a drip, was taped to her left arm. The drip bag hung from a metal frame, allowing the ketamine to seep slowly and continuously into her system. On the floor beneath her was stretched an expanse of clear plastic sheeting.

Beneath the gallery was a dark kitchen area, with pine cupboards, a tall refrigerator, and a microwave oven beside the sink. Three stools stood empty by a breakfast nook. To my right, on the wall facing the gallery, hung an embroidered tapestry with a pattern similar to the sofa and chairs. A thin patina of dust lay over everything.

I checked the hallway behind me. It led into a second bedroom, this one empty but for a bare mattress on which lay a military green sleeping bag. A green knapsack lay open beside the bed and I could see some jeans, a pair of cream trousers, and some men's shirts inside. The room, with its low, sloping roof, took up about half the width of the house, which meant that there was a room of similar size on the other side of the wall.

I moved back toward the main room, all the time keeping Rachel in sight. There was no sign of Woolrich, although he could have been standing hidden in the hallway at the other side of the house. Rachel could give me no indication of where he might be. I began moving slowly along the tapestried wall to the far wall of the house.

I was about halfway across when a movement behind Rachel caught my attention and I spun, my gun raised to shoulder level as I instinctively assumed a marksman's stance.

"Put it down, Birdman, or she dies now." He had been waiting in the darkness behind her, shielded by her body. He stood close to her now, most of his body still hidden by her own. I could see the edge of his tan pants, the sleeve of his white shirt, and a sliver of his head, nothing more. If I tried to shoot, I would almost certainly hit Rachel.

"I have a gun pointing at the small of her back, Bird. I don't want to ruin such a beautiful body with a bullet hole, so *put the gun down.*"

I bent down and placed the gun gently on the ground.

"Now kick it away from you."

I kicked it with the side of my foot and watched it slide across the floor and spin to rest by the foot of the nearest chair.

He emerged from the shadows then, but he was no longer the man that I had known. It was as if, with the revelation of his true nature, a metamorphosis had occurred. His face was more gaunt than ever and the dark shadows beneath his eyes gave him a skeletal look. But those eyes: they shone in the semidarkness like black jewels. As my eyes grew more accustomed to the light, I saw that his irises had almost disappeared. His pupils were large and dark and fed greedily on the light in the room.

"Why did it have to be you?" I said, as much to myself as to him. "You were my friend."

He smiled then, a bleak, empty smile that drifted across his face like snow.

"How did you find her, Bird?" he asked, his voice low. "How did you find Lisa? I gave you Lutice Fontenot, but how did you find Lisa?"

"Maybe she found me," I replied.

He shook his head in slow disappointment. "It doesn't

matter," he said softly. "I don't have time for those things now. I got a whole new song to sing."

He was fully in view now. In one hand he held what looked like a modified, wide-barreled air pistol, in the other a scalpel. A SIG was tucked into the waistband of his pants. I noticed that they still had mud on the cuffs.

"Why did you kill her?"

Woolrich twisted the scalpel in his hand. "Because I could."

Around us, the light in the room changed, darkening as a cloud obscured the slivers of sunlight filtering through the skylights above us. I moved slightly, shifting my weight, my eye on my gun where it lay on the floor. My movement seemed exaggerated, as if, faced with the potential of the ketamine, everything shifted too quickly by comparison. Woolrich's gun came up in a single fluid moment.

"Don't, Bird. You won't have long to wait. Don't rush the end."

The room brightened again, but only marginally. The sun was setting fast. Soon there would only be darkness.

"It was always going to end this way, Bird, you and me in a room like this. I planned it, right from the start. You were always going to die this way. Maybe here, or maybe later, in some other place." He smiled again. "After all, they were going to promote me. It would have been time to move on again. But, in the end, it was always going to come down to this."

He moved forward, one step, the gun never wavering.

"You're a little man, Bird. Do you have any idea how many little people I've killed? Trailer park trash in penny-ass towns from here to Detroit. Cracker bitches who spent their lives watching Oprah and fucking like dogs. Addicts. Drunks. Haven't you ever hated those people, Bird, the ones you know are worthless, the ones who will never amount to anything, will never do anything, will never contribute anything? Have you ever thought that you might be one of them? I showed them how worthless they were, Bird. I showed them how little they mattered. I showed your wife and your daughter how little they mattered."

"And Byron?" I asked. "Was he one of the little people, or did you turn him into one of them?" I wanted to keep him talking, maybe work my way toward my gun. As soon as he stopped, he would try to kill both Rachel and me. But more than that, I wanted to know why, as if there could ever be a why that would explain all of this.

"Byron," said Woolrich. He smiled slightly. "I needed to buy myself some time. When I cut up the girl at Park Rise, everyone believed the worst of him and he ran, all the way back to Baton Rouge. I visited him, Bird. I tested the ketamine on him and then I just kept giving it to him. He tried to run once, but I found him. In the end, I find them all."

"You warned him that the feds were coming, didn't you? You sacrificed your own men to ensure that he would lash out at them, to ensure that he died before he could start raving to them. Did you warn Adelaide Modine too, after you sniffed her out? Did you tell her I was coming after her? Did you make her run?"

Woolrich didn't answer. Instead, he ran the blunt edge of the scalpel down Rachel's arm. "Have you ever wondered how skin so thin . . . can hold so much blood in?" He turned the scalpel and ran the blade across her scapula, from the right shoulder to the space between her breasts. Rachel did not move. Her eyes remained open, but something glittered and a tear trickled from the corner of her left eye and lost itself in the roots of her hair. Blood flowed from the wound, running along the nape of her neck and pooling at her chin before it fell on her face, drawing red lines along her features.

"Look, Bird," he said. "I think the blood is going to her head."

His head tilted. "And then I drew you in. There's a circularity to this which you should appreciate, Bird. After you die, everybody is going to know about me. Then I'll be gone—they won't find me, Bird, I know every trick in the book—and I'll start again."

He smiled slightly.

"You don't look very appreciative," he said. "After all, Bird, I gave you a gift when I killed your family. If they had lived, they'd have left you and you would have become just another drunk. In a sense, I kept the family together. I chose them because of you, Bird. You befriended me in New York, you paraded them in front of me, and I took them."

"Marsyas," I said quietly.

Woolrich glanced at Rachel. "She's a smart lady, Bird. Just your type. Just like Susan. And soon she'll be just another of your dead lovers, except this time you won't have long to grieve over her."

His hand flicked the scalpel back and forth, tearing fine lines across Rachel's arm. I don't think he even realized what he was doing, or the manner in which he was anticipating the acts to come.

"I don't believe in the next world, Bird. It's just a void. This is Hell, Bird, and we are in it. All the pain, all the hurt, all the misery you could ever imagine, you can find it here. It's a culture of death, the only religion worth following. The world is my altar, Bird.

"But I don't think you'll ever understand. In the end, the only time a man really understands the reality of death, of the final pain, is at the moment of his own. It's the flaw in my work, but somehow, it makes it more human. Look upon it as my conceit." He turned the scalpel in his hand, dying sunlight and blood mingling on the blade. "She was right all along, Bird. Now it's time for you to learn. You're about to receive, and become, a lesson in mortality.

"I'm going to recreate the *Pietà* again, Bird, but this time with you and your lady friend. Can't you see it? The most famous representation of grief and death in the history of the world, a potent symbol of self-sacrifice for the greater good of humanity, of hope, of resurrection, and you're going to be a part of it. Except this is the anti-resurrection we're creating, darkness made flesh."

He moved forward again, his eyes terrifyingly bright.

"You're not going to come back from the dead, Bird, and the only sins you're dying for are your own."

I was already moving to the right when the gun fired. I felt a sharp, stinging pain in my left side as the aluminum-bodied syringe struck and I heard the sound of Woolrich's footsteps approaching across the wooden floor. I lashed out at it with my left hand, dislodging the needle painfully from my flesh. It was a huge dose. I could already feel it taking effect as I reached for my gun. I gripped the butt hard and tried to draw a bead on Woolrich.

He killed the lights. Caught in the center of the floor, away from Rachel's body, he moved to the right. I found a shape moving past the window and I loosed off two shots. There was a grunt of pain and the sound of glass breaking. A finger of sunlight lanced into the room.

I worked my way backward until I reached the second hallway. I tried to catch a glimpse of Woolrich but he seemed to have disappeared into the shadows. A second syringe whacked into the wall beside me and I was forced to dive to my left. My limbs were heavy now, my arms and legs propelling me with difficulty. I felt as if there was a pressure on my chest and I knew I would not be able to support my own weight if I tried to rise.

I kept moving backward, every movement a huge effort, but I felt certain that if I stopped, I would never be able to move again. The creaking of boards came from the main room and I heard Woolrich breathing harshly. He barked out a short laugh and I could hear the pain in it.

"Fuck you, Bird," he said. *"Shit, that hurts."* He laughed again. "I'm going to make you pay for that, Bird, you and the woman. I'm going to tear your fucking souls apart."

His voice came to me as if through a heavy fog that distorted the sound and made it difficult to tell distances or direction. The walls of the hallway rippled and fragmented, and black gore oozed from the cracks. A hand reached out to me, a slim, female hand with a narrow gold loop on its wedding finger. I saw myself reach out to touch it, although I could still feel my hands on the floor beneath me. A second female hand appeared, flailing blindly.

bird

I backed away, shaking my head to try to clear the vision. Then two smaller hands emerged from the darkness, delicate and childlike, and I closed my eyes tightly and gritted my teeth.

daddy

"No," I hissed. I dug my nails into the floor until I heard one crack, and pain coursed through the index finger of my left hand. I needed the pain. I needed it to fight off the effects of the ketamine. I pressed down hard on the injured finger and the pain made me gasp. There were still shadows moving along the wall, but the figures of my wife and child had gone.

I was conscious now of a reddish glow bathing the hallway. My back struck something cold and heavy, which moved slowly as I pressed against it. I was leaning against a half-open reinforced steel door, with three bolts on its left side. The central bolt was a monster, easily an inch in diameter with a huge open brass lock hanging from it. Red light seeped out from the crack in the door.

"Birdman, it's almost over now," said Woolrich. His voice sounded very close now, although I still could not see him. I guessed he was standing at the very edge of the corner, waiting for me to finally stop moving. "The drug is going to stop you soon. Throw the gun away, Bird, and we can get started. The sooner we start, the sooner we finish."

I leaned back harder on the door and felt it give fully. I pushed back with my heels once, twice, a third time, until I came to rest against a set of shelving that reached from ceiling to floor. The room was lit by a single red bulb, which hung unshaded from the center of the ceiling. The windows had been bricked up, the brickwork left uncovered. There was no natural light to illuminate the contents of the room.

Opposite me, to the left of the door, was a row of metal shelving, perforated bars holding the shelves in place with screws. On each shelf sat a number of glass jars, and in each jar, glowing in the dim red light, lay the remains of a human face. Most were beyond recognition. Lying in the formaldehyde, some had sunken in on themselves. Eyelashes were still visible on some, lips bleached almost white on others, the skin at their edges tattered and torn. On the lowest shelf, two dark faces lay almost upright against the glass, and even though they had been violated in this way, I recognized the faces of *Tante* Marie Aguillard and her son. I counted maybe fifteen bottles in front of me. Behind me, the shelving moved slightly and I heard the sound of glass knocking against glass and the slick movement of liquid.

I raised my head. Row upon row of bottles reached up to the ceiling, each bearing its faint, white, human remains. Beside my left eye, a face leaned against the front of a jar, its empty eyes gaping, as if trying to peer into eternity.

And I knew that somewhere among these faces, Susan lay preserved.

"What do you think of my collection, Bird?" The dark bulk of Woolrich moved slowly down the hallway. In one hand, I could see the outline of the pistol. In the other, he rubbed his thumb along the clean line of the scalpel.

"Wondering where your wife is? She's on the middle shelf, third from the left. Shit, Bird, you're probably sitting beside her right now."

I didn't move. I didn't blink. My body lay slumped against the shelves, surrounded by the faces of the dead. My face would be there soon, I thought, my face and Rachel's and Susan's, side by side forever.

Woolrich came forward until he stood in the doorway. He raised the air pistol.

"Nobody ever lasted this long before, Bird. Even Tee Jean, and he was a strong kid." His eyes glowed redly. "I gotta tell you, Bird: in the end, this is going to hurt."

He tightened his finger on the pistol and I heard the sharp crack as the hypo shot from the barrel. I was already raising my gun as the sharp pain struck my chest, my arm achingly heavy, my vision blurred by the shadows moving across my eyes. I tightened my finger on the trigger, willing it to increase the pressure. Woolrich sprang forward, alive to the danger, the scalpel raised to slash at my arm.

The trigger moved back slowly, infinitesimally slowly, and the world slowed down with it. Woolrich seemed to hang in space, the blade curving down in his hand as if through water, his mouth wide and a sound like a wind howling in a tunnel coming from his throat. The trigger moved back another tiny measure and my finger froze as the gun boomed loudly in the enclosed space. Woolrich, barely three feet from me now, bucked as the first shot took him in the chest. The next eight shots seemed to come together, the sound of their firing joining together as the bullets tore into him, the 10 millimeter rounds ripping through cloth and flesh before the gun locked empty. Glass shattered as the bullets exited and the floor became awash with formaldehyde. Woolrich fell backward and lay on the floor, his body shaking and spasming. He rose once, his shoulders and head lifting from the ground, the light already dying in his eyes. Then he lay back and moved no more.

My arm gave in under the weight of the gun and it fell to the floor. I could hear liquid dripping, could feel the presence of the dead as they crowded around me. From a distance, there came the sound of approaching sirens and I knew that, whatever happened to me, Rachel at least would be safe. Something brushed my cheek with a touch light as gossamer, like the last caress of a lover before the time to sleep, and a kind of peace came over me. With a final act of will, I closed my eyes and waited for the stillness to come.

EPILOGUE

I turn left at the Scarborough intersection, down the steep hill, past the Maximillian Kolbe Catholic church and the old cemetery, the fire department on my right, the late evening sun shining bleakly on the expanse of marshland to the east and west of the road. Soon it will be dark and lights will appear in the houses of the locals, but the summer houses on Prouts Neck Road will not be lit.

The sea rolls in gently at Prouts Neck, washing slowly over sand and stone. The season is over now and behind me the bulk of the Black Point Inn looms darkly, its dining room deserted, its bar quiet, the screen doors of the staff dormitories locked down. In the summer, the old and wealthy from Boston and upstate New York will come to stay, eating buffet lunches by the pool and dressing for dinner, the candlelight reflecting on their heavy jewelry and dancing around the table like golden moths.

Across the water, I can see the lights of Old Orchard Beach. A chill wind is coming in over the sea, tossing and buffeting the last of the gulls. I pull my coat tightly around me and stand on the sand, watching the grains swirl and twist before me. They make a sound like a mother hushing her child as the wind raises them from the dunes and lifts them like the shapes of old ghosts before laying them to rest again.

I am standing near the spot where Clarence Johns stood all those years ago, as he watched Daddy Helms's man pour dirt and ants over my body. It was a hard lesson to learn, *harder still to learn it twice. I recall the look on his face as he stood shivering before me, the desolation, the realization of what he had done, of what he had lost.*

And I want to put my arm around the shoulders of Clarence Johns and tell him that it's all right, that I understand, that I bear him no malice for what he did. I want to hear the soles of his cheap shoes slapping on the road. I want to watch him skim a stone over the water and know that he is still my friend. I want to walk the long walk home beside him and hear him whistling the only three bars he knows of some tune that he can't get out of his head, a tune that returns again and again to haunt him as he makes his way along the road.

But instead I will climb back in my car and return to Portland in the waning autumn light. I have a room at the Inn at St. John, with big bay windows and clean white sheets and a separate bathroom two doors down the hall. I will lie on my bed as the traffic passes beneath my window, as the Greyhound buses arrive and depart from the terminal across the street, as the street people push their shopping carts filled with bottles and cans down the sidewalk and the taxi drivers wait silently in their cabs.

And in the gathering darkness I will call Rachel's number in Manhattan. The phone will ring—once, twice—and then her machine will kick in: "Hi, no one can come to the phone right now, but . . ." I have heard the same message again and again since she left the hospital. Her receptionist says that she cannot tell me where Rachel is. She has canceled her college lectures. And from my hotel room, I will talk to the machine.

I could find her, if I chose. I found the others, but they were dead when I found them. I do not want to chase her down.

It is not supposed to end this way. She should be beside me now, her skin perfect and white, not scarred by Woolrich's knife; her eyes bright and inviting, not wary and haunted by the visions that torment her in the night; her hands reaching for me in the darkness, not raised to ward me off, as if even my touch might cause her pain. We will both reach an accommodation with the past, with all that has taken place, but, for now, we will each do so alone.

In the morning, Edgar will have the radio playing and there will be orange juice and coffee on the table in the lobby, and muffins wrapped in plastic. From there, I will drive out to my grandfather's house and start working. A local man has agreed to help me fix my roof and mend my walls, so that the house can be made habitable for the winter.

And I will sit on my porch as the wind takes the evergreens in hand, pressing and molding their branches into new shapes, creating a song from their leaves. And I will listen for the sound of a dog barking, its paws scraping on the worn boards, its tail moving lazily in the cool evening air; or the tap-tap-tap on the rail as my grandfather prepares to tamp the tobacco into his pipe, a glass of whiskey beside him warm and tender as a familiar kiss; or the rustle of my mother's dress against the kitchen table as she lays out plates for the evening meal, blue on white, older than she is, old as the house.

Or the sound of plastic-soled shoes fading into the distance, disappearing into the darkness, embracing the peace that comes at last to every dead thing.

ACKNOWLEDGMENTS

A number of books proved particularly valuable in the course of researching this novel. Chief among them was *The Body Emblazoned* (Routledge, 1995), Jonathan Sawday's brilliant study of dissection and the human body in Renaissance culture. Other works to which I returned included F. Gonzalez-Crussi's *Suspended Animation* (Harcourt Brace & Co., 1995); Denis C. Rousey's *Policing the Southern City* (Louisiana State University Press, 1996); Luther Link's *The Devil* (Reaktion Books, 1995); Lyall Watson's *Dark Nature* (Hodder & Stoughton, 1995); and the *Crime Classification Manual* (Simon & Schuster, 1993) by Ressler, Douglas, Burgess, and Burgess.

On a more personal note, I wish to thank my agent, Darley Anderson, without whom *Every Dead Thing* would not have seen the light of day. I also wish to acknowledge the faith, advice, and encouragement of my editor at Hodder & Stoughton, Sue Fletcher, and Bob Mecoy, my editor at Simon & Schuster in New York.

POCKET BOOKS
PROUDLY PRESENTS

THE

REAPERS

BY JOHN CONNOLLY

Out now in hardcover
from Atria Books

Turn the page for a preview of
The Reapers . . .

Sometimes, Louis dreams of the Burning Man. He comes to him when the night is at its deepest, when even the sounds of the city have faded, descending from symphonic crescendo to muted nocturne. Louis is not even sure if he is truly asleep when he comes, for it seems to him that he wakes to the sound of his partner's slow breathing in the bed beside him, a smell in his nostrils that is both familiar yet alien: it is the stink of charred meats allowed to rot, of human fats sizzling in an open flame. If it is a dream, then it is a waking dream, one that occurs in the netherworld between consciousness and absence.

The Burning Man had a name once, but Louis can no longer utter it. His name is not enough to encompass his identity; it is too narrow, too restrictive for what he has become to Louis. He does not think of him as "Errol" or "Mr. Rich" or even "Mr. Errol," which is how he had always addressed him when he was alive. He is now more than a name, much more.

Still, once he was Mr. Errol: all brawn and muscle, his skin the color of damp, fertile earth recently turned by the plow; gentle and patient for the most part, but with something simmering beneath his seemingly placid nature, so that if you caught him unawares it was possible to glimpse it in his eyes before it slipped away, like some rare beast that has learned the importance of staying beyond the range of the hunters' guns, of the white men in the white suits.

For the hunters were always white.

There was a fire burning in Errol Rich, a rage at the world and its ways. He tried to keep it under control, for he understood that, if it emerged unchecked, there was the danger that it would consume all in its path, himself included. Perhaps it was an anger that would not have been alien to many of his brothers and sisters at that time: he was a black man trapped in the rhythms and rituals of a white man's world, in a town where he and those like him were not permitted to roam once dusk fell. Things were changing elsewhere, but not in this county, and not in this town. Change would come more slowly to this place. Maybe, in truth, it would never come at all, not entirely, but that would be for others to deal with, not Errol Rich. By the time certain people started talking aloud about rights without fear of reprisal, Errol Rich no longer existed, not in any form that those who once knew him could have recognized. His life had been extinguished years before, and in the moment of his dying he was transformed. Errol Rich passed from this earth, and in his place came the Burning Man, as though the fire inside had finally found a way to bloom forth in bright red and yellow, exploding from within to devour his flesh and consume his former consciousness, so that what was once a hidden part of him became all that he was. Others might have held the torch to him, or sprayed the gasoline that soaked and blinded him in his final moments as he was hanged from a tree, but Errol Rich was already burning, even then, even as he begged them to spare him from the agonies that were to come. He had always burned, and in that way, at least, he defeated the men who took his life.

And from the moment that the died, the Burning Man stalked Louis's dreams.

Louis remembers how it came to pass: an argument with whites. Somehow, that was often how it started. The whites made the rules, but the rules kept changing. They were fluid, defined by circumstance and necessity, not by words on paper. Later, Louis would reflect that what was strangest of all was the fact that the white men and women who ran the town would always deny that they were racist. *We don't hate the coloreds*, they would say, *we just all get along better when they keep themselves to themselves.* Or: *They're welcome in the town during the day, but we just don't think they should spend the night. It's for their own safety as much as ours.* Curious. It was as hard then as it was now to find anybody who would admit to being a racist. Even most racists, it seemed, were ashamed of their intolerance.

But there were also those who wore such an epithet as a badge of honor, and the town had its share of such people as well. It was said that the trouble started when a group of local men threw a heavy pitcher filled with urine through the cracked old windshield of Errol's truck, and Errol responded in kind. That temper of his, that fury that he kept bottled inside him, had erupted, and he had tossed a length of two-by-four through the window of Little Tom's bar in reprisal. That had been enough for them to act against him, that and their fear of what he represented. He was a black man who spoke better than most of the white people in the town. He owned his own truck. He could fix things with his hands—radios, TVs, air conditioners, anything that had a current flowing through it—and he could fix them better and cheaper than anyone else, so that even those who wouldn't allow him to walk the town's streets at night were happy to let him into their homes to fix their appliances during the day, even if some of them didn't feel quite as comfortable in their living rooms afterward, although they weren't racists either. They just didn't like strangers in their home, particularly colored strangers. If they offered him water to slake his thirst, they were careful to present it to him in the cheap tin cup set aside for just such an eventuality, the cup from which no one else would drink, the cup kept with the cleaning products and the brushes, so that the water always had a faint chemical burn to it. There was talk that maybe he might soon be in a position to employ others like him, to train them and pass on his skills to them. And he was a good-looking man too, a "nigger buck" as Little Tom had once described him, except that, when he said it, Little Tom had been cradling the hunting rifle that used to hang above his bar, and it was clear what being a buck implied in Little Tom's world.

So they hadn't needed much of an excuse to move against Errol Rich, but he had given them one nonetheless, and before the week was out, they had doused him in gasoline, hanged him from a tree, and set him alight.

And that was how Errol Rich became the Burning Man.

Errol Rich had a wife in a city one hundred miles to the north. He'd fathered a child with her, and once each month he would drive up to see them and make sure that they had what they needed. Errol Rich's wife had a job in a big hotel. Errol used to work in that hotel too, as a handyman, but something had happened—that temper again, it was whispered—and he had to leave his wife and child and find work elsewhere. On those other weekend nights when he was not seeing to his family, Errol could be found drinking quietly in the little lean-to out in the swamps that served as a bar and social hub for the coloreds, tolerated by the local law as long as there was no trouble and no whoring, or none that was too obvious. Louis's momma would sometimes go there too with her friends, even though Grandma Lucy didn't approve. There was music, and often Louis's momma and Errol Rich would dance together, but there was a sadness and a regret to their rhythms, as though this was now all that they had, and all that they would ever have. While others drank rot gut, or "jitter juice" as Grandma

Lucy still called it, Louis's momma sipped on a soda and Errol stuck to beer. Just one or two, though. He never was much for drinking, he used to say, and he didn't like to smell it on others first thing in the morning, especially not on a working man, although he wasn't about to police no other man's pleasures, no sir.

On warm summer nights, when the air was filled with the burr of katydids, and mosquitoes, drawn by the heady mix of sweat and sugar, fed upon the men and women in the club, and the music was loud enough to shake dust from the ceiling, and the crowd was distracted by noise and scent and movement, Errol Rich and Louis's momma would perform their slow dance, unheeding of the rhythms that surrounded them, alive only to the beating of their own hearts, their bodies pressed so close that, in time, those beats came in unison and they were one together, their fingers intertwined, their palms moving damply, one upon the other.

And sometimes that was enough for them, and sometimes it was not.

Mr. Errol would always give Louis a quarter when their paths crossed. He would comment upon how tall Louis had grown, how well he looked, how proud his momma must be of him.

And Louis thought, although he could not say why, that Mr. Errol was proud of him too.

On the night that Errol Rich died, Louis's Grandma Lucy, the matriarch of the house of women in which Louis grew up, fed Louis's mother bourbon and a dose of morphine to help her sleep. Louis's momma had been weeping all week, ever since she heard of what had passed between Errol and Little Tom. Later, Louis was told that she had gone over to Errol's place earlier that day, her sister in tow, and had pleaded with him to leave, but Errol wasn't going to run, not again. He told her that it would all work out. He said that he had gone to see Little Tom and had apologized for what he had done. He had paid over forty dollars that he could ill afford to cover the damage and as compensation for Little Tom's trouble, and Little Tom had accepted the money gruffly and told Errol that what was done was done, and he forgave him his moment of ill temper. It had pained Errol to do it, but he wanted to stay where he was, to live and work with people whom he liked and respected. And loved. That was what he told Louis's mother, and that was what Louis's aunt told him, many years later. She described how Errol and Louis's momma had held hands as they spoke, and how she had walked outside for a breath of air to give them their privacy.

When Louis's momma eventually emerged from Errol's cabin, her face was very pale and her mouth was trembling. She knew what was coming, and Errol Rich knew it too, no matter what Little Tom might say. She went home and cried so much that she lost her breath and blacked out on the kitchen table, and it was then that Grandma Lucy took it upon herself to give her a little something to ease her suffering, and so Louis's momma had slept while the man she loved burned.

That night, the lean-to was closed, and the blacks who worked in the town left long before dusk came. They stayed in their houses and their shacks, their families close by, and nobody spoke. Mothers sat and kept vigil over their children as they slept, or held the hands of their menfolk over bare kitchen tables or seated by empty grates and cold stoves. They had felt it coming, like the heat before a storm, and they had fled, angry and ashamed at their powerlessness to intervene.

And so they had waited for the news of Errol Rich's leaving of this world.

On the night that Errol rich died, Louis can remember awaking to the sound of a woman's footsteps outside the little box room in which he slept. He can recall climbing from his bed, the boards warm beneath his bare feet, and walking to the open door of their cabin. He sees his grandmother on the porch, staring out into the darkness. He calls to her, but she does not answer. There is music playing, the voice of Bessie Smith. His grandmother always loved Bessie Smith.

Grandma Lucy, a shawl draped around her shoulders over her nightdress, steps down into the yard in her bare feet. Louis follows her. Now all is no longer dark. There is a light in the forest, a slow burning. It is shaped like a man, a man writhing in agony as the flames consume him. He walks through the forest, the leaves turning to black in his wake. Louis can smell the gasoline and the roasted flesh, can see the skin charring, can hear the hissing and popping of body fats. His grandmother reaches out a hand behind her, never taking her eyes from the Burning Man, and Louis places his palm against her palm, his fingers against her fingers, and as she tightens her grip upon him, his fear fades and he feels only grief for what this man is enduring. There is no anger, not then. That will come later. For now, there is only an overwhelming sadness that falls upon him like a dark cloak. His grandmother whispers, and begins to weep. Louis weeps too, and together they drown the flames, even as the Burning Man's mouth forms words that Louis cannot quite hear, as the fire dies and the image fades, until all that is left is the smell of him and an image seared upon Louis's retina like the aftermath of a photographic flash.

And now, as Louis lies in a bed far from the place in which he grew up, the one he loves sleeping soundly beside him, he smells gasoline and roasted meat, and sees again the Burning Man's lips move, and thinks that he understands part of what was said on that night so many years before.

Sorry. Tell her I am sorry.

Most of what follows is lost to him, wreathed in fire. Only two words stand out, and even now Louis is not certain if he interprets them correctly, if the movement of that lipless gap truly corresponds to what he believes was uttered, or to what he wants to believe.

Son.

My son.

There was a fire inside Errol Rich, and something of that fire transferred itself to the boy at the moment of Errol's death. It now burns within him, but where Errol Rich found a way to deny it, to temper its flames until at last, perhaps inevitably, it rose up and destroyed him, Louis has embraced it. He fuels it, and it, in turn, fuels him, but it is a delicate balance that he maintains. It needs to be fed if it is not to feed upon him instead, and the men he kills are the sacrifices that he offers to it. Errol Rich's fire was a deep, scorching red, but the flames inside Louis burn white and cold.

Son.

My son.

At night, Louis dreams of the Burning Man.

And, somewhere, the Burning Man dreams of him.